AROUND THE WORLD SERIES

THE ROAD AHEAD & THE BIG UNEASY

A.E. RADLEY

HEARTSOME PUBLISHING

SIGN UP TO WIN

Firstly, thank you for purchasing the *Around The World Omnibus* I really appreciate your support and hope you enjoy the book!

Every month I run a competition and randomly select three subscribers from my mailing list to win free eBooks. These books can be from my back catalogue, or one of my upcoming titles.

To be in with a chance of winning, and to hear more about my upcoming releases, click the link below to subscribe to my mailing list.

http://tiny.cc/aeradley

REVIEWS

I sincerely hope you will enjoy reading the Around the World Omnibus.

If you do, I would greatly appreciate a short review on your favourite book website.

Reviews are crucial for any author, and even just a line or two can make a huge difference.

THE ROAD AHEAD

DEDICATION

For Emma.

CHAPTER ONE

"EXCUSE ME! SORRY!"

Rebecca rushed past an elderly couple. She looked at her watch and started to run towards the terminal building. Time was running out. She had to catch her flight, she couldn't afford to miss it. Around the corner, she almost collided with another elderly couple.

Apparently, the Algarve was full of them. Slowly meandering around, not caring if they were in the way. Usually appearing to be in a world of their own. They eyed her with confusion, probably wondering what the fuss was about. The concept of time seemed to be lost on most of them.

"Sorry!" she called over her shoulder as she sidestepped them and sprinted towards the airport entrance.

She knew she shouldn't have relied on the taxi service her hotel recommended. It seemed a little too much of a coincidence that the lazy receptionist shared a surname with the taxi driver. When he'd finally turned up, he seemed less interested in getting to the airport and more interested in his telephone call. So much so that they missed the turn to the airport, adding to the delay.

The automatic doors parted, and she entered the building. She slowed her running to a jog, looking around in confusion. The departures terminal was packed with people standing around. Angry-looking people. Arms were folded, and a combined murmuring of displeasure filled the air. Something was definitely up.

Rebecca took a few steps forward and looked up at the ceiling monitors. Her eyes widened. Each and every flight on the departure board was marked as delayed.

"No, no, no," she whispered to herself.

A businessman was standing beside her, looking at his phone and shaking his head.

Rebecca turned towards him. "Excuse me, do you know what's happening?"

He looked up. "Some massive computer failure. Knocked out air traffic control in all of Portugal and Spain. Everything is grounded."

Rebecca swallowed. "Everything?" She removed her heavy backpack and lowered it to the floor.

He nodded. "Yeah, speak to a check-in assistant, but that's what they told me." He held up his phone for her to see the screen. "And that's what the news says."

"Did they say how long it would be?" Rebecca felt cold fear grip at her. She had to get home, she didn't have time for delays.

"No idea, could be ten minutes, could be ten hours. Personally, I don't think it will be that long. It can't be." He lowered his phone and gestured to the growing crowd. "This close to Christmas, they'll be calling everyone in to get it sorted out."

Rebecca looked around at the people in the departure hall. In her mind, people and planes were like water and glasses. Water spilt from a glass always looked like so much more compared to water contained in one. It was the same with people. Sat on a plane, the number of people looked reasonable, but sprawled out in an airport, they seemed like enough to fill hundreds of flights.

She turned back to the businessman. He looked authoritative, some kind of higher-up executive, she assumed. In her experience, people like that didn't always have the best grasp on reality. They assumed that their personal assistant, faithful Marjorie, would fix everything in a jiffy. They didn't know that Marjorie had sold her kidneys, killed a man, and bribed law officials to do what needed to be done because she had a large mortgage, three children, and a beagle, and needed her job whatever the cost.

"Thanks," she said. She picked up her bag and made her way through the crowds to the check-in desks.

The long row of desks was manned by exhausted-looking staff who seemed to be struggling to maintain a customer-facing smile. Luckily, there were no queues. Most people had given up speaking to the airline staff and were now standing around looking discontent, delivering filthy looks to any staff member who made eye contact.

Hoping against hope, Rebecca walked towards a free desk.

"Hi, Rebecca Edwards," she introduced herself to the woman. She took her passport and her boarding pass from her pocket and handed them over. "I'm due to fly to Heathrow, but I hear there is a delay?"

"All flights are delayed at the moment. There is a computer problem and no flights can land or take off." The woman didn't even make a move to pick up her passport or boarding pass.

"Right," Rebecca said. She chewed her lip. "Any idea of time?"

"As soon as we hear anything, it will be announced over

the speaker and on the screens." The woman pointed up towards the screens that hung from the ceiling.

"Okay…" Rebecca knew that there was nothing more to be done, but she couldn't bring herself to walk away from the desk. She lowered her heavy bag to the floor again, her mind racing as she wondered what to do next.

The illogical part of her felt that standing around the check-in desk would somehow help her predicament. The desk was a critical part in the whole boarding process. Somehow, being there gave her hope. But in her heart, she knew it was futile.

"I'm sorry, there really is nothing I can do." The check-in assistant offered an apologetic smile.

"I really need to get home," Rebecca said. She leaned on the high check-in desk, pushing aside a stand-up marketing message regarding the airline's award-winning customer service. "When do you think the next plane will leave?"

"I'm sorry, but I don't have any information to give you." The assistant, Beatriz if her nametag was to be believed, tapped some buttons on her keyboard while squinting at the screen.

"I know it's not your fault," Rebecca added.

She watched as an irate German woman yelled at the poor check-in assistant beside her. She'd never understand how someone could be so mean, especially to the people on the front line. Yes, the airport had a massive computer failure. Yes, planes were grounded. Yes, it was the twenty-third of December. But that was no reason to take it out on the minimum wage check-in assistants.

"Sorry about all the people shouting at you, it must really suck," Rebecca said. She knew she didn't have to apologise for someone else's behaviour, but she wanted to.

The German woman left, blasting out obscenities as she went.

"It is a busy time of year," Beatriz replied. "Many people want to get home. The air traffic control systems have been down since early this morning, and we have no idea when they will be back up and running. It isn't just Faro Airport that's affected, it's many airports throughout the country. And in Spain, too."

"Must be horrible for you to have to deal with it," Rebecca sympathised. She fretted with her hair tie. She couldn't imagine having to tell hundreds of irate passengers that news, over and over again.

"In all my years of flying, I've never seen such incompetence!"

Rebecca winced at the British voice. She turned to look at who had taken over from the German woman to be in the running for rudest passenger of the morning.

The woman was approximately in her forties and wore a black skirt suit. Her long, blonde hair was perfectly styled in soft curls that fell to her shoulders. Rebecca glanced down at the woman's feet, noting a plaster cast on one foot, which looked at odds with the business attire. For a brief second, she wondered what had happened and felt a pang of sympathy towards her.

"I need to get back to London, now. How are you going to make that happen?" the woman demanded. She smacked her passport onto the check-in desk.

Rebecca's eyes widened at the tone. Her sympathy at the woman's cast evaporated. She turned back to Beatriz.

"Wow," she whispered and tilted her head towards the loud woman. "Rude."

Beatriz smiled and nodded in agreement.

"Don't know why she's complaining, she should fly her broom home," Rebecca muttered.

Beatriz chuckled. She looked thoughtfully at Rebecca for

a moment. She leaned forward, gesturing for Rebecca to do the same.

Rebecca stood on her tiptoes and pivoted forward. She wondered why airport check-in desks were often so high. She was hardly short, but even she struggled to see over them sometimes.

"There were two planes to London due before yours," Beatriz explained, gesturing around the busy airport.

Rebecca turned around. She regarded the angry passengers standing around, most of them shaking their heads. The occasional tut could be heard.

"I can't say when the computer system will be up and running, but even if it sprang to life right now, the two planes from this morning would take priority. We don't have enough planes to take everyone today, and we can't divert from other airports as it's so close to Christmas."

Rebecca's heart rate picked up as she began to understand the reality of the situation.

"All of the other airlines will be fully booked," Beatriz concluded.

"You're telling me that my chance of getting home for Christmas is bad, right?" Rebecca guessed.

Beatriz nodded. "By plane, yes."

Rebecca frowned. "Is there another way? What about the trains?"

"Altogether impractical, miss. To travel from Faro to London, you would have to get to Lisbon, then take a night train to the Spanish-French border. Then, you'd have to switch to travel to Paris, and then switch again for the high-speed rail to London." The assistant frowned as if to emphasise her point. "A lot of transfers, and it could be expensive."

Rebecca's heart sank. "Not to mention the timing. I'd never get home for Christmas."

Something about her plight must have resonated with

Beatriz. The woman gestured for Rebecca to come a little closer. She did the best she could, standing on the very tips of her Converse All-Stars. "Very soon, these people are going to realise that time is running out, and they are going to look for alternative methods of transport. You can, technically, drive to London and get home for Christmas. But there will be a limited number of cars available for hire…"

The penny dropped. Rebecca slowly nodded as she understood. Beatriz smiled, picked up Rebecca's passport and boarding pass, and handed them back to her.

"I'm sorry, Miss Edwards, there's nothing I can do," she said loudly.

"Thank you, thank you so much," Rebecca whispered as she grabbed the items and hoisted her rucksack onto her shoulder.

"You better hurry," Beatriz advised quietly.

"I will, thank you again," Rebecca said. She turned and looked at the airport signage, searching for a pictogram of a car and her way home.

CHAPTER TWO

ARABELLA HENLEY awkwardly stalked the departure hall, leaning heavily on her crutch as she did. She couldn't believe the incompetence she was facing.

Air travel predated computers, and yet it was supposedly completely impossible to take off while the system remained down. No matter whom she spoke to, she couldn't get a proper answer on how long it would be until the situation was fixed.

She'd spoken to three separate customer service advisors, all of whom were completely useless. In the end, she had demanded to speak to a manager, and they'd sent her a four-teen-year-old boy. She chewed him out and then requested another manager. A grown-up emerged, only to mansplain that the computers were all down.

Of course, she already knew that the computers were all down. That was obvious. What she wanted to know was what they were going to do about it. And how, precisely, she was going to get back to London. Unsurprisingly, no one seemed to know the answer.

Eventually, she had grabbed her crutch and limped away

from the check-in desks. If she'd stayed there a moment longer she would have been arrested by the Portuguese police for throttling a member of the staff.

As she left, she heard the assistant mumble something in Portuguese, presumably something not flattering. She decided to ignore it. She knew she was a difficult customer, maybe even rude. But that was how you got things done. That was how you ensured that people didn't walk all over you. Business was tough, life was tough, and so she was tough.

She stopped her circles of the departure hall. She leaned against a pillar and let out a sigh. The terminal building was busy. Extremely busy. It seemed that everyone wanted to get somewhere for Christmas.

"Do you know how long the computers have been down?" she asked a nearby couple. She knew they were British, she could tell by the pink skin and the dreadful clothes.

"Since this morning," the man replied. "We were supposed to take off at six o'clock."

She nodded and turned away, not wanting to encourage further conversation. She wanted information, not friendly chatter and new best friends for the next few hours. She looked at the clock on her phone, it was eight in the morning. The system had been down for at least two hours.

She glanced around the terminal building again. There were hundreds, probably even thousands, of people. All standing around, waiting for information.

She'd seen this before. When ice had closed Heathrow for a day, the results had been disastrous. A lack of planes, lack of runway take-off slots, and an abundance of people had led to severe delays. And that was a major London hub, more prepared to deal with large-scale problems than Faro on the Portuguese coast.

A middle-aged couple caught her eye. They were calmly piling their bags onto an airport trolley. Trying to look discreet, trying not to draw attention to themselves. Trying but failing. The look of panic in the man's eye gave him away.

What are you up to? she wondered.

The mother grabbed her escaping toddler by the wrist and pulled him towards the exit. The man was already hurriedly pushing the airport trolley that way, seemingly trying not to run.

Arabella watched them with interest, her gaze drifting up towards the airport signage.

"Of course," she mumbled to herself.

Rebecca felt faint. "I'm sorry, could you repeat that again?"

"Two thousand five hundred and fifty-eight euros."

She knew she couldn't afford it. Even so, she desperately tapped the amount into the conversion app on her mobile phone. It looked just as hideous in British pounds.

"It is one of the last vehicles we have."

She looked up and read his nametag. "Look, Jose, it's nearly Christmas and I have to get home. Surely you can help me out?"

Jose shook his head. "I'm sorry, there are many people in that terminal who would be willing to pay for that vehicle."

Rebecca heard the door to the car hire office open behind her. She turned to see a couple with a toddler hurry in and approach the desk next to her.

"We need to hire a car to drive back to England," the man explained to Jose's colleague.

Jose raised his eyebrow and looked at Rebecca. "See?"

Perhaps in the spirit of the holiday, this young family would like to car share back to the UK.

She tried to get the couple's attention, but they purposely busied themselves with their toddler and their phones to avoid eye contact. *Christmas spirit, my arse.* She was running out of options.

"Can I pay half now, half later?" Rebecca tried.

"No. Maybe try one of the other hire agencies?" Jose gestured towards the door with his pen.

"They're either closed or don't have any cars," Rebecca said. Inspiration struck her. "What about bikes? Do you have any bikes I can hire?"

Jose shook his head. "We don't hire out bikes."

He tapped on his keyboard and nodded towards the couple.

"We are now down to one vehicle. If you want to secure this vehicle, I would need to hold it for you now with a credit card. Can you afford it?"

"Maybe." She pulled her wallet out of the inside pocket of her leather jacket and grabbed two fifty-euro notes. She put them on the table. "Please, hold the car for me, I just need to make a phone call and get someone to transfer the money to my bank."

Jose looked at her sceptically. She couldn't blame him. The chance that anyone had the money to lend her was extremely slim, but he didn't know that. And she had to try.

He picked up the notes and put them under his keyboard.

"Ten minutes," he told her.

"Thank you, thank you." She scurried away from the desk, sat in one of the waiting chairs, and pulled out her phone. She scrolled through her contact list, wondering who on earth she should call. Even if she did find someone who happened to have that kind of money rubbing a hole in their pocket a few days before Christmas, she had no idea how she'd pay them back.

She started to compose a text message that she could send to as many people as possible. She only had ten minutes. And that was if Jose kept his word.

She looked at the couple with the toddler. People from the airport were obviously starting to figure out that getting to wherever they were heading in time for Christmas was going to be difficult.

Rebecca knew that she needed to get in a car and begin the mammoth journey home soon. Not that she even knew how long it would take. She hadn't really stopped to consider the journey, the route, the time. She shivered. One problem at a time.

The automatic door opened. Rebecca looked up to see the rude woman with the cast limping into the hire office.

Shit, she thought and started bulk selecting her contacts.

Arabella entered the car hire reception. There were two people serving, one dealing with the couple with the toddler that Arabella had followed on the way over. The other had his back to her as he organised paperwork behind the desk.

Along the side wall some scruffy girl was texting. She presumed she wasn't in the queue, but even if she was, she wouldn't be for much longer.

She approached the desk and balanced her crutch against the side of it.

"I need a car, automatic, and I'll be driving it to England," Arabella said, drawing the attention of the man who was supposed to be serving.

"I'm afraid we don't have any automatic vehicles," he said as he turned to face her.

She rolled her eyes. "Fine. A manual will do."

He tapped on his keyboard. "That will be two thousand five hundred and fifty-eight euros."

Arabella chuckled and got her mobile phone out of her pocket. "You certainly know how to take advantage of a systems failure." She pulled her credit card from the mobile phone case and slid it across the counter.

"Hold on, Jose, you're holding that car for me!"

Arabella turned towards the scruffy girl and raised her eyebrow. "Apparently, he isn't."

"I'm sorry, but this lady has the means to pay immediately," he said. "You don't."

"I gave you a hundred euros!"

He picked up two fifty-euro notes from under his keyboard and held them out towards the girl.

The girl stood up and snatched the money back. "I can't believe this! You won't give me ten minutes to transfer some funds, but you'll give the car to someone with a broken leg."

He frowned and looked around the corner of the desk. He looked at Arabella's cast and winced. He pushed the credit card back across the counter.

"Sorry, I cannot let you have this car."

"What?" Arabella cried. "I can still drive, it's nothing. Just a minor... fracture."

"Fracture, broken," the girl mumbled.

"It would invalidate our insurance; my boss wouldn't allow me. This is a very expensive car," he explained.

"I'll buy more insurance. You can double the fee for hire, whatever you like, I need this car," Arabella told him firmly.

He shook his head and stood steadfast. "I'm sorry, I'm unable to lease any vehicle to you if you are not fully fit and able to drive it."

"I want to see your manager immediately," Arabella demanded.

"He's not here," Jose replied.

"This is unbelievable; how do you expect me to get home?"

He gestured towards the girl. "Maybe she could drive you? You are both going to England. She cannot afford a car, you can afford one but cannot hire one due to your leg. And it will be better for the environment to car share."

Arabella stared at him. The last sentence appeared to be his attempt at humour. An attempt that she didn't find particularly funny now. She looked at the girl. Being sat next to the girl for a two-hour *flight* would have been torturous, but driving all the way back to England with her?

"I'll do it," the girl said. "I have to get back to England. I'll drive all day and all night if you want."

Arabella looked from the girl to the assistant, wondering when they'd start laughing and admit it was all a practical joke. That moment seemed to be less and less likely the longer she watched them.

"Do you really think I'm just going to hop in a car with someone I don't even know? I don't even know her name." Arabella laughed derisively.

"Rebecca Edwards, that's my name. Look, we both want to get home. He's right, we can either do this together or both be stuck here."

Arabella bit her lip and critically looked the girl up and down. She knew her options were limited, but she wasn't about to agree to jumping in a car with an unknown quantity until she knew it was her *only* option.

"And you have a full and clean driving licence?"

Rebecca nodded. "Never even had a parking ticket."

Arabella thought of her cast-iron mail rack at home with unpaid parking tickets overflowing. She was sure the speed camera in Kensington High Street had snagged her the last weekend. If it had, she may well be disqualified from driving.

"Where do you need to get to?" Arabella sighed as if the whole thing was a massive inconvenience to her personally. Which it felt like it was. So she wasn't a saint. But that was no reason for whatever higher beings might exist to be testing her so.

"Croydon. You?"

Arabella winced. Croydon was a dive. Of course it would be Croydon.

"Putney," she replied. It was some twisted kind of fate, their respective destinations were less than an hour away from each other. Geographically speaking. In terms of humanity, they were a million miles apart.

For a moment, Arabella was going to say no. It was her go-to reaction when she found herself trapped in a situation she didn't relish. Often, she'd even say no at her own cost, just because she could. Technically, she could say no. She could wait to see what the airport situation was, bully her way onto the first flight to London.

But then she ran the risk of being home late. Alastair and her father wouldn't be happy about her missing the Christmas Eve party. She knew there was already an argument awaiting her when she got home, she didn't need to add to the situation.

The automatic doors slid open. She turned to see a man walk in, he had the gleam of desperation in his eye.

Decision made.

"We'll do it," she said. She held out her credit card for Jose. "Get us that car."

CHAPTER THREE

"Oh my god, this car is brand new!" Rebecca squealed as they approached the vehicle. "A brand-new Mercedes. No wonder they wanted so much for it. I think we probably own a quarter of it by now. Well, you do."

Arabella massaged her temples. It was as if the girl had never seen a car before.

"More like a headrest," she corrected. "Now, our first stop is to return to the terminal building."

Rebecca looked over the car roof at her. "Why?"

"To get our luggage, obviously." Arabella opened the passenger door and regarded the seat. Getting in with her skirt and cast wasn't going to be pretty.

"I have my luggage," Rebecca said. She held up a tatty backpack for Arabella to see.

"That's your luggage? One bag?"

"Yep, hand luggage only. No extra fees and no chance it will get lost. Or accidentally flown to Azerbaijan."

Rebecca opened the driver's door. She reached into the car and pulled a lever and the boot slowly opened.

"Well, it doesn't change anything. We still need to go and get *my* luggage."

Rebecca placed her bag in the boot. "Don't tell me you just left your luggage in the airport? That's a security risk, you know. Someone's probably blown it up by now."

Arabella pinched the bridge of her nose. "I didn't just leave it lying around. I left it with the first-class lounge."

"There's a first-class lounge?" Rebecca closed the boot and walked to the driver's door.

"There's *always* a first-class lounge. Are we going to debate this forever or are we going to get going?" Arabella lowered herself into the car, careful to disguise the wince she felt bubble to the surface. The last thing she wanted to do was to show her new, no doubt troublesome, travel companion any weakness.

For all she knew the girl could be a murderer, preparing to mug her and then leave her on the side of the road somewhere. She'd already made a mental note to mention her kickboxing classes early in the journey.

Rebecca got into the car. "Do you want me to put your crutch in the back?"

"No." Arabella held onto the crutch. Which she now considered her improvised weapon, if needed.

Rebecca closed her door. "Fine," she mumbled. She put her seatbelt on and adjusted the mirrors. She started the engine and felt around for the seat controls.

Arabella narrowed her eyes as the girl moved a fraction of an inch back, and then forward. And then up, and then down. After a few minutes, she'd had enough.

"Are you enjoying yourself? Would you like to have a ride on the toy train inside the terminal?"

Rebecca continued adjusting the seat. "If I'm driving us all the way to England, I need to make sure I'm set up correctly."

"Of course. I'm just a little concerned that by the time you're perfectly comfortable, Christmas, and indeed New Year, will be a distant memory."

Rebecca ignored her and took her time adjusting the steering column before diverting her attention to the mirrors.

Finally, after what seemed like an eternity, she turned to Arabella.

"Right, I'm ready."

Arabella looked at her, wondering what the holdup was now. "Well? Do you want a round of applause? A medal?"

"Belt up."

"I beg your pardon?"

"Seat belt." Rebecca snapped her own seatbelt into place.

Arabella sighed. She reached around and grabbed her seatbelt and pulled it across her body, clicking it in place. "Happy now?" she asked.

"Oh, yeah, I'm ecstatic," Rebecca replied sarcastically.

Rebecca put the car into gear and then glided out of the parking space.

Arabella got her mobile phone out of her pocket and opened her navigation app. She wondered just how long she was going to be stuck with the snarky, potential murderer.

She clicked her home address and then requested directions from Faro Airport, Portugal. The app sprang into action, a revolving circle promising that it was thinking about the conundrum.

The map of the local area that she had been using grew smaller as the map zoomed out to take in both locations. Suddenly, most of the Western side of Europe was visible. Portugal, Spain, France, and England filled her screen.

"Umm, do you wanna hop out?" Rebecca asked.

Arabella pulled the ticket receipt out from her inner jacket pocket and held it towards Rebecca without looking up from her phone.

"It would be quicker if you went, what with my leg. I'll mind the car."

A few seconds passed before Rebecca left the car, slamming the door behind her harder than was necessary for a new vehicle. She was clearly used to older cars. Arabella made a mental note to explain the features of modern cars to the girl once she'd retrieved the luggage.

But, for the moment, she was distracted. Looking at the map and wondering if she had put in the details incorrectly. It seemed ridiculous that the journey would take twenty-four solid hours. An entire day. She looked at the time and shook her head. She'd barely have enough time to have a shower and get to her hair appointment and massage before the party started.

She looked out of the window at the terminal building.

"Where is she?"

She looked at her watch and then sighed. This journey was going to be hell.

"Hi, I'm here to pick up luggage?" Rebecca asked as she approached the snooty-looking woman who manned the desk to the first-class lounge. The first-class lounge which had been impossible to find. Presumably hidden away from any old someone who might accidentally stumble into the luxurious surroundings and offend the proper clientele.

"Luggage for?"

Rebecca held up the luggage tag and looked at it. "Arabella Henley," she read. She then handed the tag to the sour-faced woman.

The woman looked at the luggage tag and then at Rebecca with uncertainty.

"She has a broken leg, she asked me to come to save her

the journey." It was sort of true. She hadn't exactly asked. Arabella didn't seem to be the kind of person who asked favours. But Rebecca needed her, and so she'd put up with the rude behaviour. For now, at least.

"Oh, I remember." The woman nodded and picked up the telephone.

"Yeah, she leaves an impression," Rebecca muttered.

A quick conversation in Portuguese took place and then the phone was hung up. "It will be brought out in a moment. Wait here."

Rebecca tried to smile politely but knew she had probably only managed a constipated wince. The inference was clear. Wait here. Do not tarnish our first-class lounge with your presence.

She looked at her mobile phone for the first time since sending her message pleading for money. She scrolled through the replies. As she suspected, everyone was broke. They all wished they could help but ultimately couldn't. A few offered suggestions, none that were that useful.

Now she was stuck with some snobbish woman who was going to treat her like mud on her shoe until they got back to England. She still hadn't had a chance to discover just how long that journey would be, or even to plan a route. Part of her was in denial. She hoped that the whole situation was some terrible dream and that she was actually asleep on the Heathrow flight, whizzing her way back home.

"Miss Henley?" a male voice asked.

She looked up. "Close enough."

He gestured to a trolley beside him.

"You have *got* to be kidding me."

CHAPTER FOUR

"AT LAST. WHERE HAVE YOU BEEN?" Arabella asked.

"Picking up Kim Kardashian's shoes," Rebecca gestured to the trolley laden down with five pieces of luggage in various sizes.

It seemed that first-class passengers still had to contend with wobbly trolley wheels. She'd struggled through the terminal, dropping a couple of pieces of luggage along the way and angrily shoving them back onto the stack.

"Who?"

She stopped by the car and stared at Arabella's confused face, where it was poking out of the open passenger window.

"Are you kidding me? You don't know who Kim Kardashian is?"

"Is it relevant to getting my luggage in the car and beginning this journey?"

Rebecca shook her head in dismay. This woman was going to be the death of her. She opened the boot of the car and moved her solitary rucksack out of the way. She started moving the bags from the trolley to the boot. She paused and moved some of the bags around. It was like an expensive Tetris puzzle.

"Do make sure—"

"If you tell me to be careful with your luggage, I swear I will throw it under the next bus," Rebecca shouted back.

She continued moving the heavy bags and cases around, eventually finding a way for most of them to fit. Her own bag would have to go on the back seat. Which would probably suit Arabella, who probably wouldn't want her luggage to be sitting handle to zip with Rebecca's aged rucksack.

She shouldered her rucksack and pushed the trolley back towards the terminal. She jogged back, slamming the boot and depositing her bag on the back seat. Then she hopped in the driver's seat. Finally, she could get out of this airport and get on with the journey home.

"We need to head for Seville, then north towards Bilbao, then into France, past Bordeaux, up to Calais, and across the Channel," Arabella informed her.

Rebecca reached for the engine start button with one hand, the other reaching for her seatbelt. "How long is that going to take?" she asked.

Arabella waved her hand. "Oh, you know these things, always overestimating. I'm sure if we get going we can knock around twenty percent off."

"How long does it say?" Rebecca asked again.

"I forget, twenty hours I think."

"Twenty hours?" Rebecca turned to stare at her.

"More like twenty-four with the time you wasted adjusting your damn chair."

"Shit, I didn't think it would be that long..." Rebecca began to worry. She was meant to be hurrying home. She'd expected to be home by the afternoon, now that was impossible.

"It will just be longer the more we sit here," Arabella

pointed out unhelpfully. "Seriously, I could just drive the car myself. I don't even know why I agreed to this farce."

Rebecca barked out a laugh. "Yeah, right, I see you wince every time you move your leg. You might be able to drive a little, but twenty-four solid hours of driving? You'd never make it."

"My leg is just fine, it's a fracture... nothing serious," Arabella defended.

"Right, if that's what you want to tell yourself." Rebecca reached into the back seat. She felt in the front pocket of her bag and pulled out her sunglasses.

Slipping them on her face she put her hands on the wheel. "Right, first stop, Spain."

Arabella leaned her head on the headrest and looked out at the countryside. It wasn't whizzing by. It was barely moving. Rebecca seemed to be one of those people who abided by every speed limit, even when the situation was dire. She checked the map again, wondering how much time she'd save if she could convince the girl to pick up the pace. She really didn't want to cancel her hair appointment at Carlucci's, but it looked horribly likely.

"You know, they're not as pedantic with speeding here as they are back home," Arabella offered.

"I'm not worried about being caught speeding."

"Oh, good. Well, you don't have to drive slowly for my benefit."

"I'm not. I'm driving the speed limit so we won't die in the event of a high-speed collision."

Arabella rubbed her temples. "If you drive properly then we won't have a high-speed collision."

Rebecca shook her head, not taking her eyes off the road.

"I'm one factor. There's other drivers, weather conditions, road conditions. There's a reason why speed limits are set. It's to maximise our chances of survival if something goes wrong. I want to get home as much as you do, but I want to make sure I get there in one piece."

"I knew all of those advertisements regarding road safety were damaging our youth," Arabella said. "Fine, do continue to drive like a sloth."

"Thank you for your permission, I'll drive like a sloth. Who happens to be going seventy miles an hour."

Arabella rolled her eyes and continued to look out of the window. Her hair appointment was seriously in jeopardy. In fact, if Rebecca insisted on driving like a ninety-year-old, the whole Christmas Eve party could be in jeopardy. She wondered if she should call Alastair to let him know, or if that would just make him worry more.

At the moment, he was probably blissfully unaware of her predicament, assuming that his fiancée was about to board a flight home. She had a few more hours before she needed to tell him what had happened. She could be in France by then. Which sounded a lot better than being in Portugal.

Anything that delayed the conversation would be a bonus at this point. She knew Alastair would relish the opportunity to tell her again that she was wrong to go to Portugal. They'd argued about the point solidly for four days before she'd finally gone anyway.

"Spain!" Rebecca cried. "One country down."

Arabella looked at her watch. They had only been driving for forty-five minutes. It was a good sign, but it was just the tip of the iceberg.

"Just all of Spain, France, and the English Channel to go," Arabella muttered. "An hour and a half and then we'll be in Seville."

"Great, thanks so much for the encouragement," Rebecca replied sarcastically.

Arabella glanced at her, noticing her hands were tightening over the steering wheel. The girl confused her. She was in her late twenties, casually dressed, and with little regard for her appearance if her unkempt long, brown hair and her lack of makeup were anything to go by.

At first, Arabella had thought of her as a free spirit type of person, someone who drifts around with no real job and probably believes in the healing powers of crystals. And yet she fastidiously kept to the speed limit.

Now she looked frustrated, but she didn't elaborate on what was vexing her.

"What did I say?" Arabella asked.

Rebecca laughed. "You really don't know, do you?"

"Know what?" Arabella demanded.

Rebecca shook her head and focused on the road ahead, closing the topic of conversation with her silence.

Arabella leaned on the headrest again and looked out of the window. It was going to be a very long journey.

CHAPTER FIVE

REBECCA DIDN'T THINK she could take much more of Arabella's constant driving tips, directions, and updates as to how long the journey would take. They'd been in the car for under an hour, and already she wanted to put Arabella in the boot with her expensive luggage.

If Rebecca celebrated another milestone in their journey, Arabella was quick to point out how many more they had to overcome. The woman was impossible to please and it was making Rebecca stressed.

She looked at her hands, her knuckles white from clutching the steering wheel. She released her death grip a little and took a cleansing breath. She rolled her shoulders to relieve the tension. She wasn't going to allow Arabella to get to her. She didn't deserve that power over her.

I need to get to know her, humanise her a bit, Rebecca thought. *This is a weird situation. She's on edge. Once we break the ice, she'll be better. Hopefully.*

"So, what were you doing in Portugal, if you don't mind me asking?" Rebecca asked politely.

"Completing the paperwork for the sale of a client's villa," Arabella said.

"Oh, cool."

"Not particularly. These countries always insist on paperwork being signed in person and cash in brown envelopes."

"Henley!" Rebecca suddenly clicked the pieces into place. "As in Henley's Estate Agents?"

"That's the one." Arabella sounded bored.

Henley's Estate Agents were well known in London. They had an office in every town, sometimes more than one. The offices were more than the average estate agent, they were beacons of modern design. Smooth angles, bright colours, faddish lights. Each branch was different, a piece of artwork in its own right. All were known for their luxurious comfort. Clients would be offered drinks from a range of fifty teas while they sat on leather sofas buying expensive properties.

Rebecca had never been in a Henley's. She'd never had the pay packet to be able to afford to step foot in one. She was sure an invisible scanner at the door would detect her financial status and a trap door would dispose of her before any of the staff members could be disturbed by her presence.

"I thought you only operated in London?" she asked.

"We have an international office, mainly Europe but some American properties, too. Mainly holiday homes. You know what it's like, after a few weeks exhausting yourself in London, you need a break in the sun."

"Absolutely," Rebecca replied. Of course, she thought the very idea was pretentious and unnecessary, but she was trying to make friends with the woman. She wasn't about to say that those kinds of riches were obscene. It wouldn't be right for her to say that she believed that vast wealth should be equally distributed and not held by the few. In their luxury holiday villas.

"You say you sold your client's villa?" Rebecca asked. "How will they take a break now?"

She didn't really care how Mr and Mrs Yah-Yah were going to rest themselves from the exhaustion of champagne galas and theatre opening nights. But it was the only topic of conversation she had open to her and she needed to bond with this woman somehow.

"They bought a yacht. They didn't want to be tied down to bricks and mortar."

"Of course." Rebecca shook her head slightly. This was going to be a tremendously long journey.

"I presume you were there working, too?" Arabella sniffed. "Some kind of bar work? Waitressing?"

Rebecca couldn't see Arabella, but she could feel the judgement radiating off her. The moment she met Arabella, she felt she knew everything she needed to know about her. But she'd given the snobbish woman the benefit of the doubt and tried to speak to her, to get to know her. Arabella apparently didn't do the same. She's taken one look at Rebecca and made up her mind.

It had been a short effort, but Rebecca had already had enough of being nice. It was clear that Arabella was judgemental, rude, and condescending. Everything Rebecca hated in a person.

"Yeah, bar work. And dancing, you know? Gotta make a living, right?" Rebecca lied.

"W-well, yes, I suppose so, yes," Arabella stuttered.

"And the tips are amazing, well, they are where I work, if you know what I mean." Rebecca elbowed Arabella meaningfully.

"Eyes on the road," Arabella whispered, clearly uncomfortable with the conversation.

Serves you right, Rebecca thought.

She'd never tended bar in her life; she was one of those

people who could only carry two drinks at a time, one in each hand. People who could carry three or more were like sorcerers. And as for dancing, two left feet.

But the comment had shut Arabella up for the meantime. Rebecca let out a breath and started to relax her grip on the steering wheel.

Arabella shifted uncomfortably in her seat. The Mercedes leather seats were sinfully comfortable but not when you had a cast, and not when you were embarking on a journey through four countries. Certainly not when you were trapped in the car with a prostitute.

She should have known. The long, brown hair, the thin, muscled body, and the ripped clothes. She knew rips were supposedly the fashion, but it just looked so messy to her.

She chanced a quick glance at Rebecca. They hadn't spoken for an hour. Not since Rebecca had told her about her employment and Arabella had been stunned into silence.

She'd briefly considered if she would survive opening the door and rolling to safety but decided to stick with her luggage. She was fairly sure her insurance wouldn't cover her for a duck and roll out of a moving vehicle.

She should have listened to Alastair and stayed home. She should have sent someone else to complete the sale. It was just her pride and her feeling of losing control that made her see the job through to completion personally.

The wedding was three months away and already her workload was being distributed to others. Of course, she'd agreed to give up work once they were married, but she was surprised at the speed with which the date was arriving. Not that she could complain. Who wouldn't say no to a life of leisure?

Not that she currently felt she'd ever get to see that life. It was looking less and less likely that she would even make it home. Rebecca was probably going to kill her and leave her body somewhere in the Spanish countryside.

The girl was probably backpacking her way around Europe without a penny to her name. And now she was in a luxurious car with a named partner of one of London's most exclusive estate agencies.

Rebecca obviously knew that Arabella had money. She'd paid the exorbitant fee for the car hire, she had designer luggage, Rebecca had seen the credit cards in her wallet. She swallowed nervously. The girl knew a lot about her, and Arabella couldn't even remember her surname. She was certain the girl had said it at some point, but she'd instantly disregarded it as useless information.

She needed to get some information on the girl, something that would help the police to track her down in the event they ever managed to find Arabella's body in the scrubland.

"We should stop at the next station and get something to eat and drink," Arabella suggested.

"You sure you want to stop? That might add some precious minutes to our schedule," Rebecca replied.

"There's no point in arriving dehydrated."

"Fine. I'll stop at the next garage I see."

Arabella shifted nervously in her seat again. Rebecca didn't want to stop, presumably afraid that her face would be picked up on any CCTV present at the garage.

She wondered if she should contact Alastair. She didn't want her sister getting her hands on the Royal Doulton collection of ceramic coasters. Alastair wouldn't be aware of their value and would probably hand them over without thinking.

"You're in luck, there's a station," Rebecca said. She

pointed towards the roadside sign promising that a petrol pump would be appearing in two kilometres.

She mumbled a reply and turned to look out of the window again.

Alastair would probably just tell her she was being silly. He always accused her of overreacting. Maybe sometimes she did overreact, but sometimes she was spot on. Of course, he only ever remembered the times she was wrong. She hated that he was right, that she shouldn't have gone to Portugal. Especially so close to the Christmas party. So she couldn't call him. She'd rather be murdered, knowing that her sister was finally going to get the precious coasters than listen to another round of 'I told you so'.

Rebecca started to indicate. Arabella looked at the upcoming garage with a sneer. Rundown would be putting it politely. Under normal circumstances, she'd never even consider slowing the car near such an establishment. Thank goodness she wasn't intending to go inside herself.

"Should I top up with fuel, so we don't have to stop again for a while?" Rebecca asked.

"Yes," Arabella answered. Anything to get Rebecca out of the vehicle for a while so she could do what she needed to do.

Rebecca pulled up beside a petrol pump. She reached into her jacket pocket and pulled out a tatty-looking wallet.

"I'll pay," Arabella said quickly. She handed over a handful of euro notes. Rebecca took them and placed her wallet on the centre console between them.

"Get me a water, and some kind of juice. No added sugar, though. If they have any fruit, that would be good too. But no pears, I hate Spanish pears."

"I doubt they'll do fruit in there," Rebecca said as she turned off the engine.

"Then get me some crackers, plain. No added salt."

"I really don't think they are going to have many healthy options, maybe you should come in and have a look—"

"No," Arabella said. "No, you go. You'll be quicker. My leg slows me down…"

"You seem nimble enough when you want to be," Rebecca pointed out.

Before Arabella could reply, Rebecca opened the car door and exited the vehicle. As the door slammed shut, Arabella let out a sigh. She watched as Rebecca examined the fuel cap and the petrol pump.

"Hurry up," she muttered.

She leaned back in her seat, listening to the sound of the fuel cap being unscrewed. A few seconds later she heard the rumbling of the old petrol pump and the whooshing of fuel entering the tank.

After what seemed like an age, she heard the click of the petrol flap being put back into place. She looked up and watched as Rebecca walked towards the garage.

As soon as she was out of sight, Arabella picked up the wallet from the centre console and opened it up. She slid the plastic cards out so she could look at them. There was a bank card and a credit card in the first compartment.

"Edwards, that was it, Rebecca Edwards," she whispered.

Next she saw a gym membership card and a library card. She looked up to check that Rebecca was still in the garage. Luckily the girl still seemed to be shopping.

Arabella turned her attention back to the wallet. There were a couple of photographs, one of Rebecca and an older woman and another of Rebecca and a younger woman. Arabella briefly wondered if they were previous victims but quickly pushed that thought aside as the older woman had a strong family resemblance, presumably her mother.

Then Arabella found what she was looking for, the driver's licence. She took the plastic card out of the wallet and snapped a couple of pictures of it with her phone. She noted that a Croydon address was printed on the licence. At least that part of the story appeared to be true.

Twenty-seven, she thought. *Practically a child.*

Her heart pounded in her chest. She quickly put everything back the way she found it and laid the wallet back on the centre console. She concentrated on controlling her breathing, trying to get herself under control before Rebecca returned.

At least now the balance of power felt a little more equal. She knew things about Rebecca. Okay, small things, like the fact that she was a member of a gym and a library. But she also had an address.

If she was going to be hacked to pieces and left by the side of the road, at least she'd know that Rebecca would be caught while lifting weights in a seedy Croydon gym. And probably given a substantial fine for overdue books at the same time. She looked the type.

CHAPTER SIX

REBECCA WALKED BACK to the car slowly. She was enjoying stretching her legs and being out of the car, in the fresh air, away from Arabella.

She knew she had to try to keep the peace. Arabella certainly wasn't going to make any attempt. If they were going to get home without sitting in awkward silence for twenty-two hours, it was going to be down to her. As much as she didn't want to, she knew she'd need someone to talk to for the sake of her own sanity.

She opened the car door and got in.

"They had fruit, but you wouldn't have wanted it," Rebecca said before Arabella had a chance to open her mouth.

She closed the car door and started to take items out of the plastic carrier bag.

"Water, and a plain orange juice with no added sugar." She handed the items to Arabella. "In the absence of fruit, I got you some wholefood cold-pressed fruit and nut bars. That was the only thing that wasn't crisps or chocolate." She emphasized her point by pulling a packet of crisps and a small box of biscuits out of the bag.

Arabella took the juice and examined the bars.

Rebecca opened the box of biscuits and put the bag with the remaining items in the back footwell. She fished the notes and coins out of her pocket and handed them back to Arabella.

"What's this?"

"The change," Rebecca told her through a mouthful of chocolate and marshmallow. She picked up her wallet from the centre console and put it back into her jacket pocket. "I suppose you thought I'd keep the change?"

"No... not at all. I just... forgot."

"Mm." Rebecca wasn't taken in by Arabella's unconvincing tone.

"What... are you eating?" The posh woman was hiding something. She'd tried to change subjects but was now unable to mask her disgust at Rebecca's food choices.

Rebecca flashed her eyes in excitement. "Mallomars. They're a biscuit and marshmallow covered in chocolate. Only the best thing mankind ever invented. Want one?"

Arabella wrinkled her nose. "No, thank you."

She shrugged and pulled another two out of the bag. "Suit yourself." She then started the engine and pulled on her seatbelt. She checked her mirrors and started moving, eager to join the motorway again and get some of the long journey done.

A phone rang. Rebecca glanced to her side and watched as Arabella examined the screen and then cancelled the call. She didn't say anything, and the air was starting to thicken again. Rebecca knew it was up to her to try to lighten the mood.

"So, how did you get into the estate agency business?"

Rebecca asked, fishing for any topic of conversation that would stop them from sitting in silence.

"My father set up the company," Arabella replied curtly.

"And you wanted to join?"

Arabella shrugged. "It was never really mentioned. It was obvious that I'd go into the family business."

"Do you enjoy it?"

"I enjoy working."

Wow, she's hard work, Rebecca thought.

Arabella's phone rang again. She hurriedly cancelled the call.

"You can take that if you want," Rebecca offered.

"I know, you're not the reason I'm not answering."

Rebecca rolled her eyes at the tone. "Fine, I was just offering."

"It's my fiancé," Arabella admitted.

"Oh, he's probably worried about you." Rebecca wondered why she was cancelling the call. She seemed cold, but avoiding her fiancé seemed odd, even for her.

Arabella snorted a laugh. "Maybe. More likely that he is looking forward to gloating."

"Gloating? Why?"

"He didn't want me to come to Portugal, he wanted me to send someone else."

"Why?"

"You ask a lot of questions."

"Well, I don't have much else to do. We're going to be stuck together for a while, so we might as well talk about something."

Arabella remained silent for a few moments. "We're getting married, and he wants me to stop working. He wants me to wind down my work duties in preparation for that."

Rebecca blinked. "Wow, I have a billion questions."

"I don't expect you to understand; it's obvious that we live different lives."

Rebecca clenched her jaw. "I can still relate to other people. Just because I live my life doesn't mean I can't understand someone else's."

The phone rang again. Arabella let out a deep sigh. Rebecca thought for a moment that she was weighing up the best avenue available to her, continuing a conversation with her or speaking with her fiancé.

Finally, she opted for her fiancé.

"Hello, Alastair," Arabella answered neutrally.

Rebecca could hear the muffled sound of a male voice on the other end of the phone, but not clearly enough to make out any words.

"Yes, it's been... yes, well... I was..."

Rebecca tried to pretend she wasn't listening, but it was impossible. Arabella didn't seem to be able to get a word in. Normally she would have found it funny, someone putting Arabella in her place, but she almost felt sorry for the woman. She was supposed to be marrying this man. A man who she clearly didn't want to talk to. A man who now seemed to refuse to listen to her.

"I'm in a car, driving back. I'll be back in plenty of time," Arabella claimed. She paused. "Well, I don't know exactly where we are now. Close, I'm sure."

Rebecca looked at the screen on the dashboard and realised she could busy herself with setting the on-board satnav system. At least that way she wouldn't be fully focused on the awkward conversation happening beside her.

"We don't need to talk about that now," Arabella said in a softer tone. "There's someone here."

Rebecca tried to ignore the conversation, tried to focus just on programming the satnav and driving the car, but she couldn't help herself.

"I'm... car sharing. She's driving." Arabella leaned towards the passenger door. "Of course, yes. Just some girl. We'll be home soon."

Rebecca muted the volume on the satnav. The last thing she needed was a booming voice announcing that they would arrive at their destination in twenty-two hours' time.

"I know," Arabella whispered. She cleared her throat. "Yes, I will."

Rebecca almost felt sorry for her. Almost.

"I know. Well, there's not a lot I can do about it now."

Alastair's voice got louder, still indistinct, but he clearly wasn't happy.

"What's done is done." Arabella tried to lean further away from her. "It will be fine. I'll make sure of it."

Rebecca glanced at the screen as it calculated the journey to London. The map zoomed out and out. Eventually it showed the whole of France, Spain, and the bottom of England. If she hadn't been aware what she had taken on before, she was now.

"Now that isn't fair, you know that—Alastair? Alastair?" Arabella looked at the screen. She sat upright in her seat again and coughed delicately. "We... were disconnected."

"He was mad?" Rebecca asked, not wanting to acknowledge Arabella's obvious lie.

"A little," she confessed.

"Sounded like more than a little."

"He's very stressed with work at the moment," Arabella defended.

Rebecca laughed. "Wow, that old one, eh?"

Arabella glared at her. "What do you mean by that?"

"I mean that he was shouting at you and made you feel bad and you just defended him by saying he's having a hard time at work. That's no excuse. Did he even ask if you're okay?"

Arabella opened her mouth to reply but closed it again. She looked down at her phone.

Rebecca chuckled. "I'll take that as a no."

"I already know that he's worried about me, he just doesn't show it in that way."

"In what way?"

"Verbally."

"Wow. He can't even ask if you're okay. And you're marrying him?"

Arabella turned to her. "Yes, I am. And I'm lucky to have him, you don't know anything about him. Anything about us. Who are you to judge?"

"Me? I'm a nobody." Rebecca shrugged her shoulders. "I just think that the person you choose to spend the rest of your life with should treat you well. You shouldn't be avoiding their calls. You should want to talk to them, lean on them, know that they have your back."

Arabella didn't reply. Rebecca knew she had her ear, so she carried on. "Your partner should listen to you, not talk over you. You should be a team. With mutual respect."

Arabella laughed bitterly. "Nice dream world you live in."

"It's not a dream world," Rebecca defended.

"So, you're like that with your boyfriend? I didn't hear you having a beautiful, mutually respectful conversation with him."

"That's because I'm single and a lesbian. But," Rebecca added quickly before Arabella could say anything, "I have been in relationships like that. In fact, all of my relationships have been like that."

"Oh, you're—"

"Gay, yes," Rebecca said. She didn't mind coming out to people. And what was Arabella going to do if she didn't like it? Throw herself out of the car?

"Alastair isn't that bad," Arabella said, apparently ignoring Rebecca's admission.

"Do you love him?"

"Of course. Why would I be marrying him otherwise?" Arabella laughed.

"Lots of people agree to get married without being in love." Rebecca shifted in her seat. "I just think he should have been nicer to you, that's all."

Arabella turned to look out of the window. Rebecca glanced at her a couple of times before returning her attention to the road.

Clearly the conversation was over.

CHAPTER SEVEN

ARABELLA PUT her hand down the side of her seat and felt around for the controls. The throbbing in her leg was getting worse, and she needed to adjust her position. Ideally, she needed to walk around and stretch her leg out, but she wasn't about to admit that to Rebecca.

Especially as they had been sitting in silence for nearly three hours.

Arabella wanted to say something to explain and defend Alastair. But the more she thought about it, the more she realised that she couldn't. As much as she hated to admit it, Rebecca was right. Alastair didn't respect her. Deep down, she'd always known that, and it hadn't bothered her.

She'd always prided herself on knowing the value of her own self-worth. She was well-educated, from a good background, and great at her job. If she did say so herself.

Alastair was handsome, rich, and the right fit. Her father adored him. Everything seemed right. Of course, it wasn't a fairy-tale romance, she didn't think those kinds of relationships existed. They were just for Disney movies. Encouraging children to want to grow up and not scare them with the reality of what life was really like.

But Rebecca seemed to believe in them. She'd spoken of respect and being a team. Arabella knew that she didn't have either of those things in her relationship with Alastair.

She'd replayed the conversation with him over and over in her head. She'd deliberately put forward a strong and well-composed image in Rebecca's presence. An image that had crumbled the moment she spoke to Alastair.

She had felt embarrassed. She'd stumbled over words, struggled to say what she wanted to say. Then she had been unable to finish a sentence. The whole conversation had been a disaster.

Her fingers grazed over a set of buttons on the side of the chair. She pressed one and sighed in relief as the chair slid backwards. She then pressed a different button and the chair started to recline. The blood flowed to her leg, and she wiggled her toes.

"Are you okay?" Rebecca asked.

"Fine."

"Are you sure, we could—"

"I said I'm fine," Arabella snapped.

Rebecca slowly nodded. She gripped the wheel tighter and sat a little straighter.

That was when Arabella felt something she wasn't all that accustomed to.

Guilt.

The girl was just being kind after all.

From her reclined position, she took the opportunity to properly examine Rebecca. The odds of her being a murderer or a thief had dropped substantially. Arabella knew not to trust anyone fully, but the girl did seem to be genuine. She'd shown more care and concern for Arabella in the last four hours than Alastair had in the last four months.

She knew that Alastair didn't wear his heart on his sleeve like Rebecca seemed to. They were just fundamentally different people. It wasn't like one was right and one was wrong.

But different people they were, and speaking to Rebecca as she would speak to Alastair wasn't appropriate.

"I'm sorry," Arabella said. "My leg twinges a little and it makes me snappish. I apologise."

"How did you break it?"

Arabella bristled at the memory. "I fell down some stairs."

"Ouch."

"Yes, marble stairs."

"Wow, sounds like you're lucky it wasn't worse."

Her mind flashed back to the evening in question. She'd been at a party at a hotel, losing track of time. Suddenly it was closing in on midnight and she realised she had to hurry to get home. A misstep had her falling down a flight of fifteen hard and unforgiving steps. The doctors at the A&E had said much the same thing her travelling companion did.

"Yes, I suppose I was lucky," she admitted.

"My ex broke her ankle," Rebecca said. "She was playing tennis, and she slipped and fell badly. Freak accident kind of thing."

"Sounds painful."

"Yeah, I had to look after her for two weeks. The doctor said she wasn't allowed to put her weight on it. So, I had to help her get dressed, get to the bathroom and stuff. Getting her drinks and snacks."

"Also sounds painful," Arabella commented with a wince. The idea of having to care for someone else in that way made her skin crawl.

"No, it was fun," Rebecca assured.

"Fun? How on earth could it be fun?" Arabella genuinely

wanted to know what kind of PR spin Rebecca was going to put on caring for an invalid.

Rebecca smiled. "We spent lots of time together, we watched movies, cuddled. I couldn't fix her, but I could take away some of the discomfort. You know when you're sick and someone brings you a drink or something to eat? When you have a cold and someone brings you some tomato soup just at the moment you need it?"

Arabella thought for a moment. She'd never had that. Then again, she'd never offered it to anyone else either.

"No, not really," she admitted.

"Even when you were a child?" Rebecca asked. She seemed surprised.

Arabella laughed. "Oh, especially not when I was a child. We were just left to get on with things."

"Wow, well… take it from someone who knows, it's nice to care for the people you love. It's nice to be that person, to make someone feel better. Even if you can't necessarily fix them. Not so they can reciprocate. Just for the sake of doing the right thing and being kind to others."

Arabella looked up at the girl in surprise. The bartending, possibly whoring murderer with an apparent heart of gold.

"Are you rolling your eyes at me?" Rebecca asked with a chuckle.

"Absolutely," Arabella joked. "Non-stop since you started talking. I'm concerned I'll get a migraine."

"Ha, ha." Rebecca shook her head, but a smile still graced her lips.

"You're a unique specimen, Rebecca Edwards," Arabella said.

"Thanks, I think." Rebecca laughed. "Seriously, though, if your leg is hurting then you should probably get out and walk a bit when we next stop. It's just going to get worse otherwise."

"Fine, next time we stop for fuel I'll do a couple of laps of the car."

Rebecca nodded her agreement.

Arabella sighed and moved her head from side to side. No matter how luxurious the surroundings, she didn't like long journeys. Now she was stuck in a car, not even halfway through Spain and already she was exhausted. There were miles to go. Over a thousand of them according to the satnav screen.

She glanced at Rebecca again.

For the first time, she wondered if Rebecca would have the stamina to drive them home without stopping. Of course, Arabella had told her that she must, and Rebecca had agreed. But could she actually do it? A whole day's worth of solid driving was a big ask. But the girl seemed determined.

Now she thought about it, she seemed *very* determined. Of course, the time of year brought that out in people.

"I assume you are driving home to spend Christmas with your family?" Arabella asked.

"My mum," Rebecca said.

"I see. And she lives in... Croydon, did you say?"

"Yeah. I promised I'd be home in time for Christmas. We spend every Christmas together no matter what."

Good, that means she's invested in getting home as quickly as I am.

"I'm sure she'll be very happy to see you," Arabella said.

"What about you? What are you doing for Christmas?"

"Well, there's a big party every Christmas Eve at my father's house. And then on the day itself it will be my father, sister, Alastair, and I. Some family members and business associates will come and visit us throughout the day."

"Of course. Peace and goodwill to all men and business associates," Rebecca said.

Arabella chuckled. "I know it's unusual to talk about

business at Christmas, but we do. It's not all presents under the tree and homemade pies at my house."

"Sounds awful."

Arabella laughed. "You really speak your mind, don't you?"

"I don't mean to be rude, I'm just saying that, in my mind, Christmas is for family. You exchange gifts, eat treats, watch television. You just be together."

"Sounds awful," Arabella joked.

"You say that now, but you haven't tasted my homemade Christmas pies," Rebecca said.

CHAPTER EIGHT

THE SUN WAS orange and hazy, low in the sky. They'd been driving for seven hours, and Rebecca was feeling a numbness creeping up her backside. Arabella had been adjusting her seat on and off for the past four hours, clearly trying to get comfortable. Now she was partially reclined. Sat so low that she was unable to look out of the window.

Rebecca had been watching the icon of their car on the satnav screen throughout the journey. It seemed to slowly crawl its way across Spain. Even now they seemed to only be two-thirds of the way across the country. She'd never really taken into consideration just how big Spain was before.

Apparently, it was easy to *say* that you were driving across two countries, but a different matter entirely to be *doing* it.

She knew that she needed a break. Even though she desperately didn't want to waste any time. She needed the bathroom, to walk around a little, and to stretch her back and legs out.

"I'm going to need to stop for a few minutes," Rebecca said.

She waited for Arabella's acerbic response.

"Good idea."

She glanced at Arabella in surprise. The older woman pressed the button on the side of her chair. The motor started to whir. She slowly rose.

"You look like a terrible Bond villain," Rebecca commented.

After another thirty seconds, Arabella finally arrived at an upright position. "Where's the next services?"

"We seem to be in the middle of nowhere. I've not seen any services as such, the odd petrol station that looks rundown but nothing else."

"Well, that can't be as bad as the place we stopped before."

Rebecca snorted. "The places we've been driving past make that look like a palace. We're really out in the sticks."

Arabella got her phone out and started to tap away on the screen. "There must be somewhere around here where we won't catch tetanus."

Rebecca looked around the road. For as far as she could see in all directions, there was nothing. Scrubland and the odd wreck of a building. Closed hotels and bars were few and far between.

"We're in the middle of nowhere," Arabella announced.

"I told you." Rebecca smothered a yawn behind her hand.

"What was that?" Arabella asked.

Rebecca frowned. "Nothing."

"That wasn't nothing, you yawned."

"It was just a small yawn, nothing much. I'd drink more of my energy drink, but I don't want to do that until I know we're near a bathroom."

Arabella looked up at the scenery. "Maybe we should pull off the road? Look for a town?" She looked back at her phone and started to tap in a new search.

"There's a garage about forty minutes up the road we're on," Arabella said. "It's a dive, but it promises to have a bathroom, petrol, and food. Or we can turn off and be at a garage in twenty minutes, but we will be heading generally away from our route."

Rebecca pressed lightly on the accelerator pedal, pushing the car ever so slightly over the speed limit. It wasn't something she was comfortable doing, but she wasn't about to start going backwards.

"I can hold on for forty minutes, you?"

"As long as you're sure?" Arabella asked. "I mean, I don't want you to kill us both."

Rebecca rolled her eyes. "You nearly said something nice then."

"I've said plenty of nice things," Arabella defended.

"Must have missed them." Rebecca winced at her own tone.

She didn't want to speak to Arabella like that, it wasn't in her nature to be rude. She was just getting frustrated with the situation. She desperately wanted to be home and her back was aching, but that was no reason to take it out on a *nearly* innocent bystander.

"Then you'll just have to pay more attention, I'm not likely to repeat them," Arabella said with a jokey tone.

Rebecca smiled. It would have been easy for Arabella to reply sarcastically, but she hadn't.

Maybe she's not that bad, Rebecca thought. *Just takes a while to get through the thick skin.*

"I'll listen out for them," she promised.

"On reflection, I'm not sure I want that walk around the car after all," Arabella said as they pulled into the garage and came to a stop.

Rebecca leaned forward and wrapped her arms around the top of the steering wheel. She looked at the rickety old shack. The building looked like it was made of scraps of wood and metal and was precariously close to the edge of a steep cliff.

There were no petrol pumps, just tyre tracks that had burrowed a groove into the ground in front of the building. A cardboard sign, written in marker pen, hung clumsily by a single nail on the door. The light of the setting sun made it all the more ominous.

"How's your Spanish?" Rebecca asked, indicating the sign.

"Ring for service," Arabella translated.

Rebecca looked at the old-fashioned brass bell that hung by the door. "Right, so I should—"

Arabella grabbed her forearm and spun to face her. "Do we want to do this? This is the kind of place where innocent travellers like you and I go missing."

Rebecca scoffed. "Says who?"

"Movies!"

"Yeah, on a Halloween fright night special, maybe. The last movie I saw was a musical. No one died. In fact, everyone was happy and dancing."

"Why am I not surprised?"

Rebecca shook her head and removed Arabella's hand from her arm. "I'm going to ring the bell. If an axe murderer appears, beep the horn to warn me, okay?"

She opened the door and got out of the car. Stretching her hands above her head, she enjoyed the sounds of her lower back cracking. She walked towards the shack, examining the property for any signs of life as she went.

An old caravan was parked around the side of the building, but she couldn't tell if it was lived in or abandoned.

A thought occurred to her that the whole place might be abandoned. They may have driven forty minutes to find a closed garage. Maybe the next one was an hour away. She was pretty sure her bladder wouldn't survive that kind of wait.

She reached up and rang the bell a couple of times, hard.

She took a step back and looked around for any attendants. She looked at Arabella, who had shrunk back into her seat and was anxiously looking around.

Suddenly the door opened.

"Si?"

Rebecca spun around to address the elderly man standing there. "Oh, hi, do you speak English?"

The man looked from her to the car. He was a frail, tiny thing. "Gas?"

"Yes." Rebecca nodded her head. "And, a bathroom? Toilet?"

The man looked at her with a frown.

"Lavatory?" Rebecca tried.

He smiled and nodded in understanding. He indicated around the building, the opposite side to the caravan, towards the cliff. Rebecca wondered if he was suggesting she find a bush.

"Thank you," she said. "Um, I mean *gracias*!"

She turned to see Arabella struggling to get out of the car.

"Jesus," she mumbled under her breath. "Why doesn't she ask for help?"

The man disappeared back into the shack, and Rebecca walked over to the car to assist Arabella.

"You okay?"

"What did he say?" Arabella asked, pulling her crutch from the car and leaning awkwardly on it.

"He said 'gas'," Rebecca said. "And I said yes."

"Is there a bathroom?"

"Apparently around the corner." Rebecca gestured with her thumb. "Are you okay?"

Arabella struggled to stand straight, leaning heavily on the crutch. "Yes, just a little stiff."

"Same here."

She heard a noise and turned around to see the Spanish man exiting the shack with a large petrol canister that was half the size of him. He walked over to them.

"*Hola, hola,*" he greeted Arabella. He looked at the car and made an unlocking gesture towards it before looking at Rebecca.

"Oh, right, yes… *sí,*" she said. She walked around the car, leaned in through the driver's door, and unlocked the petrol flap.

The man immediately opened the flap and started to undo the cap.

"I'm going to the bathroom," Rebecca announced.

"Don't leave me here," Arabella whispered through clench teeth.

"You're welcome to come, but no listening."

"How crass," Arabella muttered.

She struggled to pivot herself. Rebecca moved to stand beside her and easily slipped her arm around Arabella's waist.

"Lean on me," she instructed. "You need to get blood flow back into your leg."

Arabella slightly leaned on her but seemed insistent on doing the majority of the work herself.

They started to walk away from the car, Arabella occasionally turning to look at the man.

"What if he steals the car?"

Rebecca turned and looked at the car. She gestured to the shack. "Then you get the caravan and I get the garage."

"I'm telling you," Arabella said. "This is where we're going to die."

"Do you always overreact this much? I'm surprised you even got in a car with me. What if I was a murderer?"

Arabella was silent, only the sound of the dusty ground under her crutch and plaster cast was audible.

"Oh my god, you thought I was a murderer, didn't you?" Rebecca laughed.

"I was cautiously concerned about you; I didn't know who you were," Arabella defended. "I mean, look at you."

Rebecca shook her head and laughed some more, ignoring the comment about her appearance. "So, the natural assumption was that I was a murderer?"

"I'm not sure what's so funny," Arabella said. She pulled away from Rebecca and started to walk on her own.

They approached the side of the building. A narrow path near the cliff edge led to a wooden outhouse that had seen better days.

Arabella stopped walking and turned up her nose at the rundown structure.

"I suddenly don't hear nature calling so loudly," she said.

"Tough, we're not stopping again until we get to, like, France. I'll go first," Rebecca said.

"Oh, yes, you do that. I'll just wait out here with the murderer," Arabella called after her. "Well, the new murderer, I suppose."

Rebecca smiled to herself and walked towards the wooden outhouse. She had to admit, Arabella wasn't quite the worst travel companion in the world. Now and then, she could actually be quite funny. Unfortunately, those bouts of humour were sprinkled in between judgemental comments.

She opened the door to the outhouse and peeked inside, holding her breath as she did. She looked around, pleasantly surprised at what she found. A clean, modern toilet. A sink.

Soap. It was luxury compared to what the exterior of the building had promised.

She attended to her needs and then left the outhouse, ready to tell Arabella about the five-star facilities she'd discovered. Looking up the path, she couldn't see Arabella anywhere. She frowned and started to take a step forward.

"Rebecca, look at this."

She turned and looked at the back of the shack. "Arabella?"

"Around here, look at this."

She walked around the back of the garage and saw Arabella standing on the edge of the cliff. Rebecca walked up beside her in awe. The raised position allowed for miles and miles of uninterrupted views. Mountains in the distance, animals grazing, the odd farmhouse. The view was unlike anything she'd seen before. And the way the evening light shone on the valley was casting beautiful shadows and shades of reds and oranges.

"Wow," Rebecca breathed.

"Isn't it amazing? We couldn't see this because of the angle of the road, but we appear to be quite high up."

"Wait right here," Rebecca instructed. She took off at a sprint, running around the building and back to the car. The attendant looked at her with a kind smile. She returned the smile and retrieved her backpack from the back of the car.

She opened the worn flap, removed a couple of items of clothing, and then pulled out her camera. She paused and regarded the lens for a moment before digging in her bag for her wider-angled lens.

The man looked at her and smiled. "Click, click," he said, gesturing to the camera and then to the building.

Rebecca nodded. "Sí!"

She sprinted back around the building. This was what she loved about travel, you never knew where you might come across the most amazing shot. The view had been completely hidden behind some rundown old buildings. Many people would have driven straight by without having any idea of the wonders that lay a few metres away.

Back at Arabella's side, she raised her camera, took a shot, and then looked at the screen, examining the lighting data. She made a couple of changes to the ISO settings and then tapped the shutter again. She meticulously framed the view, adjusting the lens focus by a fraction each time she took a new shot.

She was lost in her own world, taking distance shots, close-ups, and everything in between. She knew from experience that the chance of her fully documenting the view was unlikely. Photos could never live up to the actual experience. Sometimes, though, tiny details could only be picked up in post-production.

The light was fading. This meant she must rush to capture the scene, as it grew more beautiful with every passing moment. As the winter sun set, the colours became richer and cast dramatic shadows across the valley.

"Hello? Earth to Rebecca?"

She lowered her camera and looked at Arabella in confusion. "I'm sorry?"

"I've been talking to you, but you've been in your own little world," Arabella grumbled.

"Sorry, I... I didn't hear you. What did you say?"

"I was commenting that your camera looks very expensive. Professional, even."

Rebecca looked down at her kit. "Oh, yes, it is."

"I thought you worked in a bar?"

Rebecca smirked. "Yes, you did. I might have misled you."

Arabella raised an eyebrow. "You don't work in a bar?"

Rebecca shook her head.

"You let me believe—"

"No, you assumed that because I don't look like you, I must have some low-paid, temporary job. So… I didn't give you information otherwise." Rebecca lifted her camera and took another shot. The sun was setting over a mountain and the light it cast was too beautiful to miss. "I'm a professional photographer. I was in Portugal doing a shoot for a band. Fun work but doesn't pay much."

"You're a photographer?" Arabella repeated, clearly taking a while to catch up with events.

Rebecca lowered the camera. "Yup. Not a stripper, or whatever you thought I was when you totally judged me by my appearance."

Arabella's mouth curled into a grin. "Well, you got me. I apologise for my assumptions about you."

Rebecca couldn't help herself, something about Arabella's stance, her smile, the way the wind blew gently through her hair. She raised her camera, wanting to capture the moment. She snapped a couple of pictures before Arabella began to laugh and bat the attention away with her hand.

"Oh, don't, I'm terribly unphotogenic."

"Are you kidding me?" Rebecca cried. "You're beautiful."

Arabella laughed and looked down at the canyon floor, obviously embarrassed by the attention.

Rebecca lowered her camera. "I'm sorry, I'll stop." She smiled.

"Good." She adjusted her hand on her crutch. "I'm going to use the bathroom. I assume it wasn't too horrible, as you survived?"

"You'll be pleasantly surprised," Rebecca reassured her.

"Good. You can continue taking your pictures, but no more of me." Arabella started to walk away. "I know where that can lead, I saw *Carol*," she joked over her shoulder.

Rebecca burst out laughing. "I thought you only watched slasher flicks."

Arabella paused and turned around. "It was practically a thriller. I was on the edge of my seat the entire time. They were lesbians, I was terrified they'd be killed."

She turned and started walking towards the outhouse again. "Thank goodness for a happy ending," she called back.

CHAPTER NINE

ARABELLA LOOKED at the time on her phone. It was seven in the evening. They'd been driving for ten hours and were about to enter France.

At the outset, the journey had seemed doable. Now, not even halfway in, it seemed ridiculous to think they could drive back to England in one sitting.

Despite stopping and admiring the amazing view at the petrol stop a few hours ago, she was again feeling the pain of sitting still. Her leg was numb, as was her back and her backside. But worse than that, she could feel herself drifting off to sleep. The mind-numbing country views had given away to nothing but darkness. As soon as the sun had set, she'd longed for an abandoned farmhouse or scrubland as far as the eye could see.

Her efforts to engage Rebecca in conversation had been futile. It seemed that the girl didn't want to speak about herself or her personal life. And the more she retreated into her shell, the more Arabella tried to prise her out of it. With no success.

She now knew that Rebecca was not a bartender, a

dancer, nor a prostitute. She was a photographer. Who lived in Croydon and wanted to get home to spend Christmas with her mother. Other than that, she was a mystery. Oh, and she was gay.

Arabella didn't even know why she wanted to know more about Rebecca. At first, she had wanted to learn more about her potential murderer. To somehow make a connection between them so Rebecca would be less likely to mug her and leave her for dead in an abandoned farmhouse.

But that wasn't the case anymore. Now she trusted Rebecca. As much as she trusted anyone, anyway.

She looked at the road and spied a promising sign up ahead.

"France," she said. She turned to Rebecca and smiled.

Rebecca didn't return the smile. She sat forward, focusing rigidly on the road. She looked exhausted.

"Another country down," Arabella tried again.

"Yup," Rebecca bit out.

They hadn't known each other for long, but Rebecca's silence was worrying. Arabella returned her attention to the road. They were passing over a bridge, with the promise of a toll booth up ahead. She looked at the satnav and saw that they had another thirteen hours to go. They weren't even halfway home. Rebecca looked utterly exhausted.

"Maybe we should stop?" Arabella suggested carefully.

"Ha! You're the one going on about how long this is taking and how late you'll be for your party. No, we keep going."

Arabella frowned at the outburst and turned to look out of her window.

"I'm sorry," Rebecca said. "I'm just a little tired, I didn't mean to snap at you. I'll get my second wind soon."

"It's okay, it's a lot to take on," Arabella said. "I do think we should stop."

"What time does your party start?"

Arabella looked at Rebecca. She knew what she was thinking. She wanted to work backwards from the start of the party and tell Arabella that they didn't have time to stop. Suddenly she felt an uncomfortable guilt for having pressured Rebecca so much at the start of the journey.

"Well, it starts at nine," she lied. "But it goes on until Christmas morning. I don't have to be there at nine."

"What about your hair appointment? You said that it was imperative that you made that appointment. And your massage, let's not forget your massage," Rebecca mimicked Arabella's tone.

She let out a sigh. "I may have said that in order to encourage you to drive a little faster. At this point I'll just settle for turning up to any of the party. You know, alive. And not wrapped around some tree in France because you crashed due to exhaustion."

"I'm fine," Rebecca argued.

The car slowed to the toll booth, and Rebecca pressed the button to open her window. They'd been through countless tolls in Spain, Arabella complaining at the ridiculous cost of each one. She thought they were all a scam, the country extracting money out of road users with no alternative.

The automatic booth flashed up an amount. Rebecca picked up a large handful of coins that she had stored in the cup holder. She looked at the coins with a frown on her face. Something she'd not done before.

It suddenly became obvious that Rebecca was struggling to identify the denominations of the foreign currency. Something that hadn't happened before and was clearly another sign of her tiredness.

Arabella waited a few moments before picking the correct coins out of Rebecca's cupped hand and holding them for her to take.

Rebecca took the exact change and threw it into the automatic change counter. A few seconds later the barrier opened.

"I'm fine," she repeated.

"Okay," Arabella replied.

Of course, she knew that Rebecca wasn't fine. They needed to stop, and a ten-minute break at a petrol station in the middle of nowhere wasn't going to cut it. They needed to stop for the night.

She wasn't even the one driving, and she was finding it almost impossible to keep her eyes open. They couldn't go on, even if Rebecca seemed adamant to do so. Arabella couldn't believe that she was just doing it so she'd get home in time for the party.

She assumed there was another reason for Rebecca's desire to get home as soon as possible. Probably to watch some inane television program, some overly advertised Christmas special perhaps. Or to participate in some tradition that her family upheld every year, eating a mince pie, or unwrapping one present before sitting in front of the television in a drunken stupor and a onesie.

Well, that wasn't going to happen if they carried on the way they were. They had to stop and rest for the night. And she had to make it happen.

She unlocked her phone and opened her accommodation application. She hoped that it wouldn't be too difficult to find somewhere to stay so close to Christmas.

"What are you doing?" Rebecca asked.

"Playing Angry Birds," she lied.

"I don't see you as an Angry Birds kind of person."

"Oh, I love it." She tapped in her requirements for the search filter. "Those birds. Being… angry."

"Yeah, I can tell you're a real fan."

"Why don't you talk about yourself?" Arabella changed the subject.

"What do you mean? I talk about myself."

"Not really. You lied about your profession, supposedly to teach me a lesson about making assumptions. Aside from that, you've evaded many of my questions."

Rebecca chuckled. "I've not *evaded* your questions."

The spinning search icon appeared while her phone sought out a connection. "If you say so."

"Ask me something, something I've supposedly evaded."

"There's nothing specific, just that you don't say anything."

"Maybe there's nothing to say? Maybe I'm just boring?"

"You've flown to Portugal to photograph a band, that doesn't sound *too* boring."

"Thanks, I think. And that was just one job. Their original photographer dropped out at last minute and they asked me to do it."

"You don't sound like you wanted to do it?" Arabella asked. She thumbed through a few hotels, checking for available rooms and a green light to indicate that the owner was online. No point in booking a last-minute room and surprising the host by turning up ten minutes later.

"I didn't. Didn't really want to be away from home, you know?"

Arabella laughed. "Not really. I wanted to be away from home."

"How come?"

Arabella paused as she thought about her reply.

She knew the answer, she just wasn't ready to verbalise it yet. Luckily, she was saved from the awkward truth by the search result providing its response.

"Take the next left."

"What? Why?"

Arabella sighed. "Just do it."

She was thankful that she had all her details saved on the application so she could take advantage of one-click booking. She felt the car starting to slow down and knew that Rebecca was doing as she had asked.

"What are we doing?" Rebecca sounded frustrated.

"Continue up this road for a kilometre and then turn right." Arabella quickly went back into her search result to secure another bedroom. While she didn't think Rebecca was a murderer, she wasn't about to share a room with the girl either.

"Arabella?" Rebecca asked, anger creeping into her voice.

She secured the second room and lowered the phone.

She turned to Rebecca.

"We're stopping. I've booked us in at a local bed and breakfast. No arguments. There's no way you can carry on like this. We'll stop for the night and get started early in the morning. By my calculations, we should get into London around seven in the evening on Christmas Eve."

"No, I told you, I'm okay to carry on, I—"

Arabella leaned over and put her hand on Rebecca's knee. "You're unable to keep your eyes open, you're smothering yawns, you've drifted lanes seven times in the last hour and that is only going to get worse. I know you're desperate to get home. But Christmas will wait a few hours longer. You're exhausted, and you need to rest."

She removed her hand and leaned back, waiting to see if Rebecca would argue the point or give in and accept that it was time to rest.

"You know, if this is an excuse to seduce me, forget it. You're not my type," Rebecca joked.

Arabella laughed. "Damn, you got me," she replied.

Rebecca sighed, seemingly resigned to the fact that they

would have to stop. "Okay, so where is this bed and breakfast?"

Arabella breathed a sigh of relief. She picked up her phone and accessed the map. "It's about ten minutes away. It seems to be in the middle of nowhere, but then a lot around here seems to be in the middle of nowhere. Luckily for us that means it has two rooms available at short notice."

"But we start again early in the morning, right?" Rebecca pressed.

"Absolutely, I'm used to an early start, so whatever time you want to set off is fine by me."

Rebecca nodded. She slowed down and started to indicate right. "This road?"

Arabella looked at the map on her phone and then at the fog-covered road. The further they moved from the main road, the thicker the fog seemed to become.

"Yes, seems to be the one."

The road was narrow and set between two tall stone walls. The farther they went, the thicker the fog seemed to get.

"I can hardly see," Rebecca said.

"Just go slowly," Arabella said calmly.

She didn't feel calm. The fog was so thick that she could barely see the end of the bonnet. If another car came from the other direction they would be stuck. There was no room to pass with the stone walls on either side of them.

Arabella held her breath as Rebecca slowly navigated the road. She saw an email come in from the bed and breakfast owner, confirming their bookings and advising them that they were expecting their arrival. She quickly typed a response back to say that they were in the area and would arrive momentarily.

She looked up again and swallowed. The road was so narrow and the fog so thick. If she'd known this was the road in, she would have chosen somewhere else. On the bright side, the adrenaline rush was sure to wake Rebecca up for a while.

After a few heart-stopping moments, the walls ended, and the road expanded to two lanes again.

"Where now?" Rebecca asked.

"It should be up here on the right," Arabella replied after checking the map on her phone.

Rebecca slowly drove, leaning forward and looking out of the window to the right.

"Are you sure? I mean, if you wanted to kill me and leave me out here—"

"Don't be silly," Arabella said. "It's here. Somewhere."

She looked at the phone again and then at the GPS map on the car dashboard.

"It should be a few more metres," she said.

A brick wall started to emerge through the fog. As they continued to crawl forward, the wall gave way to a large, open wrought-iron gate.

"Whoa." Rebecca stopped the car and looked at Arabella. "Bed and breakfast? Are you kidding me?"

Arabella looked at the mansion beyond the open gate, shrouded in wispy fog. A pebbled driveway led to a set of stone steps which in turn led to an imposing front door. Two large lanterns illuminated the door. It was very gothic, presumably very grand-looking in good weather. However, in the fog it just looked eerie.

"It said Château de Bernard, but everything is a Château around here," Arabella argued. She looked at her phone and then at the building again. "This must be it."

"What if it isn't?" Rebecca asked.

"Then we apologise and drive out again." Arabella pointed towards the gate. "Come on, let's go."

CHAPTER TEN

"You know, I'm suddenly feeling wide awake," Rebecca said. "Maybe we should, you know, keep going?"

Arabella glared at her.

"Okay, I'm going, I'm going." Rebecca took Arabella's phone, the booking receipt open and visible on the screen. She opened the car door and got out.

She swallowed hard as she looked up at the imposing building. It looked like something out of a crime drama. This was where Countess McDeath lived, appealing to the police that she was feeding her horses at the time of the murder, the tiny fact that she was feeding the horses body parts of the victim only coming to light at the end of the show.

Arabella rapped on the window, and Rebecca jumped. She turned and stared at her. Arabella waved her away from the car and pointed towards the front door.

"Wish I was the one with the broken leg," Rebecca muttered.

She turned back towards the house. The house that was surrounded by an eerie fog. Why couldn't Arabella have picked somewhere a little less creepy? A generic chain would have been just fine. Not that she suspected many of them were available in the French countryside.

The wind started to pick up, and she wrapped her leather jacket around her body, only now realising that she was driving north in winter. It was going to get a lot colder. Although not as cold as she felt now, the atmosphere chilling her more than the weather ever could.

She took a steadying breath and made quick work of the front steps. Before she had time to reconsider, she pulled on the large metal hoop to ring the bell. She'd not seen an old-fashioned doorbell in person before, but she'd watched enough period dramas to know what it was.

She heard a dim chime sound inside the house. As tired and exhausted as she was, she hoped that the house was empty. Everything gave her the creeps about the building. She wanted to be back in the car and making her way home.

The sound of footsteps became audible. She took a tiny step back and glanced towards Arabella in the car. She knew that if anything happened, the older woman would be out of the car and charging an assailant with her crutch in a matter of moments. She was struck by the thought that Arabella, an unknown quantity half a day ago, was now her security blanket.

The door swung open.

"Miss Henley, I'm assuming?"

An elderly British lady stood in the doorway. She was tall and extremely thin. She wore a tartan skirt suit, and her hair was swept up into a bun. She looked like the kind of person who had never worn a pair of jeans, but she was smiling and seemed friendly enough.

"I'm Rebecca, Rebecca Edwards. Miss Henley's in the car. We were just checking we have the right place," Rebecca replied.

"Indeed, you do. I'm Mary Davenport, and this is

Château de Bernard. Shall I ask my husband to help with the bags?"

Rebecca shook her head, she didn't think Arabella would want some unknown person touching her luggage. Nor did she want to ask an old man to drag Arabella's seventy-two cases up the stone steps.

"No, thank you. We're not sure what we're bringing in and what we're leaving in the car."

"Not a problem, I was just getting some tea ready. Would you both like some tea? Maybe some sandwiches?"

Rebecca felt her heart soar at the thought of a hot cup of tea. "Yes, please, that would be amazing."

Mary nodded and stepped back into the house, leaving the door open.

Rebecca hurried down the stairs and opened the car door. Arabella was literally on the edge of her seat, hands wrapped around her crutch.

"This is the right place," Rebecca confirmed.

Arabella let out a relieved sigh. "Ah, yes, well, I did know that. Of course it is."

Rebecca rolled her eyes. "Yep, of course you did. Anyway, we need to get our luggage in. And by our luggage, I mean yours. What bag do you want? Notice I said bag, singular."

Arabella balked. "I need at least three!"

"No, you don't. You're infirm, and I'm not dragging your entire wardrobe up and down those steps."

"Isn't there a bellboy?"

Rebecca pursed her lips. "No, this is someone's house. The woman who greeted me is about a hundred years old, and I'm not going to ask her husband to carry our things."

Arabella visibly deflated. "Fine. But I need two bags, one is my makeup case."

Rebecca chuckled. "You need a *case* of makeup?"

"We can't all be twenty-seven."

She narrowed her eyes. "How do you know I'm twenty-seven?"

Arabella paused for a second. "You told me, during your incessant blathering on."

"Hey, I don't incessantly blather—"

"Don't just stand there, help me out of the car."

Arabella opened the passenger door and started to try to edge her way towards it. Rebecca shook her head. One moment Arabella was bordering on nice, the next she was as cutting as ever.

She held the door open as Arabella tried to pivot herself out of the vehicle. Rebecca frowned. Arabella had seemed pretty spry before, but now she appeared to be struggling. She assumed that it was something to do with being stuck in the same position for so many hours.

In a sudden burst of movement, Arabella launched herself up out of the car. Her crutch gave way on the shingled driveway and Arabella pitched forward. Rebecca quickly moved in and grabbed her by the upper arms to hold her up. Arabella panted hard at the shock of slipping and almost falling.

"Thank you," Arabella murmured.

"That's okay, I'm not staying in this place overnight by myself," Rebecca joked.

"Your concern for my wellbeing is heart-warming." Her tone was light.

Rebecca waited for Arabella to right herself and hold onto the top of the car. Once she was sure that she was steady, she bent down and grabbed the abandoned crutch.

"So, was she cleaning a meat cleaver with a bloodied rag when she opened the door?" Arabella asked.

Rebecca laughed. "Don't! I'll never get any sleep!"

"Good, one of us needs to keep an ear out for bumps in the night."

Arabella took the crutch from Rebecca and adjusted her stance. She let go of the car and pivoted to face her.

"Thank you," she mumbled again. "Shall we?"

Arabella bit her lip. She took in the decor while her host was away preparing tea and sandwiches. At first, she had just seen a very large but old-fashioned sitting room. Fabric wingback chairs and leather sofas. The kind of thing you would expect in an older property, especially one that welcomed guests on a regular basis.

Mary Davenport had led her in, treating her as if she were an invalid. She'd guided her to a wingback chair in front of the fire. As soon as Arabella had sat down, a footstool had been dragged across the room and her plaster-covered leg was being hoisted on top of it.

With the promise of fresh tea, Mary had left the room, which allowed Arabella the time to see the other occupants of the room: shelves upon shelves of porcelain dolls. Arabella had often visited houses of clients who were collectors. Sometimes their collections lived on the odd shelf throughout the home, sometimes an entire room was dedicated to it. But she'd never seen anything on this scale.

She guessed that there were at least two hundred dolls in the room. They were on shelves, on the coffee table, one even sat on the sofa. All of them stared at her. Their dead eyes looking right her.

Even the large Christmas tree in the corner of the room had a few smaller dolls hidden in the branches, like something out of a gardener's worse nightmare.

"Hey, you should see upstairs, Jesus." Rebecca stopped dead in the middle of the room and followed Arabella's gaze. "Oh, they're in here, too."

"They're upstairs?"

"Oh, they're *everywhere*," Rebecca told her. She pulled her leather jacket off, the heat from the fire making the room overwhelmingly hot. "They are on the stairs, like in the corners, ready to grab your ankles. On the landing. Sitting in chairs on the landing. On windowsills. On the second set of stairs, on the second landing."

Arabella bristled at the idea. She was suddenly even more pleased to have Rebecca with her.

"None of this was in the photographs online," Arabella said. "It just said charming bed and breakfast, not fog-obscured gothic mansion owned by geriatric doll-collecting maniac."

"Shh." Rebecca turned around to see if she could see their hosts.

"Have you seen the husband?" Arabella asked.

"No, why?"

"Do we know that there *is* a husband?"

Rebecca glared at her. "Stop, I'm already freaked out."

"I'm serious. I've only seen her. He's not upstairs?" Arabella tried to twist her body around so she could see the door. Only now was she wondering why her host had put her in a chair with her back to the door.

"Well, I didn't do a full search, but I didn't see him."

Arabella raised her eyebrow and remained silent.

Rebecca opened her mouth to speak but stopped as Mary entered the room again, a tea tray in her hands.

"Oh good, you're both here. I made some sandwiches. How are you both settling in?" Mary asked.

Arabella remained silent and looked at Rebecca, indicating that she was to answer.

"Very well. You have a lovely home," Rebecca replied.

Arabella nearly snorted a laugh but managed to stop herself just in time.

"And thank you so much for the sandwiches," Rebecca continued, glaring at Arabella while Mary busied herself with putting the tray onto a coffee table.

"You're very welcome; I'm afraid you'll struggle to find anywhere else to eat around here. We're a little out of the way," Mary said.

Arabella raised her eyebrow again and looked at Rebecca. Rebecca shook her head and rolled her eyes.

"Do you live here alone?" Arabella asked.

"No, with my husband, Jonathan."

"I look forward to meeting him," Arabella said.

"Oh, I'm sure he'll come and introduce himself at some point," Mary said. "I'll leave you girls to it, ring the bell if you need me."

Mary gestured towards an old-fashioned brass button by the fireplace. By the time Arabella looked away from the bell, Mary had gone.

Rebecca picked up the plate of sandwiches and offered it towards Arabella. She looked at it with a sigh.

"Yeah, I know it's not wholegrain, seeded rye bread with an avocado and hummus filling, but it will have to do," Rebecca told her.

Arabella was about to deny that was what she was thinking. But another look at the starchy white bread sandwich and she couldn't stop herself grimacing.

"Eat one," Rebecca pressed.

She picked up a sandwich and took a small bite. It wasn't too bad, even if it did remind her of the sandwiches she ate at school many years ago.

Rebecca moved the table nearer to them so they could both reach the tea and sandwiches. Rebecca sat down, kicked off her ankle-length boots, and started to wiggle her toes.

Arabella stared at the dolls. Mainly because they were staring at her. "Do you collect anything?"

"Not really."

"Not really sounds like you do but you don't want to admit to it," Arabella said.

"It's not really a collection, as such. But every time I do a new photoshoot, I take a test shot to check my settings. I always print and keep that test shot. Everyone gets to see the final shots that make it to print, but only I have those first images. They might be out of focus, too much ISO, too little, incorrect f-stop. Whatever. Sometimes they are fine. But it's something that only I have, and I like that."

Arabella smiled. It wasn't a collection in a traditional sense, it was documenting her own life. Like a visual work diary, a reminder of her projects. She could see the appeal; she had kept the particulars from the first properties she had ever sold.

"What about you?" Rebecca asked. "Do you collect anything?"

"Keys," Arabella replied. "Old keys. My grandmother had a rusty old key that she dug up in her garden, and I was absolutely fascinated with it. It was the kind of key that you draw when you were a child. Very simplistic, but big and important-looking. When I started working in the estate agency, it seemed an appropriate collection to keep."

"Sounds cool. I suppose you have keys that have a cool story and huge price tag attached." Rebecca picked up another sandwich.

"A few," she admitted. "I do have one that is the key to some of the shackles used in the Tower of London. Who knows what that key could say if it could talk."

"Shackles? Didn't think of you as the bondage type." Rebecca winked as she sipped tea.

Arabella laughed. "Oh, there's a lot you don't know about me, I'm sure." She returned the wink.

She enjoyed the back-and-forth banter she shared with

Rebecca. It wasn't like the conversations she had with her friends. It was on the edge of being risqué, but she knew it was all in good humour. She didn't feel she had to watch what she said.

Rebecca snorted. She picked up the plate of sandwiches and held it out towards Arabella. She took another sandwich, only now realising how hungry she actually was.

"When's your wedding?" Rebecca asked.

"Soon." She took a large bite of the sandwich. The need for real food outweighed her knowledge of just how much sugar she was ingesting.

"Do you have everything sorted out and planned?"

"Most of it."

"Wow, you seem so excited," she said with a touch of sarcasm.

"Have you ever been married?" Arabella changed the subject.

"Nope."

"Been asked?" she fished.

"Nope."

"Asked someone?"

Rebecca hesitated a moment. Her cheeks started to show some colour.

"Aha," Arabella said knowingly. "So, what happened?"

Rebecca shrugged. "She said no. She said I was too young." She wiggled her toes and watched them, trying to look like she was unfazed by the fact. Trying, but failing.

"How old were you?"

"Twenty-three."

Arabella nodded. "You were too young."

Rebecca rolled her eyes and flopped back in her chair. "Wow, judgemental much?"

"Not judgemental, just older than you." She tossed the

crust of her sandwich onto the plate. She wasn't about to completely destroy her waistline.

"So, because you're older than me, you automatically know better than me?"

"Yes, I'm an oracle. Like Yoda."

Rebecca laughed. Her irritation evaporated at the well-placed joke. "Don't tell me you watch *Star Wars*?"

"I may have seen it once or twice," Arabella confessed.

"Well, Yoda or not, just because you're older than me doesn't mean that you know better than me."

"Maybe," Arabella allowed. She lowered her cast from the footstool and leaned forward to prepare herself a cup of tea.

Suddenly something occurred to her. "You say that she said you were too young? So, how old was she?"

Rebecca's eyes drifted towards the fire. The blush that was light on her cheeks grew in richness and started to encompass her ears.

Interesting, Arabella thought.

"In her forties…"

Arabella nearly dropped the milk jug.

"Late… forties," Rebecca continued.

"How late?" Arabella asked, unable to stop herself.

"Nine," Rebecca whispered.

"You were twenty-three and she was forty-nine? That's… that's… twenty-six years difference. She was more than twice as old as you."

Rebecca shrugged. "I loved her, and she loved me."

"What happened?"

Rebecca tore her gaze away from the fire and reached for another sandwich. "She let me go. Her words. She said she loved me, and I know that she did. But she thought she was trapping me in a life where she would be growing older and older as I'd be coming into my prime. Again, her words.

"I wanted to prove to her that I loved her, that I'd stick

by her. So, I proposed. But that was the beginning of the end. I thought that making that ultimate promise would be the proof that I didn't care about her age, that I just wanted to be with her. But it made her think about the future, what we were doing. And she broke up with me."

Arabella slowly stirred her tea, her mind racing in a hundred different directions at once. She couldn't imagine a twenty-three-year-old being in love with a forty-nine-year-old. Hell, she wasn't even sure she knew what love was herself.

"How did you know you loved her?"

Rebecca looked at her. "How do you know you love Alastair?"

"Humour me?" Arabella requested.

Rebecca let out a sigh and sat back in her seat. She brought her legs up, hugging her knees to her chest. "I enjoyed her company. Every moment we were together was something I enjoyed. I never spent a minute with her and thought it was a minute I would rather be doing something else. She made me laugh, made me think, made me hope, wish, dream. She listened to me, told me when I was wrong, agreed with me when I was right. We'd argue about things, not fight, just express a difference of opinion. Debate, I suppose. And we both learnt something new, about the subject, about ourselves, and about each other. I grew as a person, which is the purpose of life."

Arabella blinked. "Is it?"

Rebecca looked at her. "I think so. I would hate to think that I graduated university and then never changed. I had my opinions and that was that. I want to be challenged, I want to learn new things, I want to be more today than I was yesterday."

Arabella played with her necklace as she considered what Rebecca had said. She didn't have a pithy reply, nor a sarcastic comment. In fact, now she was left wondering if the scruffy, young photographer was right. Maybe Rebecca knew the purpose of life and she didn't.

"Look, I don't mean to be rude, but I have to go to bed," Rebecca said, she smothered a yawn with the back of her hand.

Arabella looked at her watch, suddenly remembering the reason for the stop.

"Of course, no problem."

"I told Mary that we'd be leaving at six, she said she would leave some breakfast out for us." Rebecca stood up and gathered her boots.

She stepped forward and handed Arabella a key.

"Your room is up the stairs and at the end on the left, it has a three on the door. I'm up the next flight of stairs at the top of the house. Will you be okay getting up there?"

Arabella took the key and nodded. "I'll be fine. But thank you."

"Okay, text me if you need anything."

"I will, goodnight."

"Night."

Rebecca picked up her jacket and walked out of the room.

Arabella let out a breath and leaned back, staring at the ceiling.

This trip was the journey from hell. Not because she was trapped in a house with a thousand creepy dolls, not because she should be home by now, and not because she was stuck with someone she hardly knew.

It was hell because it was giving her time to think. Something she had been avoiding for weeks. But miles of staring at nothing left little time for anything but reflective thought.

She knew that she didn't love Alastair, and that he didn't love her.

Not really.

Not in the true sense of love. But it had never mattered before. Getting married was just a formality, a step in the process of life. She knew it was her lot in life to get married, stop working, have children, be a mother, and… that was it. It was what the women in her family did.

Some juggled a career and being a parent, but Alastair and her own father had been adamantly against that. They wanted Arabella to stay home. Staying at home would be about as much work as going to an office. There would be coffee mornings, luncheons, dinner parties, charitable balls, and all other kinds of events to organise. Alastair had even joked that she was technically changing career from an estate agent to a party planner.

Arabella didn't want to be a party planner, but it was too late now. The wedding was fast approaching, announcements had been made and invitations had been sent.

Everyone knew.

To pull out now would be embarrassing, to say the least. And then what would she do? If it wasn't Alastair, it would be someone else. While Alastair wasn't perfect, he wasn't as bad as some that had gone before him.

She sighed again.

It was just this damn trip that was giving her doubts. Rebecca and her strange outlook on life were shaking everything up. Rebecca seemed to live in a dream world. A world where people were endlessly kind and respectful of one another. Where love existed, outside of fairy tales and Disney movies.

She's a creative, they're always a little odd, Arabella reminded herself.

She was young and naive. In a few years, she'd be married to someone who wasn't the love of her life, just someone who fit the role. Just like everyone else.

"Has your friend gone to bed?"

Arabella looked up to see Mary had entered the room.

"Yes, she's been doing a lot of driving, she's very tired."

"She said all the way from Portugal? It's a very long way. And back to England before Christmas?"

"Hopefully," Arabella said.

"Make sure you book yourself on a ferry, they do become quite booked up."

"I plan to do it in the morning before we set off," Arabella reassured her.

"Oh, good. It is so important to get back home for Christmas, isn't it? I'm sure you both have a lot of people expecting you?"

Arabella thought of the Christmas Eve party, filled with people all wanting to talk to her about business or gossip about other partygoers. Then she thought of Rebecca, seemingly going home just to spend Christmas with her mother. Planning to watch the same shows they watched every year, eat the same things they ate every year. Both heading home for Christmas traditions, but both so widely different from each other.

"Yes, lots of people," Arabella answered. "Will you be spending Christmas here?"

"We will, we invite the locals and we have a big Christmas dinner. It's a mix of French and British foods and traditions. I thought I'd never break with my British traditions, but, I have to say, the French tradition of eating oysters at Christmas is something I really enjoy. Sometimes you need to mix things up a bit, keep things fresh."

Arabella smiled.

Here she was, judging some elderly lady with her probably make-believe husband and her ten thousand porcelain dolls, who goes on to have a more well-rounded view on

Christmas traditions. Willing to accept changes, even at her later stage in life.

"That sounds lovely," Arabella said diplomatically. She was too tired and too fragile to have any more personal conversations. She just wanted to go to bed and wake up feeling different. The exhaustion and stress of travel were causing her to question decisions that could not be questioned. She knew that with some sleep and some time, she would be back to normal.

"I better get some sleep as well," she said. "Thank you so much for the tea and the sandwiches, they were very much appreciated."

"Of course, my dear." Mary looked at her foot. "Will you be all right with the stairs?"

"Absolutely." Arabella picked up her crutch and stood up. "It's just a minor fracture, hardly the need for a full cast, but the doctor wanted to be safe."

Mary didn't seem satisfied with the response and continued to look at her with a sympathetic expression. Arabella hated appearing weak, especially in front of strangers.

"Well, good night," she said. She quickly made her way to the door, ignoring the twinge of pain that rushed up her leg at the sudden movement.

CHAPTER ELEVEN

REBECCA CHANGED LANES. She used the opportunity of looking in her wing mirror to glance at Arabella. The woman had been quiet since they'd left the that morning. Something seemed to be up.

Rebecca wondered if the creepy porcelain dolls in her bedroom had prevented her from sleeping. Rebecca had been certain that she'd not be able to sleep when she'd seen the countless dolls, but she'd been so exhausted that she'd quickly fallen into a deep slumber. Maybe Arabella hadn't been so lucky.

But it seemed Arabella wasn't about to admit to anything. She'd told Rebecca that she'd slept fine when she'd enquired over breakfast. Since then, it had been four hours of polite comments and very stilted conversation.

Eventually, Rebecca had given up, not wanting to push Arabella who clearly didn't want to talk to her.

She was surprised that she cared so much about the silence. They'd had periods of silence in the car before, but this felt different. She could feel that something was on

Arabella's mind. The car was thick with the emotion radiating off of the older woman.

Arabella's phone rang. The atmosphere became impossibly thicker.

"It's Alastair," Arabella announced after glancing at the screen.

"Are you going to answer it?" Rebecca asked. "I'd try to give you some privacy, but... you know. I suppose I could find somewhere to stop?"

"No, it's fine, I... I'll take the call."

Rebecca tightened her grip on the steering wheel, attempting to focus more fully on the road and ignore what was happening beside her. She hated that such a strong and independent woman could be reduced to an uncertain bag of nerves by some *man*. Especially some man that she was due to marry.

"Hello, Alastair," Arabella answered the call.

Rebecca could hear mumbling on the other end of the call. At least this time he sounded calmer. While she couldn't make out the words, she could tell that his speech pattern was slower and softer.

"We're a little more than halfway through France..."

Rebecca looked at the GPS screen. It was true, they were halfway through France. It was Christmas Eve, but they were well on their way. They'd get there just before Christmas Day, but they would make it.

"Well, we stopped overnight." Arabella's tone became defensive. "Because we couldn't drive solidly." She paused and sighed. "The hire company wouldn't let me drive at all because of my leg, so I'm relying on my travel companion."

There was a long pause.

"They literally wouldn't allow me to drive. Something about invalidating insurance," Arabella explained. "Well, I suppose I *could* have..."

Rebecca knew what he was saying without hearing him. He was suggesting that Arabella should have driven through the night. How anyone could suggest that was beyond her.

She'd seen the winces, the tightened facial expressions. Whether or not Arabella wanted to admit to it, she was in pain from sitting so long in one position. Driving would only exacerbate that. How could someone who supposedly loved her suggest that she put her life in danger by driving through the night?

"What's done is done," Arabella was saying to Alistair. "We'll be there before the midnight toast."

Rebecca winced at the sound of the raised voice on the other end of the line. Alastair was clearly not happy with that predicted timeline.

"There's not a lot I can do now. We're getting a ferry in a few hours and then we'll be driving up from Dover. I think we'll be at the house between nine and ten. It's the best I can do, Alastair."

Rebecca smirked at the firm tone that Arabella had used.

Clearly, she did have some backbone when talking to the man.

Arabella sighed. "They'll have to accept me as I am, I'm afraid. I can't exactly do my hair in the car, can I?"

Rebecca felt her jaw drop open.

She looked at Arabella and shook her head in shock before looking back at the road. She couldn't believe the audacity of the man. He couldn't just be satisfied that Arabella would be home in time, he had to comment on what state she would arrive in?

Not that Rebecca could ever imagine Arabella looking less than perfect. Despite the long journey, the pain in her leg, and the lack of rest, Arabella had appeared at breakfast looking stunning. Another skirt suit, hair styled, makeup applied.

Rebecca had immediately felt tiny in comparison. Until Arabella had commented that she looked well rested. The small compliment had oddly sent her heart soaring.

"Yes, I have calculated the hour time difference, I'm not a complete idiot," Arabella argued.

Rebecca smiled. Maybe Arabella was going to be okay with Alastair after all. Maybe yesterday she was at a low ebb and now she was back to full power, ready to tell him what's what.

"Fine, fine, I'll do my best, but don't expect me before nine. Please tell Daddy. Goodbye, Alastair." Arabella angrily stabbed the end call button and let out a sigh.

Rebecca tried to relax herself back into her chair.

Since the start of the call, her body had tensed. She took a couple of deep breaths, brought her shoulders down away from her ears, and released her grip on the steering wheel a little. She couldn't tell if it was general conflict that made her uncomfortable or the thought of Alastair himself. She'd taken an instant dislike to him based on the one phone call Arabella had previously had with him. She knew nothing of the man, other than he seemed like an old-fashioned fossil who didn't really care about Arabella at all.

Not that any of that should matter.

It wasn't like Arabella was anything to her. They were simply sharing a journey home, nothing more and nothing less. Travel companion, that's what Arabella had called her. In a few hours, they would part ways and then they would probably never see nor hear from each other ever again. This was just a strange twist of fate.

She looked at the GPS screen again. Arabella had programmed in the port as their destination. That way they could see if they would, in fact, make it to the ferry.

So far, everything looked good, but Rebecca knew that one heavy batch of traffic could change everything. The thought of missing the ferry caused a cold sweat to break out. She needed to get that ferry, she needed to get home.

"Rebecca?"

She blinked, shaking herself out of her thoughts. "What?"

"You're speeding. Quite a lot." Arabella didn't sound angry, just surprised.

Rebecca looked down at the speed display. She took her foot off of the accelerator and applied the brake.

"I didn't know you had it in you," Arabella said.

"I didn't mean to." Rebecca watched the speedometer like a hawk. Once it was down to the correct speed, she released a breath. Her eyes flicked up to the rear-view mirror, something had caught her eye.

"Shit," she murmured.

"What?" Arabella asked.

Rebecca gripped the steering wheel tightly. She indicated and started to slow down and pull over. "The police are behind us."

Arabella turned to look behind them. "Oh, for god's sake, we don't have time for this."

"I know." Rebecca indicated and started to pull over.

"The one time you decide to speed, you do it in front of a *police car*?"

"I didn't do it on purpose! I didn't even know I was speeding."

"Then maybe you shouldn't be driving!"

Rebecca pulled the car over onto the hard shoulder. Her heart was beating out of her chest. She'd never driven over the speed limit. She'd never been pulled over by police. The one time she got distracted and allowed her lead foot to drift over the speed limit, she was being flagged down. She had no idea what to do, what to say. What was about to happen.

"This is ridiculous, we don't have time," Arabella was saying. "I can't believe you were foolish enough to—"

"Just stop," Rebecca sighed. "Okay? Please? Just stop. You can scream and shout all the way to Calais, once they let us go."

Arabella let out a long sigh and folded her arms. She turned her head to look out of the passenger window.

Rebecca took a deep breath and watched as the police officer approached the car.

CHAPTER TWELVE

Arabella grabbed hold of her handbag, ready to get out of the car and away from Rebecca as soon as she could. The debacle with the French police had taken over forty minutes. She'd counted each minute, gradually becoming more frustrated as each ticked away.

They had laboriously wanted to check every single detail of every piece of paperwork. They'd even phoned England to see if everything was in order with Rebecca's licence. On Christmas Eve, which had obviously taken ages.

Luckily, they had *just* managed to catch the ferry. After five hours of driving in complete silence. They'd stopped once for fuel and to get some food, a stop that would have made any Formula 1 pit manager proud.

Rebecca had wisely chosen to stay silent throughout the journey, clearly sensing the anger radiating from Arabella. The few times the girl had tried to say anything, Arabella simply held her hand up to silence her. Shaking her head to indicate that now was not the time.

She still couldn't believe that the girl was idiotic enough to endanger their entire journey by speeding, right next to a police car. And then panic when questioned by the police, stuttering and making them look suspicious when she couldn't answer basic questions. The whole thing was a delay and extra stress that they didn't need.

The ferry staff directed them towards their bay. The very second the car had come to a stop, Arabella unclipped her seatbelt and reached for the door handle.

"Hey, where are you going?" Rebecca asked.

Arabella paused and turned to face her. "I need some time on my own. If that's quite okay with you?"

Rebecca sighed. "Are you still angry about the police? I apologised so many times, I didn't mean—"

Arabella opened the car door and got out. She leant against the car and reached for her crutch. Rebecca was around the car in a few moments, trying to help.

"I'm perfectly capable of doing this myself," Arabella bit out. "What do you think I did before you came along?"

"I'm just trying to help," Rebecca argued.

"Help by getting me home."

"I am."

Arabella grabbed her crutch and pivoted away from the car, slamming the door behind her. She started to walk away, keen to get some distance from Rebecca.

But Rebecca didn't seem to understand and was following her.

"Look, I apologised. I don't know what else you want me to do."

Arabella spun around. "I expect you to think of someone else for a change. I need to get home, I need to be at this party. It may seem silly to you, but it's my life. Just because you want to hurry home to eat Christmas cake with your mum, that doesn't mean I expect you to jeopardise my journey home."

"So, you getting home to get to your family is more

important?" Rebecca stepped close. "Is that what you're saying?"

Arabella stood tall. "Yes, I am."

Rebecca stared at her for a long, silent moment. "Fuck you, Arabella." She turned and walked away.

"Oh, very mature!" Arabella called after her.

She continued towards the ferry's elevator to get away from the car deck and into some fresh air. She jabbed the button and waited. She couldn't believe that the girl had spoken to her like that. On a crowded ferry, too.

When the lift arrived, she stepped in and quickly selected the top deck. The doors slid closed and she leaned against the wall of the tiny elevator.

Rebecca was just as childish and naive as she thought she was when she first met her. Assuming the girl had a grain of intelligence had obviously been a mistake. If she couldn't see that her actions had the potential to jeopardise their entire trip, then Arabella didn't know how she could explain it to her.

From the moment the police let them on their way, with a hefty fine, they had been against the clock. Unable to race along for fear of other police officers seeing them. Being stopped once was one matter, being stopped again was entirely different. They wouldn't get off so lightly if they were stopped again. If you could call forty minutes' inquisition light.

And so, they were forced to obey the speed limit. The whole debacle was ridiculously stressful. And why? Because Rebecca had made a stupid mistake. She was supposed to be helping Arabella get home, not sabotaging her from ever getting there. She momentarily imagined herself stuck in a French prison.

The elevator doors opened and shook her from the thought.

She walked out and looked around. To her left was a large restaurant with large forward-facing windows. To her right was a shop and a grubby-looking casino. Directly in front of her were doors leading to the deck. A woman wearing a hideous sweater with a large Christmas tree on the front stood on the deck. She looked frozen and had one hand on the Santa hat atop her head, keeping it in place despite the strong winds.

Arabella shook her head and walked into the restaurant. She stopped in the doorway. The place was crammed with people. The sound of everyone speaking, laughing, even singing, was deafening. She turned and left the restaurant again.

She eyed the door to the deck. It may be cold, but at least it was quiet.

She wrapped her coat around her and walked out onto the deck.

The cold winter air hit her immediately, but it wasn't as unpleasant as she thought it would be. Being cooped up in a car for so many hours had given her a greater appreciation of fresh air. She walked a little until she found a set of moulded plastic seats bolted to the deck. She lowered herself into a chair and stared out at the bustling docks.

She was still angry at Rebecca for swearing at her. That had been completely uncalled for. Just because she wasn't ready to accept an apology for the girl's ridiculous lack of judgement didn't mean she deserved to be shouted at.

She turned and looked in through the windows, wondering if she could spot Rebecca anywhere. Not that she cared where the girl was. She just wanted to avoid a second round of arguing. She turned a little more, squinting as she looked into the restaurant. She hoped Rebecca would have the common sense to get a proper meal, she couldn't continue the journey on just sweets.

Arabella turned back and looked at her watch. She couldn't believe it was Christmas Eve. She was supposed to be at home, preparing for the party. Right now, she should be reconsidering her choice of outfit. She'd soon be on her way to her hair appointment, then to get her nails done. Of course, she'd be on the phone with the event planner endlessly, fixing any last-minute issues.

She felt a pull to pick up her phone and text Alastair about some of the finer party details that she was sure he would forget. But she knew that would just invite criticism as to her absence. No, he would have to deal with it all himself. She might be on her way to being a housewife who dealt with those issues, but she wasn't quite there yet. He'd have to manage this one alone.

She twisted herself around again, looking for Rebecca. She wondered if the girl was aware that she wasn't allowed to be on the car deck when the ferry departed. She wouldn't put it past her to stubbornly try to sit in the car for the hour and a half journey. She wondered if she should call her. Or ask a member of staff to check on her.

She turned back to face the dock. She didn't know why she even cared.

Sure, Rebecca had the keys to car. But if she decided to leave without her once they were in Dover, Arabella could pay a taxi driver to take her home if needed. It wasn't like she needed Rebecca any more.

She stood up, readjusting her crutch as she peered back into the ferry.

She didn't *need* Rebecca any longer, but it would be the simpler choice to continue as they were rather than find an alternative method of transportation.

After a few moments she realised it was futile, there were too many people and she'd never be able to pick out Rebecca in the crowd. Especially if, as she suspected, the girl didn't want to be found. She sat back down again and let out a sigh. Soon this nightmare trip would be over.

Once the ferry had started to move, the temperatures had taken a dramatic dive and the wind had increased tenfold. Arabella knew that the sea air would play havoc with her hair, and she had to be at a party in a few hours. There was only so much that dry shampoo could do.

She'd gone inside and walked around the decks, feeling relief at being able to stretch her injured leg. After a while, she'd found a quieter deck, one with mainly seating and had walked slow laps.

Before she knew it, the ferry was slowing. The white cliffs of Dover could just be seen through the forward windows, despite the setting sun.

Somehow, she had managed to walk for ninety minutes without realising it. Her thoughts had been tied up with the party, her future, and, for some reason, Rebecca.

She hated that the girl was so prominent in her thoughts. It was hard to get her out of her mind, surely the result of having spent so much time with her recently. And the result of her flip-flopping personality. One minute she was a petulant child in a car hire offer, preventing her from getting the vehicle. The next she was thoughtful, kind, and maybe even funny. The next she was cursing at her aboard a ferry.

She really didn't know what to make of her.

After what felt like an endless wait, the ferry finally docked at Dover. The captain announced that the stairs and elevators to the lower decks were now open. A swarm of people rushed past her, desperate to be the first down the stairs. Not that it mattered. They'd all have to wait for everyone to be in their cars anyway.

Arabella hated herd mentality.

She queued for the elevator, finally getting in on the eighth journey, sandwiched between two prams of screaming children. She wondered if maybe she should've stayed at Faro and waited for the flights to start again. Surely that would have been better than the situation she found herself in now?

Finally, she escaped the elevator and the children. She looked around to get her bearings, still not seeing Rebecca anywhere. Her heart beat a little faster as she worried that the girl had fallen overboard or was maybe stuck in one of the ridiculously small toilets with their spring-loaded doors.

She hurried towards the rental car, looking in as she arrived. There she was. Sitting at the wheel, like nothing had happened.

Arabella opened the door and got in. She adjusted her crutch, surprised that Rebecca didn't help as she had done all of the other times. *Showing her true colours now.*

"Are you going to apologise?" Arabella asked bitterly. She slammed the door shut.

"No. And I don't think we have anything else to say to each other," Rebecca said.

Arabella fidgeted with her seatbelt. "So, what? You expect us to sit in silence for the next two hours?"

"That sounds preferable."

Arabella looked at the girl in surprise. She sat bolt upright, focused straight ahead. Her cheeks were flushed, and she wore her sunglasses despite it being almost dark outside.

Has she been crying? she wondered.

"Fine," Arabella said.

"Good," Rebecca replied coldly.

CHAPTER THIRTEEN

TRUE TO HER WORD, Rebecca didn't say a word for the entire journey to Putney.

She almost spoke up as they passed the turning for Croydon. She wondered briefly if she could stop and leave Arabella to make her way home. But she'd made a deal with Arabella. As much as she wanted to be out of the car, she knew that Arabella shouldn't be driving. Especially after sitting in one position for so long, her leg must have been in agony.

She'd never forgive herself if the older woman got into an accident on the way to Putney. So, she continued on. An hour away from Croydon. Where she wanted to be. Where she needed to be. And from Putney, she'd drop the car off and somehow make her own way back.

Arabella had been on her phone for the majority of the trip back. The incessant sound of text messages arriving had started to irritate Rebecca, but she got the impression that that was part of Arabella's idea, to attempt to irritate Rebecca enough to speak.

She'd also become suddenly fascinated with the window

controls and the car climate control system. Opening and closing windows and adjusting the temperature from hot to cold to hot again.

Seemingly anything to get something out of her. Not that Rebecca was going to fall for such childish ploys.

She just kept driving. Even though she was exhausted, even though her eyes rotated from being painfully dry to just too tired to keep open. Even though her legs were numb from sitting in the same position for so many hours. Even though she was hungry and thirsty, she kept driving. The sooner this was all over, the sooner she could get on with her life.

Arabella had reprogrammed the GPS to go directly to her home address. Rebecca continually looked at the screen, counting down the minutes. She felt sweet relief when the ETA dropped to under an hour. She felt almost euphoric when the time dropped to the single digits.

"This one on the left, just park outside," Arabella said as the clock hit one minute.

Rebecca looked up at the large white wall and open gates. As she had suspected, it was a mansion. Cars lined the drive inside the gates as well as the outside street. The lights gleamed through the windows, through which she could clearly see people drinking from champagne flutes.

"Looks like you made it to your party," Rebecca commented dryly.

"Yes, though I'll have to slip in the back way so I can get ready. Can't have anyone seeing me like this."

Rebecca blinked. "Why not? You look great."

Arabella looked at her for a moment, her expression clearly showing that she was torn between accepting the compliment and making a snide remark about the end of the silent treatment.

Before she could make her decision, Rebecca saw a man

appear by the side of the car and tap on the window. Arabella jumped and turned around to see what the noise was.

She opened the car door.

"Alastair, thank goodness," she said.

"Come on, before anyone sees you." He looked in the car at Rebecca. "Thanks for driving her."

"You're welcome," Rebecca mumbled.

Yes, as she suspected, she hated him. He was a little older than Arabella. She supposed he'd be considered classically handsome. He wore a tuxedo well enough. But Rebecca hated him on sight.

She quickly turned off the engine and got out of the car. She opened the back door and threw her rucksack over her shoulder. She closed both of the doors and held out the car key for Arabella.

"There you go, enjoy your party." She turned to leave.

"Wait!" Arabella called.

Rebecca paused and slowly turned around.

Arabella whispered something to Alastair. He nodded and left. Arabella walked towards Rebecca, eyeing her up and down as she did.

"Well, that was an interesting trip. Thank you for driving me, I wouldn't have made it back here without you."

"I know. Is that it?" She folded her arms.

Arabella sighed. "No, it's not. I ordered you a taxi, it will be here in a moment."

"You... what? Why?"

"You'll never be able to get a taxi at this time of night on Christmas Eve and I'm sure public transport will be horrible. It's all paid for, you don't need to worry about that."

Rebecca licked her lips. "Oh... I..."

She didn't know what to say.

She didn't expect any kindness from Arabella considering how she had treated her on the final leg of their journey.

Even if she had deserved it, Arabella hadn't known *why* she deserved it. Arabella didn't know why Rebecca was rushing home.

"Thank you," Rebecca finally said. She stood awkwardly, not wanting to make eye contact.

Arabella looked at her phone. "He's just around the corner, he'll be here in a moment."

"Okay." Rebecca looked up, eager to see headlights and her escape route.

"So, I'll say goodnight. Again, thank you." Arabella seemed rooted to the spot, unwilling to leave just yet.

Probably waiting for a thank-you in return.

Rebecca looked up at her. "You're welcome. Thanks for paying for the car. And everything. I really appreciate it."

It was true, she did appreciate it. Even if she had wanted to kill Arabella on the ferry.

Arabella smiled. "Merry Christmas."

A car pulled up beside them. "Rebecca Edwards?" the driver called out of the open window.

Rebecca held her hand up to indicate she was coming. "Merry Christmas, enjoy your party."

Arabella chuckled. "Oh, these parties aren't for enjoyment. But I'll do my best. Goodbye, Rebecca."

"Bye, Arabella."

Rebecca watched as Arabella turned and walked through the gate. It felt weird to say goodbye. She'd never see Arabella again.

Unless she suddenly won the lottery and wanted to buy a property in Portugal. But Arabella would probably have quit work by then if Alastair had his way.

She turned and walked towards the taxi. She got into the back seat, relieved not to be driving any more.

The driver wore a Santa hat.

"Merry Christmas," he greeted.

"Merry Christmas," she replied.

"Croydon, right?"

"That's right."

"Rosemont Avenue?"

Rebecca frowned as she wondered how Arabella knew her home address. She shook her head, it was irrelevant now.

"Actually no, change of plan. It's near there, though…"

CHAPTER FOURTEEN

ARABELLA SAT at her makeup table, styling her hair. Luckily no one had seen her enter the back door of the house and make her way to the guest bedroom. Now she just needed to make herself as presentable as possible, get changed, and make an appearance downstairs.

The door flew open, and Alastair entered the bedroom.

She regarded him in the mirror. He met her eyes, and she could tell he was furious.

"How long do you think you'll be? I've been making excuses all night."

"Why did you make excuses? Surely the air traffic failure was in the news?"

Alastair snorted a laugh and sat on the edge of the bed.

"Like I'm going to tell people that you were stranded in Portugal so close to Christmas."

She spun around and looked at him. "Why ever not?"

He rolled his eyes. "Because that just screams poor time management. And people will ask why you were there and why we didn't send a junior, you know, like I suggested in the first place."

"I wanted to go," Arabella ground out.

"I know, and look how that ended up." He got to his feet and gestured for her to face the mirror again, eager for her to hurry in her preparations.

She sighed and turned around. She sought him out in the mirror and watched as he paced behind her.

"That's very distracting," she informed him.

He paused and met her eyes again. He folded his arms. "I hope you got it out of your system?"

"Got what out of my system?"

"Ignoring me, ignoring my advice. This need to always go it alone and do things yourself. If we're going to get married, I need to know that you'll listen to what I say. I don't mean that in a nasty way, I don't mean I'm the boss. I just mean that sometimes you should listen to me. Sometimes I know what's best."

"Best for who, Alastair?"

"Best for us. Best for the business."

She broke eye contact, picked up her lip gloss, and leaned closer to the mirror.

"I suppose I'm just struggling to understand why my stepping aside from the business is what's best for the business."

"I don't mean that," he argued. "Don't twist my words. We agreed that it would be better for you to be at home and me at the office. A division of labour. You know I can't sit in ladies' coffee mornings and persuade those women to persuade their husbands to put their rental business with us. And it's not just coffee mornings, it's charity events, balls, auctions... they need to be organised and it's just not a man's job. You know that."

A knock on the door stopped Arabella from delivering the argument that was on the tip of her tongue.

She turned to face the door. "Yes?"

Her father entered the room and smiled at her. "You're back."

"I am." She returned the smile. "Sorry I'm late, Daddy."

"You're here now, that's the main thing. Will you be down soon?"

She nodded. "In a few moments."

"Wonderful." He turned his attention to Alastair. "Come on, Alastair, there's some people I need to introduce you to."

Arabella let out a sigh of relief when they both left the room. She stretched out her back and turned her head from side to side to release the pressure. Sitting in a car seat for so long hadn't done her back any favours. Her eyes flicked to the small clock on the dressing table. She wondered if Rebecca was nearly home.

She returned her attention to applying her lip gloss. She really didn't know why she was wasting another moment thinking about the girl. She needed to forget about her and focus on the party.

CHAPTER FIFTEEN

ARABELLA WALKED into the kitchen and politely smiled at the waitress who was pouring champagne into glasses. She hurried through and into the utility room, closing the door firmly behind her.

She placed her crutch by the wall and leaned against the door, hoping to have a moment to herself. She had no idea what was wrong with her. Usually, she enjoyed the Christmas party.

But this one was torturous.

Probably because people kept talking about the wedding and her stepping down from the firm.

She heard a light knock on the door and froze in fear.

"Arabella?"

She sighed with relief and took a step back to open the door. She gestured for her best friend to hurry in.

Miranda walked in. "Why are we hiding in the utility room?"

Arabella closed the door and leaned on it again. "I can't take it."

Miranda rested against the washing machine and sipped

from her champagne glass. A perfectly manicured eyebrow rose questioningly.

"Can't take what, exactly?"

"All the talk about the wedding. People asking who will be looking after my work accounts. Asking about babies and telling me how lucky I am to have a man like Alastair. I can't take it."

She sucked in a deep breath.

Miranda frowned. She put her glass on the worktop and took Arabella by the upper arms.

"Take some deep breaths. I'm sure you're just exhausted, driving home... even if you weren't actually the one doing the driving... must have been exhausting."

"That's not it." Arabella shook her head. "It's all this, all these people telling me how excited I must be about quitting work. But I'm not. I love working—"

"And you'll love being a wife. It's a different kind of work," Miranda reassured.

She shrugged out of Miranda's grip. It was her turn to take her friend by the shoulders.

"Miranda, listen to what I'm saying. I don't want to quit work. I'm not looking forward to my own wedding."

She stared at Miranda meaningfully.

She watched as Miranda's eyes widened in understanding.

"Okay," her friend said solemnly. "Okay, but I don't think you should make any rash decisions now. You're tired, stressed, it's Christmas. You don't want to say or do something you might regret."

Arabella allowed her arms to drop to her sides. She leaned back against the door. Miranda was right. Making a hasty decision now could have potentially disastrous repercussions. While she felt certain at the moment, who was to say her feelings wouldn't change in a few hours?

She was exhausted. Sleep had been in short supply over

the last few days and her stress levels had been ridiculously high.

"I'm just saying, take some time to think about it," Miranda continued. "Go through the motions. Give yourself some time to really think about what you're doing. If you pull the plug on you and Alastair now, there might not be any going back."

Arabella chuckled bitterly. "Aren't you supposed to be telling me what a great catch he is?"

Miranda took a step back and picked up her champagne glass.

"Let's be honest, neither of us were ever the kind of people who believed in love. We both knew that marriage would be about finding someone pleasant on the eyes and someone you could stand to spend the next ten or so years with."

Arabella swallowed. Even the idea of spending ten years with Alastair wasn't appealing to her at the moment.

"For us, marriage is more of a business transaction than anything else. Alastair obviously brings a lot of money and investment capital to Henley Estates. Which makes the business happy and your father happy. It makes Alastair and his family happy. Does it make you happy?"

Arabella threw her hands up in the air for a moment. "I don't know. It did. I thought it did. But now… I'm not so sure. Aren't we supposed to be a partnership, working together? It feels like I'm being pushed to one side to support him as his career grows. It's like I'm losing my identity. But then, I have to wonder if my happiness is worth more than everyone else's?"

"Yes," Miranda said firmly. "Darling, if we were having this conversation in the 1950s then I'd be telling you to pull yourself together and get on with it. But this is the twenty-first century. We're not subservient to men anymore. We're our own people. And your happiness is just as important as everyone else's."

Arabella let out another sigh. She looked down at the floor and shook her head. "What do I do?"

"You need a bit of breathing space. But I don't think hiding out in the utility room is going to work for long," Miranda said.

Right again. Arabella felt a tightness in her chest. Each time she heard someone moving in the kitchen she felt sure her refuge was about to be discovered.

Suddenly an idea struck her.

She snapped her head up and looked at Miranda. "Can you cover for me?"

"Sure, what's the plan?"

"I'm going to head outside for a bit. Catch my breath."

Miranda smiled warmly. "Good, take some time. Don't make any big decisions now. Get the holiday season out of the way and see how you feel then."

Arabella nodded. "I will, thank you."

They exchanged a quick hug, and Miranda left the utility room to return to the party.

After a few moments, Arabella took a fortifying breath and left the room, too. She headed towards her father's study where she'd dropped off her handbag. She grabbed the bag and waited for a quiet moment before slipping out of the back door of the house.

She crept around the side of the property, cursing the gravelled driveway beneath her crutch. She hoped no one would notice her painfully slow escape.

She walked out of the gate and towards the hire car, still sitting where Rebecca had parked it.

She unlocked the car and slipped into the driver's seat.

She closed the door again. After a few moments, the interior light started to dim, and she sat in the darkness.

Hiding from her own party.

She tossed her handbag onto the passenger seat. What she thought of as *her* seat. She looked around the inside of the car. Flashes of memories from their journey came back to her. When she had ordered Rebecca to get her luggage, when they had listened to Spanish dance music, when they had stopped at the most beautiful vista Arabella had ever seen.

Getting stuck in Portugal hadn't been a part of her plan, but it had happened. And it had changed her. Shaking her from her daily routine long enough to stop and think about her life, where it was heading.

Since leaving university, life had been a conveyor belt. Her work, her future, all mapped out along the belt. She'd never realised before that it was possible to step off the conveyor. Everything had always been planned. She used to feel like she was the one planning it, but now she was beginning to wonder.

She shifted to try to find a more comfortable position. As she did, she felt something beneath her foot. She looked into the dark footwell and frowned. She leant forward and felt around the carpeted area. Her hand gripped something, something plastic and hard.

She lifted it up and held it towards the streetlight to see what she'd found. She turned the piece of plastic over and saw that it was a lens cap from a camera.

Rebecca must have dropped it, she thought.

She gripped the lens cap in her hand. She bit her lip and looked towards the house.

She'll need this, her lens is probably very expensive. It might get damaged, she thought.

Escape seemed very appealing.

She knew it was an excuse. She wanted just an hour or two away from the party to gather her thoughts, and this was the perfect excuse. She unlocked her phone and accessed the photo she had taken of Rebecca's driving licence. She started the engine and input the address into the GPS.

CHAPTER SIXTEEN

ARABELLA PULLED up outside the house, only now realising that her knowing the address would take some explaining.

She looked out of the car window. Rebecca, it seemed, lived in a standard 1930s semi-detached, similar to thousands of other government-built homes on the outskirts of London. Outskirts that were now considered a part of the city itself. The houses weren't much to look at, but they were highly sought after and often high in value as London became more congested and popular.

Arabella frowned. The house looked empty. The lights were off, the curtains open, revealing no sign of life. Maybe this was Rebecca's house, but the girl was with her mother somewhere else?

Although, she wondered if a jobbing photographer could afford the high Croydon property prices, even to rent.

If the property were occupied, maybe it was just the front lights that were off. Maybe the family were gathered in a room in the back.

The lens cap wouldn't deliver itself. Arabella decided it was time to be brave and get out of the car and ring the bell.

She opened the door and shouldered her bag. She awkwardly adjusted her crutch and started to walk up the garden path. Her work instincts kicked in and she started to examine the garden, noting that it was unkempt. Clearly Rebecca's mother wasn't very green-fingered. She approached the front door, noting the slight peeling paintwork on the wooden frame as she rang the bell.

"Are you looking for Allison?"

Arabella turned around to see the neighbour leaning on the short garden fence. He wore a ridiculous Christmas sweater emblazoned with a snowman.

"Actually, I'm looking for Rebecca?"

"I've not seen her for a few days, she'll probably be up at the hospital with her mum."

"Hospital?"

He frowned, his face suddenly a stark contrast from his jovial sweater. "Oh, you don't know? Allison took a bad turn a couple of weeks ago. They didn't think she'd last the night, but she's a fighter. Scary how it can come back, isn't it? One moment you're in remission and the next…" He shuddered.

"Yes, frightening," Arabella agreed.

The ground felt shaky beneath her feet. Her constant nagging to get home for a work party suddenly seemed pathetic. Rebecca was racing home to her sick mother. And she hadn't said a word about it.

"Anyway, she's up at the Royal Victoria."

"Thank you," Arabella said softly.

She started back towards the car. Her mind was spinning as she analysed conversations they had shared on the drive home. Some fresh perspective on Rebecca's words made her rethink so many of her assumptions about the girl. A girl who was going through so much, seemingly on her own.

"Merry Christmas," the neighbour called out.

"Merry Christmas," Arabella called over her shoulder without much heart in it.

She got into the car and threw her crutch into the passenger footwell. She remembered Rebecca's implosion on the ferry. Suddenly it seemed very clear why she had acted the way she had. Arabella had practically told her that her Christmas party was more important than Rebecca getting home to her mother. With no idea that her mother was sick, dying by the sound of it.

"So stupid," she mumbled to herself.

How had she shared so much time with Rebecca and not known something so important about her? Rebecca had obviously not wanted to discuss the matter. But Arabella couldn't help but feel that if she had tried a little harder to connect, she might have noticed something was up.

But she'd been so swept up in her own drama that she hadn't given a second thought to Rebecca's life. Getting home to the party and dealing with Alastair's inevitable sulk had been her entire focus.

She'd assumed that Rebecca was worrying about getting back to her mother to put on a ridiculous party hat and eat a Christmas cupcake, nothing more.

She wondered why Rebecca hadn't said anything.

She felt cold at the knowledge that she knew for sure that she would have. She would have instantly mentioned her dying mother to anyone in earshot. Not for sympathy, but to expedite her way home. If she felt that playing the dying parent card would have got her the hire car, she would have used it in a heartbeat. She placed a hand over her stomach, feeling sickened at the knowledge.

But Rebecca hadn't said a word.

In fact, she seemed to go to lengths to not mention it at all. And now Arabella felt like the most horrible person in the world. Complaining about getting back to her champagne-quaffing associates when Rebecca was going through serious mental anguish. Stranded in Portugal away from her dying mother, a mother who apparently wasn't due to last the night two weeks ago.

Royal Victoria, Arabella mused. She knew where it was. And she still had the lens cap. She'd pop in, give the cap back, and offer Rebecca her sympathies.

That way she wouldn't feel like such a monster. It was selfish, but she wanted to alleviate some of her guilt.

CHAPTER SEVENTEEN

ARABELLA HAD ALWAYS WONDERED how some ideas could go from great to terrible in a matter of seconds.

Seeing Rebecca had seemed like a great idea on the way to the hospital. Even when she was parking the car and then entering the main entrance, she'd felt good about her decision.

She'd roamed the hospital corridors for ten minutes, looking for the cancer wards. All the while she'd been assured of her plan. It had never crossed her mind that she might be doing the wrong thing.

But the moment she overheard Rebecca's voice through an open doorway to a hospital room, she'd wondered what the hell she was thinking.

She stood awkwardly outside, now adding eavesdropping to her list of crimes, and realised how stupid she was being.

Rebecca didn't want to see her, she meant nothing to the girl. Rebecca had most likely been ecstatic to get rid of her after the journey from hell. Being forced to share a car with, and financially rely upon, a woman who must have seemed like an absolute monster.

And now she'd effectively stalked her. Photographing her driver's licence, going to her house, speaking to her neighbour, and now roaming hospital hallways. For what? A camera lens that probably cost less than five pounds.

It had been an excuse, and she knew it.

She just needed to escape her own life for a while. Because she couldn't cope with her privileged lifestyle. Because champagne gave her a headache and her millionaire fiancé was being problematic.

So, she wanted to see Rebecca. She wanted to revisit the recent times where she didn't have to think about her own problems. Times where she could freely joke and not worry about what the future would bring.

And that was how she found herself clutching a lens cap, standing in a hospital corridor, eavesdropping on Rebecca's hushed voice. Wondering what the hell she'd been thinking, and wondering if she could get out without being seen.

She started to turn around and saw a nurse looking at her with a curious expression. To escape, she'd need to walk right past her. There would no doubt be questions. She wondered if she could be arrested for entering the hospital without good reason. She wasn't eager to find out.

There was little choice, she had to go into the room. She swallowed. She'd have to style it out, walk in with confidence like she was doing something natural. Something that anyone else would have done.

She took a couple of steps and crossed the threshold. The room was dim. The harsh ceiling lighting was off, and a couple of smaller lamps gave a softer light. Rebecca sat in an upholstered chair, her legs under her, a warm drink in her hands.

The older woman from the photographs in Rebecca's wallet sat in the bed. She was propped up with cushions. She looked extremely pale and thin, but she smiled the same smile. A number of wires slipped from under the bedding and into a variety of machines lined up by the bed.

The bedside table held countless cards and flowers. A couple of miniature Christmas trees and poinsettias were included in the mix.

Arabella realised she had been there a few seconds and needed to announce her presence before the situation got even weirder. She tapped on the open door with her knuckle. Both women looked at her.

She looked apologetically to Rebecca. "I'm sorry, I—"

"Oh, is this Lucy?" Allison asked excitedly. She looked groggily from Arabella to Rebecca a few times. "See? I told you she'd make it. Everyone comes home at Christmas."

Lucy? Arabella wondered. *Who's Lucy?*

Rebecca quickly got to her feet, placing her mug on a side table. She looked panicked and raced to stand beside Arabella.

"Um, yeah, yeah, this is…" Rebecca stared at Arabella meaningfully. "This is Lucy."

Arabella instantly knew that saying she wasn't Lucy would result in immediate and painful loss of life.

She looked at Allison. "Yes, I'm Lucy. Nice to meet you, Mrs Edwards."

"Mum, I just need Lucy's help with something, I'll be back in a second," Rebecca said.

Arabella felt herself being dragged out of the room, something she knew she fully deserved. She struggled to keep up and not trip over her crutch.

Rebecca dragged them across the corridor and into an empty office. She slammed the door behind them.

"What the hell?" Rebecca demanded.

"I'm so sorry," Arabella said quickly.

"How? *How* are you here?"

Arabella picked the lens cap out of her bag and held it up. "You dropped this, I thought you might need it."

Rebecca stepped into her personal space and stared coldly at her. "Do you have some kind of tracking device on me? Did you microchip me? How are you here, Arabella?"

"I saw your driver's licence, I went to the address and the neighbour said you'd be here."

"Fucking Steve." Rebecca shook her head. She plucked the lens cap out of Arabella's hand. She took a step back and raked her fingers through her hair. "You're really telling me you left your party to deliver this? After telling me multiple times that the world would probably end if you didn't get to your party in time?"

"Who's Lucy?"

Rebecca nearly growled. "None of your business."

Arabella raised an eyebrow. "Well, as I am Lucy, I think it is my business."

"You need to leave. Now."

"Won't your mum wonder where Lucy has gone?"

"Are you enjoying this?" Rebecca asked in exasperation.

Arabella paused for a second. She'd slipped right back into bantering with Rebecca without a thought as to the serious situation they were in.

"No, I'm sorry. That was uncalled for. I… I don't know why I came. I had to get away from the party, and I found the lens cap and wanted to return it. I didn't stop to think about how inappropriate it might be until I actually got here. I'm sorry, I know this is really strange. I don't have an agenda, I just genuinely wanted to return your property."

Rebecca leaned back against a desk, her arms folded over her chest. She looked at her feet and let out a sigh.

"I'm sorry about your mum," Arabella said. "Really. I realise now how selfish I must have sounded during the trip."

"Thank you," Rebecca said after a few moments of

silence. "It wasn't that I didn't trust you. I just... didn't want to talk about it. You know what I mean?"

"Not particularly," Arabella admitted. "I'm lucky enough to never have been in such a situation."

Rebecca slowly nodded her head, still not making eye contact with Arabella.

"Lucy is the name of the girlfriend I made up. My mum, she worries about me, you know?" Rebecca mumbled as she looked up. Her eyes were red and her cheeks tearstained.

Arabella wasn't sure what to say. She opened her mouth, and then closed it again. The last thing she wanted to do now was say the wrong thing and ruin the tentative truce that had formed between them.

"I had a breakup," Rebecca confessed. "A really bad one. My mum was worried about me, and then she got sick again. So, I made up *Lucy*. I just wanted to tell her that I'd be okay, that I had someone who would be there for me and look after me when she couldn't be here anymore. It helps her."

Arabella slowly nodded. "So, she's never met Lucy?"

"No, there was always a good excuse. And Mum has been pretty sick, so she doesn't always remember stuff. I feel bad for lying to her. It is for her. I want her to know that it's okay to let go. Know that I'll be okay."

A thick silence filled the air.

"I'm sorry that I got involved," Arabella said.

"It's okay," Rebecca said. "At least now she's seen Lucy. I'll just tell her you had to go again. Mum is pretty out of it, the nurses say that it won't be much longer. They were surprised that she's lasted this long."

Arabella couldn't believe they were having such an honest and heart-breaking conversation. As if they were talking about a breakfast order. She'd never been good at emotional conversations. She never knew what to say. She often wondered if she should say anything at all.

"Are you here on your own?" Arabella finally asked.

Rebecca frowned in confusion. She slowly nodded.

"Would you like me to stay?"

Rebecca looked stunned. For the first time in the short time she had known her, Arabella saw Rebecca lost for words.

"I don't mind," Arabella added.

"Why would you do that? What about your party? And what about Alastair?"

Arabella just shrugged her shoulders. Suddenly everything seemed so insignificant. So pointless.

The very idea of returning to her party and drinking champagne and discussing business deals seemed ludicrous. How could she possibly return to that knowing that Rebecca was alone in hospital with her dying mother?

"I have nowhere else to be," Arabella said. "If you'd like the company, then I'll stay. I don't wish to intrude more so than I have already. But I don't like the idea of you being here on your own. I'm happy to pretend to be Lucy. I just think some company might be a good idea?"

Rebecca shook her head. "I can't ask you to do that."

"You're not asking, I'm offering."

Arabella realised that she *wanted* to stay. Even though it felt like it might just be the hardest thing she'd ever done. She'd mercifully never spent much time in hospital. Her health and that of her family had always been good. Heart-wrenching hospital scenes had been nothing more than on-screen entertainment.

She shivered slightly at the thought of spending time in a hospital room, visiting someone she didn't even know. Part of her wanted to take the opportunity not afforded to everyone else in the building and leave.

After all, who willingly chose to spend Christmas Eve in hospital?

But the bigger part of her wanted to stay. For the first

time in a long time, Arabella was thinking about someone else other than herself. It felt good, but it also felt terrifying.

"What have you told your mum about Lucy?" Arabella asked.

Rebecca's eyes scanned her face, looking for any hint of a lie. She tugged her sweater sleeve down and rubbed the wetness from her cheeks.

"Not a lot, not anything important anyway. I just mentioned dates we'd been on. Stuff like that. But you don't have to do that, I don't want you to have to do that—"

"It's my fault. If I hadn't barged in, it wouldn't have happened. And if I just left now, then surely that would look odd?"

Rebecca slowly nodded. "Yeah, I suppose it would. It just feels so weird."

Arabella snorted a laugh.

"It is weird," she assured. "But it's been weird ever since I met you."

A grin started to form in Rebecca's face. "I suppose it has," she agreed.

"So, tell me what I need to know."

CHAPTER EIGHTEEN

IT SEEMED INSANE. But then, lately, everything seemed insane. Over the last few years, Rebecca's life had been turned upside down.

She would never forget the terrible moment when her mother told her the news of her cancer diagnosis. It took weeks for the news to properly settle in Rebecca's mind. During that time, she just went through the motions. She was as strong as she could be and did whatever needed to be done.

Eventually, she understood and accepted that her mum was fighting a horrible and invisible illness. And for a brief while, it made her stronger. But her real strength came from a listless state where she ignored the reality of what was happening. She lived in a place where a fake smile was her best friend.

She wasn't denying the truth of what was happening. She'd accepted it and decided to push it to one side.

The news of remission wasn't as joyful as Rebecca had imagined it would be. In the back of her mind, she had always wondered if it would ever *really* be over. She celebrated and made fanciful plans with her mum for the future, but she knew they'd never really come to pass.

When the cancer came back, it was stronger than ever, shocking Rebecca with the ferocity with which it dissolved her mother's personality right before her eyes.

But Rebecca had made her mother a promise, to never let cancer win. The first day that she sat Rebecca down and told her the news, she had pleaded with Rebecca not to become sad, not to let the cancer define her.

And Rebecca tried her best. Every time she started to feel sad, she would think of the good times. Knowing that soon her mother would be gone, and she would have a choice between remembering the good times or remembering the end.

It wasn't easy, but Rebecca had luckily inherited her mother's positive personality.

Her mother didn't want to talk about her illness, but she had little else to say. And so, Rebecca had become the focus of conversation, her job, her life, her relationships.

Endless questions about finding someone new had caused Rebecca to create Lucy. Lucy embodied reassurance that Rebecca wouldn't be alone.

It was a lie, but a kind one. One that Rebecca could happily live with.

Now she hoped that Arabella would be able to keep the lie alive.

"Mum?" Rebecca whispered softly.

Her mum slowly opened her eyes. The beginnings of a smile curled on her lips. "Is it still Christmas?"

Rebecca smiled and nodded. "Yeah, you didn't think I'd let you sleep through Christmas, did you?"

A glimmer of a memory shone in her mother's eyes. "Did I… was Lucy here?"

Rebecca took a step to the side, she turned and looked

Arabella. She prayed that Arabella would be able to carry off a decent performance.

Arabella took a small step forward and smiled. She looked scared.

"Hello, Mrs Edwards," Arabella said.

"Please, call me Allison. It's so nice to finally meet you. Rebecca speaks about you all the time. And I must apologise for the way I look."

Rebecca opened her mouth to speak, but before she got the chance Arabella replied, "There's nothing to apologise for."

"Look at you both, standing over me. Pull up a chair," her mum insisted.

Rebecca dragged the chair that she had been in earlier and positioned it by the bed. She gestured for Arabella to sit down. She crossed the room and retrieved the other chair from the corner and placed it beside Arabella's.

"Did you do something to your leg?"

Arabella balanced her crutch against the side of the chair, using the opportunity to give Rebecca a questioning sideways glance.

"She slipped," Rebecca said. "Nothing serious, you know what doctors are like."

Her mum laughed. "That I do," she agreed.

"I'm very sorry, Lucy, but I can't seem to remember what it is you do for a living?"

"She works in an estate agency, remember, Mum?" Rebecca said, knowing that her mum could hardly retain any information these days. The exhaustion had set in, and nowadays they just had the same conversations over and over again.

She had thought it was bad before she went to Portugal, but little did she know that was merely a taster of what was to come. She wished she had never left. Not that it mattered now.

"Oh yes, I remember now." She closed her eyes for a moment.

Rebecca wondered if she would drift off to sleep, but her eyes fluttered open again. She looked at Arabella and smiled.

"So, do you get to look at people's houses?"

"Yes, it's a very good career for a nosy person. Which I am." Arabella winked.

Rebecca smiled as her mum let out a small chuckle.

"Me too, I know it's wrong, but the best part of a party is getting to have a nose around the host's house."

Arabella laughed. "Oh yes, but then you run the risk of getting caught. Part of my job is looking around, opening cupboards and wardrobes. They can't hide anything from me."

Rebecca tuned out the conversation. She leaned back in her chair, allowing the exhaustion to slowly wash over.

For the first time in a long time, she wasn't the only person looking after her mother. She hadn't realised how exhausting the process was. But now, with Arabella beside her taking the strain, she felt like she could take a few seconds to herself. Her eyes fluttered closed, and she listened to the soft tones of the two women speaking.

CHAPTER NINETEEN

"SHE'S ASLEEP," Allison said.

Arabella glanced to her side. She suspected that Rebecca had fallen asleep a while ago. She hadn't particularly noticed, in fact she'd been enjoying talking to Allison. She turned back to face the woman.

"Yes, she must be exhausted," she said. Suddenly, she wondered if Rebecca had said anything about their journey home. She'd wait to see what information Allison provided, and hopefully get a reading on what she knew.

"She is," Allison agreed. She lovingly watched her daughter. "She is very brave, I've put her through hell."

"No," Arabella disagreed. "You mustn't think like that."

"I don't." Allison let out a soft sigh. "Not really. Becky and I agreed, when all this started, that the cancer was like a third person in our relationship. It wasn't to define me, and it wasn't to define her, or us. It was just something that was there, like a bad smell. The worst thing about cancer is it takes your identity away. I'm no longer Allison Edwards, I am a cancer patient. And I didn't want that. I wanted to make sure that I was Allison Edwards, Rebecca's mum."

Arabella nodded. She didn't really understand. She was trying her best, but even she knew that Allison was just touching the surface of such a deep topic.

"And when I go, I don't want Rebecca to still feel that the cancer hovers around her. I want her to be happy, I don't want her to remember all of this." Allison gestured around the hospital room. "I want her to remember before, and then I want her to build a new life. A happy life. I know you two haven't been seeing each other for long, but I get a good feeling about you."

Arabella swallowed nervously.

She wasn't comfortable with lying to Allison about something so important. Up until now they had just made small talk. And she had done so willingly in the knowledge that she was helping a dying woman feel more comfortable at the end of her days.

But it sounded like the conversation was about to drift into something more serious. And Arabella wasn't good at serious, heart-to-heart conversations.

She didn't want to be making promises to a dying woman, promises that she knew she could not keep. She agreed that Rebecca was as unique, special, and deserving as Allison thought she was. Rebecca did deserve Lucy, the made-up perfect girlfriend.

"Rebecca is amazing," Arabella said. "And I know that she is going to have a great life. She'll never forget you, the good times, I mean. She never talks about all this." Arabella gestured around the room. "She talks about you, but never about the third person in your relationship."

Allison looked relieved. She let out a shaky breath. She'd noticed that Allison's breathing had become more laboured since they'd been talking.

It was clear that Allison was extremely ill. Now and then her eyes would begin to close, and then open again. When they open they were brighter, more determined. She clearly didn't want to rest.

"Thank goodness," Allison whispered. "Knowing that she'll be okay, it makes it easier."

Arabella nodded.

She couldn't imagine being in Allison's position. She didn't think she could be selfless enough to care about someone else when in such terrible pain herself. But then again, maybe the end of your life brought such clarity. She hoped that it would be a long while before she had to find out.

"Are your parents still with us?" Allison asked.

"Yes, they're divorced. I don't see my mother much, but they are both alive and well."

Allison's eyes started to close again.

Arabella let out a soft breath and gently leaned back in her chair. They had been talking for a while, and now it was probably time to let Allison rest. She sat very still and looked at her hands in her lap. She hoped that if she remained quiet, Allison would start to drift off to sleep and get the rest she desperately needed.

As the silence wore on, she became aware of heavy foot-steps in the corridor towards the hospital room. Footsteps that she instantly recognised.

Thankfully, Allison had fallen asleep. Arabella grabbed her crutch and carefully manoeuvred herself around Rebecca. She walked out of the room as quietly as possible, coming face-to-face with Alastair in the corridor as she did.

His eyes sparked with fury. He was still dressed in his tuxedo. In his clenched hand was his mobile phone.

"What are you doing here?" she asked through clenched teeth.

"What am *I* doing here? What are *you* doing here? Are

you injured?" He looked over her body, searching for any sign of damage.

"I'm fine," Arabella reassured him.

"Fine? Then why you are in hospital? And why didn't you say anything? You suddenly disappeared, and the next thing I knew... you were here."

"I can't explain now, I'm visiting a friend. Well, a friend's mother anyway."

His face became even redder with anger. He sucked in a breath and took a step back. He stared at the ceiling and shook his head.

Arabella rolled her eyes. She'd seen his fits of anger before, and she was beyond being affected by them.

She noticed Rebecca stood in the doorway, a questioning look on her face. Arabella shook her head to indicate she was fine.

Suddenly, the shock of seeing Alastair cleared, and the question as to why she was seeing Alastair at all reared its head.

"Wait a minute, how did you know I'm here?"

Alastair lowered his head and looked at her. A sheepish expression crept onto his face.

Arabella's eyes went wide. Her gaze drifted to the clenched fist holding his mobile phone. She glared at him. She couldn't believe he had the audacity to track her, like a microchip on a puppy.

"You have some kind of tracking software, don't you? You... you, my god, Alastair! I never gave you permission to do that."

"I did it in case of emergencies, you know, in case you ended up in the hospital." He looked around the corridor as if proving his point.

"I don't care why you did it, you should have let me know. You should have asked."

"You're my wife."

Arabella took a shocked step back.

"I am *not* your wife, and we'll be talking about this," she promised. Her eyes drifted towards Rebecca. "But not now. Now, I have to be here."

Alastair turned, seeing Rebecca for the first time. He laughed and turned back to Arabella. "Her?"

Arabella held one of her crutch towards Rebecca. Rebecca took it from her. She used the other crutch to stride towards Alastair and jabbed him hard in the chest with a pointed finger from her free hand.

"I'm staying here. You are leaving, I will call you when I can."

She could feel his breath on her face, but she didn't take a step back. She stared into his eyes. She could tell he was analysing what was happening and deciding on the best course of action. She doubted he would come to the right choice.

"I'm not leaving without you," he said. "You have to come back to your father's house. People are asking about you. What do you expect me to say? That you're... suddenly best friends with some hippie child?"

"Leave now." Arabella knew that no matter how brave Alastair appeared, he was afraid of her. He'd always had trouble controlling her. It was something that Arabella secretly enjoyed. Before, she thought it was just a game of power, but now she realised that she wasn't playing a game; she was fighting to not be controlled by him.

"Don't speak, just turn around and go. Don't push me, Alastair."

He glared at her for a few seconds. He took a step back and nodded his head.

"We will talk about this later," he said in his best menacing tone.

"We will. Now, go."

He turned around and stalked away. She watched him leave, wondering what on earth she had ever seen in the man. As he rounded the final corner and disappeared from sight, she felt Rebecca's presence beside her. She turned and took the crutch from Rebecca's hand.

"Are you sure you want to stay?" Rebecca asked, her eyebrows knitted together in confusion.

"Absolutely. My thoughts haven't changed, I still think that you shouldn't be alone. And Alastair... well, his point of view is quite frankly irrelevant to me."

A small smile appeared on Rebecca's face. Arabella knew that she was making the right decision.

CHAPTER TWENTY

REBECCA COULDN'T BELIEVE the scene she had witnessed between Alastair and Arabella. She also couldn't believe that Arabella had chosen staying with Rebecca over him.

At first, she hadn't realised how much that meant to her. Not until she thought Arabella would cave in and go with Alastair. She had stood in the doorway willing Arabella to stay but assuming she would leave. She'd never assumed that she would have any company at this moment, but now that she had it, she was reluctant to let it go.

They both stepped back into the hospital room. Arabella paused and looked up at the clock on the wall. She turned to do the same and realised that it had just past midnight.

"Merry Christmas," Arabella whispered.

Rebecca smiled. "Merry Christmas," she whispered back. She gestured to her mother. "We should let her sleep."

Arabella looked towards the bed and slowly nodded her head.

"Have you eaten yet?" Arabella asked.

"No, I came straight here."

"Is there a place to get some food? I know how much you need to eat." Arabella joked.

Rebecca smiled despite herself. "Yes, they have a canteen, it's not great…"

"Surely it's better than some of the places we stopped at?"

"Well…" Rebecca kidded.

Arabella chuckled and gestured towards the door. Rebecca took a last look at her mother before stepping out and leading Arabella towards the hospital canteen.

They walked slowly because of Arabella's leg and in silence as Rebecca didn't know what to say. She wanted to offer her thanks and gratitude, but she didn't understand why Arabella was even there. And she didn't want to say anything that might rock the boat and cause her to leave. In a very short amount of time, Arabella's presence had become practically essential to her. She no longer thought she could do it on her own.

After a few minutes, they entered the canteen. A handful of people sat at tables, others forced to spend Christmas in hospital, either family members or workers. Some Christmas decorations had been hastily put up around the room. It was a sad attempt, and Rebecca wondered if it would have looked better without the decorations at all.

They browsed the offerings on display and, eventually, both decided on sandwiches. Arabella almost asked for coffee from the bored-looking employee, until Rebecca placed a warning hand on her forearm and softly shook her head. They both decided on tea, as it was difficult to ruin.

They sat by a window that overlooked the hospital entrance and ate in silence. In no time, Rebecca had finished a sandwich, not realising how hungry she had been. She hugged the mug of tea in her hands, enjoying the warmth.

"Thank you," Rebecca said.

"Don't mention it."

"No, I have to. I really appreciate you being here."

Arabella silently folded the sandwich wrapper and moved it to one side. She pulled her mug of tea towards her, mirroring Rebecca's pose.

"May I ask why you never said anything? I mean, you're perfectly within your right to keep it to yourself. I just wonder why you never mentioned it?"

Rebecca stared into the tea. "I think I wanted to be treated normally, to not have to worry about everything happening here. I could just be normal for a few minutes, or a few hours. No one looked at me with pity, no one hesitated every time they wanted to speak, in case they said the wrong thing."

"But I did say the wrong thing," Arabella pointed out. "And you ignored me for hours as a result. And shouted at me on the ferry."

"I'm sorry about that." Rebecca adjusted the mug in her hands.

"And you let me blather on about my party…"

Rebecca looked up at Arabella, chewing her lip anxiously. "I didn't mean… I didn't want you to…"

"I know you didn't," Arabella reassured her. "I just feel a little silly. Going on about how imperative it was for me to get home. When your need was so much greater."

Rebecca shook her head. "I didn't want it to be like that."

"Like what?"

"You know… about me."

"It should be about you."

"But I don't want that. I don't want to be the girl whose mum is dying of cancer."

Arabella smiled sadly. "You're very much like your mother."

"I'll take that as a compliment."

"Do." Arabella nodded.

Rebecca took a sip of her tea. She'd been wrong, they could ruin tea. She put the mug back on the table and continued to use it as a hand warmer.

"I felt guilty," Rebecca admitted.

"About?"

"About being in Portugal. Before I left, she was okay. I mean she was still *dying*, but it wasn't as near to the end as it is now. The chance came up to go to Portugal, get a bit of extra money and make my agent happy. I went, and she started to go downhill. I shouldn't have left."

"You couldn't have known that would happen. If you'd known, would you have stayed?"

"Of course."

"There you go then. You can't judge yourself on the unknowns," Arabella said matter-of-factly.

Rebecca clamped her lips together to prevent from chuckling out loud. Arabella had such a black-and-white view on the world.

"You know it could happen any day now," Rebecca said. "I mean she could, you know."

"Yes, I had assumed." Arabella looked down into her tea mug.

"And you're, you're okay with that?" Rebecca asked.

"Well, I'm prepared for it," Arabella said.

Rebecca watched as the older woman became lost in thought, staring into the milky tea. She couldn't understand why someone so desperate to get home to a Christmas party would suddenly abandon it to spend time with her.

Arabella was a mystery. One moment kind, another moment... not so kind. Now she was demonstrating the utmost kindness.

"I don't get it," Rebecca admitted.

Arabella's eyes met Rebecca's. "Get what?"

"You. Being here."

"I'm not sure I do either," she confessed. "But I am."

Rebecca picked up her mug and quickly gulped it down. "There's a visitors' room, it's nothing much. It has some sofas, and it's where I normally sleep when I stay the night here. I don't stay in Mum's room, I like to let her sleep. When she rests, she is not in pain."

Arabella sipped her tea. "Okay, that sounds like a good idea."

Rebecca blinked, not sure if Arabella was understanding what she was saying.

"I mean, I'm going to try to get some sleep," Rebecca clarified.

Arabella nodded. "Yes, I agreed that it's a good idea."

"So, you'll be heading home?"

"No. I'll be staying with you, if you want me to, that is? You said sofas, so I assume there's room for both of us?"

Rebecca wanted to say yes. She desperately wanted to say yes. The visitors' room, while appreciated, was lonely, dark, and scary. But it was no place for Arabella to stay. Arabella and her posh luggage. Arabella and her posh party dress.

She knew it was time to let Arabella off the hook.

"It's fine, I'll be okay," Rebecca said. "I appreciate what you're doing, but I'm okay on my own. You go back to your party, or back home. Whatever."

Arabella regarded her carefully, her eyes never wavering as they took in Rebecca. Rebecca had a feeling that she was being analysed, that her every thought was being read.

"No, I'll stay," Arabella said finally. "I said I would, and I think you want me to."

Rebecca stuttered for a second. "I... it's... I mean..." She trailed off, after realising she had nothing to say.

She did want Arabella to stay. She didn't understand how Arabella had suddenly become her support network. The idea of going through the next few hours alone was something she dreaded.

"So, it's decided then," Arabella said. She finished her tea, grabbed her crutch, and got to her feet. "Lead the way to this visitors' room, I can see by the look in your eyes that it isn't exactly the Hilton. But as long as it doesn't have creepy porcelain dolls staring at me while I sleep, it will be a step up in the world compared to last night."

"Wow, was that only last night?"

Arabella looked down at Rebecca and nodded her head. "Yes, it's hard to believe that twenty-four hours ago we were in a creepy French château. Wondering whether the husband even existed."

Rebecca laughed. She stood up and gathered their empty mugs. "I'm sure he was just busy, or shy."

"Yeah, sure he was," Arabella muttered with a sly smile.

CHAPTER TWENTY-ONE

THE VISITORS' room was just as dire as Arabella expected it to be. It had no windows and was lit by dim lamps that appeared to have been donated to the hospital directly after the War.

Three uncomfortable-looking sofas, two ugly armchairs, and a stack of blue rubber-coated mattresses filled the room. A door led to an en-suite bathroom.

Arabella wondered, not for the first time, or even the tenth time, what exactly she was doing. She wanted to stay, that much was obvious to her. But *why* she wished to stay still wasn't entirely clear.

Rebecca stood in the middle of the room, her hands tucked into her jeans pockets. She looked around the room apologetically.

"So, this is it," Rebecca said. "As I said, it's not much. But it's better than sleeping in the chair in Mum's room."

Arabella placed her bag on an armchair and sat on the edge of one of the sofas. She balanced her crutch on the wall beside her and started to remove her shoes. Rebecca walked over to a cupboard and open the door to reveal some sheets and pillows.

"It just sucks that it's happening at this time of year, you know?" Rebecca said. "Mum has always loved Christmas. It's always been her favourite time of year. We had so many traditions, things we'd always do. I know lots of families do; I suppose that's what makes Christmas what it is."

Arabella's family had never really had Christmas traditions. At least not anything that would find its way into a cute holiday movie. She took the offered pillow and sheet from Rebecca and made herself comfortable on her temporary bed.

"We always have mince pies. And Christmas cake. We eat far too much food," Rebecca said. "Not that we'll be doing any of that this year."

Arabella remained silent. She got the impression that Rebecca very rarely spoke about what was happening. Arabella would let her speak. Partly because she knew Rebecca needed; to get it all out. And partly because she had no idea what else to say.

She was still discovering how little she knew about Rebecca, how she had no idea how to comfort the girl. But, for some reason, Rebecca seemed to appreciate her presence. As long as that was the case, Arabella would stay.

"Mum's not really got much of an appetite at the moment," Rebecca explained. "I know she'd want me to have a normal Christmas. I don't think I can."

"I think you have to do what's right for you," Arabella said. "I know you're trying to do what's right for your mum, and that's important. But you have to look after yourself as well."

"That's what Mum keeps saying," Rebecca said.

Rebecca turned around and started making up a bed on the sofa opposite Arabella. Arabella watched as she quickly laid the sheet down, tucking it into each corner as if she had done a hundred times before. Rebecca sat down, removed her boots, and stretched on the sofa, reaching her arms above her.

Arabella watched, unable to drag her eyes away from Rebecca. She wanted to help, but she had no idea how. She could see that the girl was tense, ready to leap into action at a moment's notice. She couldn't blame her, but she knew Rebecca had to rest.

The worst was yet to come.

"Get some sleep," Arabella instructed.

Rebecca looked at her and let out a sigh. "I don't think I'll be able to," she admitted.

Arabella could see the exhaustion in Rebecca's face. She knew that the girl would fall asleep within seconds once she permitted herself to.

Arabella adjusted her sheeting and pillow and laid herself down. In a million years she never would have thought that she would be spending Christmas Eve on a second-hand sofa in a hospital waiting room. With a woman she barely knew.

Maybe it was the feeling of doing something for someone else, of doing something charitable, but it felt like the right thing to do.

"Just close your eyes," Arabella said softly. "Think of all those things about Christmas that you love." She sighed dramatically. "All those sugary treats, pies, and cakes, ridiculous paper hats, and whatever other ludicrous traditions that you hold so dear."

Rebecca snorted a laugh.

Arabella smiled. She turned her head, seeing that Rebecca was still staring up at the ceiling.

"I'm pretty sure I just told you to close your eyes."

Rebecca turned to regard her and slowly nodded her head. Her eyes fluttered closed.

"It's Christmas Day, so imagine that Father Christmas—"

"Santa," Rebecca corrected.

Arabella chuckled. "Very well, Santa, is making his way around the world delivering presents all the good boys and girls. Is that not how it goes?"

"Something like that," Rebecca agreed.

"Eating one hundred metric tons of Christmas treats and drinking gallons of milk or brandy, depending on the property value of the house he is visiting."

"This bedtime story is a little different to what I remember from being a kid," Rebecca said with a laugh.

"Well, it's the one you're getting. Now, stop interrupting. I'm pretty sure that there is something about reindeer."

CHAPTER TWENTY-TWO

DISTANT NOISES BEGAN to invade the quiet space, but Rebecca was used to it. The sounds of the nurses beginning their day, usually at an ungodly hour, had become her new alarm clock. She turned to lay on her back. She opened her eyes and stared at the ceiling.

Another day, she told herself. *Christmas Day.*

As she started to remember the events of the previous day, her head snapped around to look at the other sofa.

She winced.

Arabella was gone. Folded sheets sat atop a pillow on the arm of the sofa.

She blew out a breath. She couldn't blame the woman. At least she had waited until she had gone to sleep.

She looked at her watch. Her eyebrows rose in shock, it was already nine! She couldn't believe she had slept so long. She hadn't had a full night of sleep for weeks. She quickly felt guilty, her mum would have been woken that morning by a nurse.

She sat up and ran her fingers through her hair and rubbed her face. She pulled on her boots, stood up, and gathered the linens from her bed. She rolled them into a ball and threw them on top of Arabella's neatly folded sheets. She'd deal with them later. Right now, she had to pretend to enjoy what was bound to be the worst Christmas of her life.

She put her hand on the door handle and paused while she took a deep breath. Once she had exhaled, she put a smile on her face and walked out of the room.

She turned the corner and walked the few steps up the corridor towards her mother's room. The moment she crossed the threshold, she froze. Her jaw dropped, and she stared at the room in shock.

"Morning, darling, Merry Christmas," her mum said.

Rebecca tore her eyes away from the rest of the room and looked at her mother. She was so stunned she couldn't form any words.

"Isn't it amazing? It was all Lucy, you know."

"L-Lucy?" Rebecca stammered.

She looked around the room, tinsel and brightly coloured paper decorations had been hung. A tacky blow-up Christmas tree, complete with integrated hanging decorations, sat in pride of place on the table in front of the window. Another table was filled with Christmas treats, mince pies, Christmas cake, cookies, and lots more. A bottle of champagne, and what looked like non-alcoholic wine, sat on the bedside table beside some crystal-cut champagne flutes.

"Yes, she bought too much tinsel so her and Abigail, you know the new morning nurse, have gone to share the wealth with the main ward."

Rebecca looked to her mother. She was sat up in bed, a paper hat on her head. In her lap, a box of her favourite Christmas chocolates. And, much to Rebecca's amazement and relief, she seemed to have eaten a few.

It almost looked normal. If you could ignore the hospital

bed and equipment, it could nearly be a real Christmas. Rebecca felt tears start to flood her eyes and quickly turned away. Crying was not allowed. She knew that once she started, she wouldn't stop.

"We thought we'd let you sleep in," her mum said. "Get some rest after your long trip."

Rebecca pretended to analyse the blow-up Christmas tree, she smiled at the very thought of Arabella puffing out her cheeks, blowing up the hideous, tacky decoration.

"Thank you," Rebecca said.

"She cares about you," her mum said. "A lot."

Rebecca didn't answer. She didn't know what to say. Maybe Arabella did care about her, maybe it was some kind of guilt. At this point she didn't know. And that probably wasn't going to change in the near future either.

"Ah, you're up."

Rebecca turned around to see Arabella walking into the room. A chuckle escaped Rebecca's lips as she noted the paper hat on her head.

"One word about what is on top of my head, and you will regret it," Arabella said with a smirk.

Rebecca held up her hands. "Wouldn't dream of it," she replied, but she was unable to keep the smile off her face.

"I was worried you'd sleep away Christmas," Arabella gently chided.

Rebecca noticed Arabella looking towards her mother with a frown. Arabella walked over to the side of the bed and took the box of chocolates away from the sleeping woman.

"She's been drifting in and out all morning," she explained. She placed the chocolates on the bedside table. Then she picked up a mince pie and held out towards Rebecca. "Breakfast?"

"When did you do all this?" Rebecca took the mince pie

and started to peel the foil tray away from the delicious pastry goodness.

"I woke up early, I thought I might as well get a start on making Christmas. I may not have a white fluffy beard and wear a red suit, but I thought I'd do."

"You do," Rebecca whispered. "Thank you for this, it's... incredible."

"Well, it's only just started," Arabella said.

"Shouldn't you be getting home? Aren't they going to miss you?"

Rebecca really didn't want to bring it up. She didn't want Arabella to go, but she also didn't want Arabella to feel obligated to stay. Because surely that could be the only reason that she was staying?

"I keep telling you, I'm staying," Arabella said. "Now, come on, I have something for you."

"For me?" Rebecca frowned.

"Yes, for you. Come on." Arabella turned on her crutch and walked out of the room. Rebecca quickly followed her, surprised at the speed with which Arabella could move when she wanted to.

They walked down the corridor and back towards the visitors' room. Rebecca wondered what else Arabella had up her sleeve.

Arabella opened the door and walked in. She paused in the middle of the room and nodding her head towards a wrapped Christmas present on Rebecca's sofa. Rebecca stared at the present. She hadn't even thought of getting or giving any presents this year. Seeing a Christmas present beautifully wrapped, with ribbons and a bow, took her by surprise.

"Don't just stare at it," Arabella said. She placed her crutch next to her sofa and sat down.

"You got me a present?" Rebecca asked.

"Well, the evidence would indicate that that is the case, wouldn't it?" Arabella rolled her eyes.

"Why did you get me a present?"

"Because it's Christmas," Arabella replied. "Are you going to open it or not?"

Rebecca sat tentatively next to the box.

"I promise it's not a porcelain doll."

Rebecca chuckled. She gently picked it up and placed it on her lap. She found the ends of the ribbon and delicately pulled. She felt like such a fraud, ordinarily she would have ripped the parcel open in seconds. But in Arabella's presence, with the older woman still dressed to the nines from her Christmas Eve party, Rebecca acted with a decorum she never knew she had.

After carefully removing the ribbon, she searched for where the paper had been taped down and began to slowly pick at the tape.

"We'll be here all day if that's how you open gifts," Arabella commented.

"Shush you."

Rebecca sped up slightly, starting to rip the paper. Excitement was building within her, but she tried to keep it down. After all, it was quite likely that Arabella had bought her a joke gift. She removed the wrapping paper and put it to one side. A plain cardboard box sat in her lap.

"I put it in that box, so it would be easier to wrap," Arabella explained.

Rebecca open the top of the box. She peered inside and saw a label. Her eyes widened in surprise. She reached her hand into the box and pulled out the contents. The box dropped to her feet, and she stared at the Manfrotto backpack.

"It's better than that tatty old rucksack you have," Arabella said. "You wouldn't want to damage your camera."

Rebecca turned the camera bag over in her hands, examining it from all angles. It was perfect. It would perfectly contain all of her travel things, with a safe space for her camera, lenses, and equipment. She knew because she had longingly stared at it in a shop window for a number of months. The hefty price tag always made it an impossible purchase.

"I can't accept this, I know what this cost," Rebecca said. She looked up at Arabella. "How did you even manage to get it?"

Arabella spread her hands in obvious gesture. "This is London. You can get anything at any time."

"It's incredibly generous, too generous. I'm sorry I can't accept it."

"You can accept it, and you will. In the not-too-distant future the handle on your rucksack will snap and your camera, and your livelihood, will be broken. Besides, it's Christmas."

"I didn't get you anything." Rebecca stared back down at the bag. Her fingers ran over the logo.

"You're sharing Christmas with me. And let's not forget, you drove me home from Faro."

Rebecca laughed. "You paid for the car," she reminded Arabella.

"I had no idea how argumentative you could be," Arabella said. "I might just complain to your mother. Accept the damn bag."

Rebecca gripped the bag lovingly and bit her lip. Arabella was right, her rucksack was dangerously in need of repair. It wouldn't be long before it broke, she'd been lucky that it hadn't broken and damaged her camera equipment already.

"Thank you, really, thank you... for everything. I don't know how you did this, but I really appreciate it."

Arabella smiled. "Well, when you get up at a reasonable

time and set your mind to something, you can get a hell of a lot done."

"So I see!" She hugged her bag to her chest. It smelt of future adventures.

"I arranged for a Christmas dinner to be delivered to the ward. Yes, I spoke with the head nurse first. I imagine whatever they had planned to serve would have been… shall we say, less than desirable? Anyway, it's on the way and hopefully we can convince your mother to have a couple of bites."

Rebecca blinked. "Y-you arranged for Christmas dinner to be delivered to the entire ward?"

Arabella grabbed her crutch and pushed herself off the sofa to stand. "Yes, as I said, when you get up at a reasonable time you can get a hell of a lot done."

"Did you get any sleep?" Rebecca asked.

"Some." Arabella nodded. "But, to be honest, sleep escapes me at the moment."

Rebecca assumed as much. Arabella did seem to be a woman escaping from something. She'd watched the interaction between Arabella and Alastair with great interest. Of course, she had never made her dislike of the man a secret. And she had to admit she had been secretly pleased to see them argue, especially to see Arabella stand up for herself. She knew Arabella could do better. Much better.

"I'm sorry to hear that," Rebecca said.

Arabella shrugged. "It is what it is. But at least that means I get to spend Christmas here, as long as you'll still have me?"

"Absolutely, you're like my very own little Santa," she joked.

Arabella rolled her eyes. "Careful, I could still go home, you know."

"Please don't," tumbled from Rebecca's lips before she

had time to stop it. "I mean, if you still want to stay, I'd still like you to be here."

Arabella looked down at her kindly. "I still want to stay."

Rebecca chuckled bitterly. "I honestly can't think why, but I'm glad you're here."

"I know things are grim. But no matter what happens, your mum smiled this morning. She ate some Christmas chocolates, and, for a couple of moments, things seemed normal. That's what you need to hold onto."

Rebecca put her bag to the side and stood up. "You're right. Let's go and be festive."

CHAPTER TWENTY-THREE

ARABELLA STOOD outside the hospital's main entrance. She pulled the jacket she had borrowed from Rebecca around her shoulders.

Snow had been falling steadily for the last few hours. She looked out at the snow-covered car park in front of her. Any other day it would have been a beautiful sight, a perfect wintry Christmas scene. But this wasn't any other day; this was the day that Rebecca had lost her mother.

It happened so fast. One moment they were eating Christmas dinner, drinking the non-alcoholic wine, reminiscing about Christmases gone by. The next Allison's eyes had started to flutter closed. A few moments later, she opened her eyes and started to look around in confusion. Something had clearly been wrong. Rebecca rushed to get a nurse.

By the time the nurse arrived, Allison had closed her eyes again and drifted off into an endless sleep.

Arabella hadn't known what to do. She'd never been in that kind of situation before, she didn't know how to act or what to say. She stood uselessly in the room, watching as

Rebecca flopped into a chair and stared helplessly at her mother.

They remained like that for ten long and agonising minutes. The low sound of Christmas music continued to stream through Arabella's phone. It seemed utterly surreal.

The head nurse had entered the room and started speaking to Rebecca in hushed tones. Arabella had taken the opportunity to get some fresh air. Remembering that she was still wearing a thin party dress and knowing that snow had been falling thick and fast, she had grabbed Rebecca's jacket.

She had hoped that the fresh air would give her a sense of clarity. That things would seem better, that she would be able to figure out what to do next.

Sadly, it was too much to ask of fresh air. She felt just as confused, lost, and helpless as she had inside the hospital.

She felt guilty. She worried that she had overexcited Allison, that her desire to create a perfect Christmas had resulted in the woman's premature death. The nurse had explained she could have passed at any point within the last few days. And that it was just bad luck that it happened to be Christmas Day.

Arabella hoped that was true. She certainly hoped that Rebecca would see it that way. She wondered why on earth she had stayed. Had she just ended up making things worse?

The automatic doors slid open. Arabella looked up to see Rebecca step outside. Rebecca rubbed her arms in protest at the chilly air, she wore jeans and a thin sweater.

Arabella immediately started to remove the jacket from her shoulders, but Rebecca held her hand up.

"It's okay," Rebecca reassured her.

Arabella paused. "Are you sure? It's freezing out here."

"I'm sure." Rebecca rubbed her hands together. She stood beside Arabella, leaning on the wall.

"I don't know what to do," Rebecca admitted softly.

"What do you mean?"

"I have all this paperwork to fill in, and I should probably go home. But I don't want to. I feel like I should stay here. It's so weird to try to understand that I don't need to be here anymore. And I don't want to be home either. I feel... untethered."

Rebecca stared out at the white blanket of snow, lost in thought.

"Rebecca, I'm *so* sorry," Arabella said.

She slowly turned to regard Arabella, a frown on her face. "Why?"

"I shouldn't have done so much, it was all just too much. I wanted to make a perfect Christmas. Clearly, it taxed your mother."

Rebecca shook her head. "No, no, don't think this was your fault. It's amazing that she even got to *see* Christmas Day. She's had good days and bad days for the last few weeks. There's been many times when I thought I'd lose her. The fact that she got to see Christmas Day, and that you made it so amazing, means more to me than I can ever say."

Arabella looked into Rebecca's eyes, unable to detect a hint of a lie.

"I will never be able to thank you enough for what you did today. I think today was the first day in a long time that Mum forgot that she was ill. She had fun, she had a great day. If I could... if I could *choose* which day would be her last day, then it would probably be this day."

Arabella felt relief. All she wanted to do was help. The thought that maybe she had caused irreparable damage had been too much to bear.

She looked at her watch, it was six o'clock in the evening. She hadn't heard from any of her family all day. Alastair had clearly said something to prevent them from getting in touch. She didn't feel like going home either.

"Let's go somewhere," Arabella suggested.

Rebecca looked at her in confusion. "Like where?"

"I don't know. Let's go somewhere, see something. Away from here."

Rebecca turned and gazed out at the heavy snow falling on top of cars. She looked so lost. Arabella's heart clenched at the sight.

"You know, when my grandmother died... I went to the cinema," Arabella said.

A disbelieving smile crossed Rebecca's face.

"The cinema?"

"Yes. I went with my two cousins," Arabella explained. "And we went to see some children's movie; we were all in our late teens. It was two-fifteen on a Tuesday. We heard she'd died and just had no idea what to do. Everything seemed so strange. She'd been ill and in hospital for a while. It was just a matter of time until she died. I think we'd all grieved her for a long time before she died."

Arabella took a few steps forward, leaving the safety of the canopy and now stood directly in the snow. She held out her hand and watched as snowflakes began to land and dissolve in her palm.

"We didn't want to eat, didn't want to stay home. We didn't know what to do. Nobody ever really explains to you what to do when somebody dies. Especially if you've been mourning that person for some time. You're not going to burst into tears, throw yourself on top of your bed, and be inconsolable for a few hours. And yet you're not just going to get on with your life either."

Arabella watched as the snowflakes melted. She let out a sigh. She lowered her hand and turned back to face Rebecca.

"And so, we did something utterly bizarre, and went to the cinema. We bought tickets to the only thing that was playing at that time of day. We walked in and doubled the audience. And all six of us watched some mind-numbing children's film, I couldn't tell you what it was even about now."

Arabella chuckled and shook her head. "At one point, my younger cousin leaned close to me and whispered in my ear that our grandmother just died a few hours before, and now we were at the cinema, and how weird it felt. And I agreed with her, but neither of us could think of a single other thing to do."

Rebecca slowly nodded her head. "I understand what you mean, I'm not ready to grieve. I've been grieving on and off for months. And, as much as I hate myself for thinking this, there is a small part of me that is relieved that she is no longer in pain."

She started to cry. Arabella rushed forward and pulled her into a one-armed hug.

"It's going to be okay, we're going to get through the rest of this day together," Arabella promised.

Rebecca sniffed and nodded her head against Arabella's shoulder.

"I just don't know what to do," she mumbled.

"And that's okay. There's no rule book for these situations. Don't be so hard on yourself."

Arabella tightened her arm around Rebecca, grasping her crutch in her other hand. Soft sobs shook the younger woman, and Arabella knew she'd do anything to make everything better.

"I have an idea," she said. "Do you trust me?"

"Of course," Rebecca answered without hesitation.

She paused for a moment. She didn't think she'd ever heard someone have such faith in her, especially someone she hardly knew. She swallowed and cleared the wayward thought from her mind.

"Good, then I have an idea."

CHAPTER TWENTY-FOUR

REBECCA LOOKED around the familiar interior. A few hours ago, she would have given anything to have been out of the car. Now, she was almost relieved to be back in it. Although, she was going to have to have a word with Arabella about driving to the hospital with her foot in the cast.

She rubbed her face with the palms of her hands.

Everything seemed blank. Confusing didn't begin to cover it. She felt like she was waking up from a long, deep sleep. One where her life had been indefinitely on hold.

She didn't know what normal felt like anymore. It had been replaced a while ago. Life had been surreal for so long that she now struggled to remember the real world from the fake.

She couldn't believe that she had burst into tears on Arabella's shoulder. She knew she could be forgiven for crying, her mother just died. But it seemed like Arabella was the only thing holding her together at the moment. It wasn't fair on Arabella. Fate had thrown them together, nothing more.

The passenger door opened. Arabella bent down and poked her head in.

"Could you open the boot?"

Rebecca pulled the lever.

She noticed three hospital orderlies standing behind Arabella, all carrying boxes. Arabella directed them to put the boxes in the boot, reminding them not to damage her precious luggage that was still there.

In a matter of moments, they were done and walked back towards the hospital. Arabella slammed the boot closed and took her seat in the car.

"You *drove* here?" Rebecca chastised immediately.

"No, I flew here," Arabella replied. She pulled her seatbelt around her, clicking into place. "But, look at me, I'm wearing my seatbelt." She smiled.

Rebecca rolled her eyes and shook her head. She put her own seatbelt on.

"So, what did, um, what did they say?" Rebecca asked hesitantly.

Arabella's face turned serious. "After you said goodbye, I sat down with the head nurse and filled out the most important paperwork as best I could, based on what you told me. The rest is in one of the boxes. There is a leaflet explaining what you need to do, and someone from the hospital will call you in the next three days. All of her belongings are in the boxes."

Rebecca swallowed. "Thank you for dealing with that."

"My pleasure. I'm a lot better at dealing with paperwork than I am with people."

"You seem to be very good at dealing with people," Rebecca commented.

Arabella smiled wryly. "You wouldn't have said that two days ago."

She was right. Two days ago, Rebecca would have considered throttling Arabella without feeling much guilt at all.

"I've gotten to know you. You are a lot softer than you would have people believe."

Arabella chuckled. "I deny everything. Anyway, I have an idea about a place to go. If you're up for driving?"

"It's Christmas Day, isn't everything closed?" Rebecca asked.

"Asked by someone who has clearly never left their house on Christmas Day. The country may have ground to a halt on Christmas Day forty years ago, but not these days. Now, are you going to drive, or do I have to?"

Rebecca started the engine. "Where to, O navigator?"

CHAPTER TWENTY-FIVE

"This is freezing," Rebecca complained.

"It certainly is," Arabella agreed. "I'd offer you another drink, but you insist on driving." Arabella sipped from her plastic wineglass.

"Do I need to remind you again that Jose would not be happy with you invalidating his insurance by driving the car?"

"Jose isn't here," Arabella pointed out.

Rebecca laughed. She leaned on the handrail and looked out over the front of the boat. She regarded the pretty, twinkling lights of London. Lights that she would have been able to appreciate more if there wasn't a strong wind filled with snowflakes blowing in her face.

The idea of taking a cruise ship on the Thames had seemed like such a good idea. Right up until the moment they actually did it.

Luckily, Arabella had stopped off at her house and picked up a thick winter coat and scarf. Arabella's house was a smaller but no less impressive mansion than her father's the night before. The lights had been off. Arabella said that Alastair would probably, and hopefully, still be at her father's house.

After the short stop, they had driven towards the City, looking for something to do. Much to Rebecca's surprise, the roads were quiet but certainly not deserted.

Arabella was right, Rebecca had always assumed that everybody was indoors with their family on Christmas Day, despite knowing that London was a large and diverse city, consisting of many different cultures and religions. Somehow, she'd never stopped to think about the countless people who didn't celebrate Christmas, or those who just celebrated Christmas in a different way to herself.

As they had driven deeper into the City, the crowds had started to grow. Bars, restaurants, and shops were open. People scooped handfuls of snow from fence railings and parked cars and threw them at one another.

Seeing other people just doing their own thing helped Rebecca to not feel so alone.

Arabella had directed Rebecca to park in what was clearly a no-parking area. The older woman claimed that no parking enforcement officers would be out on Christmas Day. She also unexpectedly made a big deal of her cast and her sudden inability to walk too far.

A few moments later and they were at the dock, awaiting the cruise ship's arrival with a few other partygoers. Rebecca had asked Arabella if it was booze cruise. Arabella had chuckled, asking if she looked like the kind of person who would frequent such an event.

The second they got on the boat, Rebecca remembered why she didn't much like boats.

It wasn't that she got seasick, in fact she loved the feel of being on the water. It was the elements, in warmer climates, the sun would beat down mercilessly. In colder climates, like today, the biting wind felt ten times worse on open water.

But, despite the discomfort of the cold wind and the flakes of snow, she had to admit that she felt energised and alive. Something that she hadn't felt a couple of hours before.

Never in her wildest dreams would she ever have considered getting on a cruise ship on the Thames on Christmas Day.

"This is nice," she admitted.

Arabella blinked in surprise. "Aren't you the person who was *just* complaining about how cold it is?"

"Oh, it's cold, freezing. But this, this is nice." Rebecca pointed to the view.

Arabella leaned on the railing and smiled as she looked at the unique mix of old and new architecture.

"Yes, it is. London has always been my favourite city. Obviously, I'm biased. I live and work here. And I was born here. But there's something about London, the architecture, the people, the soul of the city."

"Aw, that's quite poetic," Rebecca said.

"Of course it is, I'm a saleswoman. It's in my blood." Arabella gestured to the buildings with her hand. "I could sell you any one of these."

Rebecca laughed. "You may be the best saleswoman there is. And you may well make me *want* to buy one. But I could never afford one."

Arabella shrugged. "That's what loans are for."

"Buying office blocks?" Rebecca asked.

"Why not?"

"Oh, I see, and what do you think I should do with this office block you just sold me?" Rebecca asked, a smirk on her face.

"Rent it out, make a profit. Buy another, from me, of course." Arabella winked.

"Of course," Rebecca agreed. "Until I own half of London?"

"Absolutely. And then you'll have your own private yacht to take night-time tours on Christmas Day. And appreciate the view of your empire."

"I don't think I'm an office block kind of person."

Arabella looked at her with a wistful smile. "You're right. I think you need to build a portfolio of apartments instead. Residential. Not as much profit but more security."

"Do you have a portfolio of apartments?"

"A small one, yes. Not as many listings as I'd like. I've often forgone good deals to sell them to my clients. A tactical decision while building up Henley's."

"You really love it, don't you? Work, I mean. You talked about it a lot in the car, and I can see how passionate you are about it now."

Arabella looked down at the water.

"I do love it," she admitted. "But, I don't know, it's complicated."

"That's what people say when they are scared of the truth," Rebecca said.

Arabella chuckled and looked up at her. "Oh, is that so?"

"Yep." Rebecca nodded her head. "People only ever describe something as complicated when they know what they want isn't what other people want. Like, when someone is married but they want a divorce. They'll tell someone else that it's complicated. Because they know that they want a divorce, but they don't want to get a divorce because that will be messy and scary. Complicated is a great word to stop people doing something that will end up being really messy."

Arabella regarded her silently. The smile slipped from her face.

Rebecca felt dread run up her spine, colder than the icy winds bouncing up from the waters below. She wondered if she had gone too far, if her big mouth had got her into more trouble.

"I'm sorry, I shouldn't have—"

"No, no, it's fine," Arabella reassured her. She tore her eyes from Rebecca and looked down once again at the choppy waters below them. "I was just wondering why I don't have a friend in my life who is as honest as you are."

"Self-preservation?" Rebecca guessed.

Arabella grinned. "Most likely."

A waiter made his way along the deck, expertly balancing a tray of drinks. Arabella stood up and turned to face him.

"Can I have another champagne, and can my friend here have a hot chocolate?"

The waiter nodded and hurried away to get their orders.

Rebecca looked in surprise from Arabella to the departing waiter. It had been a while since someone had ordered for her. Especially ordered exactly what she wanted.

Arabella looked startled.

"If you don't want to drink it, you can hold it and get some warmth from it," she explained.

A slight blush appeared on Arabella's cheeks as she realised that she had ordered for Rebecca without asking what she wanted.

"I like hot chocolate," Rebecca said, eager to quell Arabella's embarrassment.

Arabella turned to face the water. "You're right, I am scared of the truth. I am using the word complicated as a shield of sorts. It's not complicated at all, if I'm honest with myself."

Rebecca was surprised to hear the admission. It was so softly spoken that it was nearly eaten up by the engine noise and the waves.

She took a step closer, leaning on the handrail beside Arabella and looking out at the illuminated cityscape.

She remained quiet, wishing that Arabella would speak again.

After a few moments, the woman let out a sigh. "I don't want to marry Alastair. I think I've always known that, I just didn't see any other option. He's a nice enough man. Trust me, I've dated worse. But I'm… well, I'm trapped in this engagement now. I don't expect you to understand, but my life has been mapped out for me. There are certain things I'm expected to do. And I always knew that, and I was always comfortable with that. But now the time is here, I'm scared. But it's too late to turn back now."

"It's never too late," Rebecca promised.

Arabella laughed bitterly. "Oh, it is, believe me. Everyone knows about the engagement, everyone is planning for the wedding, and what comes after. To pull out now would be such a public disaster. Not to mention that it wouldn't change anything. If I didn't marry Alastair then I'd just end up marrying someone else. Better the devil you know."

"Yeah, you're right," Rebecca agreed. "Because, like, it is the dark ages and you're totally going to be auctioned off to a man anyway, so you might as well pick this one, right? And getting married means that your life is over. You need to stay home and let the men deal with the business while you pump out babies and arrange dinner parties."

Arabella looked up at her. She raised her eyebrow.

"Ouch," she said without feeling.

"I just don't get it," Rebecca continued. "You're brilliant, you're intelligent, impressive, you're clearly an important part of the business. Why do you have to give all that up?"

"I—"

"Actually, I don't want to hear your answer," Rebecca cut her off. "Just answer me this question: do you want to? Do you want to marry someone you obviously don't love? Do you want to give up work? And, do you want to be some weird Stepford Wife?"

"That's not the point," Arabella countered.

"Yeah, it is. It's completely the point. Come on, Arabella, you just saw how short and unfair life can be. I may not know you that well, but I know you are motivated and you seem to like challenges. You must have a list of things you want to accomplish in your life? Have you done them? Or will you do them after you're married? I can't see you having a bucket list that consists of making the perfect omelette, whisking eggs into a perfect velvety scramble or whatever you have to do to make a perfect omelette. I just don't think they are the accomplishments you want to tick off, but maybe I'm wrong?"

The waiter returned. "Excuse me."

Rebecca turned around and smiled at him. "Thank you," she said as she took both of the drinks, handing the champagne to Arabella.

Arabella mumbled her gratitude and took the glass, retreating back to her view of the dark water.

"I'm sorry," Rebecca muttered.

She didn't know why she felt the need to push Arabella. It was like she had a personal mission to stop her from giving up work and, more importantly, marrying someone she didn't love.

But she didn't know why it was so important to her. She hardly knew Arabella and she was trying to fix her life.

"You don't need to apologise, you're right," Arabella confessed. "I got myself into a mess, and I need to get myself out of it. I'm not quite sure how to do that, but I will. I shan't spend the rest of my days making award-winning omelettes."

Rebecca smiled so hard it hurt her cold cheeks. She wrapped her hands tightly around the hot chocolate mug, enjoying the feeling of warmth against her cold palms.

"I should thank you," Arabella continued. She still leaned on the handrail, but now turned to focus all of her attention on Rebecca. "Seriously, you've been a pain in my side since the moment I met you, but I am so glad I met you."

"You have a funny way of saying thank you," Rebecca pointed out.

"You opened my eyes, and that's not an easy thing to do," Arabella carried on, ignoring her comment. "If I'd caught that plane and flown home as planned, I don't think I ever would have addressed that nagging feeling in the pit of my stomach. So, thank you."

Arabella took a step forward and placed a soft kiss on Rebecca's cheek.

Rebecca cursed that she had stood in the cold wind for so long that her cheek was numb. To make up for the dulled nerve endings in her cheek, she quickly inhaled the complex aroma of Arabella's perfume.

"You're welcome," Rebecca managed to say. She was relieved when she got the words out and realised that she hadn't stuttered or squeaked. "And thank you, I couldn't have managed today without you."

"Oh, you would've been fine." Arabella returned to her place, leaning on the handrail.

Rebecca wanted to step closer but knew it was inappropriate. She was emotionally drained, as was Arabella. But Arabella was also tired and probably on her way to being drunk. And Rebecca didn't know if she just wanted some human comfort or if what she was starting to feel for Arabella was something more.

She noticed Arabella shiver slightly.

"Maybe we should head inside?" she suggested.

"We can't enjoy the view from in there," Arabella commented.

"I can," Rebecca replied with a sigh as she gazed at Arabella. "I—I mean, the windows are fine. We can... see the view through the... the windows."

Arabella was too busy deciding what to do with her glass as she looked at her crutch to catch Rebecca's rambling. Rebecca reached out and took the champagne glass from her.

"Thank you." Arabella adjusted her crutch and made her way slowly towards the door to the interior seating area.

Rebecca followed her, chastising herself for her slip.

Arabella was straight, and Rebecca didn't want to fall into the lesbian stereotype of hitting on any attractive woman with a pulse. She could just be friends with Arabella, especially as the friendship would probably only last a few more hours. Until Arabella sobered up and realised that she was hanging out with someone so far below her status. Eventually Arabella would decide that it was time to go home, and that would be the end of whatever it was they had.

Rebecca was grateful that she'd had Arabella's help and companionship as long as she had. She knew that time was running out and now she just needed to enjoy the company, build some positive memories of this terrible and messed-up Christmas Day.

CHAPTER TWENTY-SIX

Two Weeks Later

Arabella hung up the phone. She pulled her laptop closer and typed some notes into the system.

"Helen, can you get the contract ready for Mrs Simmons? She wants to come in this afternoon to sign," she called out.

Arabella's assistant Helen entered her office. "I'll get it printed out in a moment; any idea what time she will be here?"

Arabella laughed. "As usual, she's not been helpful enough to provide a time."

Helen took some files from Arabella's out-tray and put the morning post in the in-tray. She fussed around the desk, removing screwed-up pieces of paper and picking up the three used coffee mugs.

"Make sure you take some time to have lunch today. I know it's busy, but you have to eat."

Arabella looked up at her assistant and smiled. "Thank you, I'll do my best."

"Don't think I don't recognise that tone."

"What tone?" Arabella asked.

"The one you use to appease customers," Helen pointed out. "That means you won't do whatever you say you will do."

Arabella opened a file on her desk and started to read through the papers.

"You know it's January, right? Our busiest time of year? Everyone who put their life on hold for December has suddenly woken up from their turkey-induced coma and wants everything done yesterday."

Helen let out a long-suffering sigh. She stood in front of the desk and looked impatiently at her.

"Fine, fine. I will *try* to make some time," Arabella reassured her.

She had no idea where she would find that time, though. The pile of work on her desk was growing exponentially each day. She pressed some buttons on the keyboard to print the document she was working on.

"We have to get the new keys cut for Monmouth Street," Arabella said. "I suppose I could do that on my way back from my dinner appointment with the Chinese investors."

"It's already done. They're in my desk drawer," Helen replied.

She pointed to a high stack of files that sat on the floor beside Arabella's desk. "Are those to be filed?"

Arabella glanced at them and felt a pang of guilt for letting them grow into an unmanageable mess over the past few days.

"Yes, but I'll do it," she said.

"I can do it," Helen offered.

"It's my mess, I'll clean it up later this afternoon," Arabella offered.

Helen raised an eyebrow and shook her head. It was taking a while for Helen to get used to the new Arabella. The post-Christmas Arabella.

She turned around to see why her printer hadn't sprung to life. A message regarding the toner flashed on the small screen. It wasn't a surprise, January really was a hectic month and the device had been spitting out contracts like they were going out of fashion.

She turned back to her laptop and reprinted the document in the main office instead.

"Well, if you change your mind, let me know," Helen instructed gently.

Helen was the kind of person who wouldn't take any crap from Arabella, but still knew who was boss. Arabella enjoyed working with her because she knew that Helen wouldn't hesitate to tell her off if necessary.

She leaned on the desk and pushed herself to standing. She picked up her crutch and started to make her way to the main office to get her freshly printed documents, hoping that toner was holding up better.

"I'll be fine," she reassured Helen as they left her office.

The shop was buzzing with people, and she quickly looked around to check that everything looked satisfactory. All staff members were on the phones or speaking directly with customers.

She walked to the corner and saw her documents shooting out of the top of the printer. Once the job was finished, she picked up the still-warm papers and started to check through the details one last time.

"Can I help you?" she heard the receptionist say.

"I'm here to see Arabella Henley," a familiar voice replied.

Arabella heart beat a little faster. She pretended she

hadn't heard the conversation and glanced up at the glass window in front of her to check her reflection. She didn't know why it mattered to her, but she casually tamed her hair regardless.

"Miss Henley?" the receptionist asked as she approached.

"Yes?" Arabella asked, wishing she'd bothered making a note of the new girl's name. It would look better if she knew her name.

"There's a Miss Edwards here to see you."

Arabella took a calming breath before looking up and towards Rebecca. She tried to look calm and put together, but she wasn't sure she was managing it.

Rebecca stood nervously in the reception area, holding a large bouquet of flowers and waving at her. Arabella raised her hand to wave back, but, at the last minute, thought better of the geeky gesture. She turned it into a gesture for Rebecca to come and join her.

"Thank you," she said to the receptionist, giving her permission to go back to her desk.

"Well, hello there, Miss Edwards," Arabella said once Rebecca had approached her. "Lovely to see you again."

"Hi," Rebecca replied. Her eyes roamed over Arabella quickly. "You're looking good… I mean well, you're looking well."

Arabella grinned. She could cope better with her own nerves if she knew Rebecca was just as nervous.

"Thank you, you do too."

"These are for you." Rebecca gestured to the flowers.

"They're beautiful, you didn't have to do that, though."

Arabella noticed a few members of staff were starting to stare at them. It wasn't unusual for a grateful client to bring in a gift, but Arabella didn't work on cases alone, so they would all know that Rebecca was not a client.

"I wanted to. It's not much, but I wanted to say thank

you." She looked around. "Is there somewhere you want me to put them?"

"Oh, yes, let's go into my office," Arabella said. She grabbed her crutch and started to wedge the papers under her arm. Rebecca took the papers from her.

"Don't want them to get creased," she explained.

Arabella found herself speechless. She briefly wondered why she so readily accepted help from Rebecca but shunned it from everyone else. She pushed the thought to one side and turned to lead them towards her office.

"Helen, could you get a vase?" she asked as she crossed the threshold.

Helen looked up from the filing cabinet, from Arabella to Rebecca with a smile.

"Of course, Miss Henley. Would you like tea and coffee?" Helen asked.

"Yes, please," Arabella quickly replied. She purposefully didn't ask Rebecca. If she made the assumption, then the girl would be forced to stay out of politeness.

At the very back of her mind she remembered the numerous tasks she had to do today. Now they seemed to fade in significance. She could take a few minutes.

She gestured to a chair in front of her desk and placed her crutch in their usual place by the filing cabinet. She took the flowers out of Rebecca's hands and looked at them in more detail.

"These are lovely." She'd seen a lot of bouquets in her time in property management, these somehow seemed brighter and fresher than the others that had come before.

"I'm glad you like them, you're hard to buy for," Rebecca said. She took the proffered seat and looked around the office.

"I am not," Arabella argued.

Rebecca chuckled. "Are we disagreeing already? I've barely sat down."

"I'll disagree with you if you make ridiculous statements." Arabella sniffed and put the flowers down gently on the edge of her large desk. She sat in her chair and looked at Rebecca.

"How are you?"

Rebecca paused her inspection of the office and looked at Arabella.

"I'm okay. Getting back out into the real world."

Arabella's heart sunk at the thought of Rebecca only now picking up the pieces and rebuilding her life. The last two weeks of her life had passed in a blur of activity. The thought of Rebecca having slogged through each day ate at her.

She had wanted to get in touch with Rebecca but knew that she had already intruded far too much. She had to keep reminding herself that they were not friends. Circumstance and nothing more had brought them together. Rebecca didn't want to hear about Arabella's life, and she didn't need support from her either. She presumably had hundreds of friends who could offer her much better support.

"Nice office," Rebecca commented. She angled herself around to take in the large, modern space.

"Thank you. I like it."

Rebecca chewed her lip.

"Out with it," Arabella demanded.

The girl laughed. "I was just wondering how to ask something without sounding really nosey."

"That ship has clearly sailed, what do you want to know?"

"Alastair?" Rebecca asked, a light blush appearing on her cheeks.

"Gone," Arabella said.

"Oh." Rebecca sounded surprised. She pointed to Arabella's finger. "I thought you might have had second thoughts?"

Arabella looked at the large diamond ring that still sat on her engagement finger. She toyed with it, spinning it distractedly.

"Not everyone knows, so we're keeping up appearances for a while. He's moved out, but it takes a while to tell everyone, without spooking investors."

"I'll pretend I understand what any of that means." Rebecca grinned. "I'm just glad you're not marrying him. He was an idiot."

Arabella chuckled. "Tell me what you really think, why don't you?"

There was a knock on the door.

"Come in," Arabella called out.

Helen entered the room with a tray. She placed it on the desk and looked at the flowers.

"Would you like me to deal with the flowers for you?" Helen asked.

"Yes, please," Arabella said.

She looked at the tray in front of them. It was the standard client tray with teas, coffee, and biscuits. She picked up the two cups and saucers and placed them on her desk.

"Oh, these are lovely," Helen said as she picked up the flowers.

"Yes, they are. Miss Edwards has good taste," Arabella said, winking at Rebecca.

Helen took the flowers and left the room, closing the door behind her.

"The last time I was called Miss Edwards I was at school. It normally came just before the phrase 'you'll be staying after school'," Rebecca said.

"Were you a bad girl?" Arabella asked, a light heat on her

cheeks at the unintended double entendre. "Tea or coffee?" she asked quickly to gloss over the misstep.

"I had my moments," Rebecca said. "Coffee, please. I bet you were a proper goody two-shoes at school."

Arabella poured coffee into one of the cups and pushed it towards Rebecca.

"Help yourself to milk and sugar. Actually, you're right, I was a goody two-shoes as you call it. I was a prefect, then head girl."

Rebecca leaned forward and picked up the tiny silver tongs and started to load up her coffee with sugar cubes.

"Did you ever have detention?"

Arabella poured herself some hot water and added a teabag. She leaned back in her chair while she waited for it to infuse.

"Once," she confessed. "I was caught kissing a boy behind the gym building when I should have been in a science lesson."

"Tell me you weren't missing biology? That would be hilarious." Rebecca stirred her coffee.

"No, sadly it was chemistry. And I didn't find any of that behind the gym building either." She leaned forward and pulled the teabag out of the hot water. "I suppose you were always in detention?"

"Not *always*," Rebecca replied. "But quite a lot."

They shared a quiet laugh. It soon petered out, and the silence became stifling.

"I'm sorry I didn't call," Arabella finally confessed.

"I didn't call either," Rebecca said before she could make further excuses. "I'm sorry for dropping by unannounced. I just wanted to say thank you, again. Not that a single bunch of flowers is any comparison to all that you did for me."

"You don't need to thank me at all. I'm glad I helped in some small way."

Arabella felt a pain in her chest. She knew that this was it, the beginning of a goodbye. They'd said goodbye in the early hours of the twenty-sixth of December, but it hadn't felt permanent. Rebecca was still grieving, and Arabella hadn't wanted to push the issue. But there really was nothing else left to say.

Rebecca chewed her lip.

Arabella cocked her head to the side. She wondered how the girl managed to get by in life with her heart always on her sleeve. "What is it?" she asked.

"Dammit," Rebecca said, "you have to stop doing that."

"I'm not doing anything, you have a tell, you chew on your lip." Arabella gestured to her face.

Rebecca licked her lips and appeared to force her face into a neutral expression. Arabella suddenly wished she hadn't mentioned the tell, it was cute, and she'd miss seeing it. She secretly hoped that Rebecca wouldn't be able to prevent herself from doing it in the future. Should she ever see her again in that future.

"I… was wondering if you could help me? There's this house thing. A legal thing. I've been looking online, but I really don't understand all the legal jargon. Like, I looked at a lot of websites and none of them made sense. Is that a thing? Are we being conned, so we have to use solicitors? Are all websites really hard to understand so we seek out professional advice? And my mum's solicitor is always busy. He never calls me back. And he's a jerk."

Arabella laughed at the long-winded explanation. "What do you need?"

Rebecca reached into her jacket pocket, produced a couple of envelopes, and slid them across the desk towards Arabella.

"I'm the executor of mum's will. I'm the only one left so it had to be me. And she gave me everything, including the house. But I don't want to keep it. I'm living there now, but I'd like to sell it, but I need... something. Sounds like prostate?"

"A grant of probate," Arabella said.

She took the envelopes, slid her glasses on, and started to read through the familiar documents.

"I'm sorry to call on you again," Rebecca said as she read, "and this is totally not the reason I gave you the flowers. I got the flowers as a thank-you for what you did before. So, don't feel obligated to help me again if you can't, or... don't want to. I can just call the solicitor again—"

"I'm happy to help. Besides, I hear he's a jerk." Arabella nodded towards the plate of biscuits. "Help yourself; let me just read through these documents."

Arabella read the papers, enjoying the companionable silence. Rebecca had only been in the office under five minutes and already she felt like a weight had been lifted. Suddenly the hectic workdays and the sideways glances from staff faded. The end of the engagement hadn't been officially announced, but office gossip pool already had its suspicions. It had been a hectic but fraught couple of weeks.

"I'm sorry, I feel really bad bringing work to you, you're clearly busy," Rebecca apologised again.

"Not too busy to help a friend," Arabella said without thinking.

"Are we friends?" Rebecca asked softly.

Arabella stopped reading and looked up at her. "I thought so?"

Rebecca smiled. Somehow, it lit up the room.

"Cool, I thought you were just being nice because you felt bad for me or something. You look really nice in glasses, by the way."

Arabella stumbled a little upon hearing the compliment. "Th-thank you. And in response to your statement, no, I'm not being nice because I feel bad for you. I'm being nice because I consider us friends. Odd, highly mismatched friends, but friends nonetheless."

Rebecca reached for another biscuit and continued to look around the room. "Do you like these pieces of art?"

Arabella looked at the modern paintings on the wall.

"Not particularly, they came with the office space. Part of the design."

"How long has this been your office?"

Arabella lowered the papers to her desk as she thought about the question.

"I'm not sure. Six, maybe seven years?"

Rebecca looked at her in horror.

"You've been in this office for that long, and you still have the original art on the walls? Art that you don't like? Do you have any personal effects in here?"

Arabella looked around the room, keen to point out a personal item that she could claim. But the truth was, there were none. She worked long hours, but she'd never felt the need to personalise her office space. It was a place to work, somewhere to see clients. Nothing more.

She looked at the paintings on the wall. She'd never really liked them. But then she'd never disliked them enough to take them down.

"You need a grant of probate," Arabella said, trying to change the subject back to a more neutral topic. One where she felt more qualified to answer. "You'll need to fill out a couple of forms, a probate application and an inheritance tax form. You'll need the death certificate and copies of the will. You'll also need to swear an oath."

"Swear an oath?" Rebecca looked at her incredulously.

"The English law system, I'm afraid. After your application has been sent off, you should receive a grant of probate within about ten working days."

"I have to *swear* an *oath*?" Rebecca repeated.

Arabella chuckled. "Yes, just to say that what you are including in your application is true, you're not signing up a cult."

"So, I need to speak to the jerk," Rebecca surmised.

"Unfortunately, yes, you do," Arabella confirmed. "And you'll need to have the house valued in order to fill in the inheritance tax form."

Rebecca slumped back in her chair. "Why is it all so complicated? Like, isn't this the one time when everything should be really easy?"

"Who's your solicitor?" Arabella asked.

"Mr Grindey, at Aldershot, Parker, and Jerk," Rebecca sighed.

"Oh, yes, I know them." Arabella nodded.

Rebecca looked up at her. "Oh, I didn't think about that. I suppose you deal with solicitors a lot?"

"Unfortunately, every single day," Arabella replied. "Robert Grindey is a particular nuisance, very hard to get hold of him. But his secretary is rather amenable. I could contact her and get your case moved to Jonathan Parker? He is much easier to deal with."

"That would be amazing. I've been calling Grindey every day, three or four times a day, and he never calls back."

"Sounds like Robert. I'll give them a call. I can also value your house for you, if you like? That is, if you don't feel it would be a conflict of interest?"

"I'm going to need to get you more flowers," Rebecca said.

"I also accept chocolates," she joked.

"I'll remember that. Seriously, though, that would be amazing. Are you sure you don't mind?"

"Not at all." Arabella reached into her handbag and pulled out her day planner. She opened the book to the correct week and scanned through her appointments. For some reason, she skipped some of her shorter morning slots that were still available and looked at the evening slots. "I'm free next Wednesday at five? Maybe we could have dinner afterwards? It will take me a while to get back to Putney from your neck of the woods."

"Absolutely!" Rebecca enthused. "I'll make you dinner. Any allergies? Other than sugar, salt, and grease? You know, anything that makes food actually taste good."

Arabella laughed at the comment on her healthy eating.

"I like to eat well, I'm not young like you. if I ate all the junk you ate on the drive back, I'd swell up like a balloon."

Rebecca opened her mouth to reply and quickly slammed it shut again. Arabella wondered if it had been a compliment or a joke that had been on her mind.

"Well, then I'll make something healthy. Anything I should avoid? I don't want to kill you off before I get that grant of probate."

Arabella shook her head. "Thank you, your concern for my wellbeing, as always, is heart-warming. But, no, I don't have any allergies."

"Great, I better let you get on with some work. Sorry to barge in and add to your work pile." Rebecca stood up. She reached forward and snagged another biscuit from the plate.

Arabella stood up as well. "It was good to see you."

"Do you need the address, or do you still have it from when you stalked me the last time?" Rebecca joked.

"I still have it, is that why you're moving?" she replied with a grin.

"Nah, it's more that the house is on a giant sinkhole. Don't tell my estate agent." Rebecca winked. She reached forward and picked up the documents that Arabella had been reading. And then snagged a third biscuit. "I'll see myself out."

"Good, the biscuit budget can't handle much more."

Rebecca waved her hand dismissively and left the office, laughing as she went.

Arabella flopped back into her chair. Her cheeks were aching from all the smiling and laughing, despite the short visit. She wondered how Rebecca could disarm her so easily. It wasn't in Arabella's nature to relax around new people. There was something different about Rebecca, something warm and down-to-earth.

She looked at the new entry in her day planner. Butterflies started to flutter in her stomach. Dinner with Rebecca wasn't a new thing, they'd eaten together before. But somehow this felt different.

She blew out a breath and slammed the day planner closed.

Come on, Arabella. Get yourself together.

CHAPTER TWENTY-SEVEN

REBECCA WALKED around the house one last time. She'd let things go a bit in the last couple of weeks, so she'd spent the entire day clearing used mugs and discarded bras from almost every room.

The house had felt pretty big and lonely, and so she'd gone through a phase of making every room feel homely. Reading, drawing, surfing the internet on her favourite chair in each room. Before she knew it, she'd trashed every room.

And now Arabella was coming, so Rebecca had spent nine hours solidly tidying up and cleaning. She had even scrubbed the grout in the guest bathroom. Because Arabella seemed to demand perfection without even opening her mouth.

She was petrified that she would overlook something, but it was no use worrying now. It was two minutes to five, and Rebecca was trying her best to look like she had been casually waiting and not running around like a lunatic all day.

She'd got a pretty cup and saucer from the cupboard and drunk half a cup of coffee from it. She then placed the cup and saucer next to an open, old-fashioned hardback of *Great*

Expectations on the coffee table in the living room. A tartan blanket was folded neatly beside the place she had supposedly been sitting on the sofa. She couldn't help but take a few pictures of her setup; stock images of lifestyle aesthetics like this sold pretty well.

She caught a look at herself in the mirror. She'd had a shower an hour before, scrubbing away the smell of detergents and replacing them with the posh scents she usually only used on dates. They probably still weren't quite up to Arabella's standards, but at least it wasn't some cheap celebrity perfume that smelt like an explosion in a flower garden for half an hour before wearing off.

She'd put her hair up in a messy bun, spending far longer than she should have pulling individual strands of hair down to frame her face in a theoretically casual way. She wore a long-sleeved, oversized sweater. It was cream and had a few designer rips in it. She adjusted the neck a few times, making sure that her exposed shoulder looked casual enough.

She'd put on her smart, skinny blue jeans, too. She didn't want to look like she made no effort, after all. Casual could quickly tip into not giving a damn, and Rebecca wanted to look good, not like she'd made much of an effort, but still good.

The truth was, she'd made an enormous effort and she was now utterly exhausted and tense as she waited for Arabella's arrival.

She looked at the book and coffee set-up and rolled her eyes. It was too much. She rushed over to the table but paused as she stretched out her arms. Was it too much? And why did it matter so much to her?

In her heart she knew exactly why it mattered. But she couldn't admit to it. Down that path led a lot of trouble and heartbreak.

The doorbell sounded. She jumped in surprise. She

looked at the wall clock, it was exactly five. Of course, Arabella would be perfectly on time.

Rebecca glanced at her reflection once more before reminding herself that there was nothing else that could be done about her appearance now. She hurried down the hallway on tiptoes, not wanting to leave Arabella waiting, but also not wanting to appear to be in a rush.

She opened the door and stood to one side.

"Hi, come in," she said.

As Arabella entered the house, Rebecca took a moment to appreciate the light grey skirt suit she was wearing. She caught a whiff of expensive-smelling perfume. It took her a few moments longer than it should have to notice that something was missing.

"Hey, you don't have your crutch. Or your cast!"

"Nothing gets by you," Arabella kidded. She looked happy, a real smile gracing her lips and an extra bounce in her step.

"The cast was removed a couple of days ago. It still hurts but I'm healing and need to put weight on it and strengthen the muscles."

Rebecca found herself staring at Arabella's legs. She was allowed to do that, right? She was just noticing that the cast was gone. For a while. Really noticing.

"I'll be happy to get back into heels," Arabella said, shaking Rebecca from her inappropriate gaze.

"Not too soon, though. You don't want to put your recovery back," Rebecca pointed out.

"You sound like my father." Arabella rolled her eyes and placed her bag on the empty hallway table. She took out a leather file and a camera. "If you like, I could take pictures now as well as the valuation? That way, if you choose us to represent you, we wouldn't have to bother you again with taking photos for the advertisement."

Rebecca liked the idea of Arabella bothering her again, but she suspected Arabella didn't want to make more journeys than was necessary.

"Sounds good."

"Excellent." Arabella looked at her expectantly. "Do you want to show me around?"

Rebecca nodded and hurried to the doorway to the living room. She stepped inside, and Arabella followed.

"Um, this is… obviously… the living room."

"Is that fire gas or electric?"

Rebecca cocked her hear to one side as she regarded the device. She had no idea. Her mum had hardly used it. To her, it was just an object in the room, something she didn't even see anymore.

Arabella stepped closer to the fireplace and glanced at it.

"Gas," she answered her own question and made a note with her fountain pen on her leather-covered notepad. She took out a laser measuring device and placed it on the wall to get the dimensions of the room.

Arabella glanced at the coffee and book set-up that Rebecca had spent time crafting and smirked. Rebecca wondered what it meant. Had Arabella seen through her?

Of course she knew it had been set up. Estate agents must frequently see people pretending to live the perfect life in the perfect home, fresh coffee brewing and bread baking in the oven.

She felt a little stupid for trying to pull the wool over Arabella's eyes like that. Even if she did genuinely drink coffee from that cup and saucer and had read that book. Once. Eight years ago.

They moved into the dining room, and Arabella continued to take notes as Rebecca silently waited.

She counted how many rooms there were and dreaded the idea of pointlessly listing them all. Kitchen. Bedroom.

Bedroom. Yet another bedroom. Bathroom. Hallway. Was the hallway even a room? Would Arabella think she was silly for calling it a room?

She wondered when she had gotten so nervous around Arabella.

Arabella looked out of the double doors and into the garden. "Is there a side gate?"

"Yes, and a garage," Rebecca replied. *Good, you sound like you know what you're talking about now, keep it up.*

"And which side of the garden is yours?"

Rebecca frowned. "Um, what?"

Arabella pointed towards the nearest fence with her pen. "One of these fences is your responsibility to maintain, the other side is your neighbours."

Rebecca couldn't remember anything ever being mentioned about the fences. Nor could she remember them ever being replaced or repaired. Was this a thing? Ownership of fences? Was she such a bad adult that she didn't know? Was she the only person who didn't know? Were the neighbours laughing at her lack of fence maintenance knowledge?

"It will be in the legal documentation, I can find out there," Arabella said. "Oh, is it freehold or leasehold?"

"Freehold," Rebecca said, happy she had something to contribute.

Arabella scribbled some more notes down before looking up at Rebecca. "Next? The kitchen?" she questioned, pointing towards the next door.

Rebecca nodded and led them into the kitchen. This time she didn't announce the room, she assumed the sink would give it away. She leant awkwardly against the kitchen work-top, watching as Arabella walked around and made notes.

"You're very quiet," Arabella commented. "Not like you."

Rebecca smiled, relieved at the change of topic. "I don't want to interrupt your work."

"I'm just making notes, feel free to talk to me," Arabella said, still scribbling down more observations.

Rebecca's mind raced at a hundred miles per hour to come up with something to say. When had she lost the ability to make conversation?

"I thought I'd make omelettes for dinner," she eventually said. "Healthy but awesome, because I make the best omelettes in the world."

"That sounds lovely, I love omelettes," Arabella replied. "Shall we go upstairs?"

Rebecca blinked for a moment. Her mouth felt unnaturally dry. A split second later she realised what Arabella meant, but she also realised that she'd been still and silent a moment too long.

"Um, maybe I should start dinner?" Rebecca offered. "I'm sure you can find your way around up there, there's no secret passageway to the east tower. What you see is what you get."

Arabella regarded her for a moment, a small smile curling her lips.

"Okay, I'll call if I need anything," she said. She walked out into the hallway and made her way up the creaky staircase.

Rebecca let out a long sigh. She needed to get herself together. Spending the whole day worrying and preparing for Arabella's visit hadn't prepared her at all, it had just panicked her.

She'd somehow lost the ability to speak, which was a problem when you'd invited someone over for dinner. It wasn't done to sit in silence and then kick the guest out the moment they swallowed the last bite. Besides, she wanted Arabella to be there. She wanted to have a nice meal and discuss things.

She just needed to get herself under control.

It's okay, it's just Arabella, you can do this, she reminded herself.

CHAPTER TWENTY-EIGHT

ARABELLA WALKED into the master bedroom and had a quick look around. Everything seemed quite normal. London was awash with 1930s semi-detached houses, and as she'd observed on Christmas Eve, this one seemed no different. A little rundown, but nothing that some maintenance couldn't take care of.

She turned and walked into the second bedroom, pausing in the doorway. It was clearly Rebecca's room. Somehow it felt wrong being in there without Rebecca's presence, even though she knew she had permission.

She was also insanely curious.

Photograph collages filled the walls. Arabella looked at them with interest. Some were from the local area, some were of inanimate objects, some she couldn't even identify what they were, just shapes and colours. She stepped further into the room, taking more of an interest in the personal effects than she normally would on an appraisal tour.

A desk in front of the window was covered with random objects, from comics to perfume bottles. She smiled, Rebecca certainly had a lot of interests. It was fascinating to get a peek into her mind and her hobbies.

She caught herself snooping, so she lifted up her notepad and started to make some notes about the room. She used the laser measure and drew a small diagram, adding in the radiator and the window. House hunters loved accurate floor plans.

Arabella wondered how long Rebecca had lived in the house. Had she grown up in it? Had she moved out and come back when her mother took ill? Were these questions that Arabella had any business asking? It wasn't relevant to the house sale, and yet she wanted to know.

She turned around and walked out of the room before the urge to snoop became any stronger. It felt wrong, especially knowing that Rebecca was just downstairs, cooking her a meal. She wondered, not for the first time, why she had suggested dinner. A war was taking place inside of her. Part of her was desperate to stay away from Rebecca, part of her was coming up with new reasons to see her.

"Everything okay?"

Arabella turned around on the landing to see Rebecca walking up the stairs. She was wiping her hands with a tea towel.

"Absolutely, just finished," she said, relieved she hadn't been found in Rebecca's room.

"Great, I was just going to ask what you'd like to drink?" Rebecca started listing the entire drinks aisle of the local supermarket.

"Orange juice sounds lovely," Arabella picked one to prevent the never-ending list from sucking all of the oxygen from the small hallway.

They walked down the stairs and into the kitchen.

Rebecca poured two glasses of orange juice while Arabella activated her iPad and had a look at some of the local property prices. She'd done some research before leaving the office, probably a bit more than was technically required for an inheritance tax form. But she wanted to ensure that Rebecca was going to get the best price possible, she didn't want the girl to go with some local charlatan and settle for a quick sale.

"So, how many pennies is it worth? I know it's not in great shape."

Arabella was pleased that Rebecca had mentioned the matter of upkeep. It was always a sensitive subject to mention. Telling a house owner that their beloved home was looking a bit tired wasn't easy.

"I was going to mention that," Arabella said. "I'm going to give you two valuations. One is if you sell as is, the other is if you attend to some cosmetic issues."

Rebecca nodded and gestured towards the hob. "I am listening, I'm just going to get on with dinner while you talk."

"No problem," Arabella said. She made some notes in her book as she came to the final valuations.

"You're probably looking at 380,000 pounds if you sell as it is, but, with some work, I think you could easily get as much as 430,000."

Rebecca dropped the spatula she'd been holding. "What?!"

Arabella opened her mouth to repeat the figures, but Rebecca retrieved the spatula and started waving it towards her.

"No, never mind, I heard. Are you seriously telling me that I could get fifty *grand* more if I... what exactly?"

"New carpets, decorate all the rooms. I'd recommend a new bathroom suite, and then fix a few things like the windowsills, tidy up the garden, maybe repair the broken paving slab on the front path."

"That sounds expensive," Rebecca said as she tossed the spatula into the sink and picked a new one out of a drawer.

"Not fifty thousand pounds expensive," Arabella pointed out.

Rebecca started to pour the whisked eggs into a frying pan, her mouth contorted as she considered the matter.

"Put it this way. You can get a very nice bathroom suite for under a thousand pounds. Carpets throughout, depends on what you choose, but around two thousand for something nice. If you want to save some money, then you can do the decorating yourself. You're artsy, I'm sure you can paint walls easily enough."

"You make it sound so easy. Lick of paint, new bath, bish bash bosh. Fifty grand."

"I used to flip houses," Arabella explained. "Before I became so involved in the family business. I'd buy run-down properties and fix them up. You can make quite good money out of it."

Rebecca laughed. "I can't see you tiling a bathroom yourself. Did you have a team of decorators to do all the hard work?"

Arabella closed her notepad and stared at Rebecca with mock anger.

"I'll have you know, young lady, that I'm very handy."

"Uh-oh, I'm a young lady now." Rebecca chuckled.

"Well, you're certainly younger than me," Arabella pointed out. "But anyway, let's not drift from the subject, you were slighting my DIY skills."

"Well, I've yet to see any evidence of your supposed handiness. This could all be bluster." Rebecca managed to play along while still cooking the dinner. Which smelt fantastic and had Arabella wondering the last time someone cooked a meal for her outside of a restaurant.

"I'm an expert wallpaper hanger," Arabella said with a flourish. "Many have commented on my neat edges."

"Ha!" Rebecca scoffed with a wink. "Wallpaper is easy, what about the hard work? What about painting a ceiling? Laying a floor?"

"I've laid a wooden floor, I even own my own jigsaw."

Rebecca turned the hob off and picked up the two plates of steaming omelette and crisp-looking salad. She gestured her head towards the dining room. Arabella grabbed the two glasses of juice and walked into the dining room, surprised to see the table had been expertly laid in the short amount of time she'd been upstairs.

"You laid a wooden floor, eh?" Rebecca placed the plates on the table.

Arabella sat down and placed the linen napkin on her lap, breathing in the delicious smell emanating from her plate.

"I did," she replied. "It's remarkable what you can learn from YouTube."

Rebecca chuckled. "I never thought of you as someone who'd get hands on. I'd thought you'd get a man in to do it all."

"I don't like asking anyone else to do something I couldn't do myself, where possible. And some builders see a woman and add fifty percent to the price. I like convenience, but I like profit margins even more. The first house I renovated cost me huge amounts, and with the mortgage payments and the tax, I walked away with one hundred and three pounds. For thirteen months' work."

She picked up her knife and fork and started to slice into the fluffy omelette. "This looks incredible."

"Just something I learnt to make in Spain," Rebecca dismissed. "But wow, that's a long time for not a lot of money. I can see why you started doing it yourself. I've never really learnt how to do that kind of stuff. Even if a light bulb is out I'm worried I'll electrocute myself. And Mum was useless; I can't even remember the last time we decorated."

Arabella moaned at the delicious flavour of the omelette. "This is amazing. I'd say you should give me the recipe, but I'm to cooking what you are to DIY."

"What about learning from YouTube?"

Arabella shook her head.

"No, there's something about my brain that takes perfectly to understanding how to rewire a house, how to tile a feature wall, or even how to fix a bannister rail. But give me some basic ingredients and step-by-step instructions and it will all go to hell by step three."

"I could teach you how to cook," Rebecca offered. "I taught my mum to cook and she was useless. I had to learn to cook when I was a kid or I would have starved to death. The second I was tall enough to see the counter, I was making meals."

Arabella could see a crossroads ahead. Down one path lurked more time with Rebecca, the opportunity to become closer friends. Down the other path, sensible retreat from a situation that she knew was becoming something she wasn't sure she was ready for.

"That sounds great." Her traitorous heart answered before her head could formulate an excuse. "And I could teach you DIY."

You imbecile, Arabella's brain informed her.

"Really? That would be amazing," Rebecca enthused. "I mean, I'm all for increasing the value of this place, but I have no idea how. I'd really love your guidance. And, hey, you'll be selling it, so you're totally incentivised to help me increase the asking price."

Arabella raised her eyebrow. "Will I be selling it?"

"Well, yeah, I don't know any other estate agents..."

Rebecca paused. "Unless… unless you don't want to? Or this isn't right for Henley's? I know you're a posh firm, but you have a branch on the high street near here so I thought—"

"I'd love to," Arabella reassured. "I just hadn't assumed that we'd get the business. I thought you might speak with others before making a decision."

"Oh, you totally have the business," Rebecca reassured. "I trust you. And I need as much money as possible. I know you won't con me."

Arabella reached for the glass of juice, wondering about whether or not it was appropriate to ask why Rebecca needed the money. Her brow furrowed.

"I have to pay off Cutter Carter," Rebecca explained. "The drug drop went bad, and if I don't find the money within the next couple of months…" Rebecca broke off and started laughing hard. "Oh my god, you should have seen your face!"

Arabella realized she was gawping and put her glass down. "That was very mean."

"No, that was hilarious," Rebecca said, wiping tears from her eyes.

Arabella smiled despite the joke at her expense. She had to admit, it was a little funny.

"Fine, why do you need the money? Presumably not because of your ties to the mob?"

"No. No mob ties. I need the money for my adventure!" Rebecca exclaimed.

She dabbed her mouth with her napkin and got up from her chair. She crossed the room, opened a drawer in the sideboard, and took out a large white envelope.

Arabella watched her with interest. Rebecca was beaming as she poured the contents of the envelope onto the table.

"When Mum first got sick, I was just about to go on a backpacking trip around the world. I'd worked like a machine and saved enough money to finance part of it, planning to do odd jobs here and there to pay for the rest as I went. But the week before I was due to fly to my first stop, she was diagnosed with cancer."

Rebecca placed maps, brochures, leaflets, and scribbled notes down on the table.

"Mum made me promise that I'd one day go and travel like I always wanted to. Life's too short and all that."

Arabella pushed her half-eaten plate of food to one side, suddenly not quite so hungry. She picked up a piece of paper and read a long list of country names with wide eyes.

"So, I'm doing it. Me and Mum talked about all the things I should see and all the things I should experience. I wrote a list, like a bucket list. It made her happy to help me plan the trip, and now I'm in a situation where I can go. Nothing is keeping me here."

Arabella felt her hand tremble slightly as she held the piece of paper.

"Absolutely," she agreed.

She couldn't believe that she had just managed to find a friend, someone who she really enjoyed spending time with, someone who had opened her eyes to a new way of living her life. And now that person was leaving.

"Isn't it a bit dangerous?" Arabella asked. She put the paper down and picked up a leaflet for a tourist bus trip in Egypt. "Like Egypt, I'm pretty sure there's a Home Office advisory about Egypt."

"Yeah, but that's mainly Sinai. It's fine." Rebecca plucked the leaflet from Arabella's hand. "Besides, the more money I get from the house sale, the less I'll stay in cheap dorms and hostels."

Arabella felt a panic sweep through her. She wanted to talk Rebecca out of it, but she knew it would come out wrong. This was clearly something she had been planning for years, at the behest of her dying mother. She couldn't just stand by and let her go backpacking across Egypt and get herself sold for a camel. Could she?

If the final sale price of the house was going to directly correlate with Rebecca's safety on her ridiculous mission to see the world, then Arabella would make damn sure that the house sold for as much as possible.

She briefly wondered if it would be possible to delay the sale somehow. Surely Rebecca couldn't go if the house didn't sell at all. She wondered if there was any subsidence in the area that she would be legally bound to mention to any potential purchasers. Maybe there was a sinkhole?

"Are you okay?" Rebecca asked. "You've gone pale. Is something wrong with dinner?"

Arabella blinked and cleared her mind.

"I'm fine, just a little tired. It's been a long day." She pulled her plate closer. "And dinner is delicious."

Rebecca smiled. She swept all of the paperwork up with her hands and started stuffing it back into the envelope.

"So, do we have a deal?"

"What deal?" Arabella asked, a forkful of food paused in front of her mouth.

Rebecca rolled her eyes.

"The deal we just discussed. I teach you to cook, you teach me DIY."

"Oh!" Arabella remembered the moments before the terrifying discovery that Rebecca planned to get herself murdered in some godforsaken country.

"Yes, of course." She ate the food, chewing slowly as she began to formulate a plan.

She swallowed. "Actually, maybe I should come over and help you with the DIY projects? It's been a while since I've gotten my teeth into a project like this, and hands-on teaching is always more effective."

"Really? Are you sure?"

"Absolutely. What are friends for?"

"That would be amazing." Rebecca sipped her juice. "You know, you may have been a monumental pain in the butt on our car trip, but I'm so glad we met."

Arabella plucked a small piece of lettuce from her plate and threw it at Rebecca's face.

CHAPTER TWENTY-NINE

REBECCA SAT at the top of the platform ladders and let out a sigh. She dabbed her paintbrush at the wall, wondering how Arabella made it look so easy while she was struggling. She looked down at where Arabella was running her paintbrush neatly along the wall, just above the skirting board.

"Why does my paint look blotchy while yours looks professional?" she complained.

"Practice." Arabella stood and squinted towards the top of the wall. "You have too much paint on your brush."

"You literally *just* told me I had too little."

"And now you have too much." Arabella grinned. "Paint is fickle."

"Paint is something," Rebecca mumbled.

Arabella returned to her kneeling position and continued to paint.

Rebecca stared at the wall, hating how it was embarrassing her in front of Arabella. She was artsy, she was creative, but she couldn't paint a wall to save her life.

"Did you call the builder I suggested about the garden?" Arabella asked.

"I did, he said he will come on Monday," Rebecca replied.

She had to admit, she was enjoying herself. The conspiracy the paint had against her aside, it was homely. Just two friends, decorating a house and chatting.

Although she suspected that she was mainly enjoying the company. Arabella was fast becoming a permanent fixture in her mind.

After the successful dinner, where she had managed to kick off the nerves and have a normal conversation, Rebecca's mind had been preoccupied with thoughts of Arabella. Every day seemed to consist of casually wondering what Arabella would think or say about something.

She knew what it meant. She wasn't stupid. But she also knew that Arabella was straight and simply being a good friend. Something that Rebecca was in short supply of.

She had friends. Loads of friends. But her friends were either young and immature, or completely focused on their careers. Not to mention that Rebecca hadn't been a great friend lately. Her life had been so hectic that she'd not been very good at keeping up with friends. And when her mum had died, she received a flood of condolence text messages, emails, and Facebook updates. And then everyone had stayed away. Worried about how Rebecca was dealing with the loss and not wanting to intrude.

So, life had been a little lonely. She knew she could pick up the phone and call someone, but the truth was that she didn't want to. She wanted to stay in her little cocoon. She wanted to paint the dining room on a Sunday morning with Arabella.

"So," Arabella said with what sounded like fake casualness. "Travel."

"Yep." Rebecca scraped her paint brush against her tin, trying to remove the excess.

"You seem to have it all planned."

"I do. I've been thinking about it for a long time." Rebecca could sense Arabella's wariness.

She suspected that Arabella thought the idea of travelling around the world and staying in cheap hostels was childish and dangerous.

"Have you travelled much?" she asked, trying to change the subject.

"Some." Arabella shuffled along the floor to continue painting the skirting board. "Mainly for work these days."

"Just locations where a gazillionaire needs a holiday home to get away from the paparazzi?" Rebecca joked.

"I don't deal with anyone below a kazillionaire," Arabella replied.

"Of course, you must maintain standards."

"Indeed."

"Is there anywhere you haven't seen that you want to see? Something to tick off the bucket list?"

"I don't have a bucket list," Arabella said.

Rebecca paused, her paintbrush centimetres away from the wall.

"You don't have a bucket list?"

"No. Too much pressure. I could die tomorrow. I don't want to be laying in the street after being hit by a bus and thinking that I never got to see the sunset over the Sahara, or the Northern Lights. I'd be quite disappointed enough that I'd been hit by a bus without the added pressure."

"That... that's *so* pessimistic."

"I've never been known for my optimism," Arabella confessed. "I wasn't exactly encouraged by my parents to dream big. I had a path laid out for me and I'm exactly where I'm supposed to be."

Rebecca balanced her paintbrush on the tin and stepped down the ladder.

"You may be a part of some grand plan for Henley's to take over the London property market, but surely you've thought 'I wanna do that' at some point in your life? Not everything revolves around work. You do get some free time."

Arabella looked up at Rebecca. "You've stopped painting."

"Forget the painting, you've just told me that you have no dreams." Rebecca shook her head in exasperation. How could Arabella focus on painting at a time like this?

"I have dreams, they just don't match up to your expectations of the dreams I should have." Arabella put her paintbrush down. "I dream that we'll hire a really good receptionist next time, so that my clients are offered drinks in a timely manner. I dream that Mrs Taylor will stop messing about and just buy the damn house on Sycamore Avenue. I dream that—"

"These are all work-related. Come on, I know you have a life outside of work." Rebecca paused. "Wait, you do have a life outside of work, don't you? You must have a hobby, right?"

"I... like gardening," Arabella admitted as if it were a struggle to come up with anything.

Rebecca stared at her.

"I do!"

"You liar, you just picked that out of thin air. I can see it in your eyes."

Arabella turned away. She picked up the paintbrush and continued her work.

"We're not talking about me, we're talking about you and your travel plans."

Rebecca looked at Arabella's tense posture. She realised that she had upset her with her suggestion that she had nothing outside of work. She wondered if it were true. Arabella was the kind of person who would live for her work.

"I suggest you read the Foreign Office's online travel guidance," Arabella said. "There's a lot of information on there about countries that are not safe to visit. You can't just gallivant around the planet as if there are no consequences."

Rebecca felt her jaw open. "Gallivant?"

"Yes, it's hardly the most sensible option, is it?" Arabella scoffed. "Coming into a large inheritance, you should be putting it aside for the future. Buying a home, creating security. But you're going to spend it all on seeing the world. And then you'll presumably come back here with nothing to show for it but some knickknacks that you collected on your travels. Possibly a drunken tattoo."

"Wow," Rebecca breathed. "You really have that low an opinion of me?"

Arabella turned around. Her eyes widened as if she only just realised what she had said.

"I'm sorry, I'm sorry, I didn't mean that. That was... harsh. I apologise."

Rebecca furrowed her brow. Arabella's apology seemed sincere enough, but she was hurt. She knew the insinuation hadn't come from nowhere. There was an element of Arabella's true feelings in there.

"So, you think I should buy a small house and get a job, right?"

"It doesn't matter what I think," Arabella said softly.

"No, it does. I know I'm young, you think of me as a child compared to you and all your adult accomplishments. You think I should settle down and get on the career path, don't you? I suppose not having a stable career makes me a bit of a failure in your eyes, right?"

"I never said that." Arabella put her paintbrush down and climbed to her feet. "And I don't feel like that."

"It's okay, I get it. I know we're different people," Rebecca continued. "You have your life together, I don't. I'm a dreamer, you're practical. I'm just some loser with fanciful ideas about travelling that will amount to nothing important."

"Don't change a thing about you," Arabella said forcefully. "I shouldn't have said what I said, I'm sorry. It comes from a place of fear, I worry about you. But I don't have any right to tell you what to do."

"You worry about me?" Her breath caught in her throat.

"Of course I do. You're about to sell everything and pack a bag and go god knows where to see god knows what. You won't know where you're going to be sleeping from week to week. Knowing you, you'll walk into some war zone and get yourself killed!"

Rebecca saw real fear in Arabella's eyes. She noted that her hands were balled into tight fists.

"Yeah, but it's a *really* great bag," she joked to defuse the tension.

Arabella shook her head and marched out of the room. Rebecca rolled her eyes at herself. She always reverted to joking when she really ought to be serious. And now Arabella was mad at her.

She walked out of the room and into the kitchen where Arabella had her back to her.

"Hey, I'm sorry, I shouldn't have joked like that."

Rebecca waiting for a reply, but none came.

"I just joke when things are tense, you know?"

She shifted her weight from foot to foot.

"And it is a great bag…"

She heard a sniffle. Arabella's shoulders shook slightly.

Rebecca stared in shock.

"Are you… are you crying?" She quickly walked around to get a look at Arabella's face.

As soon as she moved, Arabella moved as well.

"Stop turning," Rebecca ordered.

Arabella ignored her. They spun around a few times like children playing chase.

Eventually, she took a hold of Arabella's shoulders and forced her to make eye contact. Red eyes and wet cheeks looked back at her. She wondered what on earth she had said to upset her so much.

"I don't want you to get hurt," Arabella mumbled. She turned to shield her face. "I keep thinking that you're going to go wander into a minefield or get taken hostage by ISIS, or… or die of exposure on a sand dune!"

Rebecca pulled her into a hug. Arabella struggled slightly. Rebecca knew she felt embarrassed at becoming upset but held on tighter. She waited for Arabella to stop resisting and give in to it.

"I don't know where you think I'm going," Rebecca whispered into her hair. "I want to see the Coliseum, bathe in the waters off Bali, and see the Sydney Opera House. I don't have any intention of wondering around Syria. I'm not going to do a weekend tour of Mosul."

"They have terrorist attacks in Bali," Arabella whispered.

"They have terrorist attacks in London," Rebecca countered. "You're in more danger here than I am."

"Thanks, now I'm worried about that, too," Arabella mumbled. She adjusted her stance and wrapped her arms around Rebecca, holding her tight.

Rebecca swallowed nervously. She wondered what to do. Arabella didn't seem like the kind of person to just break down in tears. This had obviously been bothering her for a while. Rebecca wondered if Arabella maybe felt something for her. Her heart soared at the very thought.

"Come with me," Rebecca suggested.

Arabella took a step backwards. Rebecca felt the loss keenly.

"Come with you?" Her brow knitted.

"Travel with me," Rebecca said.

Arabella wiped at her tears as she chuckled. "I can't do that. I have… I… I just can't do that."

Rebecca started to feel stupid for even suggesting it.

"I know, I— I just offered so you can see for yourself that it's safe."

Arabella took another step backwards.

"I'm sorry, I shouldn't have become so emotional. I'm not sure what's wrong with me."

Rebecca could see that she was planning to make her escape. She had seconds to decide on whether she wanted to let her go or bring up the elephant in the room.

"I think you do know," Rebecca said.

Arabella looked hesitant before shaking her head.

"Just tired, I'm sure. It's been a busy week."

Rebecca wasn't about to accept that excuse. "I think it's more than that."

She couldn't control the shaking in her voice. Nor could she predict what Arabella's reaction would be, and it frightened her. Would she laugh it off? Would she run a mile? Gay paranoia was a thing, Rebecca had seen it before.

Arabella looked at her in surprise, her mouth opening and closing as she struggled to find something to say.

Suddenly, she grabbed her handbag from the kitchen worktop and hurried away. Rebecca momentarily considered running after her, but she knew that emotions were high, which made it a bad idea. She watched as Arabella rushed through the front door and out of her life.

CHAPTER THIRTY

ARABELLA TOOK off her reading glasses and tossed them onto the desk. Reading the fine print on legal contracts was the bane of her existence. And, to her mind, the sole reason why she now had to wear glasses.

Usually she'd pass the tedious task on to one of the juniors, but she was keeping herself busy. Anything to avoid the voice in the back of her head whispering and ridiculing her for running away from Rebecca the previous month. And ignoring her calls. And passing the paperwork for Rebecca's sale on to someone else.

Helen burst into the office. Arabella jumped.

"Sorry, couldn't knock," Helen explained.

She held a large package wrapped in brown paper. It was nearly as tall as she was and only a couple of inches thick.

Arabella got up and walked over to help her.

"It was just delivered; are you expecting something?"

"I ordered a new phone case, but I'm assuming that's not it," Arabella said as they leaned the heavy package against the wall.

"Not unless screen sizes have really gotten out of control. Can I get you anything else?"

Arabella shook her head, distracted by the package. She heard the click of the door closing as Helen left the room. She started looking around the package for a delivery note. She tore at the clear plastic address label and pulled out the paper. Her heart stopped when she saw the sender's name.

Rebecca Edwards.

She took a deep breath and put the delivery slip on her desk. She regarded the package suspiciously for a moment. Then, she plucked the scissors out of her pen pot and carefully sliced the top and sides of the cardboard.

It flopped open, revealing several large picture frames. She frowned and separated the first two. Her eyebrows raised in shock and she gasped. The frames contained large photographs of the beautiful vista they'd seen when travelling in Spain.

She pulled the first frame out of the cardboard packaging and held it in front of her. It was just as beautiful as she remembered it, the sun hitting the distant mountains and casting light across the land. She placed the first frame in front of her desk and quickly picked up the second. It was another shot of the view, but from another angle. The sun had lowered a little more giving a dramatically different effect.

She held the frame up with both hands and turned to look at the dreary artwork on her walls. She walked to the other side of the room, placing the frame below the painting she disliked the most.

She returned to the cardboard box and pulled apart another two frames. An envelope fluttered to the floor.

Scooping the envelope up, she walked over to her desk and slumped into her chair. She was scared. Part of her desperately didn't want to open the envelope, afraid of what Rebecca's words would say.

But then she knew the curiosity would be too much for her to leave it unopened. She held her breath for a moment before plunging in. She pulled out a piece of paper and a photo.

The photograph was of her. She was smiling and standing in front of the vista, having just discovered that Rebecca was a professional photographer. She'd been enjoying watching the girl in her element. And being told that she was beautiful. She placed the photo and the envelope down on the desk and held the paper in shaking hands.

She unfolded the letter and took a deep breath before reading.

Arabella,

I had intended to give you these after we'd painted the dining room. You desperately needed new artwork for your office. If you don't like them, then feel free to give them away, or even throw them away. I include my favourite photo but assumed that you aren't narcissistic enough to want it blown up to a metre high like the others.

I miss you.

Rebecca

Relief swept over her. She'd expected ranting and raving, a claim that she was running away from her feelings. A hastily scribbled note about being homophobic. But Rebecca was as kind as ever, not even mentioning her terrible behaviour, running away in the middle of a project and ignoring the girl's subsequent calls.

The door burst open for a second time, and she opened her mouth to berate Helen for scaring her again. But it wasn't Helen entering the room, it was Alastair.

"I need you to sign these," he said without preamble, tossing some legal documents onto her desk.

She discreetly folded Rebecca's note and slid it into her desk drawer. She picked up the documents and started to look at them.

"The solicitor won't talk to me about anything to do with the sale of the cottage unless you sign that. Pedantic old man," Alastair grumbled.

He sat on the edge of the desk, picked up a stray elastic band, and started to play with it.

Arabella nodded in understanding.

"I'm sorry, I'd forgotten to tell him that you would be dealing with the cottage. My fault." She picked up her fountain pen and started to read through the document thoroughly, never one to sign anything without reading it.

"Not a problem," Alastair replied. "How have you been?"

"Well. Busy."

"As you like it."

She looked at him.

"Alastair," she warned.

He held up his hands. "Just a comment, I don't mean anything by it."

Strangely enough, her relationship with Alastair had actually improved since the break-up. They fought less, listened to each other more. The pressure of the wedding and the new life they were embarking on had vanished, and, instead, they were just two people working together to separate their lives.

It reminded her that Alastair did actually care for her in his own strange way. Despite initially not wanting to break off the engagement, he was now happy to do his bit to split their interests.

She returned her attention to the document and picked up where she had left off.

The elastic band pinged from Alastair's fingers and landed on the floor. Arabella rolled her eyes as he bent down and picked it up.

She signed the document and looked up to hand it back to him.

She paused in fright. He was holding the photograph of her in his hand, looking at it curiously.

"If you want my advice," Alastair said, as though he could read her thoughts, "you'll find whoever it is who can make you look this happy and build a life with them."

He took the proffered documents with one hand and held out the photograph with the other.

"I'll take that under advisement," she said. She snatched the photo from his hand and dropped it into her desk drawer.

"Do," Alastair said firmly. "You deserve to be happy. I know I never made you that happy. I wish I did, but I know I didn't. I have a suspicion who can, and I think you should grab them with both hands. Life is short."

He turned around before she could formulate a reply.

"Thanks for these." He waved the documents in the air. "I'll try to get more than a button and an old shoe for the cottage, but I can't promise anything."

CHAPTER THIRTY-ONE

"ARE YOU GOING TO BITE ME?" Rebecca asked the little crawling insect that was working its way up the handle of the shovel. "Because I'm really not into gardening and that's really going to put a massive downer on the whole thing if you end up being a bitey insect."

She leant in close and looked at it. "You totally have teeth, put those away, friend."

"Maybe it doesn't speak English?"

Rebecca jumped in fear and dropped the bug-infested shovel. She spun around to face the unexpected sound of Arabella's voice.

"The gate was left open and I heard you talking," her visitor explained, gesturing to the open side entrance to the back garden.

Rebecca's heart slammed against her rib cage. She knew sending the photos had been a bad idea. She'd gotten them printed a while ago and had no use for them, so she sent them to their intended recipient. And now that recipient was presumably about to tear a chunk out of her for ignoring the clear signals she had sent about wishing to be left alone.

She'd suspected that this might happen. But she'd kind of hoped that it wouldn't happen when she was wearing scruffy old clothes, covered in paint and mud, with her hair a complete disaster.

"Of course, I thought you'd be talking to another person. You know, like a human being. Maybe on the telephone. But, no, you were talking to some bug."

"Bugs need friends, too," Rebecca replied. She smoothed her hair down. Arabella, as always, looked pristine.

"They do. And you're a good friend."

Rebecca blinked.

Arabella didn't seem angry. In fact, she seemed nervous if her inability to make eye contact was anything to go by.

"So are you," Rebecca whispered.

Arabella chuckled. She looked to the low garden fences that surrounded them.

"Can we talk? Inside, maybe?"

Rebecca nodded. She wiped her hands on her dirty jeans and gestured towards the open kitchen door. Arabella stepped inside. Rebecca followed her, pausing to hold onto the doorframe as she divested herself of her muddy work boots.

"Can I get you a drink?" Rebecca offered.

Arabella's perfect posture slumped.

"How can you be so nice? So... forgiving? I ran out of here, and I've avoided you for a month."

Rebecca shrugged. "Even mean people get thirsty."

Arabella snorted a laugh. She shook her head. "Thank you, but no, I'm not thirsty. I just needed to talk to you."

Rebecca held a breath. This was it. The time where Arabella told her to back off. To most certainly not send gifts to the office.

"Okay," Rebecca said after the long pause.

"Firstly, I need to apologise for my behaviour. I shouldn't

have run out of here like that. I was scared. I should have stayed and talked to you, but instead I ran. And for that I truly apologise."

Rebecca felt herself shrug again.

"It's okay," she said automatically.

"No, it's not," Arabella corrected.

"I went too far," Rebecca said. "I shouldn't have pushed you, I realise that. You were worried about me travelling because you're a good friend and I made it into... something else. I just misread some signals and, well, it won't happen again."

"Maybe you didn't misread any signals," Arabella said so softly that Rebecca wondered if she had heard correctly.

She just stared. Part of her mind was jumping for joy at the possibility of what Arabella might be admitting to. Part of her was cursing her decision to spend the whole day sweating in a muddy garden. Couldn't Arabella have an awakening on a day she felt fresher?

"Th-that..." Rebecca stammered. "I-I, well..."

Arabella chuckled softly. She stepped forward and reached up her hand. Rebecca stood as still as a statue. Arabella picked some leaves from Rebecca's hair and threw them through the open door into the garden.

"When I heard about your travel plans, I panicked," Arabella said. She continued to pick the odd leaf from Rebecca's hair as she spoke. "I had mental images of something terrible happening to you. And then I had mental images of not being with you. Not being able to see you. I didn't know what it all meant, I suspected I knew, but I didn't want to admit to anything."

She smoothed Rebecca's long hair down, adjusting it lovingly. Rebecca couldn't breathe. Arabella and her expensive perfume was right in front of her. Filling her every sense with her presence.

"I printed out Foreign Office travel warnings, and medical information about the Zika virus and about malaria. I planned to bombard you with information on why you shouldn't travel. I told myself I was being a good friend, keeping you safe." Arabella chuckled again. She ran her fingers along Rebecca's cheek.

Rebecca knew she should say something, but her mind was a complete blank. On her list of things to do that day, this was not one of them. This was something that she dreamt about. Not a reality.

"You seem to have lost the power of speech," Arabella whispered.

Rebecca slowly nodded her head.

"I don't know what I'm doing," Arabella admitted.

Rebecca knew an opening when she saw one. She leaned forward, careful to keep her clothes away from Arabella's perfectly tailored suit. She approached slowly, giving Arabella every opportunity to back away. But she didn't. Their lips softly touched. Rebecca itched to bring her hands up and hold Arabella, but she knew they were caked in mud. Again, she cursed her decision to step foot in the garden that day.

She moved her lips slowly against Arabella's, wanting to lead the way but also allowing her the opportunity to control what was happening. Pushing her too fast now would ruin everything, and Rebecca couldn't take another month like the one she'd just endured.

Slow didn't seem to be the thing on Arabella's mind. She took a fistful of Rebecca's T-shirt and pulled her closer.

"Touch me," she ordered.

Rebecca's mind crumbled at the thought.

"But I'm dirty," she pointed out, wincing at how stupid she must have sounded.

"I don't care," Arabella replied. She wrapped her arms

around Rebecca, pulling her close before returning her lips to the kiss. Harder and more frantic this time.

Rebecca hesitated for a second before clasping her arms around Arabella and running her hands along the woman's back. The kiss was growing in intensity and Rebecca was getting lost in it. She wanted to get lost in it, wanted to kiss and hold Arabella for as long as she could. Worried that the moment would soon end. But if that was a possibility, she needed to know now before she got her hopes up.

She pushed Arabella away gently and took a step back.

"I need to know what this is," Rebecca said carefully. "I... I have feelings and I'm not ready to be—"

"Hurt," Arabella finished. "I know, I'm sorry. I got carried away. I'd been thinking about that all the way over here. Longer, if I'm honest with myself."

Rebecca's hands trembled at the admission.

"Don't apologise, I'm the one who kissed you," she pointed out. "But I just need to know what this is."

"I don't know," Arabella admitted. "I've never been interested in women, never even considered being with one. This is all very new to me."

"Why me?" Rebecca asked, her insecurities tumbling out.

Arabella smiled and reached up to tuck hair behind Rebecca's ear.

"You're special, unlike anyone I've ever met. And I can't stop thinking about you. Anyone would be lucky to be with you."

Rebecca felt her cheeks heat up.

"I... am going to get a bottle of water," she decided.

She turned from Arabella, walked to the opposite end of the kitchen, and opened the fridge. She was thankful for the cold air that hit her face, despite the chilly February weather outside. She quickly glugged down some water. Her mind was racing.

"I don't want to hurt you, it's the last thing I want to do," Arabella said. "And I'm only just starting to figure all of this out in my mind. It seems every time I spend a few moments with you, I completely re-evaluate my life. I was happily engaged, or so I thought. But you opened my eyes to the truth, I didn't want to marry Alastair. I didn't want to give up my work. Actually, not my work. My freedom, I didn't want to give up my life and become someone else. And, I was pretty sure I was as straight as they come but, no, apparently I'm not."

Rebecca laughed a little. "Sorry for confusing everything for you."

Arabella smiled. "I'm glad you have. I could have suddenly woken up from this fog when I was sixty and wondered what on earth I'd done with my life."

Rebecca looked at her seriously. "I haven't, like, brain-washed you, have I?"

Arabella laughed loudly. "No, I don't think so. You just woke me up."

"So, you're gay now?" Rebecca asked.

She'd heard stories about straight women suddenly deciding they wanted to test out being a lesbian. She didn't want to be Arabella's test. She cared too much about her for that. It would break her heart when Arabella stopped having fun and went back to her real life.

"I don't think so." Arabella leaned against the kitchen counter, looking pensive. "I have feelings for you, I haven't thrown myself at any other women and I don't have an urge to."

Rebecca breathed a tiny sigh of relief.

"I can't promise you anything," Arabella admitted. "All of this is extremely new, not to mention scary, to me."

Rebecca nodded, remembering how she felt when she was figuring out her own sexuality in her teens. She couldn't imagine suddenly having her life turned upside down in her forties.

"I don't want to jump into bed," Rebecca said quickly.

Arabella's face flushed a dark red. Her eyes widened, and Rebecca had to stop herself from laughing at the shock Arabella expressed.

"Me neither!" Arabella replied. "I… I don't mean that you're not… that I… I mean…"

"It's too soon," Rebecca added helpfully.

"Yes, exactly." Arabella breathed a sigh of relief. "I'm still sorting a lot of things out."

"I bet," Rebecca agreed.

Arabella still looked a little shaken.

"Are you sure I can't get you a cup of tea? Coffee?" Rebecca offered. "I can get out of these muddy clothes and we can sit down. You can tell me all about the terrible diseases I'm going to catch on my trip."

Arabella snorted a laugh. "I don't want to interrupt your gardening, you were making friends out there."

Rebecca picked up the kettle and carried it over to the sink to fill it up. "I'll live. Stay. We can chat, if you like? I've missed you."

"I've missed you, too," Arabella confessed. "And I'd love a cup of tea."

CHAPTER THIRTY-TWO

ARABELLA KICKED off her shoes and brought her legs up underneath her on the sofa. She looked nervously around the living room, wondering if she was doing the right thing. When she'd set off from the office, she'd only intended to thank Rebecca for the photos and to apologise for her behaviour.

Heavy traffic had given her more time to think. She decided an apology wasn't quite enough, maybe a quick explanation of her actions was also deserved. By the time she arrived in Croydon, she had decided that Rebecca deserved the truth. Or as much of the truth as Arabella had managed to figure out, anyway.

Rebecca entered the room with two steaming mugs of tea. She handed one to Arabella and then took a seat in the armchair beside the sofa.

"Freaking out?" Rebecca asked.

"A little," Arabella admitted.

She sipped the hot liquid. It was true, British people did fortify themselves with tea. She already felt a little braver. "I'm starting to realise that a lot of my life has been me doing what I think I ought to do. What other people want me to do. Rather than what *I* want to do. I'd never considered that until we drove back from Portugal."

"What did I do to make you change your mind?"

"You gave me a speech about how people in love should be a team." Arabella chuckled. "I thought you were young and naive. That you didn't understand how relationships worked. But then I thought that there must be some truth to it. You'd clearly experienced relationships like that."

Rebecca inclined her head but remained silent. She'd changed out of her gardening clothes and now wore jeans and a cosy-looking sweater. She'd taken the time to brush her hair and apply some light make-up. It made Arabella's heart beat a little faster to think that she had taken the effort for her. Not that she needed to. Rebecca was one of those natural beauties who looked great in any situation.

"The more I thought about it, the more I realised that I didn't want to be with Alastair. When you told me that I should marry someone because I loved them, it sounded like a crazy idea. And that's when I really started thinking and I realised something that shocked me."

Rebecca raised a questioning eyebrow.

"I don't know how to be happy."

Rebecca blinked. "What do you mean?"

"I mean what I said; I don't know how to be happy. I've never really sought out happiness. My parents were always very miserable and negative, so I have no problem identifying what I *don't* like. But finding something I like, seeking out something that will make me happy, I struggle with. That must sound stupid to you."

Rebecca shook her head. "No, no, I think I know what you mean. You've never really thought about being happy. You had a plan in front of you, so what was the point in seeing if it made you happy?"

"Exactly." Arabella sighed in relief that Rebecca got it.

She'd been worried that it sounded ridiculous. She sipped at her tea again, fortifying herself for the next round of admissions. "By the end of the trip home, I knew that I didn't want to be with Alastair anymore. But I didn't know what I did want. I snuck out of the party and had to seek you out. The lens cap was just an excuse."

"No! Really?" Rebecca feigned shock.

"Shut up, I'm spilling my heart here."

"Sorry." Rebecca grinned. "Please, continue."

"I felt a pull towards you, I tried to convince myself that it was friendship. That you were the first person I'd really been able to speak to. You weren't like other people I knew, you told me the truth and you told me when I was being ridiculous. I didn't feel I needed to pretend with you." Arabella leant forward and placed the mug on the coffee table. "I feel stupid," she admitted. "Spilling my soul like this."

Rebecca placed her mug alongside Arabella's and reached forward to take her hand. "You don't have to explain to me if you don't want to."

"It's not that, it's… I just feel that I don't know anything anymore. My life is being turned upside down, and I don't know which way is the right way up anymore. I had a plan, but now I don't think that's what I want. And suddenly what I want is important to me."

"But you don't know what you want?" Rebecca guessed.

"Exactly." Arabella ran her thumb over the back of Rebecca's hand.

Rebecca stood up and sat on the arm of the sofa, beside Arabella.

"Well, let's start at the top. Do you know what you don't want?"

"I don't want to marry Alastair," Arabella chuckled.

"Good. He's an idiot."

"Actually, he thinks I should be with you," Arabella admitted.

"As I said, really nice chap, great instincts," Rebecca added quickly. She removed her hand from Arabella's and wrapped an arm around her shoulder. It felt nice, comforting, supportive. Arabella leaned into it.

"What else don't you want?" Rebecca asked.

Arabella shrugged.

"I don't know. I love my job, but it doesn't excite me anymore. And I'm wondering if it's what I want or what I fell into."

"Well, you practically own the company, don't you?"

"Sort of," Arabella confirmed.

"Then take a break. I'm sure you can afford to take some time off. Take a sabbatical, or whatever posh people call it when they take a month off to find themselves. Maybe find Buddhism. Shall I find you a guru?"

Arabella shrugged Rebecca's arm off from her shoulders and jabbed her in the side playfully.

Rebecca giggled and backed away. "I'm sorry, I'm sorry!"

Arabella stopped her attack and thought for a moment. "What would I do with time off?"

Rebecca bit her lip.

"Out with it," Arabella pushed.

"Travel with me," Rebecca said. "My first stop on my grand tour is Scotland. Safe, secure Scotland. A short flight, no shots needed. I'm going to go to the cities and then ramble around the countryside a bit. If you can't decompress and sort your life in Scotland, then there's no hope for you."

Arabella laughed for a moment before looking seriously at Rebecca.

"Do you mean it?"

"You coming with me? Yes, absolutely. I mean, I'm not

suggesting we sleep in the same room or anything. Just travel companions. We can see some stuff, talk, get to know each other. It will be good, for both of us. No pressure, no commitments."

Arabella furrowed her brow at the idea. Could she do it? Did she dare? Taking time off work was doable. And she'd never really seen much of Scotland. Maybe a prolonged holiday was what she needed. To breath in some fresh Scottish air. And to spend some time with the woman she couldn't seem to stop thinking about.

"It's a stupid idea. I'm pushing again, I'm sorry." Rebecca stood up to return to her seat.

Arabella reached out and grabbed her hand. "Let's do it."

Rebecca turned and stared at her with a surprised grin. "Really? Like… really? You'll come with me?"

"Yes, you set the agenda, and I'll follow you. Be my guide of the Highlands. I promise I'll even eat some haggis."

Rebecca pulled Arabella to her feet and into a bear hug. Arabella breathed in the subtle scents of Rebecca's shower gel and hairspray. She'd never realised how tantalising those smells could be. Alastair had always smelt of strong cologne that she'd never enjoyed.

Rebecca was jumping up and down with excitement. "That's amazing! I promise you it will be great, you'll love it."

Arabella jumped a little with her, allowing Rebecca's happiness to wash over her. Maybe she was still learning how to find her own happiness, but appreciating and sharing in Rebecca's was becoming second nature.

CHAPTER THIRTY-THREE

REBECCA KNEW something was wrong the moment she walked into the airport. It was far too busy. After spending the last two weeks trying to convince Arabella that Gatwick would be better than Heathrow, they were now walking into unexpected crowds of people.

"Don't say a word," Rebecca said to her travelling companion.

"Would I?" Arabella said sweetly.

"Of course you would."

The check-in queue for their airline was enormous and didn't seem to be moving. A man at the front was arguing with the check-in assistant.

"Why do people do that? It's not their fault, they can't fix everything," Rebecca mumbled.

"Instinct," Arabella explained.

A man in a high-vis vest walked by them.

"Excuse me," Rebecca got his attention.

He turned and smiled at her questioningly. "How can I help?"

"What's going on?" she asked. "Is there a problem?"

"Yes, there's an issue with the automatic baggage systems, it's been like this for about an hour. Where are you flying?"

"Edinburgh."

He sucked in a breath through his teeth. "I think that one will be cancelled, you can rebook for tomorrow. If you hurry, you can get a room at one of the onsite hotels."

Arabella stepped forward, smiling at Rebecca as she did.

"Could you point us in the direction of the car hire desk?"

"Absolutely, just along that back wall." He pointed in the direction and then went about his business.

Rebecca looked at Arabella in surprise. "Really?"

"Why not? A long car journey sounds like fun. I'll even do some of the driving this time." Arabella tilted her wheeled luggage and started to walk towards the car hire desk.

"As long as we can stop off overnight at a creepy castle filled with demonic porcelain dolls, I'm in!" Rebecca said.

She smiled and quickly followed after her, into their next adventure.

THE BIG UNEASY

1

THE ARRIVAL

I t w a s another blisteringly hot day on Bourbon Street. The broken red tiles of the sidewalk were soaked with rainwater from one of the frequent and much-needed storms that were common in New Orleans during the height of summer.

The thirty-minute downpour had done nothing to cool the air. Early morning tourists walking up the iconic street complained about the unforgiving heat, but locals like Jenn Cook were simply happy for the brief respite the storm had offered. Even if it was hardly noticeable now the rains had stopped.

The doors and shutters to CeeCee's Bar were all wide open, but there was still zero airflow. Jenn plunged her hands into the ice bin behind the bar. Bottles of water and beer and half-melted ice cubes bounced around on the top of the cool water.

She blew out a deep breath and turned to face the antiquated fan that whirred behind the cash register. It blew warm air in her face, but she'd take that over no air at all.

It was ten o'clock in the morning on a Tuesday in July. Already some tourists were starting to make their way up

Bourbon Street. It may have been before lunch, but CeeCee's Bar, like so many others in the area, was open and ready to sell alcohol. Jenn had already served a few people that morning, pouring frozen cocktails into plastic to-go cups. Tourists loved the fact that alcohol was cheaply available, and that it was perfectly legal to walk around with a cup of whatever, unlike many other places.

Personally, Jenn couldn't think of anything worse than imbibing alcohol at ten in the morning, but heat made people do strange things. In fact, *New Orleans* made people do strange things.

In the five years Jenn had lived in the city, she'd seen things she would never have believed if she hadn't seen them with her own eyes. A city didn't earn the nickname 'The Big Easy' for nothing, and millions of tourists packed the narrow streets each year to see what all the fuss was about.

New Orleans had a unique culture, something that couldn't be found anywhere else in the world. A blend of jazz, architecture, history, and food made it a one-off. But it was the people who really brought New Orleans to life, from impromptu jazz sessions that would pop up on a street corner to the party animals who filled the French Quarter each and every night.

Jenn was blinded by New Orleans when she had first arrived as an unemployed twenty-three-year-old post-graduate. She had expected to use her degree to obtain a respectable office job, which would allow her to spend her evenings strolling around admiring the nineteenth-century architecture. Or to take a trip down to the Mississippi and soak up the atmosphere as she watched an old paddlewheel steamboat sail by.

That hadn't quite worked out.

She had quickly blown through her savings, and, before long, she had to abandon her hunt for work in the Business

District and turn her attention to the party zone: the French Quarter. Necessity caused her to take any part-time job she was offered. Five years later, nothing had changed. She loved her life and the freedom the multiple jobs offered her.

CeeCee's was the first place to give her a chance. Even though Jenn loved it, she knew there was no getting away from the fact that it was an absolute dive. The entire bar was only five metres by fifteen metres in size. Just enough room for patrons to walk in one of the many open doors and order a drink at the long bar.

The main selling point of CeeCee's was the brightly coloured slushie machines that churned out neon alcoholic ice cocktails all day and all night. Each machine had a scrappy piece of paper taped to it with a scribbled description of the contents: Piña Colada, Margarita, Daiquiri, Rum Punch, and the famous Hurricane.

Now and then a special would crop up, usually in the guise of a fruit or some inexplicable name like the Terminator or the Mind Number. People bought the drinks regardless of the name or presentation. That was New Orleans for you; it never claimed to be classy.

The bar was open twenty-four hours a day, mainly because the rickety old doors on the building didn't close. Five double-shuttered doors allowed entry into the bar. Half of the shutters were missing, and the others were so old they were being held together by flaking paint.

The effect was as if there was nothing separating people walking along Bourbon Street from the hypnotic churn of the slushie machines. It was easy to step in, part with a staggering eleven dollars for a souvenir cup and grab a frozen drink to go.

And many people did, no matter the time of day or night.

Each night Bourbon Street came to life and partied like it

was the last night on earth. The street, road, and sidewalk would be packed with people talking and walking from bar to bar, picking up cheap drinks as they went.

The balconies above the street would be filled with well-dressed people slow-dancing to traditional Dixieland jazz, occasionally toasting the rabble below them.

During the day, Bourbon Street was sparsely populated with curious tourists, fellow business owners, and the people who lived in the apartments that overlooked the street. But all the nightlife businesses that thrived during the darkened hours still opened their doors during the day. Which was why it wasn't unusual to find a drunk literally sleeping in the gutter outside the bar, or unsuspecting tourists being pulled into daytime shows in strip clubs.

Despite some of the seedier elements of New Orleans, Jenn adored the vibrant city and the freedom and equality it offered all who visited.

A young tourist couple entered the bar, interrupting the thoughts the rainstorm had sent her. Jenn took her hands out of the ice bin and shook the cold water off them, enjoying the feel of the cold drops on her bare legs.

"Hey guys." She blew a stray lock of long, blonde hair out of her face. "What can I get you?"

The young man ordered two of the strawberry daiquiris. Jenn picked up two plastic cups and placed them under the taps on the slushie machine. She pressed a button and watched the neon icy drink automatically drop into the cup.

She turned around to face her customers. "Got any plans for this beautiful day?"

"Melting," the woman answered with a laugh.

Jenn smiled. "It is a hot one, be careful out there."

"Where's the voodoo museum?" the guy asked.

Jenn leaned over the high bar and pointed down the street. "Keep on down Bourbon for about three more minutes. After that, you'll come to the lobster place on the corner. Turn right there and you can't miss it."

She grabbed the drinks from the slushie machine and placed them on the bar. She stabbed a straw into each before pushing them towards the couple.

"Great." He handed her some bills. "Keep the change."

"Thanks." Jenn beamed. "Y'all come back tonight for happy hour. Half price on all Hurricanes!"

The couple picked up their drinks and sauntered out. Once they left, Jenn wiped down the wet residue left on the bar and checked the temperature gauges on the slushie machines. She walked around the bar, straightening stools, and checking that everything was clean. It had only been an hour since her previous check, and with less than five customers, everything was as she had left it.

She sighed as she sat on the rickety wooden stool behind the bar and watched the street through the open doors.

A few moments later, a black sedan pulled up on the opposite side of the street. The driver's door flew open and a tall, well-dressed redhead got out. She strutted to the rear of the car where the trunk popped open.

A few seconds later, the front passenger door opened, and an attractive brunette got out of the car. Jenn thought she'd be more attractive if her expression wasn't bordering on rage. She stormed to the back of the car and started arguing with the redhead.

A nearby saxophone played a soulful jazz tune, which Jenn would have usually enjoyed. But at that moment, she was curious, and it was preventing her from hearing what was being said.

The redhead pulled a small suitcase out of the trunk and placed it on the sidewalk. She turned back to the trunk and started to pull a second, larger case from the car. As she did, the brunette picked up the small case from the sidewalk and attempted to put it back into the trunk.

Jenn laughed at the ridiculous sight of the two suit-clad women wrestling with their luxury luggage. She grabbed a moth-eaten old broom and headed to the sidewalk in front of the bar where she pretended to sweep. Luckily, the women were shouting so loudly she didn't need to strain to hear what was being said.

"I've literally had it up to here, Kathryn!"

Jenn tilted her head. The redhead was addressing the brunette. Jenn thought she looked like a Kathryn. Short-sleeved white blouse, tight black work skirt, pantyhose, and high heels. Clearly no idea how to dress for the exhausting New Orleans heat.

"Stop moving my suitcase, Erica," Kathryn shouted back.

Jenn leaned on the handle of the broom and watched as the two women struggled with the suitcase. One blocked the path to the trunk, while the other tried to get around her.

"No. I'm serious! You're staying here," Erica replied.

"I am not staying in this sordid hellhole one more minute," Kathryn replied.

Jenn raised an eyebrow. She had to admit it; Kathryn was brave to call New Orleans a sordid hellhole in a screaming match in the middle of Bourbon Street.

Stupid, but brave.

"Well, that's tough. Because I booked you into the hotel for two weeks," Erica said. "You need to get yourself together. You can't go on like this anymore."

"I'm fine!" Kathryn shouted back. "And why the hell would I want to stay in this grubby, sleazy cesspool for two whole weeks? And even if I did, what was wrong with the perfectly good hotel we just came from? Why do I have to stay with the drunks and drug-pushers?"

Jenn winced. She looked around the street to see if

anyone could hear the select adjectives this woman was using to describe their hometown.

"Because that was a business hotel, for conventions," Erica explained, like Kathryn was five. "This is a hotel and spa, for relaxing."

"I don't need to relax. I need to work," Kathryn said.

"No, you need to take some time for yourself. Time you should have taken before."

"I'm fine," Kathryn argued.

"You're not fine. And you know that. You're... you're like a husk of the person you were before the—"

"Erica!" Kathryn's shriek cut her off.

Before the what? Jenn wondered to herself. The day had been shaping up to be another quiet and dull Tuesday morning until these two turned up and put on an impromptu show.

Erica used Kathryn's distraction to toss one of the suitcases away from the car. It flopped into the road.

"New Orleans is far enough away from home for you to not cause any more problems for Mother. And if there's one place on earth that even *you* will have to eventually crack and enjoy yourself, this is it. Think of it as a vacation. A nice break."

Kathryn stalked towards her case. She picked it up and spun around, fixing Erica with a glare that could melt steel.

"A *nice* break? Are you out of your mind? *Here?*"

"Soak up the atmosphere," Erica instructed. "Take some time to reflect on... things."

"You can't *force* me to take a vacation."

Erica raised an imposing eyebrow. "If you come home before the fifth of next month, then I'll tell Mother about Addison."

Jenn deemed the threat a good one if Kathryn's shell-shocked face was anything to go by.

"You wouldn't dare," she seethed.

"Oh. I would." Erica picked up the other case and placed it on the ground. She slammed the trunk shut. "Two weeks, Kathryn. Take some time for yourself."

Kathryn dropped her suitcase and marched over to Erica. She stood in front of her, toe to toe with arms folded. "So, dragging me down here for that conference was a ruse? All so you could dump me here?"

"Yep. Gotcha." Erica smirked.

"This is ridiculous!" Kathryn flailed. "I don't need a vacation. I need to go back to work."

"You really don't," Erica replied. "There's an envelope in the front pocket of your suitcase with all the information about your hotel. Remember, if you don't stay here... I will tell Mother."

"I can't believe you're blackmailing me," Kathryn growled.

"Well, I am. And I know you don't believe me, but I am doing this for your own good." Erica got into the car and wound down the window. "By the way, I've had your cell disconnected. Just so you don't try to do any work. There's the oldest possible, non-Internet enabled burner I could find in your bag. Just in case there's an emergency. I'm not a monster, after all." She looked Kathryn up and down before rolling the window back up. "All right, see you next month!"

Kathryn pitched towards the car in what looked like an attempt to strangle Erica, but the redhead sped away.

Jenn watched as the black sedan rounded a corner and disappeared from sight. She decided the show was over and that being anywhere near the irate brunette wasn't a good idea. She gave up her pointless sweeping and went back into the bar.

Inside, she picked up a cloth and started to wipe the bar

down, wishing that someone would give her a two-week all-expenses-paid spa vacation in New Orleans.

She heard someone mumbling curse words under their breath and looked up to see Kathryn struggling into the bar with her suitcases.

Jenn let out a small sigh. It was just her luck that the troublesome woman would come in. She watched as Kathryn stacked the suitcases beside a bar stool and then sat down.

"Hey, what can I get you?" Jenn flashed Kathryn her friendliest smile.

Kathryn regarded the slushie machines and rolled her eyes. "Water."

Jenn picked up a bottle of water from the bucket of half-melted ice and placed it on the bar in front of Kathryn.

Kathryn raised an eyebrow and looked with displeasure at the wet bottle. "Do you not have cups?"

Jenn plucked a plastic to-go cup from the large stack by the slushie machine and placed it beside the dripping water bottle.

Kathryn looked at the two objects as if they were completely foreign to her. She sighed and pulled a couple of paper napkins out of the metal box on the bar. She placed one on the bar and wiped the bottle dry with the other before placing the bottle on the dry napkin.

Jenn watched with amused interest as Kathryn plucked another napkin and dried her hands before finally opening the bottle and pouring some of the water into the cup. It was the least New Orleans thing she'd ever seen.

Jenn picked another water bottle out of a box and put it in the bucket of icy water.

"So, are you in New Orleans long?" she asked.

Kathryn laughed sarcastically. "Please, like you didn't hear it all."

Jenn considered pretending she hadn't been listening but

thought she might get more gossip if she admitted it. She took the middle road and shrugged her shoulders.

Silence loomed over them.

Jenn realised she wasn't going to get anything else out of the woman. She wrapped her foot around the leg of her own rickety bar stool and dragged it over to the slow-moving fan. She picked up a magazine and started to flick through it.

After a couple of minutes of head-shaking and slowly sipping water, Kathryn bent down and opened the front pocket of one of her suitcases. She pulled out an envelope and slammed it down on the bar angrily.

Jenn attempted to ignore the brunette, but it was impossible. She watched as she noisily sighed, ripped open the envelope, and pulled out some pieces of paper.

"Hey!" Kathryn called without looking up. She flicked a disinterested hand in Jenn's direction. "Where is this hotel?"

Jenn stared at Kathryn in disbelief. Not that it mattered, Kathryn wasn't looking at her. She slowly pushed herself off of the stool and ambled back towards the bar. She snatched the piece of paper out of Kathryn's hand.

"The Royale. Nice," Jenn said with a dreamy sigh. "You want to walk down Bourbon, turn left by Dixie's Bar, and then take the next right."

Kathryn turned around and regarded Bourbon Street with a sneer. "Unbelievable," she muttered as she snatched the paper out of Jenn's hand.

"I'm beginning to understand why she dumped you here instead of driving you to the hotel," Jenn mumbled under her breath as she returned to her stool and her magazine.

She didn't bother to look up to see if Kathryn had heard her words.

"How much for the water?" the woman asked.

"On the house. Consider it some Louisiana hospitality,"

Jenn said without looking up from her magazine. "Courtesy of the sordid hellhole."

"Oh, great. You heard that?" Kathryn muttered.

"*Everyone* heard that."

A few more silent moments passed before Jenn heard Kathryn pick up her papers and shove them back into the front pocket of her suitcase. She refused to look up at the rude woman. She simply wasn't worth her time or energy.

At the sound of suitcase wheels trundling into the distance, Jenn let out a sigh and looked up to see the empty bottle and cup and a handful of screwed-up napkins lying on the bar.

2

GRUMPY TRAVELLER

ARABELLA HENLEY NODDED a silent greeting to the doorman at the Royale Hotel as she passed by. She crossed the lobby, not paying much attention to her surroundings. She was exhausted and what she most wanted was to check in, get to her room, and finally rest. She approached the front desk and lowered her handbag onto it.

"Arabella Henley, checking in," she said.

She turned around and saw Rebecca was following her. She'd been speaking to the bellboy who was now dealing with their luggage.

"And Rebecca Edwards, separate booking," she added.

She watched as Rebecca looked around the ornate lobby with fascination. Arabella followed her gaze. There was a sumptuous chandelier hanging from the ceiling. Rebecca took her phone out of her pocket and snapped a couple of pictures.

Arabella smiled to herself as she watched Rebecca taking in the splendour of the room. She'd walked straight past without a second thought, hadn't even noticed the beauty of the surroundings that entranced her travelling companion.

She knew she could do with taking a leaf or two out of Rebecca's book, learning to stop and smell the roses now and then.

"Would you like a connecting room?" the receptionist asked.

Arabella turned back to face the man. She didn't know. It wasn't something they had discussed. Was it presumptuous to request one? Did asking for a connecting room imply that she intended to use it? Worse, what did *not* requesting one say?

She sighed at her internal fretting. She was putting too much emphasis on an innocent enough question.

She nodded. "As long as the rooms are well away from the elevators."

"Hemingway stayed here," Rebecca said as she joined Arabella by the front desk.

Arabella raised her eyebrow and looked around the lobby. It was all marble columns, gold leaf, and chandeliers. "Really? I thought he liked... understated things."

"May I have your passport and a credit card?"

Arabella reached into her handbag and handed over the items. Rebecca took her rucksack from her back and did the same.

"Are you from England?" the receptionist asked once he looked over their passports.

Arabella looked at his name badge. *Tommy.* She sighed. Why did she always get the chatty ones? Especially after a long journey.

"We are," Rebecca answered. "London."

"I've always wanted to visit London," Tommy confessed.

Arabella rolled her eyes and turned away. She just wanted to check in, unpack, and maybe have a shower. If she could manage to stand up long enough to do so.

The ten-hour flight, the three-hour check-in before that,

and the hour's drive from the airport to the hotel had completely sapped her energy. She'd been looking forward to a holiday away from the stresses of work, but simply the journey to the hotel had her longing for a twelve-hour shift at her desk.

Her desk. She blew out a breath as she recalled the mountain of work she had been forced to leave for her colleagues. It had been a busy first half for Henley Estates, and staff upheaval meant that it had been busy for everyone for a number of months.

Eventually, she decided that waiting for the office to quiet down would be like waiting for a watched kettle to boil. There was no good time to take a holiday, so she might as well do it anyway.

But that didn't stop her worrying about the work she had left behind. Rebecca had reminded her that she was the boss, and she should learn to delegate and trust her staff. Which just showed how little Rebecca knew the staff members in question.

She shook the thought from her mind. She was here to relax, not fret about work.

"I need to make a copy of these, I'll be back in a moment." Tommy disappeared into a room behind the front desk.

"You get grumpy when you travel," Rebecca noted with a grin.

"I'm tired," Arabella corrected.

"Grumpy." Rebecca picked up a couple of leaflets from the desk. "You were like this in Portugal, too. I thought you were a grade A bitch, but you just don't like travel, do you? You could have mentioned that before we agreed to travel together."

"I'm *tired*," Arabella repeated. "It was a long flight."

"Long?" Rebecca laughed. "That was nothing. Just wait

until we go to the Far East. Oh god, actually, no. If you're this bad after a mid-haul flight to America, I can't imagine you after a long trip with a changeover."

Arabella felt her cheeks flush. She coughed and turned away, pretending to read some historical facts that were framed on the wall beside her.

She hated Rebecca seeing the worst of her.

"If you want to travel with me in the future, that is," Rebecca added.

"Of course, I do," Arabella said quickly.

She did. The idea of travelling with Rebecca was scary but exhilarating. Not because of where they could go or what they could see, but because of how Arabella felt. She was pretty sure she was falling for Rebecca, despite six months ago being engaged to a man and planning her wedding.

The relief at the ending of that particular relationship was still palpable.

She had Rebecca to thank for it. Without that fated trip from Portugal to London the previous Christmas, she would have blindly walked into a marriage with a man she didn't really love. Unaware of what love really was.

But with the certainty that she was doing the right thing by ending the engagement, came confusion regarding her feelings for Rebecca. They'd kissed. A few times. Tentative, unsure kisses but nothing else. No conversation, no understanding of where they were heading.

Arabella had asked for time to sort out her feelings and figure out what it meant to be, quite suddenly, attracted to a woman. And Rebecca, damn perfect Rebecca, had given her time.

And continued to do so. The long overdue conversation hung between them. Arabella was too frightened to even think about her feelings, never mind discuss them. And

Rebecca was generously giving Arabella all the time she needed.

The proposed trip to Scotland had been a disaster. It took a few weeks for the pair to even start talking again after the aborted adventure. Eventually, they picked up and continued to socialise, this time just as friends.

The free-spirited Rebecca had continued with her travel plans, taking short, solo trips here and there. Each time Rebecca went somewhere, she invited Arabella, and, each time, Arabella said no. She said no because she was scared of a repeat of Scotland, but she always told Rebecca it was bad timing or some other excuse. The enormous workload at the office had become a convenient justification.

Then Rebecca mentioned New Orleans, a trip to see a good friend of hers, and Arabella knew that she had to say yes to this particular trip. The strain on their friendship was beginning to pull a little too tightly. If she didn't say yes, she might lose Rebecca. Lose a chance at finally figuring out what she wanted.

But now they had arrived, she felt much as she had on the way to Scotland. Fearful. She swallowed down the emotion and forced herself to remain calm.

"Thank you for coming," Rebecca said softly.

"Thank you for inviting me."

"Of course. At least we made it here. Better than our first attempt to travel together to Scotland—"

"Let's not talk about that," Arabella pleaded. Clearly, she didn't need a reminder.

She heard a commotion at the front entrance and turned to see a brunette with two cases struggling to get up the short flight of stairs. The doorman was offering to help her, but she seemed determined to do it alone.

"Thank you, ladies." Tommy had returned and placed their passports and credit cards on the desk. "I have you booked into 612 and 613. A lovely view of the city. You can even see the Mississippi."

"Oh, cool!" Rebecca enthused. "And there's a roof terrace, right?"

"There is," Tommy confirmed. "On the ninth floor. There's a fitness suite and a roof terrace. Great views, especially at night."

Arabella took a step to the side to accommodate the brunette with her luggage. She regarded the harassed woman with a raised eyebrow. She was pretty sure she had that skirt.

"Kathryn Foster," the woman said. "Apparently you have a room for me?"

Arabella turned her attention back to her travelling companion.

"Told you there would be a gym," Rebecca said, continuing where Tommy had left off. "So you can keep up with your ridiculous exercise schedule that could kill a horse."

"I'm in training," Arabella explained for the fiftieth time.

"Supposedly."

"I'm doing the London marathon!"

"Supposedly," Rebecca repeated with a knowing grin.

Arabella hated how well Rebecca knew her. She'd started a strict gym schedule not long after she started questioning her sexuality. She claimed it was to get her into peak fitness to take on the annual London Marathon. In truth, it was something to fill the long and lonely nights when her mind ran rampant with questions she didn't have answers to.

She hoped that New Orleans would give her some answers. That she'd find the courage to have a proper conversation with Rebecca and figure out what they were, or what they could be.

"Shall we have an hour or so?" Rebecca asked. "We can unpack, shower... take a nap if you like, Grumpy."

Arabella smirked. "You know, I have no idea why I'm travelling with you. You're mean."

Rebecca chuckled. "Aww, can I make it up to you by buying you beignets?"

Arabella picked up her luggage and headed, blessedly, for the elevators. "If you think I'm that cheap, you're very much mistaken."

3

INVEST IN A MAP

JENN HAD BECOME a fan of the afternoon nap since moving to New Orleans. When she first arrived in the city she had mistakenly believed she would be able to work through the day and even into the evening with no ill effects.

Then, she worked straight through Louisiana's exhausting midday sun and almost certainly suffered from heat exhaustion as a result. She had stumbled along Basin Street towards her part-time job in the tourist office. When she arrived, she was immediately lectured by her co-worker, Miss Mae, who informed of the importance of the two R's—Rest and Rehydration.

Since that day, she always ensured that her hectic schedule kept her out of the furious heat from midday until two o'clock and that she always carried a full bottle of water with her.

She noticed that many tourists were also caught out by the heat. After the third occasion that an exhausted tourist passed out in front of her, she decided it was time to do something about it. She spoke to Mr Webb, her manager at the tourist office, and said that she was interested in taking a first aid course. He readily agreed, and Jenn enrolled in one, which she passed with flying colours.

It wasn't long before she realised that walking into the tourist office with her shiny new certificate was a big mistake. As one of the very few qualified first aiders on the tourism team, she was quickly signed up to be one of the many marshals along the routes of the parades that were a frequent feature of the French Quarter.

Parades zigzagged their way across the city on a daily basis, and it wasn't unheard of for there to be two parades on any one day. Half the time the locals had no idea what the parade was actually for. Not that it mattered, as most would happily cheer and wave regardless.

Jenn loved the parades. The first time she saw one, she had only been in New Orleans for two days and was eating lunch at a café on Bourbon Street. Engrossed in a local newspaper and looking for jobs, she hadn't heard the parade until it was practically in front of her.

She'd decided to have lunch at an indoor café with air conditioning and had sat at a bar table right in front of the window overlooking the busy street. Towards the end of her sandwich, and while reading, she distractedly noticed that her drink was vibrating. She stared at the rings forming on the top of the clear liquid as her brain attempted to figure out what was happening. It was then that she realised it wasn't just the drink, it was the whole table. She could hear a brass band and heavy feet marching in time to the tune.

Looking through the window, she could see a parade coming down the street. For the next ten minutes, she was absolutely mesmerised by the sight. Ceremonial uniforms with shining buttons and extravagant hats adorned with feathers were the first things she noticed. Then she became aware of the instruments, drums of all shapes and sizes and shining brass instruments that gleamed brightly in the sun. It was only halfway through that she realised the majority of the marchers were teenagers, with young dancers twirling batons and weaving in between the musicians with grace.

Crowds were stopping on the sidewalk. As they watched the spectacle making its way down the narrow street, people cheered and applauded. Everyone became caught up in the carnival atmosphere.

Jenn had asked her waitress what the parade was for. The young woman had no idea, stating there were so many displays that she lost track.

As the end of the parade passed by the window, Jenn noticed that people had randomly joined in, dancing, skipping, and clapping in time to the music. Random strangers who seemed to have nothing to do with the parade were happily getting involved and pulling other spectators along with them. With a laugh and a shrug more and more people joined the end of the party. By the end of the street, the procession had doubled in length.

That was one of the many times that Jenn found herself falling in love with the city.

Unfortunately, being a token first aider did take some of the shine off of a parade. All parades needed permits, and the organisers often provided their own first aiders. But the tourism office liked to provide a few extra bodies to help out, especially with so many tourists being caught unaware by the summer heat.

Jenn had quickly realised that nothing was less fun than watching other people watching a parade.

On the positive side, being a marshal meant patrolling the route with the police and, even though Jenn hated to admit it, she loved the uniform. If she was going to have to attend a parade and miss out on all the fun the least she could do was take in a little eye candy along the way.

"Hey, Jenn!"

Jenn looked up to see Officer Aude Durand, a beautiful black woman she often saw patrolling the parades and with whom she had struck up a conversation once or twice. Her slight French accent always made Jenn a little weak at the knees.

"Afternoon, Officer Durand." Jenn smiled back.

"You pulled the short straw, huh?"

"Yep." Jenn laughed as she tugged on her lime green high-visibility vest. "The perks of that first aid certificate are literally endless."

"At least the vest matches your eyes." Durand winked as she threaded her thumbs through her belt loops and strutted away from Jenn.

Jenn regarded the woman and sighed. Being interested in women in New Orleans was hard. Though it was one of the most gay-friendly places that Jenn had ever been to, which was undoubtedly a good thing, that meant her misfiring gaydar struggled here more than usual.

With the odds of finding a same-sex partner dramatically higher in New Orleans than in many other places, Jenn had thought it would be simple to find a girlfriend. But she hadn't factored in the famous Deep South hospitality. Everyone she met was fantastically friendly. While that was a great thing, it did mean that Jenn was now becoming an expert at hitting on straight women.

In a city supposedly bursting at the seams with gay women, Jenn could only find the straight ones. Even in gay bars Jenn seemed to spend her time befriending straight women that their gay male friends had brought along to cheer up due to some straight relationship drama.

"Oh, it's you again," a voice said. "What is that tremendous racket?"

Jenn didn't even have to turn around to know that the

acerbic voice behind her belonged to the woman from the bar earlier that day. Kathryn.

"And why are you wearing that hideous thing?" the woman continued.

Jenn kept looking across the road, not wanting to turn around and look at the irritating woman.

"I'm a first aider. There's a parade."

"A parade?" Kathryn laughed derisively. "For what?"

"Celebrating."

"Celebrating what?"

Jenn turned around. "Why, your arrival, of course!"

Kathryn regarded her with a passive expression before replying, "Sarcasm doesn't become you."

"Are *you* honestly questioning *my* personality traits?" Jenn shook her head. She turned back towards the street and wished that the parade would hurry up and arrive. The sound of the band could be heard in the distance. She desperately wished for it to be closer, just so it could drown out anything else Kathryn might say.

No luck. "I thought you worked at that dingy bar," she said, loud and clear.

"I do. I have more than one job," Jenn explained through gritted teeth.

"Well, I suppose this is a step up," Kathryn drawled. "Where is Basin Street?"

Jenn turned around and regarded Kathryn with a suspicious frown. "Why?"

Kathryn gave Jenn a pointed look. "Because I've been led to believe that there is a tourist center there and I'm a tourist."

"A few hours ago, you were furious for being dumped here. Now you're looking for restaurant recommendations?"

Kathryn sniffed. "I spoke with my sister again. We've agreed that I'll stay here for two weeks, so I might as well fill my time with something productive. Educational, perhaps. If such a thing exists here, you know, between the drinking."

The parade was starting to get closer, and a few people were beginning to gather. Jenn looked from Kathryn to the approaching parade.

"So, where is Basin Street?" Kathryn repeated.

"You know I'm not your personal map, right?" Jenn rolled her eyes.

"Well, I'd use my cell phone, but, as I'm sure you over-heard, it's from 1992." Kathryn folded her arms across the long-sleeved, blue, silk shirt she had changed into.

Jenn took in Kathryn's outfit with a shake of the head. "You changed into a long-sleeved shirt? Really?"

"I asked for directions, not fashion advice."

"It may have escaped your notice, ma'am, but it's kinda hot," Jenn said. The sound of drums was getting louder. The parade was nearly upon them.

Kathryn shrugged. "It was cold in my hotel room."

"And pantyhose? Who wears pantyhose and heels in this heat?"

"Basin Street," Kathryn articulated slowly.

"Fine." Jenn let out an aggravated sigh. "Walk up this road until you get to the Dixieland Jazz Bar, turn left, and then keep walking until you get to the church. After the church, turn right, and it's on the other side of the road. But, seriously, you might wanna get changed or at least take some water with you."

The end of Jenn's sentence was wasted. Kathryn turned and started to walk into the distance.

"And invest in a map!" Jenn shouted at the retreating figure.

4

POWDERED SUGAR

REBECCA BIT INTO THE WARM, sugary beignet and let out a loud moan. She closed her eyes and enjoyed the exploding flavours in her mouth. She chewed slowly and then swallowed. Her eyes snapped open, and she dunked the remaining part of the beignet into the pile powdered sugar on the plate.

She realised that eyes were boring into her and looked up. Even through the dark glass of Arabella's large sunglasses, she could see a raised eyebrow.

"Enjoying that, are you?" Arabella asked.

"It's phenomenal," Rebecca replied. She pushed the plate closer to Arabella. "Try one?"

She knew her beignets were safe. Arabella was fastidious about looking after her health, specifically her weight. Not that she needed to. Yes, she was a little curvy, but Rebecca thought she looked incredible. And she'd continue to do so even if she ate all the beignets in New Orleans.

Arabella's lips pursed, and she looked away.

Rebecca sighed and pulled the plate back towards her.

Arabella had been in a strange mood since they arrived. Well, since they arrived at Heathrow, to be exact.

The day before she had been excited and happily discussing what they would be doing in New Orleans. The nerves were slightly visible, but she was soldiering on in her attempt to cover them up.

Then they'd arrived at the airport, and acerbic, scared Arabella was back.

Rebecca wished she knew what Arabella was so nervous about. She had joked earlier that travel made Arabella grumpy, but she knew it wasn't that. She'd hoped the quip would get Arabella to open up. No such luck.

Ever since their abandoned trip to Scotland, Arabella had been out of sorts. Rebecca was desperate to get to the bottom of it, but any time she tried, Arabella pushed her away. So, Rebecca decided to give her space and time to figure things out. She'd rather have Arabella's company than force a permanent wedge between them.

She could tell that Arabella was trying. She was obviously struggling with something, and Rebecca figured she'd tell her about it in her own time.

"So…" Rebecca reached into her rucksack and pulled out her travel notepad. "I've written down a few things that I want to do while we're here. You're more than welcome to join me at any time. But, if you want to do your own thing, then that's fine, too."

She opened the notepad and removed the pen from the spiral spine. She placed the book and the pen in front Arabella.

Arabella turned her attention to Rebecca's list of sights to see.

Rebecca turned *her* attention to the remaining beignets.

"When are we meeting your friend?" Arabella asked.

"She's working tonight, so we decided to meet tomorrow

for dinner. I may pop over and see her before then, if she's free. She's going to message me her schedule." Rebecca licked the powdered sugar off her fingers. "She's looking forward to meeting you, if you're free. If you don't want to do dinner tomorrow, then we can meet up some other time."

"Dinner tomorrow sounds lovely," Arabella agreed. "If we have nothing planned, maybe we could explore the area this evening?"

"Sure, we could walk around the French Quarter and grab some dinner. How are you feeling? Jetlagged yet?" Rebecca asked.

"No, not yet." Arabella looked up. She smiled and reached forward and ran her thumb along Rebecca's chin.

Rebecca's breath caught in her chest. It wasn't the first time Arabella had touched her, but it was rare enough that it took her breath away every time. She tried to look unfazed, but inside she was screaming with joy.

"Sugar," Arabella explained. She wiped her thumb on a napkin. Rebecca mourned the missed chance to see Arabella lick the residue off her thumb. Or even better, to guide Arabella's thumb into her mouth and lick it off herself.

Arabella returned her attention to the list. Rebecca resisted the urge to plunge her face into the plate of sugar.

She took a sip of water and tried to calm down. She reminded herself that she'd promised to give Arabella as much time as she needed. To go from being engaged to a man to being unsure about your sexual preference in a few short weeks was bound to be disorientating. And Arabella didn't seem like someone who handled change very well.

"Remember that it's your holiday, so feel free to do whatever you want to do," Rebecca said. "The main thing is that you relax and have a great time. Let me do all the organising."

"I'll hold you to that," Arabella said. "With how my

work schedule has been lately, I'll be glad to never see another month planner ever again."

At first, Rebecca had thought that Arabella had used work as an excuse to avoid her. Then she visited her a couple of times in the office and saw for herself that it was absolute pandemonium. Apparently, everyone wanted to move before their summer holiday, and so Henley's Estate Agency was rushed off its feet for a few months. No one more so than one of their top executives: Arabella Henley.

For a while, Rebecca was seriously worried that Arabella was going to burn out. The stress definitely put a wedge between them. She'd assumed that was what had happened on the way to Scotland. But each time they argued, Arabella would come back to her, apologising for her words and behaviour.

Soon they were spending more and more time together. Sadly, it was platonic time. Arabella's sexuality was never brought up. They exchanged innocent cheek kisses but nothing more.

Rebecca enjoyed Arabella's company so much that she didn't say anything. She had previously promised to give Arabella time, and that's what she would do. It wasn't like she was in a hurry. Her mum had only passed away six months before, and her life had completely turned upside down since then. She was finding her own feet, so she had time to give Arabella, too.

She figured that things would sort themselves out eventually. And the unlikely friendship she had developed with Arabella was more important to her than potentially ruining everything by demanding answers that she was sure Arabella didn't have.

"May I?" Arabella picked up the pen and gestured to the paper.

"Sure."

Arabella drew stars beside a few of the things Rebecca had planned.

"If you don't mind me tagging along, these things sound interesting."

"I'd love you to tag along," Rebecca confessed.

In between the blow-up on the road to Scotland and finally getting Arabella to travel to New Orleans, Rebecca had undertaken a few trips on her own. She'd enjoyed them, and she'd taken some amazing pictures along the way, but something was missing. She always felt lonely.

"I think I'd like to relax tomorrow," Arabella said. She sipped at her freshly squeezed orange juice. "I was looking at the brochure for the hotel spa and it sounds wonderful."

"Cool. I was going to head out and see a couple of things, maybe catch a boat on the Mississippi. As I say, you're welcome to dinner, but if you want to take a break don't feel obligated to come—"

"Of course I'll be there," Arabella said as if it were obvious. "I'll have breakfast and dinner with you. We can just do our own things during the day. Unless you want to join me at the spa?"

Rebecca felt her eyes bug at the thought. She was thankful for her own sunglasses. She'd love to join Arabella at the spa, but she wouldn't be able to maintain a respectable distance if she did.

"No, I think I'll go out and explore. U—unless you want me to join you?" Her heart pounded in her chest.

"No... no. I'm fine on my own. Relaxing."

Red graced Arabella's cheeks.

Good, I'm not the only one struggling with this, Rebecca thought.

"Those beignets were great. I might have them for dinner, too," Rebecca joked to break the tension.

"You'll need another seat on the plane home if you do," Arabella replied.

"Totally worth it." Rebecca licked her finger and dipped it into the powdered sugar.

Arabella rolled her eyes and shook her head. "Such a child," she mumbled playfully.

5

FINE SHOES

JENN WAITED PATIENTLY for the traffic lights to change so she could walk across the busy road towards the famous Basin Street Station. The large building had been built at the turn of the twentieth century, and the frontage of red brick and large glass windows looked just as impressive today as it must have done back then.

The station building had become a hub, with the open-top double-decker tourist bus stopping on one side of the building and the famous St. Louis Cemetery Number One on the other. Inside the station was a large and grand marble-floored lobby where the tourism officers sat behind large wooden desks and handed out maps and information.

Beyond the lobby was the old station's waiting room which had been restored and contained glass display cases with historical documents and items from days gone by, when the building had been a working railway station. Jenn often spent time in the waiting room looking at the old timetables, maps, and trinkets that were on display.

A recent addition to the building was a shop that had been set up within the old ticket office selling New Orleans merchandise, most of which was overpriced and seemingly pointless, but the tourists loved it.

The traffic light changed, and Jenn hurried across the road and into the tourist office where she was immediately greeted by Miss Mae, a rotund black lady in her seventies. Miss Mae knew everything there was to know about everything. She sat, as always, in her large, worn leather chair.

"Hey, sweetie," Miss Mae greeted her.

Jenn exhaustedly smiled back at Miss Mae. "Hey. Gosh, it's hot out there today!"

Miss Mae laughed. "Oh, you ain't seen nothing, dove."

"Yeah, yeah." Jenn chuckled. "You've seen it hot enough to melt parked cars, I know."

She placed her green high-visibility vest back in the first aid bag behind one of the large desks and walked over to the water cooler where she started to fill a paper cone with ice cold water.

"By the way," Jenn said in between sips, "did a snooty-looking brunette come in here?"

Miss Mae smiled knowingly. "Oh, yeah, we saw her in here." She shook her head and chuckled as Jenn downed the rest of the water. "In her fine shoes."

"Yeah, that's the one." Jenn nodded.

"She didn't like the bus." Miss Mae pointed out of the window at the open-top bus, which was about to depart on a tour of the city.

Jenn frowned. "Why not?"

Miss Mae shrugged. "I didn't ask. She didn't seem to like much."

"No, she doesn't," Jenn agreed.

"She took a map and a few leaflets. Said she'd go and look at the cemetery."

"She paid for a tour?" Jenn questioned with surprise.

Kathryn didn't seem like the kind of person who would

want to go on a tour of the cemetery. Jenn would have bet money down at Harrah's Casino that Kathryn would have gone straight to the art museum.

"Yep." Miss Mae released a long and tired sigh and closed her eyes for a moment before looking up at Jenn. "How do you know her, dove?"

"She came into CeeCee's," Jenn said. She poured herself some more cold water. Little and often, that was the key. "Then I saw her at the parade. She wanted directions to here."

"She on vacation?" Miss Mae frowned.

"Kinda, yeah."

"She don't look like she on vacation."

"No, I think it was kind of a last-minute thing," Jenn admitted. She decided not to mention the conversation she'd overheard. It was really none of her business. Moreover, if Kathryn ever found out that anyone else knew about that conversation, she'd know who to blame. Jenn didn't want to be on the receiving end of her anger.

"She's troubled," Miss Mae said with a small shake of her head.

"She's trouble," Jenn enunciated.

"No, troubled," Miss Mae pressed. "Those big old brown eyes of hers, she seemed haunted somehow."

Jenn finished her water and threw the empty cone into the recycling bin. She rolled her eyes. Not a day went by when Miss Mae didn't use her supposed voodoo sixth sense to identify some sort of pain or suffering in a stranger passing through the tourist office.

"Nothing a vacation can't fix, I'm sure," Jenn said.

She tidied some of the leaflets that lined the desks. It didn't need doing, but she liked to keep busy.

"Are you going to be at Jack's tonight?" Miss Mae asked.

"No, I'm on the streetcar tonight," Jenn replied.

Miss Mae shook her head. "I don't know why you still do that job, dove."

Jenn shrugged. "It's fun, you meet lots of interesting people on the streetcar."

Miss Mae sneered with obvious disagreement. "But working the nightshift as a conductor on those streetcars... no, no, no."

Jenn smiled at the maternal head-shaking Miss Mae was offering her from her beaten-up chair.

"It's not as bad as you think," she placated. "Most people are just fine. Besides, it's no worse than working on Bourbon Street in the evening, and you don't mind me doing that."

"At least then I can keep an eye on ya!" Miss Mae laughed loudly.

Miss Mae might have been an older lady, but that did not stop her from getting right in the thick of things when it came to a good party. Jenn had met Miss Mae for the first time when the older woman was entertaining a large crowd at a karaoke bar on Bourbon Street.

Jenn had still been getting used to the novelty of being able to carry around an alcoholic drink and was walking up Bourbon Street sipping on a frozen daiquiri from a plastic cup when she heard the most amazing sound.

Utter silence.

She had been passing a bar with all the doors and windows thrown wide open. The place was packed with people but completely silent. While all of the other bars pumped out loud music and the sound of people talking and laughing turned into an incomprehensible rumbling over the top, this bar was quiet with expectation.

Jenn stopped and looked into the building from the road. Then suddenly a deep and beautiful female voice floated over a loudspeaker. The voice was singing a song that Jenn didn't know the words to, but that didn't stop her from feeling immediately captivated. She found her feet walking towards the bar without a second thought.

The room was small and crowded, but Jenn managed to navigate her way to the stage and was surprised to see that the owner of the voice was a woman in her twilight years. She sat on a well-worn, high-backed chair. It looked out of place in the bar, almost like she had brought it with her from her own living room.

At the end of her first song the bar exploded into whoops and cheers, applause and whistles, and the woman gave the slightest nod of gratitude before moving straight into the next song. She sang five songs in a row before leaving the stage and heading into a dressing room in the back. Jenn asked a member of the bar staff who she was and, before long, she was being introduced to Miss Mae in person.

Miss Mae took an immediate liking to Jenn and explained to her that if she wanted to listen to real jazz and hang out in the best bars, then she needed to head towards Frenchmen Street. Miss Mae scrawled some directions onto a napkin along with the names of bars with days and times scribbled beside them.

Over the next month, Jenn saw Miss Mae perform many times in many different venues, and they struck up a close friendship. Before long, Miss Mae was introducing Jenn to Mr Webb, her boss at the tourist office, and telling the man that he had to hire Jenn.

"Why don't you go on home?" Miss Mae said. She looked around the empty office lobby with her eyebrow raised in amusement. "I think I can manage all these folks."

"Are you sure?" Jenn asked, a smile drifting across her lips.

Miss Mae chuckled. "Go on, before I change my mind."

"You're the best," Jenn said. She gave the woman a quick

embrace before grabbing her rucksack that she'd left behind the desk.

"I know." Miss Mae nodded. "Repay me. Come and see me one night, maybe at The Cat?"

"Sure, I'll be there," Jenn promised.

She looped her arms into the rucksack straps, tightening them as she walked through the old waiting room. She took one last deep breath of air-conditioned air before heading out into the stifling heat.

She walked up the sidewalk beside the cemetery and almost immediately let out a groan.

Kathryn was straight in front of her. She was pensively chewing her lip as she leaned against the stark white, crumbling wall that surrounded the cemetery.

Jenn quickly decided that she'd come too far up the sidewalk to turn around. Besides, the road was too busy to cross. She was going to have to head straight towards the prickly woman.

She put her best customer-facing smile on and approached.

"Hello again," she said.

Kathryn frowned at her, seemingly disorientated. A few seconds passed before recognition washed over her face.

"Oh, it's you."

"Yes, me again."

"Are you following me?"

"What?" Jenn blinked. "No, you're the one who keeps bumping into me!"

Kathryn didn't seem to be listening. She heaved herself away from the wall, and Jenn noted that her silk blouse clung to her skin and her face was covered with a sheen of sweat.

"Regretting your outfit yet?" she smirked.

"Can you imagine being buried in one of these wall

vaults?" Kathryn asked, ignoring her question and placing her hand on the thick wall.

"Alive? No."

"At all," Kathryn clarified. "Being slid into a hole in the wall like… like an envelope in a desk drawer."

"Well, it's not quite like that," Jenn argued.

"And then… after a year and a day," Kathryn continued, "they scrape out whatever might be left of you and put someone else in instead."

Jenn looked closely at the woman in front of her to try to ascertain if these were serious words or the ramblings brought on from some kind of heatstroke.

"It's the way it's done here," she explained softly. "It's tradition, religion."

"My father died six months ago." Kathryn stared at her hand pressed against the cemetery wall.

"I'm sorry to hear that," Jenn replied. Kathryn may have been a rude, entitled pain in the backside, but Jenn was still sincere in her condolences. Family was important.

"He was buried," Kathryn said. "In the ground. And I visit him as often as I can, but it doesn't feel like it's enough. What about these people? What if they want to visit their loved ones, but someone else is in there?"

Jenn shrugged off her rucksack and knelt down. She unzipped her bag and grabbed a bottle of water. She stood again and grabbed Kathryn's hand, wrapping it around the bottle.

"I think you need to drink something. It's very hot out here."

Kathryn absentmindedly took the bottle. She gave Jenn a serious look. "Do you believe in an afterlife?"

"Not really," Jenn said.

"Not at all? You think we just, what, rot?"

Jenn pinched the bridge of her nose and took a deep

breath. "Look, it's Kathryn, right?"

Kathryn nodded.

"Kathryn, I really think you need to get back to your hotel and lie down for a while. The heat can kinda creep up on you, and—"

"I'm fine," Kathryn argued.

"Humour me." Jenn looked at the bottle of water meaningfully. "It's sealed."

Kathryn twisted the plastic cap off and took a few delicate sips of water.

"Look, I'm heading back to town," Jenn explained. "Maybe I can walk you back to your hotel?"

Kathryn shrugged and gestured for Jenn to lead the way. Jenn was relieved that she didn't put up a fight; she didn't feel like she could cope with that right now.

They walked side by side along the street.

Kathryn sighed and ran the back of her hand across her clammy forehead. "So, you live here?"

"Yep." Jenn nodded. "Five years now."

"Five years." Kathryn paused. "Why?"

Jenn laughed. "Wow. You're really rude, aren't you?"

"Just honest."

"It's a fine line," Jenn said. She pressed the button at the crosswalk. "I moved here because I wanted something different. I'd just graduated in Boston."

"Boston?" Kathryn frowned. "Well, you certainly succeeded in finding something different. What made you stay?"

The light changed, bringing the traffic to a stop. They crossed the road, Jenn leading the way.

"Probably the same reasons that makes you hate it," she admitted. "It's fun, disorganised, full of life, unexplainable."

Kathryn let out a rich, throaty laugh. "So, you have me pegged already?"

"Oh, I think you've been quite clear on your preferences. New Orleans is not one of them."

The walked down a narrow road with abandoned buildings on either side of the street. Kathryn continued to sip from the bottle of water. Jenn continued to wonder if Kathryn was suffering from the heat.

"I suppose," Kathryn said thoughtfully, "I suppose I just don't get *it*."

"Get *what*?"

"It," Kathryn repeated. She waved her hand at their surroundings. "It. New Orleans. The… I don't know, the culture, I guess? It's foreign to me. I feel like I'm out of my comfort zone."

Jenn could understand how the city could easily be outside Kathryn's comfort zone. She knew that New Orleans wasn't for everyone, but she also thought that most people could find something for them in the diverse environment, if only they gave it a chance.

"I think that's what I like about it," Jenn confessed. "I'm constantly surprised by things. I never feel like I've seen it all. It's an adventure."

"I'm too old for adventure."

Jenn laughed. "Oh, come on, you're not that old."

"Not as young as you," Kathryn said, dragging her eyes over Jenn's body.

Jenn shivered at the attention. "Not that old," she repeated.

She glanced at Kathryn. She was very attractive, something that Jenn had only recognised now that Kathryn wasn't being a massive pain. But now the woman was softening, Jenn could appreciate it.

"Too old for adventure," Kathryn repeated before sipping some more water.

Jenn regarded the brunette with a critical eye. "I'm good

at this, I think you're… thirty… five?"

Kathryn stopped dead and stared at Jenn in surprise. "How on earth did you know that?"

Jenn stopped and turned back to look at her. "I told you, I'm good at that."

Kathryn shook her head and started walking again. "Well, anyway, too old for adventure."

"You're never too old for adventure. I think if you gave New Orleans a chance, you might even find you like it here."

Kathryn laughed. "Oh, I don't think so."

"Look, I'm not suggesting a cocktail run on Bourbon Street to get wasted. New Orleans has something for everyone, I can guarantee there will be something here for you to enjoy."

"I'm pretty sure there isn't anything here for me," Kathryn argued.

"I'm pretty sure you're wrong."

"Why do you care so much whether *I* like it here or not?"

Jenn opened her mouth to reply, but the truth was, she didn't know why she cared. Kathryn had been an annoyance to her ever since she arrived, but for some reason Jenn felt compelled to make sure she left New Orleans having enjoyed her vacation. Even if it was an enforced vacation which she clearly intended to hate every minute of. For some reason, it was important that she reverse Kathryn's view of her adopted hometown.

"Because I love New Orleans," Jenn finally said, "and I honestly believe that it's rich enough and diverse enough that there will be something you'll enjoy. I work for the tourist office, it's like my mission to make people love it here."

"Hold on." Kathryn paused and placed her hand on Jenn's arm to stop her from walking. "You work at the bar, you work as a marshal at the parade, *and* you work for the tourist office?"

"Yep." Jenn looked at the manicured fingers that briefly touched her arm before fading away again. She instantly missed the sensation.

"Any other jobs I should know about? Will you be serving me breakfast in the morning?" Kathryn chuckled.

"No, but I do run a water aerobics class in your hotel on Thursday," Jenn confessed. She started walking again. Kathryn quickly joined her.

"Water aerobics instructor," Kathryn said disbelievingly. "So, a bartender, a marshal, tour guide, and a water aerobics instructor?"

Jenn bit her lip and looked down at the cracked sidewalk.

"Oh my god, there's more." Kathryn laughed.

"Technically the first aid job is part of the tourist office," Jenn explained.

"Uh-huh." Kathryn nodded with a smug smile.

"I work on the streetcars," Jenn admitted. "As a conductor."

"The trams?" Kathryn frowned.

"Streetcars," Jenn corrected. "Yeah, I'm working tonight. You should come."

"Why would I want to do that?"

"Because the streetcars are a part of New Orleans history! The Saint Charles line is the oldest continuously operating streetcar line in the world, running since 1835. In 2014, it was listed by the National Park Service as a historic landmark."

Kathryn's shoulders shook with barely contained laughter. Jenn looked up to see the woman biting her lip.

She rolled her eyes. "Okay, so that is the exact speech I give at the tourist office, but I mean every word of it. And it's accurate."

"I'm sure it is," Kathryn said with clear amusement. "It's adorable."

"And," Jenn continued, on a roll now, "we've bumped into each other three times today already, so it's obviously fate that I'm supposed to show you how wrong you are about New Orleans."

She didn't know why she was suddenly offering to show the woman around her hometown. She told herself it was in defence. She wanted to hear Kathryn take back the words 'sordid hellhole'.

They arrived at the revolving doors to Kathryn's hotel. Kathryn started to hand back the half-drunk bottle of water.

"Keep it," Jenn instructed. "And make sure you carry a bottle with you in the future. The sun can be fierce, and I can't always be here to save you from dehydration."

"Yes, ma'am." Kathryn gave Jenn a small salute.

"So, what do you say? Want to see the streetcars?"

Kathryn considered the question for a few seconds before nodding. "Well, I don't have any other plans. And, as you say, we seem destined to bump into each other anyway."

"Great." Jenn pointed towards Canal Street. "Meet you by the stop up there at nine minutes past eight."

"Very precise," Kathryn commented.

"It may be the Big Easy, but the streetcars run on time."

"Impressive." Kathryn smiled. "Thank you for the water. I do think I was beginning to feel the sun a little."

"You're welcome."

Kathryn frowned. "I've just realised, I don't even know your name."

"Jenn," she said.

"Jenn," Kathryn repeated with a smile that set Jenn's heart racing. "Well, Jenn, I'll see you tonight at nine minutes past eight."

Kathryn turned and nodded to the doorman before disappearing into the hotel lobby. Jenn watched her leave, wondering what on earth she was getting herself into.

6

STREETCAR NAMED DESIRE

JENN NERVOUSLY PACED UP and down the streetcar stop in her work outfit of black trousers, a short-sleeved white shirt, and a black tie. She was waiting for the streetcar to arrive so they could do a quick turnaround and begin the journey back down Saint Charles Avenue.

She knew exactly why she was nervous; she had spent the last couple of hours going over every single element of the interactions she'd had with Kathryn that day. The woman had undergone a miraculous transformation from rude to enigmatic in a short space of time.

As Jenn had eaten her evening meal, she stared blankly at the television in her small apartment. Mentally she was picking over every segment of the conversation they had shared during the walk from the cemetery to the hotel.

She was convinced that Kathryn had been flirting with her. So convinced that after her shower, she had spent a little extra time curling her long blonde hair and had applied a touch more makeup than she usually did for an evening on the streetcars.

She didn't know exactly what to make of Kathryn. She

had been rude and abrasive at first, but she'd also been dumped in the middle of town and clearly didn't want to be there. That would have distressed anyone, surely? Later Kathryn had showed another side to her personality. She had a streak of humour, and Jenn wondered what else was buried under the harsh shell. Maybe she'd been wrong to write Kathryn off so quickly?

Jenn's famously poor gaydar was more confused than ever. During her detailed analysis of the conversation, she'd managed to confuse herself even further. At first, she was convinced that Kathryn had been mildly flirting with her. But as doubts began to assert themselves, Jenn worried that she had read too much into things.

Luckily, the two-hour streetcar journey would give her plenty more time to analyse the situation and learn more about her new companion.

The rumbling sound indicated that the streetcar was approaching. Jenn stopped her pacing and waited for the vintage army-green vehicle to arrive at the station stop. The streetcars that ran the Saint Charles Avenue line were the original vehicles, each of them considered a heritage piece in their own right, having been built in the 1920s.

Each streetcar was beautifully maintained. The simple driver's seat at the front of the vehicle was a high wooden swivel chair with space to stand in front. The controls were heavy metal levers. The floor, walls, and window frames were all constructed from wood, and the wooden benches were all restored originals. The only modern items were the glass windows which were reinforced and could be opened to allow airflow on hot days.

Once the doors swung open, Jenn climbed on board and quickly spoke with her co-worker who was relieved to be going home after a long day of driving. Jenn's shift was thankfully a lot shorter and took in two round trips of the line, which took just over four hours to complete. The line was open practically twenty-four hours a day in the summer, but Jenn only ever worked up until midnight.

She placed her rucksack in the corner and began to change the overhead display to show the new destination of the streetcar.

"You're *driving*?!"

Jenn looked down and through the open door to Kathryn, who was looking up at her with an astonished face.

"Yep." Jenn smiled as she noted Kathryn had changed into a black tank top and khaki-coloured cargo trousers.

"I thought you said conductor?" Kathryn asked. She regarded the antiquated vehicle with a frown.

"Same thing." Jenn shrugged. She sat on the driver's seat. "So, what do you say? Trust me?"

Kathryn paused for a moment before climbing up the steep steps and into the vehicle. Jenn watched as she looked at the empty carriage with captivation.

"Is this an original vehicle?"

"Yep." She swivelled her chair around, watching as Kathryn walked down the middle of the carriage. "There are about thirty of them on the line."

Kathryn examined the features with a smile on her face. "Amazing," she breathed.

"Well, look at that, we found something about New Orleans that you like."

Kathryn rolled her eyes playfully. "If you're going to be like that I could leave again."

Jenn reached behind her and pulled a lever which caused the doors to heavily slam shut.

Kathryn stood in the centre of the carriage regarding Jenn with a smirk. She put her hands on her hips and drawled, "Really?"

Jenn swallowed thickly and released the door again.

Confident Kathryn was all kinds of scary and hot. Jenn found herself flustered as she turned back to the control panel and mindlessly fiddled with some of the switches.

Kathryn walked back towards the driver's seat and looked at the controls with interest. "So, where are we going?"

"Saint Charles Avenue, all the way to South Carrollton Avenue, then up to South Claiborne and then we turn around and head back again."

Kathryn shrugged disinterestedly as if the street names meant little to her.

"I should warn you the whole trip takes around two hours," Jenn admitted. She hoped the long journey wouldn't put Kathryn off.

Kathryn looked around the carriage, her gaze settling on a wooden bench at the front that ran against the wall. It was the closest to the driver's seat and opposite the door.

"I guess I'll sit here?" she said.

Jenn looked up as Kathryn sat herself down. She placed her arm along the back of the bench and looked out of the window.

She looks like a film star, Jenn thought.

"S—sure," Jenn said out loud. She mentally kicked herself, wondering what on earth had gotten into her.

Other passengers started to approach the streetcar. Jenn greeted them warmly as they made their way down the carriage and took their seats. Jenn looked at the old-fashioned clock on the wall. She reached up and pulled the wire that in turn rang the bell to indicate the vehicle was going to start moving.

The streetcar rattled its way down Canal Street, the open windows of the vehicle providing a nice through-breeze. Jenn could feel Kathryn's eyes upon her and focused intensely on driving. They turned onto Saint Charles Avenue and passed through the edge of the Business District.

They frequently stopped, and passengers got on and off. Jenn used the opportunity to glance back at Kathryn. She could tell that she was unimpressed with the start of the journey, presumably she had already seen the Business District and its standard metropolitan style.

Jenn smiled to herself as she remembered the first time that she had taken the streetcar to see what all the fuss was about. She had also found it boring until farther down the famous Saint Charles Avenue, where she was suddenly awestruck by the buildings and architecture. She hoped Kathryn would feel the same.

They passed through a roundabout, went under the expressway, and Jenn adjusted one of her many rearview mirrors so she could see Kathryn's bored expression without turning around. In the Business District there were no real sights to speak of, but the streetcar was now off of the road and onto a private central reservation which made driving a lot easier.

The traffic thinned out, the Business District faded away, and the Garden District took its place. Large trees began to frame the street, and slowly but surely the landscape started to change. The streetcar rattled along, occasionally stopping to let passengers on and off.

Jenn risked a glance at Kathryn. She was staring out of the open window, enthralled by the sight of the boulevard. Exquisite mansions with porches and balconies lined either side of the street; the trees and gardens were all perfectly landscaped. Churches, university buildings, stylish restaurants, and more went by, and every time Jenn turned to look at Kathryn she was relieved to see her smiling as she took everything in.

At one stop an elderly lady with a cane was waiting. Jenn stopped the streetcar and eagerly hopped down from the vehicle to assist the woman up the steep stairs. Jenn walked the woman to a seat and took her fare money. As she walked back towards the driver's seat, she bent down towards Kathryn and pointed up and out of the vehicle.

"If you look in the trees you can still see the Mardi Gras beads," Jenn told her with a grin. Kathryn looked up at spotted a few of the brightly coloured beads—tossed there back in February—and smiled.

Jenn took her seat again and rang the bell. They moved farther down Saint Charles Avenue. It was a very long road, and by the end of it there were only a couple of passengers still on the streetcar.

Kathryn got up and stood by Jenn at the driver's podium. "May I stand with you?"

"Sure," Jenn replied, "just hold on."

Kathryn nodded and held onto a grab-bar by the door. She watched with interest as Jenn drove the streetcar across Saint Charles and onto South Carrollton Avenue. Kathryn looked out of the front windows with awe as they passed by more beautiful houses, churches, schools, and parks.

"Thank you," she said softly.

"What for?" Jenn asked with a frown as she focused on the road in front of her.

"For showing me this," Kathryn replied.

"Thank you for coming, it's nice to share the journey with someone," Jenn said.

Kathryn chuckled. "Don't you always share the journey with someone? Nearly fifty other someones?"

"You know what I mean. A certain someone." She felt the blush touch her cheeks and quickly turned her attention towards the road.

"So, you drive up here and then what? Do you turn around?"

"Well, we do, but the streetcar doesn't," Jenn said.

She hooked her thumb towards the other end of the vehicle. Kathryn looked over her shoulder towards the identical driver's console at the other end of the carriage.

"Oh, I see. Very clever."

"There's a ten-minute stop when we get there," Jenn told her. "There's a shop if you want to get a drink or something."

"Sounds good." Kathryn nodded her head. "I owe you a drink or two by now."

They stopped at the end terminus, and Kathryn headed over to the shop. Jenn said good night to the departing passengers before closing down her driver's panel and walking up the carriage to the other one.

The sun had started to set, and Jenn knew that the route back would alternate between darkness and beautifully lit buildings. She hoped that Kathryn would enjoy the sight as much as she did. She smiled at the feeling that New Orleans was doing its bit to turn Kathryn's opinions around.

Kathryn returned with a large paper bag. Jenn raised her eyebrow.

"I bought snacks," Kathryn announced. "But then I realised I didn't know what you liked so I got a selection."

Kathryn climbed the steps and balanced the bag on the driver's console. She opened the bag and Jenn peered inside. There were chips, chocolate, and a large bag of marshmallow treats.

"You did good," Jenn said in a serious tone. "I think I'll keep you."

"Best news I've had all day," Kathryn said. "Literally."

Jenn plucked a chocolate bar from the bag. Kathryn took out a bottle of apple juice.

"So, I know I'm still technically a stranger," Jenn said, "but why did your sister dump you here?"

Kathryn let out a sigh and leaned against the wall of the carriage. She absentmindedly picked at the label on the drink bottle.

"Erica and I are very different. She's… she's fun, and I'm not. I take things more seriously, and everything is a joke to her. Let's just say that she thinks that everything can be solved with alcohol and a party mentality."

Jenn didn't have to ask if Kathryn thought the opposite. That much was obvious.

"So, she thinks that… whatever's bothering you… will be solved by partying it up in NOLA?"

"Apparently," Kathryn admitted. "That and there's an important deal being signed right now, and she wants me out of the way."

Jenn quirked an eyebrow. "You work together?"

"Yes, Erica, myself, and our mother set up a PR business after I graduated from college. With my knowledge, Erica's personality, and our mother's capital investment, it's gone from strength to strength."

"And now some deal is going down and they want you out of the way?" Jenn fished. Something didn't make sense. She remembered Erica mentioning a name that had Kathryn launching herself towards her sister in a murderous rage.

Addison, she remembered. *That was it.*

There was clearly a big piece of this puzzle that she was missing out on.

"Yes, they—" Kathryn paused as she noticed other passengers approaching the streetcar.

Jenn resisted the urge to slam the door closed in their faces. Kathryn wandered towards the front bench and took her seat.

Jenn welcomed the passengers on board and took their fares. The opportunity was lost, but the evening was going so well that Jenn hoped she would have another chance to find out what had happened.

A few minutes passed, and more passengers climbed aboard. As the minute hand swept onto the departure time,

Jenn closed the door and they were underway again. As soon as they started to move, Kathryn stood up and took her place beside Jenn again.

Kathryn asked questions about the buildings they passed, and Jenn answered as best she could, thankful for her near-encyclopaedic knowledge of her city.

Now and then the streetcar would jolt a little and Kathryn would almost fall into Jenn with a surprised giggle.

Jenn was amazed and mesmerised by the change in the woman. She wondered if Erica was maybe right, that Kathryn was just desperately in need of a vacation. The person who had fumed in the middle of Bourbon Street and the woman whose eyes sparkled with the fairy lights that adorned the passing houses were two different species.

They made small talk, taking the cues from their surroundings. It was never awkward, and the silences were always comfortable. By the end of the hour-long journey back, it seemed as if they had talked about everything and nothing all at once.

It was quarter past ten in the evening when the streetcar came to a stop at Canal Street. Jenn waved goodbye to the departing passengers as they filed off the streetcar.

"That was wonderful." Kathryn beamed as she turned to face Jenn. "I had no idea a simple tram journey could be so much fun."

"Streetcar," Jenn corrected as she shut down the driver's panel.

"Of course. Thank you, again. I know our first meeting was—"

"In the past." Jenn looked up. "You were having a bad day."

Kathryn smiled gratefully before looking around the streetcar. "So, what happens now? Does someone take over from you?"

"I have another journey to do." Jenn indicated the direction of travel with her thumb. "I turn around and do it all again."

"Oh." Kathryn looked around the empty carriage pensively. "Would you... would you like some more company? Or have I bored you enough for one day?"

Jenn felt her eyes light up at the prospect. "I'd love some company! Are you sure, though? It's another two-hour trip."

"Sounds good to me," Kathryn said. "We were talking so much during the journey back that the time just flew by. And the streets look so pretty in the dark with all the lights."

"Great!" Jenn hadn't realised how sad she was at the prospect of Kathryn's departure until she realised she'd be staying. Now, the long shift into the evening was looking much brighter.

7

HUNGER STRIKES

Rebecca knelt down and angled her camera up, trying to capture the beauty of St Louis Cathedral. The sun was beginning to set, turning the sky a deep purple colour. The white building with three tall, grey spires was offset by the bright background. She knew it was a shot she'd never get again.

Part of the allure of photography was capturing those moments that only came around once. She leaned down a little lower, trying to force the perspective of the towering building. She took a couple of shots and rocked back on her heels as she looked at the screen to see how the pictures had come out.

Perfect, she thought. *Might add that to iStock.*

She looked around and saw Arabella strolling through the pathways of nearby Jackson Square. She took a couple of quick shots of Arabella while she was unaware. In the distance, she heard jazz drifting through the air. She wasn't entirely sure where it was coming from, but that didn't seem to be unusual in New Orleans. An impromptu concert could be set up anywhere, at any time.

She stood up, slung her bag over her shoulder, and walked over to Arabella.

"Capture the perfect shot?" Arabella asked when she approached.

"I did," Rebecca said, thinking about the candid photographs she had taken of Arabella.

"Maybe we should find somewhere to eat dinner?" Arabella suggested.

Rebecca quickly put the lens cap on her camera and put it back into her bag. She'd suggested they eat dinner hours earlier, but Arabella wasn't feeling hungry. Which was unusual because Arabella's eating schedule was regimented.

"Sure." Rebecca looked around the square at the restaurants in sight. "Do you have any idea what you want to eat?"

"Food. Soon."

Rebecca nodded. It seemed Arabella had sailed past hungry and into starving, something that was easy to do when your body was out of sorts after a day of travel. She gestured towards a café in the distance. It looked in good condition, had a glass of wine as a logo, and was close.

When they got there, Rebecca paused to look at the menu. It was the kind of place that did everything. She was about to ask Arabella what she thought when she passed her by and addressed the waitress, asking for a table for two.

She wondered how long Arabella had been suffering in silence with hunger pangs so Rebecca could get the shot she wanted.

They were quickly seated, and Rebecca ordered a bread basket before the waitress left. She didn't know if one would have arrived anyway, but she didn't wish to leave it to chance. Arabella looked at her gratefully.

"Why didn't you tell me you were starving?"

"You were being artsy."

Rebecca laughed. "Artsy?"

"Yes, you get this faraway look, your eyes glaze over, and you drift off to take pictures." Arabella turned the page of her menu. "I don't want to get in the way."

"You don't get in the way," Rebecca said quickly. "If you're hungry in the future, tell me."

Arabella glanced up from her menu and slightly nodded her head.

"Promise me," Rebecca pressed. She wasn't accepting a half-hearted nod.

"Fine, fine," Arabella agreed.

Rebecca made a mental note to keep an eye on her. She didn't believe for one moment that Arabella would tell her if she was feeling hungry in the future. The woman was one of the most stubborn people she'd ever met.

The waitress placed a bread basket on the table and Rebecca quickly pushed it towards Arabella.

"I know white bread is a sin but eat something before you chew on the menu."

Arabella picked up a piece of bread and immediately started to eat it.

"No butter?" Rebecca asked.

One look told her that white bread and real butter would be a step too far. She picked up a slice of bread, opened a pot of butter, and started to slather it on.

"It's a crime that you can look the way you do and eat the way you do," Arabella muttered.

"It'll catch up with me," Rebecca said.

"I gleefully await the day." Arabella closed the menu. "In the meantime, I'm having a salad."

Rebecca raised her eyebrow. "A salad? You're on holiday."

"Fat grams don't identify holidays."

Rebecca knew she was onto a losing battle and decided to save the topic for another day. The waitress returned, Arabella ordered salad and sparkling water, and Rebecca ordered a burger and a beer.

"What do you think of New Orleans so far?" Rebecca asked.

"It's certainly different to anything I've seen before," Arabella replied. She picked up another piece of bread. Rebecca knew better than to mention it.

"Is that a good thing or a bad thing?"

Arabella chuckled. "I'm not sure yet. It's very vibrant and different from what I'm used to. I don't think I'm going to be out on Bourbon Street at eleven o'clock this evening. But I'll certainly enjoy a glass of wine at an outdoor café and listen to the jazz one evening."

"Sounds like a great idea, we'll have to schedule that in. Maybe tomorrow, after your spa day and before we meet up with Jenn for dinner?" Rebecca suggested. She was looking forward to a more relaxed Arabella after the spa treatments.

"Maybe. I'm sure I'll fall asleep during the massage." Arabella sat up straight and twisted her head from side to side to loosen the tight muscles. "They are going to use a new kind of body butter, it firms and smooths."

Rebecca had to stop herself before she claimed that Arabella didn't need such a thing. That road led to a lot of uncomfortable admissions about having watched Arabella closely enough to know.

"Sounds great. Good to know you're not completely anti-butter."

Arabella rolled her eyes and looked away.

The waitress delivered their drinks and Rebecca thanked her. She poured her beer into the glass provided, having learnt that Arabella wasn't a fan of anyone drinking directly from the bottle if a glass was offered.

She noticed Arabella was looking out of the restaurant windows to the seating area outside. She leaned forward and saw a female couple. They were holding hands, leaning in close, and deep in conversation.

"Cute couple," Rebecca said.

Arabella looked away, a light blush on her cheeks.

Rebecca wasn't about to let the subject drop. She continued watching the pair.

"Do you think they've been together long? Maybe this is a first date?"

Arabella sipped her water, her eyes flickering over to the window to assess the women outside.

"I don't think it's a first date, they are very touchy-feely," Arabella said.

Rebecca was about to point out that things way beyond touchy-feely often happened on first dates but thought better of it.

"Maybe," she said. "They make a good couple, though."

"We shouldn't stare," Arabella said. She turned back to face the table and looked down at her drink.

Rebecca sipped her beer. She wanted to press the point, to open a discussion about romantically involved women. But then she knew not to push an already stressed, and clearly very hungry, Arabella. It wasn't the right time.

"I suppose you think I'm a prude?" Arabella asked. "I'm not."

"I didn't say a word."

"Your silence speaks volumes."

"Silence, by virtue of being silent, speaks nothing."

Arabella opened her mouth to reply and then stopped. She closed her mouth, her lips tightening to form a thin line. "Let's talk about something else," she all but demanded.

I hope that massage tomorrow relaxes her, Rebecca thought. "Sure, what would you like to talk about?"

"Your plans for tomorrow," Arabella said quickly, clearly

having grasped the first safe subject that had sprung to her mind.

Rebecca nodded. She listed the things she had in mind to do the next day. She hadn't made any firm plans yet, but she had some ideas. As she spoke, Arabella visibly relaxed.

That masseuse is going to earn their money tomorrow, Rebecca mused.

8

MALFUNCTIONING GAYDAR

JENN WAITED for the lights to change. Out of the corner of her eye she watched Kathryn leaning against the wall of the streetcar. She'd just finished explaining all of the training she had gone through in order to become a qualified streetcar operator. Kathryn seemed suitably impressed.

The lights changed, and they started moving again. A couple of drunk young men wolf-whistled at them as the streetcar rattled by. Jenn shook her head and chuckled at their childishness.

"You have to admit, this city is obsessed with alcohol." Kathryn grinned. She'd been playfully trying to poke holes in Jenn's love affair with New Orleans for a while now.

"No more so than other places, we just have more relaxed rules." Jenn shrugged.

"But those slushie machines…" Kathryn laughed.

Jenn smiled. "Hey, it gets hot, what can I say? Some people just feel more refreshed after a frozen mojito!"

"Uh-huh."

"Don't knock it until you've tried one." Jenn gently elbowed Kathryn.

The streetcar came to a stop in front of another set of traffic lights. The junction was particularly busy, so Jenn picked up her water bottle and took a few long sips.

She felt Kathryn tapping her on the shoulder.

"Open the door," she commanded.

"What?" Jenn frowned.

"Open the door," Kathryn repeated.

Jenn turned to see Kathryn engaged in some silent conversation through hand gestures with a bartender in a run-down old bar across the street.

She laughed and opened the door. "I won't wait for you," she warned.

Kathryn took off quickly across the thankfully empty road. The bartender was already pouring her an alcoholic slushie as Kathryn waved some dollar bills in his direction.

Jenn's eyes switched from the red light in front of her to the exchange taking place at the bar. She watched as Kathryn looked both ways before running back towards the streetcar. She jumped up the steps just as the lights changed to green.

Jenn burst out laughing and closed the doors. She pulled the bell and took off the brake, causing the streetcar to start moving again. The passengers who had been watching Kathryn's alcohol dash burst into spontaneous applause. Kathryn curtsied and held her drink aloft to them.

"I would have got you one, but you're driving," Kathryn explained. "And I was against the clock."

"No problem," Jenn said. "What did you get?"

Kathryn regarded the icy drink with a frown before sniffing the top. "Red?"

Jenn kept an eye on the road as she reached up and pulled Kathryn's hand down. She took a small sip of the drink through the bright green straw.

"Mmm, strawberry daiquiri! Good choice!"

Kathryn took a sip herself and winced. "Ugh, sugar and food colouring."

"Yeah, never seen a strawberry in its life," Jenn admitted.

The trip raced by and Jenn found herself hoping more passengers wanted to board on the journey back towards Canal Street, just so they could spend some more time together. They laughed until they cried, and Jenn felt her breath restrict in her throat each time Kathryn placed her hand on her arm or shoulder when she spoke.

"Is that a casino down there?" Kathryn asked as they turned back onto Canal Street.

"Yep." Jenn nodded as she carefully navigated around the traffic and tourists on the busy street.

"Suppose you work there, too?" Kathryn laughed at her joke.

Jenn remained silent. She knew a blush was taking over her cheeks.

Kathryn stared at her. "Seriously? How many jobs do you have?"

"A few." Jenn shrugged.

"But you *do* work at the casino?" Kathryn pressed.

"Yeah, I'm not on shift for another week, though."

"Okay, I've consumed half of the world's worst strawberry daiquiri, so you'll have to bear with me here." Kathryn placed her arm around Jenn's shoulder as she drove up the busy street. "A bartender, a marshal, a tour guide, a streetcar driver, a water aerobics instructor, *and* a casino employee?"

Jenn chuckled. It was amusing to listen to Kathryn listing the jobs she knew about on her fingers.

"Yep, there's more, but you'll have to wait to see what they are," she added flirtatiously.

"Oh, will I now?" Kathryn laughed.

A few short minutes later and the journey and Jenn's shift were finished. Jenn picked up her rucksack and handed the streetcar over to her co-worker. Both she and Kathryn exited the streetcar and stood in the large central reservation on Canal Street, the streetcar tracks on either side of them and the main road on either side of that.

"I had a great time this evening," Jenn said. She leaned casually against a lamppost.

"So did I," Kathryn confessed. "Except that drink. I thought this place was famous for its cocktails?"

"You need to let *me* make you one," Jenn explained. "Not buy one for three bucks."

"Oh, do you charge more?" Kathryn raised her eyebrow.

"I think you can afford me," Jenn said. She quickly took a step forward to place a kiss on Kathryn's lips.

Kathryn jumped back, startled. "What are you doing?!"

Jenn's eyes widened as she took in Kathryn's shocked and horrified expression. Her hand covered her mouth. "Oh my god, I'm so, so sorry."

"I'm not gay!" Kathryn hissed at her. She looked around to see if anyone had been watching the scene unfold. "What... why... why did you kiss me?"

"Well... duh," Jenn said. She immediately wished she had come up with something better.

"You're... oh..." Kathryn took a deep breath. "I'm... flattered, really I am, but I'm straight. I'm sorry if I gave you the wrong impression."

Jenn swallowed. She attempted to look casual as she shook her head and held up a hand.

"It's fine, no problem... I'm the one who's sorry."

Kathryn stared wordlessly at her before finally nodding her head. "Thank you... for a lovely evening. I really did enjoy the sights. I'll... well... I... should be going."

Jenn nodded. "Okay, do you know your way back?"

Kathryn nodded, the earlier smile gone from her face and replaced with a serious expression. "I do. Good night, Jenn."

"'Night, Kathryn," Jenn said as she watched her turn and walk away.

She watched until Kathryn was out of sight and then leaned back against the lamppost and sighed to herself.

"Jenn, you idiot…"

9

LOOKING GAY

DINNER HAD BEEN A TENSE AFFAIR. Rebecca was relieved when Arabella said she wanted to head back to the hotel and go to bed.

Clearly Arabella wasn't ready to talk about same-sex relationships and was also embarrassed by her reaction to the start of the conversation. Rebecca knew that Arabella's embarrassment often presented as anger, so they'd eaten in silence save for the odd observational comment about the restaurant's interior decoration.

They walked the short distance back to the Royale, passing crowds of people laughing, drinking, and generally celebrating. Rebecca suddenly felt like she didn't want the evening to be over, she wanted to stay up a while longer and experience a little more of New Orleans.

When they entered the lobby, Rebecca paused. She turned to face Arabella.

"I'm going to have a drink in the bar, so I'll say goodnight." She deliberately didn't extend the invitation. She felt guilty for doing so, but she just needed some time to herself. If she was going to pretend that Arabella's reticence to acknowledge anything gay wasn't killing her inside, she needed some time to herself.

"Oh." Arabella seemed at a loss as she peered into the bar. "Okay, well, goodnight."

"See you at breakfast." Rebecca smiled as she passed her and entered the bar. She looked around and saw that many of the chairs and tables were taken, but there were a couple of free spaces at the bar. She approached the closest available barstool and sat down.

The bartender greeted her immediately.

"Hey, can I have a..." Rebecca scanned the optics, debating how much she wanted to forget the events of dinner versus how much of a hangover she wanted the next day. "Jack Daniels and Coke."

A napkin appeared in front of her, and, a moment later, her drink was served. The joy of a hotel bar was that service was always super speedy.

She took a sip before letting out a long sigh.

"Excuse me?"

She turned to acknowledge the brunette beside her. "Yes?"

"I'm so sorry, but I was wondering if I could ask you a question?"

The woman appeared to be drinking whisky, a couple of empty glasses lingered in front of her. Rebecca imagined that was down to the speed of intake rather than the slowness of the bar staff.

"Sure?" she said.

The woman pointed to the rainbow lapel pin that Rebecca wore on her collar. "Forgive me if I'm being rude, but I'm guessing you identify as... gay?"

Rebecca smiled. This was one of the weirdest come-ons she'd experience in a while.

"Yeah, I'm gay. But I go by Rebecca." She held out

her hand.

The woman smiled and shook her hand. "Kathryn."

"Nice to meet you, Kathryn." She took another sip of her drink. "Was that your question?"

"Not exactly."

"Then how can I help?"

Kathryn turned to face her head on. "Do I... look gay?" She gestured to her face and body with both hands.

Rebecca blinked.

Oh, boy, should have gone to bed.

She looked at Kathryn. She was smartly dressed, with mid-length, perfectly styled brown hair. There was nothing about her that screamed gay, she looked... average. Striking, but she'd fit into a crowd easily.

"Well, that's a hard question to answer," Rebecca admitted. "Gay comes in lots of different shapes and sizes. Sometimes it's easy to identify someone's sexuality, but many times it isn't. I wouldn't say you're giving off any obvious indicators of being gay. But, I'm guessing that if you hadn't seen my badge, you wouldn't have guessed my orientation either?"

"That's true," Kathryn allowed. She turned back to the bar.

"Are you?" Rebecca asked.

"Am I?"

"Gay... are you gay?"

"No." Kathryn sipped her drink.

Okay, maybe not a strange come-on, Rebecca decided. "May I ask why you asked if you look gay?"

Kathryn turned back to face her. She leaned in a little closer, as if about to divulge some enormous secret. "A woman... kissed me." She nodded sagely and sat back up. She pinned Rebecca with a knowing look, a 'Well, what do you say about *that*?' kind of look.

"Okay..." Rebecca really wished she had gone to bed

instead of heading to the bar for a drink. "So, do you know why she kissed you? Do you know her well?"

"No, I met her today. Today!" Kathryn gestured to the bartender for another drink. "We spent the evening together, and then she kissed me."

"You spent the evening together?" Rebecca quizzed. "Like a date?"

"No... no. Like, she's... well. She works on the trams, and I was with her while she worked. She drives the tram."

"Streetcar," Rebecca corrected.

"Yes, that. Anyway. We did a couple of journeys up and down the route and then she kissed me."

"Why were you with her on the streetcar?"

Kathryn knocked back the last of her whisky as the bartender placed a fresh drink on a napkin in front of her. "She asked. I'm new to the city, she wanted to show me around."

Rebecca massaged her temple. "So, correct me if I'm wrong at any point here..."

Kathryn nodded eagerly.

"You're new to town. Meet this woman. She tells you that she works as a driver on the streetcars and invites you along. You go, you spend the evening together. Right?"

"Yes, all accurate."

"Do you talk on the streetcar?"

"Yes, she told me about her life here, I told her a little about me. Nothing much, small talk mainly. We laughed and joked. Shared some food."

"This is sounding very much like a date," Rebecca pointed out.

Kathryn scrunched her face up in thought. She turned back towards the bar and leaned her head into her hand.

"Maybe she thought it was," she admitted. "You're right,

it does sound like a date. But I'm straight... so, I'm drawn back to my original question: do I look gay?"

"And back to my original answer, it's hard to say. Some people dress and style themselves so they stand out as obviously gay, and some people don't. It's impossible to know who is straight and who isn't just by looking at them these days." Rebecca tapped her badge. "Remember, we're only having this conversation because I happen to be wearing this."

"True," Kathryn agreed.

"She was being a bit presumptuous," Rebecca confessed. "I always double-check, you never know when you're misreading signals."

"Oh, it was just a peck," Kathryn said. "I won't be filing charges."

Rebecca smiled and returned her attention to her drink. She wondered what it was about women in their late thirties and older who were so confused by sexual identities. Kathryn seemed to think that she must have been inadvertently wearing a rainbow flag for a woman to have kissed her. Arabella couldn't even look at a female couple without her cheeks reddening.

Times had clearly changed a lot, people were talking more about their sexuality. People of Rebecca's generation rarely had an issue with the subject. Now Rebecca spent her time trying to reassure hot, older women.

"So, are you here with your girlfriend?" Kathryn asked.

Rebecca laughed. "No... not exactly."

Kathryn looked at her with a grin. "Not exactly; that sounds interesting."

Rebecca bit her lip and shook her head. She had come into the bar to wrap her mind around what was happening with Arabella. Who better to talk to about the matter than someone who seemed to be having similar issues.

"We met just before Christmas," Rebecca explained. "Hate at first sight."

Kathryn laughed.

"We were kind of forced to share a car journey home. I swear, at first, I wanted to leave her by the roadside in Spain. But we sort of came together. I saw another side of her. Then she helped me with some things after and we stayed in touch. We're friends. Good friends."

"Just friends?" Kathryn pressed.

"She... she was engaged to be married, but she realised she didn't love him. Soon after we got back, she broke off the engagement. We got closer and..." She blew out a breath and ran a hand through her hair. "I thought we were getting somewhere. But then it kind of morphed back into friendship. We're travelling together and I'm hoping I'll get some kind of answer as to if we're friends, or possibly more."

"You want to be more than friends?"

Rebecca nodded. "Yes, I'll take friendship. But when she said she had feelings for me, and the chance of being more than friends was presented... I knew that was what I wanted."

"She said she has feelings for you?" Kathryn sipped at her drink.

"Yes, well, it's complicated. She needed time to figure out her feelings. I gave her time and space and... maybe I shouldn't have given her so much time and space."

Kathryn patted her on the shoulder. "I think you did the right thing. Very chivalrous of you. Or whatever that word would be for a woman. Respectful?"

Rebecca laughed bitterly. Yes, she'd been very respectful. But a part of her wondered what might have happened if she had been a little pushier. Would she be in a relationship with Arabella? Or just friends and happy in the knowledge that nothing more would come of it? That would free her up to date rather than keeping herself in suspended animation.

Not that she was in any sort of hurry. Arabella was worth waiting for. She just wished she had a timeline to work to. Some indication on whether or not anything would change, and if so, when?

"I suppose I was respectful," Rebecca finally agreed. "But now I'm kind of lost. I don't know if I should ask or leave it alone. Give her time to come to me or not. And I know she's struggling with it, too. But I don't know why. She's not great at opening up."

She sat in silence for a few seconds before she realised Kathryn wasn't saying anything. She turned to look at her.

Kathryn shrugged her shoulders. "I don't know what to tell you. I thought I'd had a rough night, but it wasn't that bad. I overreacted. At the end of the day, someone found me attractive and that's a nice thing to happen. You clearly have it much worse than I do, I feel like a fraud for complaining." She smiled kindly. "I'm really sorry. I hope you and your friend manage to figure everything out."

"Thanks, me too." Rebecca let out a breath she'd been holding and relaxed her shoulders. It felt good to speak to someone, even if it didn't resolve the issue.

She knocked back the rest of her drink. "I think I'm going to head to bed; thanks for listening," she said.

"No problem. I really do hope things work out." Kathryn raised her glass to her lips. She paused and looked at the liquid woozily before putting the glass back down. "I think I better call it a night as well."

Arabella stared up at the ceiling. Her hotel room was beautiful, with original plasterwork features on the ceiling, a picture rail around the walls, and a chandelier light fitting. The bed was divine, a firm but forgiving mattress, soft pillows, and bedding that was crisp and clean yet welcoming.

But she couldn't sleep.

She'd love to say it was jetlag, or the excitement of the day, or the distant sounds of a city that definitely never slept. The truth was, it wasn't any of those things. She had been lying awake for the last three-quarters of an hour because she felt guilty.

She'd ruined dinner with Rebecca. A sudden downturn in her blood sugar levels, coupled with the embarrassment of Rebecca catching her watching a young, female couple, had caused her to become tetchy.

Once she became embarrassed, it was hard for her to snap out of it. Then she started to feel guilty for her behaviour and the whole thing escalated from there.

It wasn't until she'd returned to the hotel room, angrily scrubbed the makeup from her face, and prepared for bed that she realised she could have solved it all with a simple apology. Rebecca was infinitely understanding of her mood swings.

But Arabella felt terrible for putting her through them. It wasn't Rebecca's fault that she was a mess.

She couldn't blame Rebecca for wanting to have a drink in the hotel bar. If their positions were reversed, she'd probably want to drink away any memory of the evening, too.

She turned over and grabbed the unused pillow from the other side of the bed and hugged it to her chest. She knew she was running from her feelings. Certainly, running from something. Every time she started to even consider her feelings for Rebecca, or her thoughts towards homosexuality, her brain shut down.

It was impossible to come to any conclusions if any time you thought about something, your mind went blank.

She heard a muted clicking sound. She turned her head and listened carefully. A moment later, she heard a door closing. Rebecca had returned to her room next door.

She stared at the interconnecting door.

The need to apologise clawed at her.

She didn't quite know what to say. But she had to say something. She hugged the pillow closer to her chest as she tried to think of how to word it. She was torn between a blanket apology and an explanation. Not that she had an explanation as such.

She sat up and kicked the sheets away. She rubbed at her face and debated putting a light amount of foundation on. It was ridiculous, but she knew she was that vain. And she knew Rebecca would see right through it.

She got up and walked into the bathroom. She turned on the bright lights that surrounded the mirror. Leaning in, she looked at her reflection and tilted her head from side to side. She looked tired. But then she had been in bed for a while, of course she would look tired.

"Pull yourself together," she muttered. "Just… say sorry. End of story."

She pushed herself away from the counter and turned off the light. She checked her silk pyjamas were in order, with no undone buttons, and then walked towards the connecting door.

Before she had a chance to connect her shaking knuckles to the wood, she heard Rebecca's door open and close again.

Rebecca had gone out.

She took a few steps back. Her jaw dropped as she stared at the door in horror.

Rebecca had gone *out*.

It was the middle of the night, so it was clear to her where Rebecca was going. To see someone. Probably someone she had just met in the bar. It was the only possible explanation.

She put some distance between herself and the door. She climbed into bed and wrapped the now-cool sheets around her.

She didn't own Rebecca, and Rebecca certainly didn't owe her any explanations. She slowly lowered herself back down to the mattress. She knew sleep wouldn't come easily that night.

10

ANSWERS

ARABELLA LOOKED at her reflection in the mirror of her hotel bathroom. She leaned in close and used her finger to smooth out a stray piece of lipstick. She took a step back and fluffed up her hair.

She rolled her eyes at her behaviour and grabbed her clutch bag from the counter. She picked up her keycard and left the room, walking quickly towards the elevators.

When she'd woken up, she noticed she had a text message from Rebecca saying that she'd meet her downstairs in the restaurant for breakfast.

She'd wondered if Rebecca had knocked to try to wake her that morning. The previous evening, she'd resorted to the sleeping pills she had been saving for the flight home in order to finally get to sleep. Her mind had been spinning up until that point, and she knew sleep wouldn't come without medical intervention.

The morning sun hadn't been welcome, but she'd decided to do her best to try to turn events around. And that started with breakfast—and with trying to not feel like she had a knife in her chest while asking how Rebecca's evening had gone.

She approached the restaurant manager and gave him her name and room number. "My companion should already be here, Rebecca Edwards?"

He checked his list and nodded. "Ah, of course. If you'll join me please, Miss Henley." He snatched a menu from his podium and led her through the large dining room.

She saw Rebecca sitting in a booth by the window, watching the world go by while holding a mug of what she guessed was hot coffee. She turned and saw Arabella approaching and smiled in greeting.

"Hey, good morning."

"Good morning." Arabella took her seat.

"Can I get you some tea or coffee?" the manager asked.

"Coffee, please."

"And some more for me, please," Rebecca asked.

He opened the menu and handed it to Arabella. "I'll be back with coffee in a moment."

"So, wow, those beds are something, right?" Rebecca asked.

Arabella gripped the menu tightly. "Yes, very comfortable."

"It was like heaven," Rebecca added.

Arabella stared at the breakfast menu with an intensity that caused her to fear it might spontaneously combust in her hands. Was she really expected to discuss Rebecca's... what? Conquest? She hadn't signed up to that. She wouldn't do it.

"I don't think I've had a better night's sleep in ages," Rebecca continued on.

Arabella's jaw was so tight she wondered if she'd ever be able to unlatch it to eat her breakfast. Her eyes turned to look at the oatmeal, minimal chewing required.

"Two pots of coffee." The restaurant manager returned and placed the two silver pots on the table. "Are you ready to order?"

"I am, I'm famished," Rebecca said. She immediately ordered a plate of pancakes with fresh fruit, as well as a side plate of bacon.

Arabella lowered her menu and looked at Rebecca in disgust. Famished. She shivered at the suggestion.

Rebecca frowned. "What? Pancakes and bacon are a breakfast thing here."

"Unbelievable," she muttered and quickly glanced at her menu again. "Eggs benedict, please." Diet be damned,

The manager took their menus and departed again.

Rebecca looked at her with a confused expression. "Is everything okay?"

"Why wouldn't it be?" Arabella asked. She swiped the fabric napkin from the table and unfolded it, placing it on her lap.

"I don't know, you seem a little off..." Rebecca trailed off as her eyes drifted behind Arabella.

"Good morning!" she called out suddenly.

Arabella turned around in the booth and saw a woman walking towards them. She was in her mid-thirties, wore far too much makeup, and hadn't bothered to do anything with her brown locks.

Ah, the conquest.

"Hi there!" the slattern said. "How are you this morning?"

Arabella rolled her eyes and returned her attention to pouring some coffee. She couldn't deal with that awful American accent before she'd ingested some caffeine.

"I'm good, how are you? Headache?" Rebecca asked with a chuckle.

"Yes, a little. This must be your friend?"

"Yes, this is Arabella. Arabella, this is Kathryn. I met her at the bar last night."

Kathryn stuck her hand out and Arabella gave it the minutest of shakes.

"She wouldn't stop talking about you," Kathryn said.

Arabella raised her eyebrow. She didn't think that statement was entirely appropriate considering the circumstances.

"You have a great friend in this one," Kathryn said, jutting a thumb towards Rebecca.

Rebecca blushed and waved Kathryn away. "Go and have your breakfast, you'll need it to soak up all that alcohol," she laughed.

"You're right, you're absolutely right. Have a good day, hope to catch up with you both later."

"Good to know I'm a topic of conversation," Arabella said after Kathryn left.

Rebecca's blushed deepened. "Well, she was talking a lot, and I felt I needed to say something. She'd had a lot to drink."

"So I gather."

Arabella was reeling. Knowing that Rebecca was off having late-night trysts was one thing. Having to discuss them the next morning over stainless-steel kitchenware was another matter. And the drunken woman involved in the whole debacle wanting to greet her and shake her hand… it was more than she could take.

She was fuming. How dare Rebecca drag her all this way and then behave like that. Okay, so maybe she *was* a prude. But it just wasn't acceptable.

"You know, Rebecca—" Arabella started.

"One second…" Rebecca gestured towards the restaurant manager as he was passing. "Excuse me, I was wondering if you could organise a new room keycard for me? I went to the gym late last night, and I had to try several times before it let me in. When I got back to my room it was the same thing."

He looked apologetic. "Of course, miss. I'll get reception to get a new card for you, and I'll deliver it with your breakfast."

"Thank you, I thought I better ask now before I forget and get locked out of my room entirely!"

He nodded politely before leaving. Rebecca turned back to Arabella. "Sorry about that, I wanted to catch him before I forgot again. You were saying?"

"Y—you went to the gym last night?" Arabella asked.

"Yes, I had a quick drink in the bar, chatted with Kathryn for a bit, and then decided to go to bed. But on the way back to my room I realised how wired I was and thought I'd take advantage of the twenty-four-hour gym. They weren't kidding about the views, you'll love it up there."

Arabella felt faint with relief. She slumped back into her chair and stared at the tablecloth.

"Wow, are you okay?" Rebecca was out of her seat and next to her in a few short seconds. "You've gone really pale."

"Fine, fine." Arabella tried to sit up. She realised her hands were shaking slightly, so she clasped them in her lap. "I took a couple of sleeping pills to get to sleep last night; I think I just need to eat something."

"Are you sure?" Rebecca placed her hand on Arabella's shoulder and looked at her seriously.

She took a deep breath and nodded her head. The shock was starting to dissipate, and she was feeling better already. Rebecca hadn't gone off with some woman. She'd just gone to the gym, all perfectly reasonable. She wondered why she hadn't even considered it before.

She tried to push down the reason why she was so relieved. It was another thing she wasn't quite ready to acknowledge. Something she knew she would have to recognise sooner rather than later.

Rebecca's hand still rested on her shoulder. Arabella looked up and met her eyes.

"I'm okay, sorry if I scared you… As I say, just tired. And probably the pills. Some breakfast will do me a world of good."

Rebecca lowered her hand but continued to watch Arabella as if afraid she might shatter at any moment.

"Maybe I should stay behind today?"

"No, I don't want you to change your plans. And I'll be here at the hotel. If anything happens—which it won't—I'll be in good hands."

Rebecca didn't look fully convinced, but she slowly nodded. "Okay, but if you feel unwell again, I want you to text me and I'll come straight back."

"Agreed. But seriously, I'm fine." Arabella took a sip of coffee. Luckily her shaking hands were back under control. "Tell me what you're planning to do today again?"

Rebecca reached across the table and pulled her coffee cup closer, having apparently decided to relocate to sit beside Arabella.

She started talking about her plans. She'd already decided to head out with her camera and explore the French Quarter some more.

Arabella tuned out the details, too consumed with the happiness she felt at knowing that Rebecca hadn't hooked up with some stranger the night before.

She couldn't wait any longer, she had to figure out her feelings and take action. Rebecca was a catch, and if she didn't hurry up and make up her mind, she might lose her.

Luckily, she had an entire day relaxing at the spa to think things through and decide what she wanted.

11

STARTING OVER

JENN SLOWLY OPENED the door from her apartment building to the street. She looked in both directions, trying to determine if it was safe or not. She had half expected to see Kathryn standing right outside her building, such was the frequency of their bumping into each other the previous day.

Thankfully, there was no sign of her.

She stepped outside and hurried along the street towards her third favourite coffee shop. She decided on that one as she considered it to be the least touristy and therefore the one with the smallest chance of attracting someone new to the city. Someone like Kathryn.

After she grabbed a coffee to go, she took the long route down to the Mississippi River. She was thankfully early for her afternoon shift on one of the few remaining steamboats that took passengers out on trips up and down the river.

Not only was it a job she enjoyed, but it would give her the opportunity to take her mind off of the ill-fated kiss from the previous evening. Since it had happened, her brain had unhelpfully replayed the kiss over and over again.

Distraction would be welcome, and an afternoon on the

river was perfect for that. It was hard to be caught up in your own troubles when you were sailing along the Mississippi, regaling tourists with stories of times gone by and listening to the sounds of the live jazz band aboard.

All the stresses and worries of the day seemed to disappear when she was on the river. The gentle sway of the boat knocked them overboard, and the paddlewheel washed them away.

In the years since Jenn first started working on the steamboat, she'd taken on most jobs at some point. Now she'd progressed to the role of host, which was more of a pleasure than a job.

Being a host involved greeting people as they queued on the dockside while they waited for the ship to be prepared. She also helped them to board, and then walked around the boat during the cruise and answered questions.

She'd once joked with her boss that she was literally paid to chat with passengers. He'd quickly gotten his phone and showed her some of the online reviews the company had received. All of the reviews were extremely positive. Many mentioned Jenn personally and thanked her for her time.

The positive publicity was worth its weight in gold. And it was definitely worth the company's time to pay Jenn to chat with the passengers.

Jenn loved to chat, and most of the part-time jobs she had enabled her to speak with people from all walks of life. No matter what was happening in her own world, she knew she would be able to surround herself with people and pass the time of day with some small talk.

Now thoughts of the miscalculated kiss were rushing through her mind, and Jenn knew that she was in desperate need of some distraction. But her first job was to walk the long way around to the dock. The long way because she didn't want to bump into Kathryn as she had so many times the day before.

So, she walked out and around the tourist areas of the French Quarter before walking back along the riverside road towards the dock.

Unfortunately, there was only one way into the dock, through a paved plaza with a number of popular cafes on either side. Chairs and tables were scattered across the paved area, giving tourists the best view of the river and the ships.

She turned into the plaza and immediately came to a dead stop.

"You have *got* to be kidding me," she mumbled.

Kathryn sat at a table with a glass of water and a cup of what she guessed was coffee in front of her. She was facing away from Jenn, looking towards the river through large, dark sunglasses.

Jenn took in the scene and calculated a way around Kathryn without being seen. She knew there was an alleyway where the trash was kept—she sighed. She couldn't justify climbing over bags of trash just to avoid Kathryn. And what would she do for the next thirteen days of Kathryn's stay in the city? It would be impossible to avoid her.

The kiss had been an honest mistake, and the best way to clear the air was to apologise and try to move forward.

She took a deep breath and walked over to Kathryn's table.

Standing in front of Kathryn, she offered a shy smile.

"Hi, I'm Jenn Cook. I'm gay with the worst gaydar on the planet. I sometimes mistakenly kiss straight women, but I promise it's not a regular occurrence. And, when I do, I'm very sorry."

The sunglasses made Kathryn's eyes unreadable. Luckily, a

smile crept onto her lips and after a few short moments, Kathryn raised her hand.

"Kathryn Foster. Pleasure to meet you, Miss Cook."

Jenn shook Kathryn's proffered hand. "I'm so sorry. I —I just…"

"Don't mention it." Kathryn shook her head softly. "It was a stressful day for me yesterday. You'd been very kind, and I'm sorry I reacted in the way I did."

Jenn let out a relieved breath and finally lowered her shoulders away from her ears. She couldn't believe that Kathryn was being so forgiving. After her outburst yesterday, Jenn was sure Kathryn would be livid.

She wondered again if the first impressions she'd had of her were entirely wrong. Maybe her sister Erica was right, she thought again; maybe Kathryn was stressed beyond all reason and a vacation was exactly what she needed.

"So, we're good?" Jenn confirmed. "I don't have to sneak around the city in case I bump into you?"

"Were you?"

Jenn smiled at Kathryn's raised eyebrow that appeared from under the sunglasses. "I might have been."

"Well, you're doing a terrible job." Kathryn gestured to herself.

"Yeah, seems like fate keeps throwing us together," Jenn pointed out.

"Indeed it does. Are you going to the casino today? Or are you driving streetcars?" Kathryn took a sip of coffee. "Or maybe the tourist office?"

Jenn rubbed the back of her neck. "Um, no, not any of them."

"Day off?" Kathryn enquired with a surprised tone.

"Nope." Jenn grinned.

"Oh my god, you're going to yet another job, aren't you?"

Jenn chuckled and nodded.

"Are you trying for some kind of record?" Kathryn dead-panned. "Is someone following you and taking notes?"

"Ha-ha. No, I just like change," Jenn explained.

"I see. So, what is it today? Lion tamer? Trainee astronaut?"

"Nah, that's Monday," Jenn joked.

Even with the dark glasses, she could tell Kathryn was rolling her eyes.

"Actually, I'm working there for the afternoon," Jenn said, pointing towards the steamboat at the dock.

Kathryn turned to look in the direction she pointed. "Where?"

"The steamboat," Jenn clarified.

"Wait, don't tell me." She pretended to size Jenn up. "You're the captain?"

Jenn laughed. "No, I'm a host."

"Host? What does a host do?" Kathryn enquired with a smile.

"Help people aboard, make sure everyone is happy, point out interesting sights along the river," Jenn answered.

"Sounds like fun," Kathryn commented.

Before Jenn knew what she was saying, an invitation spilled from her lips. "Would you like to come?"

"Me?" Kathryn looked confused.

"Yes, you. Consider it our second non-date. It's a lot of fun, and a great way to see the city. I still want you to love New Orleans."

Kathryn removed her sunglasses and regarded the ship with interest. "How long is this trip?"

"Three hours. There's food included." Jenn didn't know why she was inviting Kathryn. It was as if she were a glutton for punishment.

"Maybe." Kathryn sighed and looked away from the

steamboat and up at Jenn. "I wouldn't want to get in the way. In *your* way."

Jenn nodded. "I understand. It's a large boat, but I understand if you have other plans."

A waitress appeared and placed a Caesar salad on the table in front of Kathryn. Kathryn thanked her, the waitress nodded and left them alone again.

"I'll leave you to your lunch," Jenn said. "Seriously, though, if you're at a loose end you should come along. We depart at two, and I guarantee you'll enjoy it. I'll leave a ticket for you at check-in, in case you decide to come along."

"Thank you." Kathryn nodded politely. "I'll think about it."

Jenn nodded and gave an awkward wave goodbye before walking towards the dock. As she walked, she rolled her eyes at herself. What was she thinking inviting Kathryn on board? And why did she *wave* goodbye?

On the bright side, Kathryn didn't seem to hate her, and all was forgiven. That knowledge alone added a spring to her step.

12

ALL ABOARD

JENN WALKED along the dockside while the boat was being prepared for the upcoming cruise. Passengers were starting to gather and wait to board, so she approached them and asked about their hometowns, vacation plans, and offered suggestions for restaurants and where to find the best jazz in town.

She was asked many of the same questions time and again. Best gumbo, best jazz, best beignets. She mixed it up a bit, she didn't want to sound like she had a favourite or was driving customers to a certain establishment.

It also meant she had to ensure she was up to date with what was going on in New Orleans. She didn't want to recommend somewhere that had closed a month ago. It was another reason why the job was a pleasure and a challenge.

She looked up at the gathering crowd, trying to see if she could spot Kathryn. When she didn't see her, she found she was torn between relief and disappointment.

"Jenn!"

She spun around at the sound of her name. Her English

friend Rebecca ran to meet her, and they collided in a messy hug.

"Bex!" She sprinted over and held out her arms. "It's so good to see you!"

"So good to see you, too!" Rebecca greeted her.

Jenn took a step back and looked at her friend. It had been years since they'd seen each other.

"You haven't changed a bit," Jenn said.

"Neither have you! Well, more tanned."

"And you're just as pale as ever."

"Guilty, trying to fix that, though," Rebecca said.

Jenn looked around. "Where's your girlfriend?"

Rebecca chuckled. "I told you, Arabella is not my girlfriend. Just… a friend. Who I'm travelling with."

"Right." Jenn clucked her tongue.

Rebecca playfully elbowed her in the ribs. "Hey, I'm not saying I wouldn't be happy—ecstatic, even—if it happened. It's just not happening yet."

"I hear you. So, where is your not-girlfriend?"

"Chilling at the hotel spa. She's been majorly stressed with work, so she's taking a day out to relax. She's joining us for dinner, though. She's looking forward to meeting you."

"I'm looking forward to meeting her. You don't talk about anyone else lately," Jenn joked.

Rebecca's cheeks started to redden. It was true, though; most of Rebecca's recent communications had included mentions of the mysterious Arabella. Ever since they had shared a journey over Christmas. It was clear that Rebecca was head over heels for the woman.

Jenn had tried to ferret out more information, but Rebecca had been reticent. Finally, she promised that she would dish the dirt when they met up in the summer.

"Yeah, yeah, whatever," Rebecca now sidestepped the subject. "When's this boat get moving?"

"You're coming along?" Jenn asked.

"Of course! You said I had to see it, so I here I am."

"That's great! I thought you might be jetlagged."

"I can sleep when I die," Rebecca joked. She pulled a leaflet out of her shorts pocket and opened it up. "Besides, I'm looking forward to listening to 'soothing jazz' while eating 'world-class food'."

Jenn laughed. "Hey, I didn't write that. But the jazz is soothing. And the food... well, it's not going to hurt you. Too bad."

Her walkie-talkie sprang to life, and the captain gave the all-clear for passengers to begin boarding. Jenn looked apologetically at Rebecca.

"Hey, it's fine, I knew you'd be working. I'll just hang around and entertain myself, no problem," Rebecca reassured her.

"We'll catch up later," Jenn promised.

She started the passenger boarding process, beginning by assisting a wheelchair-bound passenger up the ramp and onto the boat. She positioned the passenger and her family at the back of the boat with the best view of the enormous paddlewheel.

She watched as other customers boarded and started to make their way around the ship, seeking out the best views and the most comfortable seats. She walked around and greeted people, introducing herself and answering still more questions.

The jazz ensemble gathered in the central room in the middle of the boat, and the sound of music swept over the entire ship through its speakers. It was looking to be another wonderful day on the Mississippi.

The steamboat's whistle loudly sounded, and the ropes were untied from the dock. The large paddlewheel slowly came to life, manoeuvring the boat onto the river.

Everyone's attention was diverted to the iconic wheel as it carved its way through the water. Jenn took the opportunity to go down towards the engine room and crew area to grab a drink.

The boat was a maze of levels and stairwells. After grabbing a bottle of water, Jenn navigated her way along the boat, taking five different sets of stairs to get to the front of the ship.

The front of the boat was always empty at the start of the cruise, as passengers made a beeline for the large wheel at the back, so Jenn was surprised when she arrived on the prow's lower deck and saw someone sitting at a table reading a book. Her surprise increased as she realised that someone was Kathryn.

"You came." Jenn smiled and looked at the book Kathryn was absorbed in. "And you're reading about the streetcars?"

"Yes, on both counts," Kathryn agreed. She glanced at the front of the book. "I met someone with a passion for the streetcars, and she made them sound so fascinating I had to learn more."

Jenn smiled at the compliment. "You're missing the wheel."

"The wind is coming from the east," Kathryn pointed out. "As delightful as the river is, I don't want to be covered in it. I'll take a look at it once we turn around."

"Okay, well, I'll leave you to your book and the river. I hope you have a nice and relaxing cruise. I'll see you around."

Jenn passed Kathryn to make her way towards the rear of the boat.

"Jenn?"

She paused and turned to see Kathryn looking at her.

"Thank you for inviting me," Kathryn said, smiling.

"You're welcome."

"Hello again!" Jenn turned to see Rebecca approaching

them, but she wasn't greeting her. For some reason, she was speaking to Kathryn.

"Small world," Kathryn said, and she closed her book.

"You—you know each other?" Jenn stammered.

"Yep, we're staying in the same hotel," Rebecca said. "We met last night at the bar."

Kathryn gestured to the chair beside her. "Would you like to join me?"

"Sounds great." Rebecca dropped herself into the chair. "What are you reading?"

Jenn heard someone call her name, she was needed elsewhere. She looked at her friend and her crush and realised they were in their own world, talking to each other, completely unaware of her.

She turned and hurried away. Now she was regretting inviting Kathryn on board. How did she know Rebecca? A chat at the hotel bar? What had they discussed?

She took a deep breath to calm herself. Rebecca was a friend, and she was in love with Arabella. And Kathryn was very, very straight. The worst that could happen was some mild discomfort if Rebecca told Kathryn an embarrassing story. Or if Kathryn told Rebecca about the kiss.

She stopped walking and let out a groan. Why did they have to know each other? And why did she have to fall for straight girls?

13

REALISATION

ARABELLA LET OUT A LONG SIGH. The spa was pure bliss.
Her back had been pummelled by her technician, Dhia, for
sixty minutes. Now she was relaxing on a comfortable bed,
her hair wrapped in a towel, her face covered in some anti-
ageing, collagen-infused product that left her skin tingling.

To say she was relaxed would be an understatement. The
hotel fire alarm could sound, and she would wave it away
and tell the flames she'd be out in another ten minutes. There
was a fresh smell in the air. It smelt like the mountains
without all the fuss and bother of travelling. And she could
hear wind chimes, not annoying ones, just the occasional
chime, as well as the sound of a babbling brook.

"Everything okay, Miss Henley?" Dhia asked.

"Perfection," Arabella replied.

Her eyes were closed and all the stresses that had laid so
heavily on her just an hour ago seemed to be inconsequen-
tial. For the first time in a long time, she felt like she had
clarity in her life. Like she had time to stop and think.

There were no clients on the telephone, no junior agent

who needed to be trained, no receptionist who hung up while transferring every single important call.

It was just her.

A smile caused her lips to curl slightly beneath the mask. She missed Rebecca. While that wouldn't ordinarily be a thing to smile about, it gave her a clarity that had been absent recently.

The previous night she had been devastated at the idea of Rebecca being with another woman. She had almost fainted at breakfast when she realised that Rebecca had innocently spent the early hours of the morning in the gym.

She obviously had feelings for Rebecca. Feelings that she had never quite managed to explain. She'd spent the last few months trying to decide what she was, attempting to put an exact label on what she wanted her relationship with Rebecca to be.

When she had asked Rebecca to give her time, she had naively expected to be able to return at a later date with the exact parameters of their new relationship. She anticipated that she'd be able to tie it all up in a nice bow, place a label on it, and move on with her life.

Except that never happened. She never found a label. She could never decide what she was, or what she wanted. Half of the time, just thinking about it sent her into a panicked spiral. She wondered if her whole life had been a lie. She'd been engaged to be married to a man. Had she ever loved him? Did she know what love was? Was she even capable of love?

It was only now, in the calmness of the spa, that she realised she had missed a huge piece of the jigsaw puzzle. At no point had she spoken to Rebecca and asked for her help and guidance on her newly discovered feelings.

Instead, she'd spent most of her time avoiding Rebecca,

or worse, snapping at her while her brain did somersaults trying to come to a conclusion.

Rebecca was the one person she knew who could help her figure out her feelings. Of course, Rebecca had at some point realised her own sexuality, and she seemed very comfortable with that. Arabella couldn't imagine that had been easy, and she would bet that Rebecca had assistance in finding her way.

Of course, it was very important to her that she didn't lead Rebecca on. Whether Rebecca was a close friend, or something more intimate, she was important to Arabella. If possible, Arabella wanted to remain on good terms with her.

But she needed to talk to her. As uncomfortable as that conversation might be. As embarrassing as it could end up. She needed to tell Rebecca what was going on in her mind and ask for Rebecca's help in finding her way.

She'd asked for space and Rebecca had given her oceans of it. She'd been more patient and understanding than Arabella ever would have been. Now it was time to come clean and be open with her, to tell her what little she had worked out for herself and ask for help with the rest of it.

She'd been blinded by jealousy the previous evening, suffocated by it as she tried to sleep. Eventually, she'd had to take medication to get the mental images out of her mind.

It was time to speak to Rebecca, before she lost her to someone else.

14

WOMAN OVERBOARD

KATHRYN LOWERED her book and looked out at the river. She had to admit, it was a peaceful feeling to be sailing up the river on an original steamboat.

She regarded the woman beside her. Rebecca was taking photographs with what looked like an extremely expensive camera.

It seemed that New Orleans was a very small city, or at least the part of it that she had toured was. First, she was constantly bumping into Jenn, now Rebecca as well. She smiled to herself as she remembered Jenn's panicked look when she realised that she and Rebecca knew each other. That was definitely something to explore.

"Photographer?" Kathryn enquired casually.

"Yes. Well, freelance," Rebecca replied. "But when you work for yourself like that, work and social life kind of drift into one."

"I can imagine. It must be hard to turn off."

"Impossible," Rebecca agreed. "But it's okay, I'm doing something I love."

Rebecca replaced her lens cap and put the camera on the table between them. She looked at the book in Kathryn's lap.

"Streetcars?"

"Mmm. It was in the hotel lobby, so I thought I'd borrow it."

Rebecca nodded. "So, the kissing conductor was... Jenn?"

"It was," Kathryn confirmed. "I must thank you for your words of wisdom last night, you certainly put things into context for me."

"I'm glad." Rebecca smiled.

Kathryn leaned forward. "So, how do you know Jenn?"

"We've known each other for years," Rebecca replied. "We met when we were both visiting New York. We sat next to each other on an open-top bus tour. Been friends ever since."

Kathryn nodded. She remained silent for a moment, in the hope that Rebecca would choose to share more information. She wanted to know if Jenn had spoken about her, if the two had ever been more than just friends, everything. Suddenly, with no work to occupy her mind, this was at the forefront of her brain.

Rebecca continued to look out at the river.

Kathryn rolled her eyes. She would have to prompt the woman, it seemed. "Did she... say anything to you?"

"About you?" Rebecca asked.

"Yes, about last night."

Rebecca shook her head. "Nothing. I arrived yesterday, today was the first time we've spoken, and we haven't had much time to catch up."

Kathryn let out a small sigh of relief. The last thing she wanted was to be the butt of some joke between the two.

"But," Rebecca continued, "now I know that it was Jenn

that kissed you, I can honestly say that she's probably just as mortified about the mistake as you were."

"I wasn't mortified," Kathryn defended.

Rebecca gave her a look.

"Okay, I was… well, I overreacted," Kathryn admitted. "But I've calmed down now, and I realise it was all a big misunderstanding. I saw Jenn at lunchtime, and she apologised and invited me here. So, it's all been ironed out."

"I'm glad to hear that, Jenn's a great person. And if you're visiting New Orleans then there is no one better to show you around."

"Will she be showing you around, too? And your friend I met at breakfast?" Kathryn asked.

Rebecca smothered a small cough and returned her attention to the view. She was clearly regretting her decision to tell Kathryn about her unrequited love for her traveling companion, though Kathryn wasn't sure what Rebecca saw in the uptight and rude English woman she had been introduced to that morning.

"Y—yeah, she will," Rebecca answered. "We're having dinner tonight."

"I hope you have a nice time, and I hope you manage to figure things out with your friend… Arabella, was it?" Kathryn asked. She didn't want Rebecca to be nervous that she would blurt out her secret and cause problems for her.

Rebecca's calm and collected thoughts from the previous evening had managed to cut through the drunken fear and settle her mind.

She'd overreacted to the kiss, pure and simple. The stress of the day, and the past few months, had built up and she'd lashed out unexpectedly.

"Yeah." Rebecca nodded.

"Doesn't she like cruises?" Kathryn asked.

"She's having a spa day. She's had a rough few weeks,"

Rebecca explained. "First day of holiday, so she wanted to relax in the spa and meet up later."

She looked like she could use some unwinding, Kathryn thought. *And get the stick surgically removed from her ass.*

"Sounds like a good idea," she said aloud. "I browsed through the spa brochure myself, but I couldn't resist heading out for a coffee. I'm still not sure New Orleans is the place for me, but they do make great coffee."

Rebecca looked surprised. "You don't like New Orleans?"

Kathryn shrugged. "It's not really my kind of place." She held up her hand to ward off Rebecca's next question. "It wasn't exactly my choice to come here, long story."

Rebecca blinked. "Right... so, you're here on holiday, but you never chose to come here?"

"Essentially, yes. If I had my choice, New Orleans wouldn't be somewhere I would come and visit."

Rebecca chuckled. "No wonder Jenn took you on the streetcars. She loves New Orleans and will do anything to help people see it through her eyes."

"So I've noticed. And she's everywhere! Seriously, how many jobs does she have?"

Rebecca shrugged. "I lost count. She likes doing a bit of this and a bit of that."

"She's everywhere," Kathryn repeated incredulously.

Rebecca smiled. "She likes to work. When she first arrived here, she struggled to find a job in the city, so she came to the French Quarter and took on a few part-time jobs. She enjoyed them so much that she never left most of them, and now she likes the variation."

Kathryn couldn't imagine what Jenn's schedule must look like. She couldn't imagine not knowing where she'd be from one day to the next, or one week to the next. She liked having her own desk, her own belongings surrounding her.

"I'm sorry, I can't stand it any longer," Rebecca

announced. "Why are you here if you don't want to be here?" She threw up her hands. "I don't get it."

Kathryn smiled. "I was visiting the business quarter for a conference with my sister, we run a PR company together. I thought we were driving home, but she'd booked me into the hotel without telling me and was planning to abandon me here. An enforced vacation."

"Wow, wish I had a sister who would book me into a swanky hotel and force me to have a vacation," Rebecca said.

Kathryn laughed. "Well, let's just say I've been difficult to work with for a while. There's been a lot of family stress lately."

"I'm sorry to hear that."

"It's okay, I wasn't dealing with it very well. Erica decided to kill two birds with one stone. Keep me out of the way while a big deal is being signed in the office and force me to take a break." Kathryn stretched her legs out and rested them on a metal railing. "I hate to admit it, but I think she was right. As much as I hated being dropped here—and I really did hate that—I'm feeling a little better. I'm itching to check my email, but waking up this morning with no obligations was a very new feeling. A nice feeling."

"Sounds like you needed a holiday," Rebecca said.

"I did. So, as I said, I wouldn't have chosen New Orleans, but I'm learning to co-exist with it."

Rebecca opened her mouth to reply, but before she could formulate any words, a shout and then a splash sounded from the side of the ship.

Kathryn spun her head around. "Was that... someone going in?"

Rebecca was on her feet and rushing to the railing to see what was going on. "There's a man in the water!"

Kathryn stood beside her. They were on the bottom deck, only inches from the water due to the uniquely flat design of the steamboat. She spotted a man spluttering in the river. People were screaming from one of the top decks.

"Did he fall?" Kathryn asked.

"He looks plastered, I think he might have fallen," Rebecca replied.

A flash of movement from the back of the boat caught Kathryn's eye. Jenn was on the lower deck, looking out at the river. A moment later, she had climbed the railing and was in the water, too.

"What the hell is she doing?" Kathryn cried.

Rebecca pointed to the water where the man had vanished. "He went under."

"Shouldn't she throw a preserver to him or something?" Kathryn demanded. "Not go in there herself!"

"Did you see how uncoordinated he was? He wouldn't have caught or held onto a life ring." Rebecca moved along the deck to get a better view of what was going on. Kathryn was right beside her.

"Why isn't anyone else going in?" Kathryn asked. She looked around, hoping to spot another member of staff.

Rebecca took off her sunglasses and handed them to Kathryn. She started to climb the railing.

"Ma'am!"

Rebecca paused. A member of the crew was running towards her.

"Ma'am, step off the railing, please. We need to keep the number of people in the water to a minimum."

Kathryn looked over to where Jenn was struggling with the man, trying to pull him up so he could breath. Every now and then both their heads disappeared beneath the water line.

"She needs help!" Kathryn shouted.

"Ma'am, she is fully trained to deal with these situations. Please, let her do her job."

Kathryn wanted to punch the woman. She wanted to jump in herself, except that she knew that she wasn't a strong enough swimmer to save herself, never mind two other people.

Rebecca climbed down, but she was clutching onto the railing and staring helplessly into the water.

"How long do we wait before we do something?" she demanded.

An alarm was blaring across the ship. Kathryn had been so caught up with the drama that she hadn't even heard it begin. A few more members of the crew were gathering at the back of the ship now, pulling on ropes and preparing a lifebuoy.

She looked back out into the water. Her breath caught in her throat when she couldn't see either Jenn or the drunken man. For a brief second, they both completely vanished from sight, as if they had never been there at all.

Ice cold fear washed over Kathryn. She felt as if she were the one drowning.

Suddenly Jenn spluttered to the surface. A determined look fixed on her face, she waved over to her crew mates, and a rope was thrown into the murky water.

Kathryn gripped onto the handrail as if it were her own lifeline. She watched as Jenn caught the rope and expertly weaved it around herself, all while keeping her charge safe and above the water.

The alarm blared all around her. People on the decks above were screaming and crying, but everything faded as Kathryn focused on Jenn, willing her to get back to the safety of the ship.

It was agonisingly slow going, but, eventually, Jenn was secured to the rope and her colleagues pulled her in. Kathryn hurried towards the aft of the ship but was stopped by the crew member who had stopped Rebecca from jumping in the water.

"Sorry, ma'am, I'm going to have to ask you to remain here."

Kathryn paused. She stood on her tiptoes to look over the woman and watched as Jenn was dragged aboard.

15

ANGRY CONCERN

JENN THOUGHT back to every time she had ever complained about the stifling heat of a summer in New Orleans and wished she could feel like that again. Her teeth wouldn't stop chattering. The thick blanket that had been wrapped around her shoulders seemed to be doing no good at all.

The sensible thing to do would be to go up on deck and sit in the sun, but she needed some time to herself, away from the passengers. Not to mention no one wanted to smell her at the moment.

As soon as she had been pulled aboard, she was dragged to the calm of the staff room, a room in the middle of the ship with no windows.

She was checked over by the only other person on the ship who had a first aid certificate and was deemed to simply need to rest. This was her assessment, too. The drama quickly died down, and her colleagues quickly went back to work to leave her to recover.

She realised she was being watched and looked up. In the doorway, arms folded and with a furious expression, was Kathryn.

Jenn didn't say anything. She looked back down at the large pool of water that was forming below the wooden bench she was sitting on.

"I thought you were dead," Kathryn angrily informed her.

Jenn frowned. "You were worried about me?"

"Of course I was!"

"You seem kinda angry," Jenn pointed out, still staring at the floor.

She heard Kathryn let out a deep breath.

"It all happened so fast," Kathryn said, her tone softer now. She sat on a bench opposite Jenn.

Jenn wanted to point out that it had happened a hell of a lot faster from her perspective but figured now wasn't the time to be arguing.

She shivered again, curling into herself even more tensely and gripping the blanket tightly. When her eyes closed, she could see the entire thing as if it were happening again.

The guy was in his late thirties and had obviously been appreciating New Orleans freely available alcohol for some time before he boarded the steamboat.

The moment she spotted him, she had made a mental note to keep an eye on him. Years of working in bars had provided her with a sixth sense when it came to identifying troublemakers.

It wasn't long before he was standing on the railing, arms stretched, releasing his inner Kate Winslet. In a flash, he lost his footing and plunged into the water.

Jenn knew that he was too drunk to be able to swim, and probably too gone to even catch the lifebuoy. She radioed the incident into the captain, pulled the alarm, and ran down the steps to the lower deck before plunging into the murky water.

The water had been freezing cold, especially when she

dove under to bring the drunken idiot back to the surface. It took a few attempts to grab hold of him, she had to resort to using touch as the muddy water meant visibility was practically zero.

She knew she was racing against the clock. Not only was she getting colder by the second, but in the back of her mind she knew how notoriously difficult it was to slow or manoeuvre a steamboat. The longer she was in the water, the farther the boat would be from her, and the harder it would be to get back aboard.

It had been less than ten minutes between her jumping into the river and being pulled back on the boat. The passenger was being taken care of in the first aid room. Jenn was thankful to be away from him.

The silence was becoming thick. She could feel Kathryn's eyes boring into the top of her head, but no words were coming.

"I'm fine," Jenn finally said.

"That remains to be seen," Kathryn huffed.

Jenn let out a small chuckle. "Seriously, I'm just a bit cold, I'll warm up in no time." As if to prove her point, her body involuntarily shuddered again.

She heard Kathryn get up. A moment later she felt the woman take a seat beside her and wrap her arm around Jenn's blanket-covered shoulder. Kathryn pulled her close in a futile attempt to help warm her.

"Thank you," Jenn mumbled.

"You were under the water for so long and no one was doing anything."

"Standard procedure," Jenn admitted quietly. "Once someone has gone in, you have to wait before anyone else goes in after them or there'll be more crew in the water than on the boat."

"I thought you were dead," Kathryn repeated. The arm

around her shoulder tightened.

"Jenn, are you okay?"

She looked up to see Rebecca rushing into the staff room. She had a takeaway mug of coffee in one hand and another blanket in the other. Kathryn stood up and took the blanket from Rebecca and proceeded to wrap Jenn up in it.

Jenn poked a hand through a gap and gratefully took the mug.

"I'm fine."

"She's not fine," Kathryn argued. "As you can see, she's chilled to the bone."

"I'm fine," Jenn repeated. It was becoming a mantra.

"Can I get you anything else?" Rebecca asked. She sat on the bench opposite.

Jenn took a sip of the drink. Coffee, milky and sweet, just as she liked it.

"No, I'm good. Welcome to New Orleans," Jenn joked.

Rebecca laughed. "Yeah, non-stop entertainment."

Jenn shrugged. "We try to keep people happy. And alive."

"He better thank you for saving his drunken ass," Kathryn said. She took her seat beside Jenn and placed a hand on her back.

Jenn wished the blankets weren't so thick. She would have been cold, but at least she would have been able to feel Kathryn's hand more easily.

She suddenly remembered that she was due for a short shift in CeeCee's later. There was no way she could go there covered in Mississippi mud, and it would take her too much time to head home to shower and then head out again.

Rebecca saw her panic. "What's up?"

"I need to call CeeCee's and tell them I can't make it later. I'm due to work for a couple of hours before we meet up for dinner," Jenn explained.

"Where's your phone?" Rebecca stood up.

Jenn thought for a moment. "I left my bag behind the bar on the top deck."

"No problem, I'll grab it. Back in a few."

Jenn watched Rebecca leave. She sipped at the coffee again, relishing the warmth it brought her, even if it was temporary.

"You don't have to sit here," she said to Kathryn. "I'm okay. You should go back to the cruise. The gumbo is really good. And the jazz band, you should go listen to them play."

"Would you say it's the best gumbo and jazz in New Orleans?"

Jenn turned to looked at Kathryn curiously. "What do you mean?"

"Is the gumbo the best I will taste in New Orleans? Is the band the best I will hear?" Kathryn repeated.

"Well, no. But they—"

"Then I'm fine here. Unless you want to be alone?"

"No. I just—"

"Then I'm fine here," Kathryn insisted. "We'll just sit together, and maybe you can tell me where I can find the best gumbo?"

Jenn smiled and nodded. "Sure, I can suggest a few places. You should try Mama Dee's, great food there. And ambiance, in fact—"

"I kind of hoped you'd *show* me the best places," Kathryn hinted. "As friends, of course."

Jenn felt her eyes widen. "Oh, okay. Yes, that sounds great."

Kathryn chuckled. She reached into her bag and pulled out a small notepad and a pen. She flipped the pad open and wrote down a number before tearing the sheet of paper out and handing it to Jenn.

"The hotel number, and my room number. Maybe you

could give me a call when you have a ten-minute window between your numerous jobs."

"How about tonight?" Rebecca asked as she walked back into the staff room. "We can all have dinner together. Arabella won't mind."

Jenn was so relieved that Rebecca had offered. She'd wanted to immediately invite Kathryn out that evening, not wanting to miss an opportunity. But she didn't want to sound overly eager, nor did she want to cancel on Rebecca and Arabella.

Kathryn looked from Rebecca to Jenn and smiled. "That sounds great." She stood up and pointed towards the door. "I'll leave you to make your call and freshen up. Call me and let me know where and when to meet." She walked towards the door and paused. "As friends."

"As friends." Jenn nodded quickly.

Kathryn looked Jenn up and down one last time before leaving the staff room. She left, and Jenn listened to the sound of her walking down the narrow, echoing corridor. Once she was sure that Kathryn could no longer hear her, she turned to Rebecca and beamed happily.

"Thank you!"

"No problem," Rebecca said. She held out Jenn's bag for her. "I heard the end of the conversation—you couldn't let an opportunity like that go. I can see the way you look at her."

"Yeah, but it won't go anywhere," Jenn said. "She's straight. But she's cool, when you get to know her."

"She told me about what happened last night," Rebecca said.

Jenn felt her cheeks burn with embarrassment.

"She was at the bar, a bit tipsy. She saw my rainbow flag badge and wanted to know if she looked gay," Rebecca explained.

Jenn snorted a laugh. "What did you say?"

Rebecca sat down and shrugged. "Who looks gay these days?"

"True. You sure you don't mind inviting her to dinner with us? Will Arabella mind?"

"She'll be fine," Rebecca reassured her. "But do I need to give you the standard warning about falling for a straight woman?"

Jenn laughed. "No, I'm okay, I promise. Yeah, I have a thing for her, but she's fun to be friends with. Just... enjoying my life."

Rebecca looked at her for a moment before finally nodding her head. "As long as you know what you're doing," she said.

"I do. Well, I think I do," Jenn replied. "What's the worst that can happen?"

"Broken heart?" Rebecca suggested.

Jenn bit her lip. Rebecca was right. It wasn't fun and games to pine over someone you couldn't have. Even if she convinced herself that she was just friends with Kathryn, in the back of her mind she knew that she wanted more. And Rebecca was suffering through the same issues. She'd have to get the gossip on what was happening with her and Arabella. Later, when she'd stopped shivering.

16

PROFESSIONAL PAIN IN MY ARSE

ARABELLA HEARD Rebecca's hotel door closing. She marked her place in her book and set it to one side. She sat on the bed, able to see her reflection in the large mirror on the opposite wall. She looked nervous.

She took a deep breath before shuffling off the sumptuously soft bed. Crossing to the mirror, she looked at her reflection again and adjusted her hair a little.

She'd made the decision to speak with Rebecca as soon as she returned. No more beating around the bush, no more silent treatment, no more flares of anger. They were both grown-ups and could handle adult conversations.

Leaning in close to the mirror, she checked her mascara and then straightened the collar on her short-sleeved blouse.

An excited knock on the door sounded through the room.

"Arabella? You in there?"

Her eyes widened in shock. She hadn't expected Rebecca to call on her so suddenly. She looked around the room, checking that everything was in place.

"Arabella?" Rebecca called again.

"Coming," Arabella replied. She lunged for her book and shoved it in the drawer of the bedside table. She didn't need Rebecca knowing that she was reading a self-help book about how to empower her subconscious brain.

She took a deep breath and opened the door. Rebecca rushed into the room a second later.

"Oh my god, you will not believe what you missed today," Rebecca announced.

Arabella smiled as Rebecca plonked herself down on the edge of the bed and leaned back onto her hands.

"Jenn dove into the Mississippi River and saved a drunk man. And, let me tell you, that river ain't clean." Rebecca made a face.

"Is she okay?" Arabella asked. She pulled out the chair at the desk and sat down.

"Yes, she's fine. I was just sitting there chatting with Kathryn and then splash—"

"Kathryn?" Arabella interrupted. She felt her nails dig into the upholstered arm of the chair.

"Yes, we met her at breakfast this morning," Rebecca reminded her.

As if she needed reminding.

"So... you arranged to meet her today?" Arabella asked.

"No, I think Jenn invited her," Rebecca said. She sat up. "Anyway, I heard this splash and we looked over—"

"Jenn knows her?" Arabella asked.

"Yeah, they met yesterday. We're having dinner with them both tonight," Rebecca said quickly, clearly wanting to get onto the next part of her story. "Anyway... splash."

"Splash," Arabella agreed. She wasn't going to get anything else out of Rebecca until she'd told her story.

"Right." Rebecca's eyes flashed with excitement. "So,

there's this man in the water. Drunk as a skunk. No way he's rescuing himself. Then the alarm is blaring, and people are screaming. And Jenn just jumps in after him."

Rebecca jumped to her feet and walked over to the window to start pacing. "So, Kathryn and I are watching and they both keep going under the water. And the crew are gathering at the back of the boat, but no one is doing anything. So, I climb up onto the railing—"

"Don't you dare tell me you jumped in," Arabella demanded. She looked Rebecca over critically. She didn't look like someone who had taken an unscheduled swim in the toxic-looking river. But there was always the chance she'd done so and then had a shower and cleaned up. Not that a shower would protect her from the untold nastiness that was obviously lurking in the murky waterway.

"No, this woman stopped me before I had the chance."

"Good!" Arabella felt her hand shake at the thought of Rebecca diving into the water. Even though she knew she was safe and well, the terror of what might have happened was palpable.

"Anyway, eventually they got their act together and threw her a rope. It was a mess. Kathryn was livid." Rebecca looked out of the window, peering down at the street below.

Kathryn again. Arabella pursed her lips and turned away. "I thought we were only meeting up with Jenn for dinner?"

"We were," Rebecca replied distractedly. Something at street level had caught her attention. "But Kathryn invited Jenn out, so I thought I'd ask her to come and join us tonight."

Arabella frowned. She couldn't fathom the connections. "Can you please explain to me who Kathryn is, how she knows Jenn, how she knows you, and why I'm suddenly having dinner with her?"

So much for no flares of anger.

Rebecca turned around, confusion clear on her face. "I didn't think you would mind. I... I can cancel?"

"Who. Is. Kathryn?"

"She's just someone on holiday," Rebecca explained. "She came to the city yesterday and bumped into Jenn. Then they arranged to meet up later that evening. Jenn thought it was a date, but Kathryn's straight—"

Thank you, lord, Arabella thought.

"Jenn tried to kiss her at the end of the not-date. Kathryn came back to the hotel to have a drink, I bumped into her and she asked me if she looked gay. She saw my rainbow badge. Anyway... Jenn saw her this morning and apologised and invited her to go on the cruise."

Arabella could feel her heart rate returning to normal. Kathryn was straight. And Jenn was interested in her. No messy spanners in the works.

"Kathryn realised she overreacted after the kiss and wants to apologise to Jenn. Jenn is crazy about her, I think. Kathryn wanted to have dinner with Jenn one night while she's in town, so I invited her along with us tonight. That way Jenn can still meet up with us and see Kathryn at the same time. And I can keep an eye on Jenn."

"Keep an eye on her?" Arabella asked.

"She's got a classic crush on a straight woman, I need to make sure she doesn't get hurt," Rebecca answered.

Arabella bristled a little. Had she hurt Rebecca by not being honest about her feelings? Was this a thing in the lesbian community? Accidentally falling for straight women and having your heart broken?

"Do you mind having dinner, all four of us?" Rebecca sought clarification.

"No, the more the merrier." Of course, Arabella wasn't

over the moon about spending more time with Kathryn, but at least Jenn would be there to keep her occupied.

"I think you'll like her, you're a lot alike."

Arabella flared her nostrils. "Oh, really? And what, pray tell, do we have in common?"

No more being nice, she wasn't standing for being compared to some drunken barfly with gay panic and a terrible accent.

"Um." Rebecca's eyes widened in panic. "Well, you... she works in PR."

"P. R." Arabella raised her eyebrow. "And what, precisely, does PR have to do with me?"

"I mean she's a professional," Rebecca said. Her tongue darted out and licked her lips.

Professional pain in my arse.

"Like, she... owns skirt suits and works in an office," Rebecca continued.

Arabella stared at her. "Owns suits... and works in an office. I see. I'm glad you have such a thorough understanding of the complexities of our individual personalities to know that we'll be best friends based upon your uncanny observations of our practically identical lifestyles."

She stood up and stalked into the bathroom. She picked up her makeup bag and tossed it carelessly onto the counter. She shook her head and turned on her heel and entered the main room again.

"It's because I'm old, isn't it? She's old, I'm old. Boom. We'll do cross-stitch together. As long as our eyesight doesn't go first." She folded her arms and glared at Rebecca.

"Old? She's not—I mean **you're** not old. Neither of you are old. I mean, I don't even know how old you are!" Rebecca's eyes flicked between her and the open interconnecting door, clearly wanting to escape before she buried her leg in her mouth up to the kneecap.

Arabella shook her head and walked back into the bathroom. She angrily unzipped her makeup bag. The copious bottles of lotions and potions stared back at her mockingly.

She let out a sigh and leaned heavily on the sink. She closed her eyes and hung her head in shame.

17

OLD

REBECCA LET out the breath that had been trapped in her throat since a furious Arabella had demanded to know, essentially, if she was considered old. She knew that Arabella was insecure about her age and her looks. A few days after she first met Arabella, she had discovered that the woman travelled with a *case* of makeup.

Since then, Rebecca had noticed that Arabella never let anyone see her unless she was perfectly presented. Her hair, makeup, and clothes were always fussed to faultlessness.

Rebecca took a deep inhale of air-conditioned goodness and approached the open bathroom door. Arabella stood in front of the sink, bracing herself for impact against the white porcelain. Eyes closed, head slung dejectedly downwards.

She opened her mouth to speak when she heard Arabella mumble something. It was so quiet that it was lost immediately in the space between them.

"I didn't hear that," Rebecca said.

"Forty-three."

Rebecca swallowed. She had gotten the impression that Arabella only mentioned her age to people she had power over, or those she would soon be murdering. And she knew that now was definitely not the time to mention that she suspected that Kathryn was considerably younger than Arabella.

Arabella stood up and turned towards Rebecca with a solemn expression.

"Now you know."

Rebecca brought her hand up to her mouth in a pathetic attempt to cover her smile.

Arabella frowned. "You're... laughing at me?"

"I'm sorry, it's just you've said your age in the same way some people deliver news of a death." She couldn't help but let out a small snort. "Doctor, will he be okay? I'm terribly sorry, miss, he's forty-three."

Arabella stared at her, blinking a few times. "This isn't a laughing matter."

"I beg to disagree, it's hysterical," Rebecca said as she fought to hold back giggles. "You sound like you're telling a child that you killed their puppy."

Arabella opened her mouth, and Rebecca knew that whatever was about to come out wouldn't be pleasant. She quickly walked forward and cupped her hand over Arabella's open mouth.

"You're not old. You're not even middle-aged. Forty-three is nothing. Nothing at all. I know people say it all the time, but it's true; you're as young as you feel. And I know you worry about your looks... but you're beautiful. With and without makeup. Like, seriously... breathtakingly beautiful."

She felt her cheeks begin to heat up and realised that this was the exact opposite of giving Arabella the space she had requested. She looked up into Arabella's shocked eyes and took a hesitant step back, removing her hand from her mouth.

"Sorry." She gestured to her hand. "Didn't mean to...

silence you like that. I just wanted you to really hear what I was saying."

"You don't think I'm old?" Arabella asked, almost breathlessly.

"No, not at all. Forty-three isn't old, not these days. And you look after yourself, you eat well, you exercise…" Rebecca waved her hand towards Arabella's body. "You look amazing. Definitely not old."

"I'm fat," Arabella said as if she were stating that fire was hot.

It was Rebecca's turn to blink silently for a few seconds. "Excuse me?"

Arabella gestured towards her hips, and then her torso. "Fat. And the wrinkles around my eyes."

"Has someone told you that you're fat?" Rebecca demanded. Suddenly she wanted to board a flight back to Heathrow and throttle Alastair. She was sure it was that brainless numbskull.

Arabella looked shocked at Rebecca's harsh tone and took a tiny step back.

"Well, I am…" She gestured again to her body.

Rebecca turned around and presented Arabella with her back for a couple of moments while she let the rage pass over her. Once she was calm enough that she didn't think she would throw something, she turned back again.

"You are *not* fat. No, you're not skin and bone either. You have *curves*, which women are allowed to have. In fact, many people, myself included, think that some curves on a woman are incredibly sexy. And as for wrinkles… it happens when you live your life. You smile and you get lines, you frown and you get lines. It means you've lived your life and experienced things, and nothing is more attractive than that."

Rebecca could feel herself vibrating with anger. She couldn't believe that Arabella felt this way about herself. Sure, she knew she was insecure, but this was more than she'd suspected. How could anyone have ever said anything negative about her? They should have worshipped her, not put her down.

Arabella looked like she was caught between embarrassment and shy gratitude.

"I'm going to go and start to get ready for dinner. I need to shower and stuff," Rebecca said. She needed to get out of the small space with such a vulnerable-looking Arabella before she said something she'd regret.

Give her space, give her space, Rebecca chanted her mantra to herself.

Arabella nodded. "Meet you downstairs?"

"Sure, meet you in the lobby at seven," Rebecca said.

18

CRUISING TOWARDS A BROKEN HEART

Jenn stepped into the shower, relieved when the hot water hit her skin and started to wash off the grimy dirt from the river. She looked at the floor of the shower and grimaced at the dirty water flowing towards the drain.

The thought of a fantastic evening of great food, entertainment, and friendship helped to shake off the residual effects of the biting cold Mississippi that still plagued her.

She'd stayed in the staff room for the rest of the trip, not wanting any of the passengers to catch sight of her looking like the proverbial drowned rat. And definitely not wanting to speak to the man she had rescued. She had very little to say to him that would keep her in employment.

She spent the time thinking about places to eat and things to do that evening. She wanted it to be perfect. Everyone was new to New Orleans and she wanted to show them the very best it had to offer. Especially if that meant that she might be able to win Kathryn over a little. Within ten minutes, she had called in some favours and booked a table at her favourite restaurant.

Kathryn had very clearly stated that dinner wasn't a date,

but that didn't stop Jenn from wanting to go all out when it came to getting ready. There was nothing wrong with getting dressed up, especially after swimming in a river so dirty that you feared you'd never get the smell out of your hair again.

As she poured shampoo into her hand, she thought about Kathryn and all the interactions they'd had to date. To say that she was confused by Kathryn was an understatement. From being convinced that she was a terrible, stuck-up snob, to thinking she was one of the most enigmatic and interesting people she'd met in just a few hours.

And then from the kiss to the realisation of the enormous mistake she'd made. Jenn had run through a ton of emotions in record time.

She lathered the shampoo and worked it into her long hair, letting out a sigh at the knowledge that she'd soon feel more like herself.

She couldn't get the kiss out of her head. It had seemed so perfect. The warm evening air, the sound of the streetcars rumbling along the road, the twinkling lights from the old-fashioned lampposts.

And then there was Kathryn's angry face. Closely followed by the cold wave of dread and panic that hit Jenn like a truck. She turned the temperature of the water up a little to counteract the shiver that ran down her spine.

Jenn didn't like labels, primarily because she didn't know which one to put on herself. She'd started her sexual life being straight, then thinking she might be bisexual, then lesbian, then pansexual. She hadn't dated a man in years, but she still found some attractive. So, pansexual, if she was pushed to put a label on herself. Not that she entirely understood the need for labels.

As terrible as her gaydar had always been, she still couldn't believe how badly she had misread the signals she thought she'd been receiving from Kathryn. It wasn't like

Jenn to go in for a kiss at the end of a date unless she was absolutely certain about things.

She wondered if maybe Kathryn wasn't 100% straight. Maybe, buried deeply within her, lay someone who wasn't sure. That had certainly been the case with Jenn.

Her own first experience with a woman had been with someone who was very comfortable in their sexuality and certainly not new to the idea of a female lover, as Jenn had been. Since then, Jenn's misfiring gaydar had always directed her towards women either as experienced as her or more so.

Jenn had never been anyone's first, and she certainly had no idea about guiding a gay awakening in a supposedly straight woman. Not to mention the fact that Kathryn could actually be straight, despite some of the evidence to the contrary.

She sighed and rinsed the shampoo out of her hair.

Rebecca was right, she might be cruising straight for a broken heart. It was a dangerous game. On one hand, she'd enjoyed her time with Kathryn so much that she wanted to hang out with her more. On the other, she was deeply attracted to Kathryn and hoped for more than just friendship. But could she separate the two?

If Kathryn was absolutely straight and had no interest in Jenn, how would Jenn feel? Especially if they spent more time together. There was a real danger that the more time Jenn spent with Kathryn, the more she would fall for the woman. And that road led to a lot of emotional pain, pain that Jenn desperately wanted to avoid.

She'd always been told that she was a sensitive soul, and it was true. Jenn wore her heart on her sleeve. It had caused her many problems over the years, from falling in love with the wrong person to having people take advantage of her sweet nature.

She closed her eyes and tilted her face towards the water spray.

Why does it have to be so complicated? She wondered.

In the distance she heard her phone beep, signalling that she had forty-five minutes before she had to leave. Her phone was the only reason she ever arrived anywhere on time. She reached for the bottle of conditioner and started to pick up the pace. She had a dinner to get to.

19

EVENING RENDEZVOUS

KATHRYN SAT in the lobby of the Royale and looked around
the lavish space. Understated, it was not. But at least it wasn't
as tacky as most of the rest of New Orleans. No, that was
unfair. Much of New Orleans was very pretty. It was
Bourbon Street and some of the offshoots that were filled
with seedy establishments and the people who frequented
them.

Jenn had proved to her yesterday that New Orleans was
also a place of calm boulevards with timeless charm and
beautiful architecture. And the steamboat on the Mississippi
had been breathtakingly enchanting, up until the moment
where she felt for certain she was about to witness Jenn's
demise.

She shuddered, gripping the plush sofa below her fingers
to ground herself. She tried to ignore the feeling of dread that
had clawed at her as she watched Jenn's head dip below the
water. And she definitely ignored the fact that she had no
such concerns for the drunken man who was just as close to
perishing. He'd gotten himself into the situation by being
drunk and acting the fool.

Natural selection, she mused.

She heard someone walking across the lobby and looked up to see Arabella. She resisted the urge to roll her eyes. Dinner with Jenn was something she was looking forward to, and having Rebecca join them would certainly be enjoyable. But Arabella's stuck-up attitude at breakfast wasn't something she relished sitting through again.

Arabella was thrusting her hand towards her. "Hi, Arabella Henley. I just wanted to apologise for this morning. I'd had a terrible night and I'd yet to have coffee, so I'm afraid I was awful."

Kathryn felt her eyebrow raise off her face. Were her emotions that transparent? "That... perfectly fine." She shook the offered hand. "I was hardly at my best either. Kathryn Foster, by the way."

Arabella smiled kindly. "Then it's a great chance to start again."

Kathryn gestured to the space beside her on the sofa, and Arabella sat down. Kathryn noted that she was wearing a simple white blouse and a draped skirt that fell just below the knees. It was a print that Kathryn recognised; she owned a similar garment.

Having been dumped in New Orleans without the opportunity to pack correctly, Kathryn wore a tight navy-blue dress that she had worn one evening at the conference. It was a little more corporate than she would have liked.

Her sister Erica had taken the opportunity to hide some T-shirts and shorts in her suitcase, but they weren't suitable for dinner. It added to her feeling of insecurity, being incorrectly dressed, in a place that didn't quite suit her.

Arabella glanced at her watch. She rolled her eyes. "Rebecca is always late," she said good-humouredly.

"Sounds like my sister," Kathryn said. "She operates in

her own time zone." She paused. "Correction, more like her own planet."

Arabella chuckled. "Family… what's the saying? Can't live with them, can't live without them?"

"You have no idea." Kathryn shook her head. She wasn't about to explain her family situation to a complete stranger, but she felt for sure that whatever difficulties Arabella had with her family, Kathryn could top them and then some.

She noticed Arabella straighten slightly, her gaze captured by someone exiting the elevators. Without even turning, she knew that Rebecca had arrived.

Arabella stood up and smiled. "You look wonderful," she greeted Rebecca. She gestured to Kathryn. "And look who I found."

Rebecca was wearing a wine-red summer dress. It was lacy around the capped sleeves and stopped just above the knees. It was a complete contrast to what Kathryn had previously seen Rebecca in, but then Rebecca did seem to be a mass of contradictions, and very much her own person.

"You look stunning," Rebecca told Arabella. She quickly looked at Kathryn. "I mean, you both look stunning." Panic settled into Rebecca's eyes, and she looked back at Arabella in fear. Kathryn detected a hint of jealousy from Arabella, or maybe it was just concern on Rebecca's part that Arabella would misinterpret the compliment.

"Everyone's stunning," Kathryn said, trying to defuse what had suddenly become a tense situation. She turned away from the two women who were now shyly looking at each other.

Ridiculous, Kathryn thought. *Why are these two not together? They're obviously interested in one another.*

She turned away, and her breath instantly caught in her chest. Jenn was walking in through the main entrance of the hotel. She was wearing a simple, white, summer dress. For someone who'd been in the river just a few hours ago, she looked ready to be part of a fashion show. To say it wasn't what Kathryn had expected would be an understatement.

Jenn walked towards them, grinning happily.

"Well, you clean up nicely," Kathryn announced.

"I try my best." Jenn winked.

"Jenn, this is Arabella," Rebecca introduced the two.

Kathryn watched as Arabella and Jenn greeted each other. She swallowed hard, bringing some much-needed moisture to her throat. She didn't know what it was about Jenn, but she was strangely drawn to her.

She'd never had any feelings towards women at all. She wasn't a homophobe, but she knew her own mind and her own desires. Clearly, there was something about Jenn that she found fascinating. Surely that could be the case without her being *attracted* to Jenn. Couldn't it?

Jenn turned to face Kathryn. She frowned. "When are you going to get changed?"

Kathryn paused for a split second until she noticed the twinkle in Jenn's eyes. "Rude!" She tapped Jenn's arm with her clutch bag.

"You look great." Jenn smiled.

"I wasn't sure how to dress," Kathryn admitted. "I didn't know if we'd be going to a nice restaurant or if the best gumbo in New Orleans was served through a hole in a wall."

"If it is, then I need to get changed," Arabella joked.

Jenn laughed. "Well, the guidebooks would probably send you to some dirty little café downtown, but don't worry —I know somewhere perfect. It has seats and everything."

"Seats?" Rebecca gushed. "You spoil us."

"Sure do, stick with me. You can trust your local guide," Jenn said.

"I do," Kathryn confessed. "My tour guide is a life-saving, first aid-giving, streetcar-driving, water aerobics instructor."

"Sounds like a fascinating person," Jenn quipped. She gestured for Kathryn to take her arm.

"She certainly is." Kathryn took Jenn's arm and allowed herself to be led out of the lobby and into the city at night.

20

A HIDDEN OASIS

ARABELLA AND REBECCA walked a little way behind Jenn and Kathryn. Arabella could have quite happily ditched the idea of dinner altogether. She was ready to talk to Rebecca. Even more so after her impassioned speech in Arabella's bathroom.

She'd kept her age a secret from most people her entire life. She'd attended a small private school, and most of her classmates had resembled greyhounds being released from a racetrack gate upon graduation day. They'd been so eager to be successes that they had all sprinted off to make their fortunes and hadn't spoken to each other since.

Following university, she'd been given a prestigious role within the family business. She'd lied about her age, attempting to appear older than she was in order to fit in with the other executives.

But time moved on, and one day she realised that she was employing executives younger than she was. She'd stared at the dates of birth on employment applications, wondering if there'd been a typo, thinking that surely someone born in that year should still be in high school. She'd gotten old.

That had happened a few years ago, and now every passing year felt like a large, rusty cog hammering itself into place in an old-fashioned clock. Moving her ever closer to old age, wrinkles, and the scrap heap.

Lying about her age had become second nature, or at least keeping it a closely guarded secret had. And keeping up the illusion required many hours in front of the mirror with enough make-up to give Donald Trump a new career as a runway model. Okay, maybe not *that* much make-up.

"You okay?" Rebecca asked. "You look miles away."

Rebecca had hidden away in her room after her declaration that Arabella was foolish to worry about her age. Arabella knew why, she was giving her time. Sweet, wonderful Rebecca who put everyone else's feelings in front of her own was, yet again, doing just that.

Arabella had wanted to burst into her room. She had wanted to explain what had been going through her mind and announce that she was fed up with hiding how she felt. But this evening wasn't about her, it was about Rebecca meeting up with a dear friend. Dropping a ton of emotional baggage on Rebecca before they went to dinner would have been unfair.

She reached out and took Rebecca's hand in hers. "I'm good, really good."

Rebecca looked in surprise at their joined hands. "G—great."

"Thank you, for what you said earlier," Arabella added. "It meant a lot to me."

"I meant every word," Rebecca promised.

"I know."

They walked in silence for a few more minutes, following Jenn as she expertly navigated the traffic. They turned into a side street and found a small courtyard with cobbles on the ground and trees and ivy interlaced into a canopy above them. Fairy lights twinkled in the foliage.

Rebecca's mouth fell open, and she stared at the surroundings.

Arabella squeezed her hand. "You'll have to come back here with your camera," she suggested.

Rebecca silently nodded, still taking in the beautiful square.

Arabella could practically see the photographer considering angles and lighting, figuring out the best way to frame the shots and the ideal time of day to do so.

Jenn turned around and smiled at Rebecca's awestruck expression. "Thought you might like this place," she said.

Rebecca looked at the doorway they'd come through in confusion. "I passed this road earlier, I had no idea this was here."

"Local knowledge." Jenn tapped the side of her head. "This place has great food, and there's a jazz club in the back-room. I got all of us tickets for the show tonight."

"Jazz in the backroom?" Kathryn asked with a grin. "This place feels like a movie."

"What can I say? We inspired Hollywood," Jenn said. "Shall we head inside?"

Everyone agreed. Jenn led them further into the court-yard and through a set of wooden doors. She spoke with the waiter and soon they were walking up a set of marble steps to the second floor and onto a terrace surrounded with an ornate balcony.

Arabella looked over the balcony and down onto the busy street below. She could see tourists snapping pictures or looking at maps on their phones. On the street corner, one of the many impromptu jazz bands had set up and was playing some of the classics. It was a postcard-perfect scene.

She turned and took her seat at the stunning cast-iron

table. Jenn and Kathryn were examining the menu, and Rebecca was sipping from a freshly poured glass of water.

"Rebecca?" Arabella said softly.

Rebecca looked at her from over the edge of her glass.

"I'm very glad we came here."

Rebecca looked at her strangely, happy but obviously wondering what alien shape-shifter had taken the place of her friend.

"After dinner, maybe we could have drinks in the hotel bar?" Arabella suggested. "Just the two of us."

"S—sure," Rebecca stammered. She shakily placed her glass back on the table.

"Nothing bad," Arabella reassured. "Hopefully, quite the opposite."

Rebecca's eyes sparkled. She nodded her head and grabbed for a menu.

"Let's eat," Rebecca announced to the table.

21

SOMETHING IN THE AIR

JENN NOTICED REBECCA BLUSHING SLIGHTLY, and she wondered what she had missed between her friend and Arabella. She'd been so wrapped up in pointing out interesting dishes to Kathryn that she'd not looked up at the other couple until Rebecca had spoken.

She'd clearly overlooked something, but she wasn't sure what it was. She glanced over the top of her menu towards Arabella. She seemed nice. She was attractive and seemed to be very smart. Jenn could totally see what Rebecca saw in her.

On top of that, Arabella looked at Rebecca like she was ice cream on a hot day. How they had still not quite managed to get together was beyond her. Unless something had recently happened to move the process along? She decided that she'd grill Rebecca about it the next day. For now, she wanted to focus on Kathryn.

She noticed Kathryn's fingers were tapping away on the back of her menu, in time with the lively beat of the jazz being played in the street.

"You like jazz?" Jenn asked.

"I never really listened to it before coming here," Kathryn said.

Jenn's mouth dropped open. She stared at Kathryn, incredulous.

"You've *never* listened to jazz?"

"Nope. Not my style."

"Seems to be your style." Jenn pointed to Kathryn's tapping fingers.

Kathryn paused and looked at her traitorous fingers. "It's catchy. Let's say it's growing on me."

"I love the music here," Rebecca said. "It really brings everything to life, it's so vibrant."

"Yes," Arabella agreed, "and you're extremely lucky that all of your bands appear to be very good. Not like some of the buskers you see in London. You know, I once saw a man playing a road construction cone like a kazoo. I believe it was 'Sweet Home Alabama', but it's hard to tell at a railway station."

"I've seen him!" Rebecca exclaimed. "Victoria Station, right?"

Arabella nodded. "Don't tell me... you thought he was marvellous?"

"I did! He has some lungs to keep that up for the whole of rush hour. I gave him five quid," Rebecca said.

Arabella rolled her eyes. "It's people like you who encourage people like them."

She said it kindly, but it was obvious she meant it.

"Exactly," Kathryn agreed. She gestured towards the band on the street corner. "They have real talent, I'd happily pay them for their time. But why people insist on giving money to people who have no musical talent is beyond me. Like your construction cone gentleman."

Arabella nodded readily, happy to have an ally.

"I don't give him money because I think he's a genius

musician," Rebecca explained. "I give him money because he is probably homeless and needs the money."

Arabella opened her mouth, presumably to argue. Rebecca quickly placed a finger on Arabella's lips to silence her.

"No, we're not talking about this now. We can debate whether or not homeless people buy bread or crack with the money I give them *another* day."

Arabella looked suitably chastised and quickly nodded. Rebecca lowered her hand and continued to examine her menu. Jenn smiled to herself. She could see what Rebecca meant when she'd explained how Arabella could sometimes be a little opinionated. Rebecca had joked that she was still training her.

Jenn plucked the drinks menu from the table. "Well, you can't visit New Orleans without having a real cocktail made by a professional bartender. Anyone want a drink?"

"I'd love a Bellini," Arabella said.

"That sounds perfect. Refreshing and not too sweet," Kathryn agreed.

Jenn looked at Rebecca who nodded her agreement. She turned around and gestured to the waiter. "Can we have four Bellinis, please?"

He nodded and turned to place the order with the bar.

"I'm assuming it won't arrive in an icy slush?" Kathryn joked.

"Nope. You'll even get it in the right glass," Jenn replied.

"My, how refined!" Kathryn affected a Southern belle accent and placed her hand on her chest.

Over the course of the next two hours, the four women dined on exquisite traditional Cajun food while listening to the band play a selection of jazz classics. It was a better evening than Jenn could have ever hoped for.

Arabella and Kathryn seemed to hit it off. Once conversation started to flow, it became clear that they had quite a lot in common. Jenn was grateful for Arabella's expert conversational skills. It had led her to discover that Kathryn had been born in Brazil but had lived in New York her entire adult life.

She worked in public relations with her sister and her mother. The darkness that flashed through her eyes at the mere mention of her mother indicated to Jenn that it was best to avoid the subject altogether.

Though it was becoming clear that Jenn and Kathryn had literally nothing in common, their conversation flowed easily. A perfect example of opposites attracting, which did nothing to keep Jenn's crush from growing with each passing minute. She felt proud to be out on the town with someone like Kathryn.

The sun had set. The glow from the streetlights and the soft, glimmering lights that were wrapped around the balcony balustrades were all that illuminated them. Jenn never wanted the night to end.

Apparently, Rebecca didn't share her desire. She watched as her friend downed the last of her wine and let out a big, fake yawn. Jenn smiled to herself. She didn't know if Rebecca wanted to make herself scarce to give her some alone time with Kathryn, or if there was something else going on.

There had definitely been something strange in the air between Rebecca and Arabella all night. If Jenn hadn't been told that they weren't a couple, she would have bet money that they were. Another example of her misfiring gaydar. She slumped a little in her seat, remembering that Kathryn was oh so straight. She wished it wasn't the case, but, perfect night out or not, she was.

She realised that she had been foolish to think she could socialise with Kathryn and not get caught up in her web. Of course she'd fall for her. She'd already fallen during the streetcar trip.

"I'm so sorry, but I think I'm going to have to call it an early night," Rebecca said.

"Same for me, I think I'm starting to feel the jetlag," Arabella added.

"Oh, that's a shame," Kathryn said. "I thought you'd both be joining us for the jazz?"

Rebecca looked at Jenn, clearly having forgotten all about the show they were supposed to listen to after the meal.

Jenn waved her hand distractedly. "It's fine, I just called in a couple of favours for the tickets... I can easily move them to another night when you're not feeling so tired."

"Are you sure?" Rebecca asked.

Jenn could tell that Rebecca really wanted to leave but didn't want to cause her any difficulties.

"Absolutely," she said. "Text me in the morning and we can make other arrangements."

"You're a star." Rebecca stood and gave Jenn a hug. "Sorry, I'm just shattered."

"Yeah, right," Jenn mumbled in her ear. "I'll want all the gossip later."

Red appeared on Rebecca's cheeks, and she softly nodded her agreement. She handed her some money to pay for their dinner, despite Jenn having asked her not to. Shortly after, Arabella and Rebecca said their farewells and hurried from the restaurant.

"Jetlag can be rough," Kathryn said.

"Yeah, it can be," Jenn agreed. She didn't bother mentioning that she was pretty sure jetlag had nothing to do with their sudden disappearance.

22

THE EX, THE JAZZ, AND THE ALCOHOL

KATHRYN SIPPED wine from her glass. Jenn had chosen a wonderful vintage. She wondered where Jenn had acquired that knowledge from. She couldn't imagine it was from that awful bar where she had first met her. Everything in there was fluorescent and mixed with ice.

All in all, she was having a surprisingly fun evening. The restaurant was perfection. Not only was the food, drink, and service exceptional, but it also looked like it was a movie set. They were a stone's throw from busy Bourbon Street, littered with drunks, but it felt like they were miles away.

It was the kind of restaurant that was reviewed in magazines but rarely found in the real world. Charm and sophistication, but with all the convenience of modern-day dining.

And the company had been more than she could have hoped for. Arabella was witty and fun once you got to know her. Rebecca was delightful, and Jenn... *Jenn*. She gazed at her dinner companion, who stood at the balustrade looking down at the jazz band on the corner.

Jenn was more than she had ever expected. They'd had a great time on the streetcars the night before, but she'd really shone over dinner. She was very intelligent, funny, and kinder than anyone Kathryn had ever met before.

She didn't think she was guilty of judging books by their covers, but she'd definitely done so when she'd first met Jenn. To Kathryn, she was a bartender in a tank top and ripped denim shorts. Nothing more. Probably uneducated, definitely not someone she'd cast a second look at.

She couldn't have been more wrong. Jenn was not only educated, she was *smart*. Kathryn had met many people with qualifications coming out of their backside, but they could still be dumb as a box of rocks. Jenn had a natural curiosity about the world which had developed into a keen intellect.

The dinner invitation had originally been to reassure herself that Jenn was safe and well after the river incident. Maybe to try to apologise for her reaction to the kiss. Much to her surprise, it had turned into one of the most pleasant dinners she'd attended in a number of years.

She took another sip of wine. As she looked up again, she realised that a tall blonde woman was walking straight towards Jenn. Not towards the balustrade to look at the band, but towards Jenn.

"Grace!" Jenn announced happily when she noticed the woman beside her.

"Jenn, I thought it was you!"

The two women embraced. Kathryn narrowed her eyes, wondering who the interloper was. Didn't they know it was rude to interrupt someone's meal? Even if the food had been consumed long ago.

"Wow, it's been... what? Three years?" Jenn asked as they pulled away from the hug.

Grace nodded. "Yep. I just got back in town a couple of days ago. I was going to call you, but I've been so busy. Then I was having dinner with my girlfriend and I looked out here and there you were."

"Here I am." Jenn smiled from ear to ear.

Kathryn watched the two of them, wondering who on earth Grace was. She found herself hoping it was a co-worker from one of Jenn's many jobs. She didn't want to reflect on why that mattered to her.

"Oh, Grace," Jenn said, as she seemed to suddenly remember who she was with. She gestured toward Kathryn. "This is Kathryn, she's on vacation here."

Kathryn offered her hand. "Pleasure to meet you."

"Likewise." Grace smiled as she shook Kathryn's hand. "Anyway, I'll let you get back to your dinner. I just had to come over and say hello."

"I'm so glad you did, it's great to see you," Jenn said.

Grace pulled Jenn into another hug, placing a kiss on her cheek. "I'll call you, we'll catch up."

They exchanged farewells and Grace walked away. Jenn took her seat at the table again, watching as Grace walked away.

Eventually, the silence had dragged on too long for Kathryn.

"So…" she said.

"She's my ex. We dated for a while," Jenn admitted.

"Oh." Kathryn looked up to catch another glimpse of the blonde who had now taken her seat inside the restaurant. "Didn't work out?"

"No." Jenn shook her head. "But we're still friends. I think we were always better friends than lovers."

Kathryn could feel a blush flare on her cheeks. She didn't want to appear to have a problem with same-sex relationships; she didn't. Even if her reaction to the kiss might have been interpreted otherwise.

"I see." She forced a wide smile. "It's nice that you're still friendly."

"Life's too short. We all need friends, right?"

Kathryn chuckled. Jenn raised a questioning eyebrow at her unexpected response.

"Some of us clearly find it easier to make friends," Kathryn said by way of explanation.

Sadness flashed across Jenn's face before she quickly masked it again. She looked at her watch. "Wow, look at the time. We better get moving if we're going to catch the show."

Kathryn gestured to the band on the street. "We've seen a show."

"Oh, they're good, but this show is better," Jenn promised.

She turned around and gestured for the waiter to bring the bill.

"Obviously, I'll be paying for dinner," Kathryn said, already sliding her credit card from its compartment in her phone case.

"No, you won't," Jenn argued.

Kathryn raised her eyebrow. "Oh, no?"

"No, this is my treat." Jenn handed the waiter some cash the moment the bill landed on the table. "You can get the next one."

Kathryn decided not to dispute the matter, especially as she knew she'd rather enjoy another night of Jenn's company.

Once the bill was settled, they walked back downstairs and through a small door into a backroom that she never would have known about if she hadn't been following Jenn. The room was small but well decorated. There was a tiny raised stage at one end of the room. The rest of the room was filled with small round tables and mismatched chairs. Most notably, the room was completely empty.

"Where would you like to sit?" Jenn grinned.

"Are you sure it's tonight?" Kathryn looked at her watch and then around the empty room. "It's due to start in eleven minutes."

"This is New Orleans. It won't start on time, and people will arrive about thirty seconds before."

Kathryn smiled. "This takes some getting used to," she said.

"It's worth it," Jenn promised her.

Kathryn's smile bloomed into a laugh. She pointed to a table near the front but off to the side. They both sat down, and a waiter approached them almost immediately. Kathryn wondered if the service was always this good or if Jenn had called in a couple of favours.

"What do you think?" Jenn asked. "More cocktails?"

Kathryn bit her lip and nodded. "I'll have one if you do."

"Bellini?"

Kathryn nodded again.

"Two Bellinis," Jenn ordered.

They were soon alone again. A question had been gnawing at Kathryn's brain for a while, something she desperately wanted to know.

"This may be completely inappropriate," she started. "So, don't feel obligated to answer."

"Okay," Jenn replied, seemingly unfazed.

"How did you know you were gay?"

"Well, just to clarify, technically I identify as pansexual," Jenn explained.

"Wait, hold on." Kathryn sat up as she thought about the term. "I know this one."

Jenn laughed.

"Shh, shh." Kathryn waved her hand to silence Jenn's laughter, it was hard to think when someone was guffawing all over the place. "Oh, yeah, it's like bisexual, but…" She trailed off, not remembering exactly what it was.

"It means attraction to someone else, regardless of gender," Jenn explained.

Kathryn frowned.

"The dictionary defines bisexual as someone attracted to either men or women, although some people question that definition. Either way, pan is more inclusive because it includes people who are genderfluid."

Kathryn sat back and considered that. "That's fascinating. I rarely hear about pansexuality."

"A lot of the rainbow community is still discovering terms that they are comfortable with," Jenn explained. "But, to answer your question, I had my first non-straight thought when I was about thirteen and I saw two women kissing in the grocery store. I couldn't get the image out of my head, it was so different and kinda forbidden. A couple of years later, I was dared to kiss a girl at my school, so I did. I'm pansexual, but I favour relationships with women."

"Which would make you a le—"

Jenn put her hand up. "No. That wouldn't make me a lesbian. It would make me a pansexual in a relationship with a woman."

Kathryn could detect a little anger from Jenn. Clearly, she had misspoken. She decided to drop the subject for now. She needed to research these terms further.

The waiter placed two Bellinis on the table.

Once he had left, Jenn leaned forward. "Can I ask you a question?"

Kathryn felt her heart skip a beat. Jenn was about to ask her about her own sexuality. And she'd no doubt say the wrong thing and ruin the evening.

"Sure," she replied.

"Was that the best gumbo you ever ate?"

Kathryn let out a sigh and quickly nodded. "Absolutely delicious. The entire dinner was amazing."

Jenn opened her mouth to reply but paused when she noticed people entering the room. Kathryn turned around and saw Grace and her girlfriend walking in and taking a seat.

"We can go if you like," Kathryn offered. She wouldn't like to see her ex when she was out trying to have a good time, she wondered if Jenn felt the same way.

"No, it's fine," Jenn replied. "We're good."

"May I ask why you broke up?" Kathryn asked as she watched Grace and her girlfriend take a seat and look at the drinks menu.

"We just drifted apart," Jenn admitted wistfully. "Mind-blowing sex can't sustain a relationship forever."

Kathryn was glad she hadn't been sipping her Bellini when those words fell from Jenn's mouth.

"No, I suppose not," she managed in a whisper. She found herself looking towards Grace with a curious gaze.

They sat in silence, watching as the room filled with people. After a few minutes the room was packed, and the atmosphere was electrifying.

Kathryn noticed Grace and her girlfriend had started making out while they waited for the band to arrive. She couldn't tear her eyes away, despite really wanting to. Jenn caught her staring and looked highly amused. Kathryn made a concerted effort to angle her head down towards the table so she didn't feel tempted to snoop. She decided that the Bellinis and the wine had gone to her head.

Luckily the band soon arrived. The lead saxophonist introduced his fellow musicians, and they began to play soulful and lively jazz tunes. Kathryn had never really cared for jazz, but she had to admit that it was very enjoyable to listen to. Her eyes kept getting drawn to the back of the room where Grace was still making out with her girlfriend.

Halfway through the set the waiter took more orders, and before Jenn had a chance to speak Kathryn had ordered two more Bellinis for them.

23

READY

THE WALK from the restaurant to the hotel had been made in silence. Rebecca casually glanced at Arabella as they'd walked, noting that she seemed to be getting more nervous as they got closer to the hotel. Closer to talking.

Rebecca was just as nervous. Arabella had told her she wanted to talk. She had added that it wasn't bad, but Rebecca didn't know if Arabella's concept of a positive conversation was the same as hers.

She didn't want to talk. Talking could end everything they had. Admittedly, it wasn't much, but it was friendship with a hint of something more to come. Rebecca didn't know if she could cope with the loss of the possibility of them being something more.

At first, she had taken Arabella's words and actions to mean a positive development, but it wasn't long before negative thoughts and anxiety had turned that around. Before she'd finished her main course, she was convinced of the worse.

They walked into the hotel bar, which was thankfully quiet. Arabella pointed to a table and high-backed leather chairs in the corner. "Take a seat, what would you like to drink?"

"Just water," Rebecca replied.

Arabella raised her eyebrow. "Just water? Seriously?"

"Fine, apple juice."

Arabella looked at her for a moment, as if she wanted to say something. She broke eye contact and walked over to the bar. Rebecca wiped her clammy palms on her dress before taking a seat. Her mind was racing with a hundred different scenarios, considering all the things that Arabella may say and all her possible responses.

Despite the rapid synaptic action, she didn't know what her response would be. When Arabella pulled the plug on the idea of romance, should she look unaffected in order to save the friendship? Or should she be honest and admit how crushed she was?

You shouldn't have said anything in the bathroom, Rebecca chastised herself.

Arabella lowered a glass of apple juice and a glass of red wine to the table. "I can hear you thinking over there."

"Can't help it," Rebecca said. "I don't think I've ever had a good conversation following someone saying, 'nothing bad'."

Arabella sat back in her chair and looked at Rebecca thoughtfully. "I'm ready," she said softly.

"For?" Rebecca was confused.

Arabella chuckled. "Us. Well, exploring whatever this thing between us is."

Rebecca wished she'd ordered something stronger to drink. She sipped on her apple juice, trying to process what had been said.

"You look like I just shot your childhood pet," Arabella commented with a smile.

"I thought you were breaking up with me! Or putting a stop to the direction we were going in."

"Why on earth would you think that?"

Rebecca stared at Arabella. The woman was unreal.

"I held your hand when we walked to the restaurant," Arabella pointed out, as if that was supposed to clarify everything.

"Jenn and Kathryn were walking arm in arm, I thought you wanted to do something similar." A light bulb went off in Rebecca's head. Understanding hit her like a sonic boom. "Wait, wait… you… us?"

Arabella nodded.

Rebecca reached for Arabella's wine glass and took a long sip of the rich, red liquid.

Arabella watched her with an amused expression. "I wanted to speak with you earlier, but I didn't think it was fair to start to talk about this before dinner. I wanted to ensure that we'd have time to talk after the meal, hence asking you to have drinks here afterwards. I didn't realise you'd panic quite so much about it. I'm sorry, I should have read the situation better."

"An apology, too?" Rebecca widened her eyes and stared at Arabella. "Who are you and where is—"

"Oh, shush," Arabella cut her off. "I'm changing my mind already."

"What did change your mind?" Rebecca had to know where this was coming from. What had led Arabella to her decision?

"Firstly, I want to apologise for how I have treated you," Arabella started. "I'm aware that it must have been hard for you lately, I've been giving you mixed messages and I've been all over the place emotionally."

"It's fine." Rebecca shrugged her shoulders.

"No, it's not."

Rebecca swallowed nervously. Arabella was right, it wasn't fine. She'd been on edge for weeks wondering what they were and where they were going, the mantra of *Give her time* running over and over in her head.

"When we drove home from Portugal, I was a very different person to the person I am today. As I've said to you before, I was on autopilot. Heading towards a life, a marriage, that I was destined to have. I'd never thought once about what I actually wanted in life. It seemed like an irrelevant luxury."

"And then I came along," Rebecca said.

"Quite." Arabella smiled. "And you blew all of that order and predetermined planning out of the water. And thank goodness you did. I was sleepwalking into a nightmare, one which I surely would have woken up from at some point. Probably when it was too late. Realising that I was miserable, and my life had been wasted."

Arabella took a sip of wine. She edged back into the wing-backed chair and looked at the liquid thoughtfully.

"It was an enormous change for me. To go from planning my wedding to a man—to Alastair—and preparing to give up work... to the unknown. You woke me up, reminded me that we only get one life and it's for living the way we want to live it. But, my upbringing meant I'd never really known what I wanted."

Rebecca remembered the heartbreaking moment when Arabella told her she didn't know how to be happy. At first, she'd thought it was a dramatic statement based on some truth blown out of all proportion, but she'd soon discovered that it was true.

Arabella's parents had never been about fun or seeking happiness. They were about duty, building a career, and a family. Arabella had never stopped to look outside of that path, and a child who had never been taught what happiness was couldn't identify it as an adult.

"Going from such a set plan in life to realising you don't know anything…" Arabella shivered slightly. "It's terrifying, Rebecca. Really, it is. My only constant was you. You'd woken me up to see this new world and the possibilities within it."

Rebecca knew that Arabella had struggled with the new 'directionless' life she was living. Another reason why she had given her space. She wanted to be the one person not pushing Arabella into a certain direction.

"When I kissed you, I thought I knew exactly what I wanted. I thought we'd drift into a relationship. Slowly, but surely. But then I started to get cold feet."

Rebecca thought back to the time before their trip to Scotland. They'd shared a few kisses and cuddled a little. It had felt like Arabella was holding back, but Rebecca had just written it off as a new feeling for the previously straight woman.

"And then Scotland…" Arabella trailed off.

Scotland was a topic that Rebecca had learnt to avoid. Something happened that had nearly ripped them apart, it was just that she didn't know what had happened. So, she avoided the entire subject.

"I owe you an explanation," Arabella said.

"You owe me nothing," Rebecca replied. Sure, she wanted to know, but she didn't want Arabella to feel obligated.

"I panicked. When we realised that our flight would be cancelled, driving all the way to Scotland seemed like a great idea. I realised it would be a lot like our trip from Portugal. Sharing a car journey for so many hours, I thought it would be wonderful. I could even share the driving that time."

"What changed?"

"Realisation and expectation," Arabella said.

"You lost me." Rebecca frowned.

"I realised that we were on our way to Scotland. Our first trip together, a... tester for whether or not we were compatible as travel companions. And maybe more. And then I wondered if the expectation would be that we would... become more in Scotland. And I couldn't get that thought out of my head. I wasn't ready, but we were on the way and I felt trapped. So, when the car broke down, I was relieved."

"Relieved? More like livid," Rebecca pointed out. She'd thought Arabella had been difficult when she'd first met her in Portugal, but that was nothing compared to how she had been when they had broken down on the motorway. She'd gone crazy, and then demanded to go home. The trip was cancelled, and for a while, they didn't even speak.

"I panicked. We'd been driving for three hours, and I was terrified of what expectations you had of me and what expectations I had of myself. It was like driving towards a ticking time bomb. When the car broke down, the dam on my emotions broke with it." Arabella placed her wine glass back on the table.

"There were never any expectations," Rebecca gently said.

"I know. I realised that the moment I got home. By then, it was too late. I'd embarrassed myself, caused a huge scene, and..." She put her head in her hand.

Rebecca grabbed a nearby stool and placed it beside Arabella's chair.

"So, you hid from me for a while?"

"Yes," Arabella admitted. "I was so embarrassed. I realised I should have just spoken to you, but that seemed impossible at the time. It wasn't until later that I realised how stupid I'd been."

"Do you now know that you can talk to me about anything, at any time?" Rebecca asked.

Arabella looked up at her. There were unshed tears in her eyes as she nodded.

"And do you know that I would never have any expectations of you?"

Another nod.

Rebecca let out a sigh of relief. "Good. Because, I've seen you at your worst. And you scare the shit out of me. But you can always, always talk to me. And I'm happy to continue to give you space."

"I don't want any more space," Arabella said.

Rebecca raised her eyebrows.

"I've been using that space to hide. I've been burying my feelings. I'm not training for the London Marathon, I'm running away from my own mind. Every time I close my eyes, or pause working for two seconds, this flood of questions rushes through my brain. And every single time, I bury it."

"Why?"

Arabella shrugged. "Fear of the unknown? I don't know. But I do know that I am sick of that. I can't carry on living my life in this limbo. I've changed as a person, I'm probably still changing. I told myself I didn't want to start a relationship with you because I didn't know if I felt romantic feelings towards you, or if you were just the best friend I ever had."

Rebecca was still terrified of where this conversation was heading. She wanted to give Arabella the chance to figure things out for herself, she didn't want to push her. But she felt like there was an axe over their heads, waiting to drop.

"A—and?"

"I realised it can be both," Arabella said. "I'm still not ready. But I'm not prepared to hold you at arm's length any more either. I'm hoping to figure this out on my own, and I realise that I can't do that. I need your help. But I understand if you don't want to do tha—"

"I'll help," Rebecca said quickly.

"I may end up hurting you."

"I'll take the risk." Rebecca put her hand on Arabella's. "I know there is something between us, I feel it all the time. I hoped that you would feel it, too. But I know that it's really hard to deal with it all on your own."

"It is," Arabella agreed. "I've been holding back—burying my feelings—to try to protect us both. But all I've done is made things even harder for us. I suppose I thought I could figure it all out and then come to with a decision. As clear cut as that."

"But it's not that easy?" Rebecca guessed.

"No, it's really not that easy." Arabella smiled at her. "Help me?"

Rebecca grinned. "I'd like that. But you have to start talking to me and telling me what's going on in your brain."

"I know, I'm going to make a concerted effort to do just that."

"Good, because it won't work unless you do," Rebecca admitted. She needed Arabella to understand that she needed to start to open up. Even if it was hard, and sometimes embarrassing.

"I've been thinking about it a lot over the past couple of days. I'm fed up with being scared. I want to move on. Someone very wise told me I needed to live my life and fill it with love and happiness."

Rebecca could feel her cheeks hurting as her grin grew impossibly wide. She'd patiently waited for Arabella to come to some kind of decision, hoping for this but fearing and preparing for worse. Now she couldn't believe that her patience had paid off.

"Are you *sure* about this?" Rebecca checked.

Arabella lifted her hand and cupped Rebecca's cheek. She leaned forward and looked into her eyes.

"Very sure. I've done a lot of soul-searching, and I realise... I need you in my life. The very thought of you being with someone else..." Jealousy flashed in Arabella's eyes.

Rebecca closed the gap between them and pressed her lips to Arabella's. They shared a chaste kiss, considering they were still sitting in a public hotel bar. When Rebecca withdrew she brought her own hand up to Arabella's cheek.

"No chance of me being with someone else. I've only been able to think of you for some time now," she confessed.

Arabella smiled. "Good. I feel the same. And I am so sorry I've been up and down lately. I'm going to try my best to stop that. And obviously I'll talk to you when I feel nervous."

Rebecca lowered her hand and reached over to sip her apple juice. The adrenaline was wearing off, and she was suddenly exhausted, having been in a state of near-panic for so long.

"Are you okay?" Arabella asked.

"Yeah, just... happy," Rebecca admitted. "Really happy. And no idea what to do with myself." She laughed.

Arabella tilted her head for a moment as she considered it. "I'm happy, too. There you go... it seems I'm already learning."

24

PDA

JENN AND KATHRYN walked arm in arm down Royal Street towards the hotel, discussing the jazz set they had just listened to. Jenn was relieved that Kathryn had apparently had such a good night. She was animated and clearly excited as she spoke about the musicians and her favourite pieces of music.

It was night and day from the person who had loudly slated the entirety of New Orleans in the middle of Bourbon Street just a couple of days before.

Jenn was more confused than ever. The glances, the licking of her lips, the body language... everything pointed to a woman who wasn't 100% straight.

It didn't help that there seemed to be an abnormally high number of kissing women around them that evening. First, there had been Grace and her new girlfriend making out at the back of the jazz venue. Now, they were following another female couple who were holding hands and sneaking kisses occasionally.

"There's a lot of that around here." Kathryn gestured to the couple in front of them.

"Love?" Jenn questioned.

"Public displays of it, yes."

"Does that make you uncomfortable?"

"I'm not used to it," Kathryn admitted.

"Like jazz?" Jenn chuckled.

The couple in front of them suddenly stopped and pulled each other into a passionate open-mouthed kiss. They stepped around the amorous couple. Jenn noted that Kathryn's eyes nearly bugged out of her head at the sight.

"Like jazz," Kathryn agreed once they had moved further along the street. "Maybe it will grow on me like jazz did."

Jenn swallowed hard. It was comments like this that made Jenn question Kathryn's claim to be straight. She couldn't read the words as anything other than flirtatious.

They walked in silence for the last couple of minutes to the hotel. As they arrived Jenn gestured towards the door.

"Your home, sweet home," she said. "I had a great night."

"So did I." Kathryn swayed slightly.

She'd been doing that a lot since they started to walk home. Jenn had tried to slow her alcohol intake during the music, once she had noticed Kathryn's glazed eyes. But Kathryn wasn't really a person you argued with, and the drinks had continued to flow.

"Wonderful food," Kathryn said. She took a step forward, closer to Jenn. "Wonderful music." She stepped forward again, forcing Jenn to take a step back. She felt the cold stone wall of the hotel behind her.

"Wonderful company."

Jenn saw a glint in Kathryn's eye and knew what was going to happen a split second before it did. But it was a little too late. Kathryn lunged forward and placed a sloppy kiss on her lips.

Jenn ducked away from the kiss.

"Kathryn, you're drunk... and straight, remember?"

Kathryn pouted. "I'm not drunk."

"You are." Jenn caught Kathryn by her upper arms and held her in place. "I'm not going to kiss you while you're drunk. I won't take advantage."

Kathryn smirked. "It's just a friendly goodnight kiss." She winked seductively.

Jenn knew she had to get out of there and fast. It may have been exactly what she wanted, but she knew that Kathryn was in no state to be giving any kind of consent. She placed a swift kiss on Kathryn's cheek.

"Good night, Kathryn."

She gently pushed on Kathryn's upper arms, so she could be free of her. She gestured towards the door to the hotel.

"Good night, dear," Kathryn said. She was still smirking but seemed to understand that she wouldn't be convincing Jenn of anything this evening. She turned around and walked into the hotel.

Jenn watched her walk into the lobby before letting out a long breath. She knew Kathryn would be trouble from the first moment she saw her, but she had no idea just how much trouble that would be.

25

BOO-BOO

"Can we go to my room?" Arabella asked.

Rebecca raised an eyebrow.

"Not like that." Arabella rolled her eyes. She gestured around the bar, which was starting to become a little busier. "I just don't want to be with so many people."

"Sure." Rebecca stood up and held out her hand to Arabella.

Arabella smiled and took the offered hand. "Better get used to this. They'll be a lot of it, dating an older woman."

A shadow passed over Rebecca's face before quickly clearing. "Yes, remember, I told you about my ex?"

Arabella got to her feet. *Oh, yes,* she thought. *The forty-nine-year-old.* She'd almost forgotten that Rebecca's previous partner had been much older than Rebecca. In fact, much older than Arabella also.

She then recalled the reason they broke up. The older woman had let Rebecca go, worried about trapping her in a relationship with someone so much older. And she'd done so after Rebecca had proposed marriage.

Marriage.

Arabella had just gotten out of one engagement. She wasn't ready to dive into another. In fact, the whole debacle had put her off of the idea of marriage entirely. She wondered what Rebecca's thoughts were. And children. She'd not even considered that.

Calm down, she told herself. *There's plenty of time to talk about these things. Get your anxiety under control.*

"You okay?" Rebecca asked at the prolonged silence.

"Yes, sorry, I was just thinking."

"About?" Rebecca pressed. "You did promise you'd tell me what you were worrying about."

"Who says I was worrying?"

Rebecca chuckled and pointed her finger to the centre of Arabella's forehead, right between her eyes. "Worry Central has traffic," she said. She gently poked the crinkled skin.

Arabella relaxed her face. "We are not referring to that part of my face as Worry Central."

Rebecca shrugged her shoulder. "You might not be."

"I'm regretting inviting you to my room," Arabella joked.

"You're not," Rebecca replied, winking as she did.

"No, you're right, I'm not," Arabella said.

She reached down and took Rebecca's hand. They slowly walked through the bar and towards the elevators.

"I'm sorry we had to cut the evening with Jenn short," Arabella said. "I know you've been looking forward to catching up with her. What with her spending half of the afternoon swimming in the river, and then us rushing off after dinner…"

"It's fine. She'll understand." Rebecca pressed the call button for the elevator.

"Oh, so you'll be telling her… about us, I mean?" Arabella asked.

"Hell yes, I will. I'll be telling her the second I see her next. I'll be telling everyone I can. All the time. 'Hello, this is my girlfriend.' And 'Have you met my girlfriend?' That kind of thing."

Arabella sighed. "Must we use the word girlfriend? I feel like I'm too old to be someone's girlfriend."

The elevator arrived, and they stepped inside.

"Partner?" Rebecca suggested, selecting their floor. "Although that does sound very…"

"Very?" she asked.

"Permanent," Rebecca said. A trace of worry passed over her face.

Arabella swallowed. "I… don't want to make any promises. And I certainly don't want to hurt you. But I can't envisage me walking away from this. Not in the near future. You mean too much to me."

Rebecca looked pleased with the comment. She bit her lip. "We can pick an appropriate name for you later," she decided. "Until then, I'm just going to introduce you as my boo-boo."

"It will be the last introduction you ever give," Arabella promised.

The elevator doors opened, and they made their way towards the rooms. For the first time in many years, Arabella felt butterflies careening into her stomach walls. It was exciting. Nerve-wracking, too. She didn't know what she was doing, or what would happen next. But she did know that felt happiness.

"What do you want to do tonight?" Rebecca asked. "I have cards, we can play a game? Or watch some TV?"

"I'd love to see some of the photos you took today," Arabella replied. "I want to see New Orleans through your eyes."

Rebecca paused by her door. "Really? You're not just saying that?"

"Absolutely not, I love seeing the photos you take. Trying

to figure out why a certain scene, or object, caught your eye." It was true. She enjoyed trying to figure out what made Rebecca tick. It was a habit she had begun shortly after they met, and a subject that she didn't think she'd ever fully discover. Rebecca was different from the other people in her life, she was on a completely different path. Her own path, forged by desire, dreams, and determination.

Rebecca opened her room door. "I'll grab my camera and the cables, and I'll come through. Obviously, I won't say no to a cup of tea."

"Says the person who mocked me for bringing a travel kettle," Arabella chuckled. She pulled her room key out of her bag.

"No, I mocked you for bringing three different varieties of tea and around two hundred individual tea bags."

"And now you want one of those tea bags," Arabella pointed out. "Good thing I brought extra."

Rebecca leaned in and kissed Arabella's cheek. "Whatever you say, boo-boo."

26

A LOT TO DRINK

THE DISTANT SOUND of people going about their morning routines eventually woke Kathryn. She flopped over in the king-sized bed to lay on her back.

Her brain thrummed with a post-alcohol haze. She squinted at the ceiling, struggling to piece her memories together.

Where am I? she wondered. *And how much did I drink?*

Suddenly she sat up in bed, clutching the sheet to her naked chest in shock.

"Shit!"

Total recollection of the previous evening came to her like a tsunami crashing against her frontal lobe. She brought her other hand up to hold her head. She winced.

"Shit," she muttered again.

She had kissed Jenn Cook. She'd tried for much more, too. While she had claimed it was intended to be an innocent goodnight kiss, it was anything but.

She swallowed hard. Pain in her head pulsated like a siren. This wasn't just a hangover, this was a hangover and outright shock.

"What am I doing?" she muttered to herself. "I'm not gay. I'm not."

It even sounded weak to her own ears. She got out of bed and grabbed the white hotel-issued dressing gown and tossed it around her body. She walked over to the mirror and stared at her reflection.

"I am not gay."

She regarded herself in the mirror for a few silent moments before adding, "So why did you kiss a woman?"

Her reflection stared back at her in confusion. "And why can't you get her out of your head?"

She blew out a breath. No answer was forthcoming, because she didn't have one. It was as if she were a completely different person when she was around Jenn.

She tilted her head to one side. "I've... been under a lot of stress."

She walked over to the coffee machine, selected a pod, and placed it in the top of the device. "I'm in a strange city, alone. And lonely." She started the machine and walked into the bathroom, switching on the light.

"I'm confused... and suffering from... from emotional loss." She looked at her reflection, this one less flattering with the bright bathroom lights glaring at her. She blew out a long sigh.

"And I'd had a lot to drink."

She rubbed at her eyes before reaching into her toiletry bag and pulling out a packet of pain medication. She'd been through a lot lately, but that was no reason to take it out on Jenn.

She'd simply had the misfortune of being one of the very few people who had shown Kathryn some kindness lately. And Kathryn had repaid her by getting startlingly drunk and sending the most enormous of mixed signals. She wasn't gay, but for some reason she couldn't be trusted around Jenn Cook.

The coffee machine finished whirring, and she walked back into the main room. She picked up the cup and placed it down on the desk beside the hotel directory.

Panic coursed through her body.

Jenn would be coming to the hotel today to teach a water aerobics class. Kathryn lunged for the directory and hurriedly flipped through the pages. She quickly found the activities list and ran a shaking finger down the page.

Midday.

She turned to look at the alarm clock beside the bed.

Eleven o'clock.

She hurriedly headed for the shower, nearly tripping over the desk chair in her self-imposed rush.

The museum, she thought to herself as she turned on the shower. *I'm a tourist, of course I won't be here. Doesn't mean I'm avoiding her. Just… seeing a museum.*

27

VERY GOOD FRIENDS

Rebecca walked out onto the roof terrace of the hotel. She took a deep breath and stretched up to the sky. It was a good day. A great day, in fact, to take a dip in the pool and meet Jenn for some water aerobics before having lunch with her girlfriend.

Girlfriend. She tossed the word over and over in her mind. She smiled.

"There you are," Jenn called out from a storage room at the back of the pool.

"Here I am."

"How am I supposed to get any gossip out of you if you turn up five minutes before the class starts?" Jenn chastised her.

"Sorry, I lost track of time." She held her arms out to the side and pointed to her bikini top and shorts. "Is this suitable for water aerobics? I've never done it, so I didn't know."

Jenn put floatation noodles on the ground and walked over to her. She was wearing a black swimsuit, something Rebecca wished she had brought. Jenn eyed the bikini top before pulling on the straps a little.

"You'll be fine," she said, satisfied that the material would stay in place. "Now, spill. What was all that about last night? That big fake yawn and a sudden need to leave. You're so obvious."

Rebecca turned around a few times to check they were alone, primarily to be sure that Arabella hadn't suddenly turned up.

"Arabella told me she wanted us to have a drink at the hotel bar after dinner. To talk."

Jenn raised her eyebrow and let out a sigh. "Uh-oh."

"Right?" Rebecca nodded. "Exactly. She told me it was nothing bad, but since when has that ever been a thing?"

"People say it's not bad so that you stay calm up until the moment they drop a ton of bad news on you." Jenn nodded sagely.

"Precisely!"

"So, what was the bad news?"

"It wasn't bad news," Rebecca admitted. A grin crossed her face, she was powerless to stop it. "She wants us to give it a go, you know, being together."

Jenn's eyes widened. "That's great news!"

"I know. I mean, she scared me half to death with all that 'let's talk later' stuff. But we chatted, and she explained a few things, why she's been so up and down with me and that she's come to some realisations. And she explained what happened on the way to Scotland."

Jenn winced. Rebecca had told her about the car trouble on the way to Scotland, Arabella's subsequent explosion and the week of silent treatment. At that point, Jenn had told Rebecca that Arabella was unhinged and to stay away from her.

Not that that was ever an option for Rebecca. The second their lips had touched that first time, she was hooked.

"So, what happened?" Jenn asked.

"She was scared out of her mind. She thought that we were going away to… you know, cement our relationship or something. She worked herself into a state over it. But didn't tell me, obviously. Then, when the car broke down, she saw a way out. She apologised, but that's classic Arabella. Bottle it all up and then explode at a later date."

Jenn chuckled. "And now you're in a relationship with her?"

Rebecca bit her lip and blushed. "Okay, that sounds bad. I didn't mean it like that. I mean, she feels so much, but she's not good at expressing things. I love that about her, she's like this huge ball of emotions, but she's so used to bottling them up… when she lets them out it can be beautiful. It can also be scary as hell, but she's working on it." She sighed. "I'm not explaining this very well."

Jenn put her hand on her shoulder and squeezed. "Are you happy?"

"So happy."

"Then you don't need to explain. As long as you're happy and you think she's the one for you, then I'm happy. She seems great. I had a great time last night."

"We did, too. I'm so sorry we bailed like that, I just had to know."

Jenn laughed. "Yeah, I would have dumped you, too." She looked up. "Speak of the devil."

Rebecca turned around. Her eyes widened, and she felt a lump in her throat. Of course, she knew she'd be seeing Arabella in a swimsuit. But she hadn't actually processed the fact that she'd be seeing Arabella in a swimsuit.

"You're drooling," Jenn whispered.

Rebecca couldn't control her expression. All she could see was long, toned legs that went on and on. Not to mention creamy breasts that were barely covered. They bounced as Arabella walked towards them.

"Morning," Jenn greeted. "Ready to burn some calories?"

"Absolutely," Arabella replied. "I need to after that sumptuous dinner last night. Is that your plan? Take people out for a wonderful, fattening meal, and then get them to come to your aerobics workout the next day?"

"Yep. You got me. I get a cut from the restaurant and from the hotel, it's a great money spinner."

Arabella chuckled and turned to look at Rebecca. She raised an eyebrow and smirked. "Are you okay?"

"Nice suit. Swimming. I mean… nice swimsuit," Rebecca finally said. She winced.

"Smooth," Jenn commented. "Real smooth."

The door from the gym opened, and some more guests walked onto the roof terrace.

"Okay, I better get started." Jenn walked away and greeted the newcomers.

Rebecca's eyes were transfixed on Arabella's long neck. They only broke contact to move down towards her chest.

"I can feel your eyes on me," Arabella whispered.

Rebecca eyes snapped up to Arabella's.

"Sorry," she apologised. "I… just—"

"I didn't say I didn't like it."

Rebecca smiled. She leaned forward and placed a soft kiss on Arabella's lips.

Arabella smiled. "What was that for?"

"Because I can." Rebecca shrugged. "I'm enjoying the fact that I can do that whenever I want."

Arabella returned the kiss.

"Hey, lovebirds, you ready to get started?"

Rebecca jumped a little. She felt herself blush.

"I'm ready," Arabella said as if nothing had happened.

"Great. By the way, it's really nice to see you two together," Jenn said.

Arabella beamed happily. "Thank you, it's nice to be together."

"Don't know why, she's not a great catch," Jenn joked. "If you want an upgrade, let me know and we can hit some of the bars here."

"Hey!" Rebecca complained. "You can't pull us apart. She's my boo-boo."

Arabella rolled her eyes. "I think I might take you up on that offer, Jenn."

"I think you better. No one wants to be called someone's boo-boo."

Arabella gave Rebecca an 'I told you so' look.

"But we should go out to celebrate—damn, I'm working at Façade tonight." Jenn bit her lip thoughtfully as she looked at Rebecca. "You could come down if you like? I can leave tickets at the door?"

Rebecca and Jenn shared a look. Jenn obviously didn't know if Arabella would be comfortable with the idea of going to Façade. Rebecca didn't know either. But she was in the business of stretching Arabella's boundaries and showing her new things.

"Yeah, I think we might," she replied.

"What's Façade?" Arabella asked.

"I'll tell you later," Rebecca said. "Let's get on with the exercise so I can get back to the eating."

28

TIME TO APOLOGISE

FIVE HOURS PASSED. Five hours of Kathryn looking over her shoulder and tiptoeing around establishments in case Jenn worked there. This was the problem when you were trying to avoid someone who appeared to have a million jobs in and around the city.

First, it had been a coffee shop where she'd eaten breakfast, then one of the many museums. Following that was another café, then a small parade which Kathryn had ended up running away from the second she saw it. A while later, it was a restaurant, then the pharmacy, and, finally, a bench by the docks.

Every single location terrified Kathryn. She had been on edge the entire day, and it was starting to take its toll. Jenn was nowhere in sight. Kathryn had a pain in her neck from constantly twisting around to seek out long, blonde curls.

Kathryn remembered when she was a little girl and used to play chasing games with her father. She would run up to him and tap his arm and declare that he was 'it' before turning and running away. As soon as she started to flee, she would be overcome with terror, knowing that her pursuer was faster and stronger than she was.

Almost immediately she would begin to hyperventilate as she heard her father approaching and saying he was coming to get her. She knew her father would never hurt her, but there was something about being chased that she hated.

Now she felt like she was in a giant version of the game. One where Jenn was potentially hiding around any corner. The mere thought had Kathryn's breath quickening. She looked around at the people milling around the docks to assure herself that she was safe.

Five hours was enough. Kathryn knew she couldn't maintain this level of panic any longer. She decided it was up to her to change the rules of the game. If she was going to get any peace, then she needed to take control and confront Jenn.

She wanted to find Jenn and apologise for her behaviour. And, of course, to reiterate that she was not gay. She needed to explain that her actions were simply down to stress, alcohol, and loneliness. Kathryn winced. No, definitely not loneliness, just stress and alcohol. She didn't need to explain her woes to someone she barely knew.

She was not gay, that was the main message she needed to convey.

She needed to find Jenn. She'd spent hours trying to avoid her, now to see if she could find her. She realised that she was just around the corner from the bar where she had first met her. It was as good a place to try as any.

She started walking, considering how convenient it was that everything in the French Quarter was within easy walking distance. She supposed the city did have its charm, despite her first impressions.

As she turned a corner onto Bourbon Street, she mentally

gave herself a pat on the back that she had correctly remembered just where the rundown CeeCee's Bar was.

She stepped inside, her heart sinking when a young brunette looked up at her.

"Hey. What can I get you?"

She looked around nervously. Suddenly wondering if her new plan was such a good one. "I was looking for Jenn. Is she not working today?"

The tall, skinny brunette shook her head. "Nope, sorry, not her shift tonight."

"Oh," Kathryn said. "You wouldn't happen to know where I could find her, would you?" She suddenly released how odd it sounded for some random woman to stroll into the bar looking for Jenn. "She, um, left her phone on the table when we were having lunch, and she probably needs it…"

"Oh! Yeah, yeah, of course. Well, she's up at Façade tonight. She should be there now, setting up and stuff."

Kathryn smiled, happy that her ruse had worked. "Wonderful! I'm new in town, where is Façade?"

The young woman indicated down the road with her thumb. "Straight down the street, just beyond Jack's Lobster Bar."

"Thank you so much." Kathryn smiled and quickly left.

Finally, she had a solid plan. One which didn't involve roaming the streets of New Orleans for hours on end.

She was going to go to Façade, whatever that was. And she would tell Jenn in no uncertain terms that her sexuality was not in question. She was most definitely straight. The drunken kiss was just that, a drunken kiss. A mistake. Which she would apologise for.

What could possibly go wrong?

29

GETTING CLOSER

REBECCA SAT on the desk chair in Arabella's hotel room while she waited for Arabella to get ready. They'd had a fantastic day. A leisurely breakfast, water aerobics followed by a swim in the pool, then a visit to the casino—where Arabella had won at nearly every machine or table game she tried, and then a small shopping trip to Canal Place, followed by a quick meal in the hotel's restaurant.

It was the perfect vacation day. Rebecca couldn't have planned anything better if she'd tried. And she knew all of that was down to being with Arabella. She'd always loved spending time with her, it was no exaggeration to say that they had become the best of friends.

But things were different, less than twenty-four hours after Arabella had admitted her feelings. There was a lightness between them now. As if some wall had been knocked down.

"Why won't you tell me where we're going?" Arabella called from the bathroom.

"Because it's a surprise," Rebecca replied. That wasn't entirely true. She wanted to see the surprise on Arabella's face.

Arabella appeared in the doorway, holding a tube of mascara. One eye had been painted to perfection. The other was bare.

"It's not a surprise, it's some kind of joke. I saw the way you and Jenn looked at each other. And then the refusal to tell me exactly what it is. You're messing with me."

"I am," Rebecca confessed. "I'm taking you somewhere that I think you'll like, but honestly I don't know what your reaction will be."

Arabella paused. She narrowed her eyes to regard Rebecca. It was a ridiculous look, considering the mascara situation.

"And, if I don't like it?"

"We'll leave," Rebecca said. "I want you to experience new things, go to places you wouldn't normally go. But I don't want you to have a bad time. If you don't like anything, we'll move on. I promise."

That seemed to calm Arabella's concerns. She nodded and walked back into the bathroom.

Rebecca smiled to herself. Arabella was certainly being more communicative lately, and she welcomed it. She'd spent weeks wondering what was going on inside her head, pondering where a sudden mood swing had come from. She hoped her openness continued.

"If you introduce me as that ridiculous name again, I'll tear you limb from limb," Arabella called from the bathroom.

"Sorry, didn't quite catch that, boo-boo," Rebecca said, barely able to keep a straight face.

Silence.

She wondered if Arabella was ignoring her. A moment later, her question was answered. No, Arabella wasn't ignoring her. She swept out of the bathroom with a murderous look over her face.

"Stop calling me that," she demanded, a glint of humour in her eye.

As she got closer, Rebecca grabbed her by the arm and pulled her onto her lap. She wrapped her arms around Arabella and silenced her with a kiss.

Arabella melted against her, wrapping her arms around Rebecca's shoulders and returning the kiss with enthusiasm.

Rebecca hadn't expected the kiss to take that kind of turn, not that she was complaining. Not at all. In fact, now she found she wanted more. She placed her hands on Arabella's waist and quickly stood up, manoeuvring Arabella onto the desk in front of the chair. She pressed Arabella back against the wall with her own body, never once breaking the kiss.

Arabella's hands started to roam Rebecca's body, working their way down her back and up her sides. Her fingers gripped eagerly, like she couldn't get enough.

Rebecca surged impossibly closer, pressing her front against Arabella's. Her mind was short-circuiting. This was what she had dreamed of and hoped for. She just hadn't expected it right now.

At the back of her mind, a little voice questioned if Arabella was ready for this kind of kiss. She seemed ready, but Rebecca wasn't going to take any risks and ruin the day they'd had.

She broke the kiss and leaned her forehead against Arabella's as she took a couple of deep breaths to calm herself down.

"Well," Arabella said, "that was…"

Rebecca closed her eyes, praying for a positive response.

"Incredible," Arabella finished.

Rebecca smiled. "You're incredible."

"And you're the reason we're going to be late," Arabella told her. She placed a flat palm on Rebecca's chest and pushed her back. She slid from the desk. "I can't believe you hoisted me up there like some…"

"Some?" Rebecca asked. She knew Arabella had enjoyed it, her flushed cheeks gave her away.

"Never mind." Arabella brushed down her dress. She turned around and looked at her reflection.

Rebecca looked over her shoulder. Arabella's lipstick was a mess, her hair was mussed, and some of her mascara that hadn't dried was smudged. She looked a mess. A beautiful mess.

"Your fault we'll be late," Arabella said, her eyes meeting Rebecca's in the reflection.

Rebecca held up her hands. "My fault."

Arabella turned around again. She placed one hand on Rebecca's chin and held her face in place, with a finger from the other hand she cleared away lipstick.

"Leave it," Rebecca suggested. "Let everyone know."

"I didn't know you were such an exhibitionist," Arabella joked. She placed a quick kiss on Rebecca's lips and then walked back into the bathroom to finish getting ready.

Rebecca looked at her reflection. She looked just like someone who had recently been in a passionate lip-lock. While she didn't mind the fact, she thought it best to clean herself up a little.

She walked through the open interconnecting door into her own room, smiling ear to ear as she went.

30

ECHO

Kathryn was so busy mentally preparing her speech that she barely gave the fluorescent sign for Façade a second thought. She walked straight into the building.

She passed a couple of women and entered what looked like a nightclub. A large bar area took up the middle of the room and around the large and dimly lit room were tables and chairs, as well as plush sofas and armchairs. Two large stages on either side of the room were professionally lit.

Kathryn wondered if live jazz was played of an evening. Everywhere in town seemed to advertise live jazz.

She walked over to the bar and nodded at a young woman cleaning some glasses. "Hello, is Jenn here?"

The woman frowned at her. "Well, yeah, she's probably getting ready."

"Could you get her for me?"

The woman looked very uncertain. "She's getting ready."

Kathryn wanted to roll her eyes but decided against it. "I need to speak to her, it's very urgent."

The young woman sighed. She put down the glass and the cloth and walked out of the bar area and across the room.

Kathryn shook her head. *What's her problem? And how much time does Jenn need get ready to pour a few drinks?*

She walked around the bar area for a bit before sitting on a stool. She stared at the enormous range of drinks on offer and wondered how anyone in New Orleans managed to get anything done.

Someone sat down on the stool next to her.

"Decided to get here early and get the good seats, huh? I like that."

Kathryn turned to regard the woman beside her. She was a large lady, probably in her early forties. She wore a white tank top which displayed a variety of tattoos on both her arms. She had short hair which had been gelled into impressive spikes.

"Yes." Kathryn nodded, unsure of what to say. Apparently, there were good seats and bad seats, and somehow, she'd managed to get a good one. Maybe the day wouldn't be a complete waste.

"Well, you picked a good night for it. I hear the show tonight is going to be amazing! I'm Echo, by the way."

Kathryn took the woman's offered hand. Echo shook her hand with a vice-like grip.

"I'm Kathryn. Echo is an interesting name. Is it a nickname?"

"Well, kinda." Echo snorted a laugh. "But I can only tell you about that when we've shared a vodka slammer."

Kathryn smiled. Echo seemed to be yet another of the larger-than-life characters she was meeting on her trip.

"I've never had a vodka slammer, but it sounds like fun."

Echo looked at Kathryn with a knowing grin. "You're not from around here, are you?"

Kathryn shook her head. "No, just visiting."

"Well, if you need anyone to show you around town, I'm

your woman," Echo pointed to herself with her thumb. "Really, if you need anything at all."

"Thank you, that's very kind." Kathryn smiled.

"Er, Kathryn?"

Kathryn turned around. Jenn was approaching them, a frown on her face as she looked from Kathryn to Echo.

"Oh, Jenn. There you are." She turned back to Echo. "Excuse me a moment."

"I'll be sure to save your seat," Echo offered.

"That'd be great."

Kathryn lowered herself from the barstool. She gestured for Jenn to follow her out of earshot from her new acquaintance. She didn't want to air too much dirty laundry in front of a stranger.

"What are you doing here? And why are you talking to Echo?" Jenn hissed as soon as they were far enough away.

Kathryn was taken aback by Jenn's attitude. She blinked. "I'm sorry?"

"Why are you here?" Jenn demanded.

Kathryn really didn't appreciate her attitude one bit. Okay, she'd messed up, but Jenn was behaving abysmally.

"What do you mean? I can go wherever I like," Kathryn replied.

"No, really, why are you here? You shouldn't be here."

"Well, I came to *apologise,* but I don't know if I want to anymore!" Kathryn argued.

"What?" Jenn frowned in confusion.

"I came to apologise," Kathryn repeated. "For the kiss," she added in a whisper.

"Oh."

"I wanted to explain that I didn't mean to give you mixed signals. I was very tired and emotional. I'd had too much to drink and I was... well, I shouldn't have kissed you. I'm not gay."

Jenn snorted a laugh.

"Is something funny?" Kathryn demanded. She was apologising, and Jenn was laughing in her face. What had gotten into her?

"Nothing," Jenn said.

"Well, it must be something. I guess you think it's funny that I tried to kiss you despite being straight. But I'm sorry, that's just the way it is. I'm completely straight."

Jenn bit her lip, looking like she was trying to prevent another laugh.

"Really," Kathryn demanded. "What's so funny about that?"

"Nothing at all." Jenn shook her head but was still smiling.

"You think something is amusing," she pointed out. "You know, I don't know if you've had a bad day, but you need an attitude adjustment."

"What?!"

"You heard me." Kathryn folded her arms and stared at Jenn.

"What did I do?"

"Demanding to know why I'm here as if I'm not allowed in some… music… bar… place!" Kathryn replied. "And asking me why I'm talking to my new friend."

"New friend?" Jenn folded her arms and laughed softly. "Okay. Whatever."

"I think that kiss—that drunken kiss, I might add—went to your head. And you think you own me or something." Kathryn laughed derisively.

Jenn held up her hands. "You know what, Kathryn? Fine. I apologise for my behaviour. I was wrong, you were right. Clearly, you are not gay, and I understand that the kiss was just a mistake."

Kathryn hesitated a moment. Something felt off, but

she'd triumphed and won the battle of words and so she was satisfied.

"Yes, well… thank you."

"Now," Jenn smiled. "You go and spend some time with your new friend. Don't let me stop you."

Kathryn frowned at Jenn's smile. Something was definitely wrong. Maybe Jenn didn't like Echo. She glanced at the woman at the bar. Yes, she might be perceived as a bit rough around the edges, but Kathryn wasn't going to let stereotypes put her off. Echo seemed perfectly polite and, at the moment, infinitely nicer than Jenn.

"Fine, I will." She nodded her head sharply to emphasise the point.

"Fine," Jenn repeated. She shook her head and chuckled as she turned and walked towards the staff room.

Kathryn frowned. Something was very wrong, but she wasn't going to let Jenn have the upper hand. If Jenn wanted her to leave and not hang out with Echo, then Kathryn would stay and would talk to Echo all damn night.

She returned to the barstool and let out a sigh.

"Problem?" Echo frowned.

"Not really." Kathryn shook her head. "She was being possessive, but I put her in her place."

"Good for you! So, are you and her?" Echo gestured between them with her finger.

Kathryn balked. "Me and Jenn? No, no, nothing there at all."

Echo looked at her for a couple of seconds before grinning. "Kathryn, can I buy you a drink?"

"You know, that sounds like just what I need."

31

FAÇADE

ARABELLA SAW a queue of people at the door to Façade. She looked at the neon flashing lights and frowned. "What is this place?"

"You'll see," Rebecca replied.

She rolled her eyes. Rebecca still refused to tell her anything. Not that she was worried. Rebecca had yet to lead her wrong. She knew Arabella's limits, and while she might push on them a little, she never went beyond them.

They joined the queue, and Arabella realised everyone in the queue was a woman, even the security guard at the door.

Is this a gay bar? she wondered to herself. If it was, she couldn't understand the secrecy. Did Rebecca really think she was such a prude that she wouldn't be able to cope with a gay bar?

The queue moved quickly, and they were soon in the venue. There were stages at each end of the room, a variety of chairs and tables in between, and a large bar in the middle of the room.

Her eyes focused on someone familiar sitting at the bar.

"Is that... Kathryn?" Arabella asked in surprise.

Rebecca followed her gaze. "Yeah, she's looking a bit drunk."

"Seems to be a common theme with her," Arabella pointed out.

"Hey, she's on holiday. Don't judge."

"I thought you hated her for messing your friend around?" Arabella asked.

"No, I hate that she messed my friend around," Rebecca corrected. "But I don't hate *her*."

Arabella smiled at yet another example of Rebecca's compassion. If someone had upset her friend the way they had Jenn, Arabella wouldn't be so generous.

"Do you mind if we go and sit with her?" Rebecca asked.

"If you'd like to..."

"Yeah, I want to know why she's here. And what's going on with her and Jenn."

"Oh, so you want to meddle?" Arabella laughed.

"No." Rebecca smiled. "Just... fish for information."

They approached Kathryn and the woman she was talking with. They were so deep in conversation that they didn't notice Arabella and Rebecca beside them until Rebecca delicately coughed.

Kathryn turned around and beamed when she saw them. "Hi!"

Oh dear, drunk as a skunk, Arabella thought.

"Hi, we didn't expect to see you here," Rebecca said. She gestured to the two stools beside her. "May we join you?"

"Absolutely," Kathryn said. "This is my friend, Echo. Echo, this is Rebecca and Arabella. They're English."

Arabella felt her eyebrow raise in amusement. She didn't think she'd ever been introduced like that before. She shook hands with the interestingly named Echo and took her seat, leaving a space between herself and Kathryn. If Rebecca really wanted to sit with her, she could sit *next* to her.

"Can I get anyone a drink?" Arabella offered.

"That's very kind of you," Echo immediately spoke up. "I'll have another beer."

"White wine would be lovely," Kathryn said.

"Rum and coke for me," Rebecca ordered as she sat down.

Arabella made eye contact with bartender and ordered the drinks, getting herself a white wine as well.

"So, you seen the show before?" Echo asked.

"I have, Arabella hasn't," Rebecca answered.

Arabella looked over to the stages. *Show*, she thought. *Hmm.*

"How about you?" Rebecca asked.

"I have, but this one hasn't," Echo said with a gesture towards Kathryn. "I keep telling her, she's in for a real treat!"

"Yes, you do," Kathryn said. She sounded a little glazed, and Arabella felt sorry for her. She wondered how the woman had found herself in some kind of gay bar with Echo. She couldn't imagine it was planned.

"So, you know what the show is?" Rebecca asked. She sounded cautious.

"No, but Echo says it's amazing," Kathryn said.

The bartender served the drinks, and the conversation ended.

Rebecca leaned in close to Arabella. "Okay, this is weird. Why is she here?"

"I've no idea," Arabella said. "Could Jenn have invited her?"

"I doubt it," Rebecca replied. "I don't see why she'd invite her to—"

Suddenly the lights in the bar dimmed. Music started blaring through wall-mounted speakers.

Arabella looked around the audience, noting that the predominantly female crowd had started clapping loudly and wolf-whistling. She noticed that Kathryn was looking around in confusion as well. Wherever they were, and whatever they were about to see, it was clear that it was only her and Kathryn who were out of the loop.

A single spotlight appeared on the main stage.

Jenn Cook stepped into the light, wearing a tight, floor-length red dress with slits up each leg to her hips.

The crowd roared with excitement as Jenn winked and blew kisses at them.

"It's a burlesque show," Rebecca shouted in Arabella's ear about the din.

Arabella looked at Rebecca in shock, and then leant forward to look at Kathryn. The woman had practically swallowed her own tongue at the sight of Jenn on the stage.

This should be interesting, Arabella thought.

"Are you okay to stay?" Rebecca asked.

"Absolutely," she replied. She wasn't about to miss both shows: the one Jenn was putting on, and Kathryn's reaction to it.

She turned to face the stage and started to applaud with the rest of the audience.

3 2

WHAT A SHOW

THE SHOW ENDED, and the room was soon awash in cheers and applause. Arabella turned to look at Rebecca who was eyeing her curiously.

"What did you think?" Rebecca asked.

"It was amazing," Arabella replied while clapping her appreciation.

Rebecca sagged in relief. Clearly, she'd been concerned that Arabella might not have enjoyed such a risqué art form. She could understand Rebecca not explaining what the show was beforehand, she wasn't sure she would have gone if she had known. But she was so happy that she had.

She'd never seen a burlesque show before, she'd made assumptions about them, but she was pleased to find that—in this case—she was wrong. The show was undeniably naughty but also extremely classy.

It had been a little unsettling at first to watch one of Rebecca's friends as she danced, swivelled, teased, and, ultimately, undressed. But she'd soon got into the show and could appreciate the artistic content, as well as the incredible bodily strength that Jenn possessed. She'd made a mental note to talk to Jenn about her workout routine.

She looked down the bar at Kathryn. Echo was standing above her, applauding so loudly that Arabella was deafened by it. Kathryn wasn't reacting at all. She seemed to be in her own world, staring at the empty stage in a stupor.

Arabella cupped her hand to Rebecca's ear and whispered, "Someone clearly enjoyed the show."

Rebecca cast a casual glance towards Kathryn before turning back to Arabella with a grin.

The applause was starting to die down, and they could hear each other again.

"Man, what a show!" Echo shouted.

"Indeed, it was," Arabella agreed.

Echo ordered another round of drinks. Arabella regarded Kathryn's pale face and thought that the last thing the woman needed was another drink.

Echo put her hand on Kathryn's shoulder. "Man, that show was incredible. You tapped that?"

Kathryn was still staring at the stage, completely unaware of her surroundings.

"Hey, earth to Kathryn?" Echo asked.

Kathryn slowly turned to look at Echo. "Oh, I'm sorry, I was miles away. What did you say?"

Echo smiled. "I asked if you've tapped that?"

Kathryn recoiled. "No! Absolutely not!"

Rebecca looked at Arabella with a raised eyebrow. Arabella unashamedly watched the interaction.

Echo chuckled and held up her hands. "It's okay, I'm not the jealous type. I know how to share my toys."

Arabella almost snorted a laugh. Supposedly straight Kathryn had somehow—and judging by the look on her face, *mistakenly*—found herself in a burlesque lesbian bar. With a new girlfriend called Echo who had been plying her with drinks for some time. She watched Kathryn swallow hard and realised with a chuckle that the same fact was now dawning on Kathryn.

Echo put her arm around Kathryn. "After this, I was wondering if you wanted to go on to Shady's? It's not as classy as it is here. There the girls take it all off, not just down to their panties like they do here."

Arabella covered her mouth to contain her laughter. Yes, Kathryn had got herself into quite the mess.

Kathryn's mouth opened and closed a few times as she struggled to know what to say. Arabella regarded her a little more closely. She nudged Rebecca. "I think she's about to go," she said.

"Go?" Rebecca asked.

She gestured towards Kathryn with her head.

Echo seemed none the wiser in regard to Kathryn's unstable state.

"Unless you want to go back to my place?" Echo suggested. "We could crack open a couple of beers and I can give you a hands-on demonstration of why they call me Echo."

Kathryn's eyes fluttered closed just as Rebecca turned around. A split-second later, Kathryn was out for the count, Rebecca catching her before she fell to the floor.

33

ALL A MISUNDERSTANDING

JENN SAT in her light blue silk kimono, eating potato chips from a large bag on the dressing table in front of her. The air-conditioning unit in her small dressing room was silently blowing out ice-cold air. She watched the rise and fall of Kathryn's chest, strictly for medical reasons, of course.

Five minutes earlier, a quick knock at her door from Monica had informed her that they'd had a 'fainter' in the bar. It wasn't uncommon that the heat, or the excitement during some of the racier shows, would get to one of the audience.

As the dressing room was one of the few places where there was a door, a sofa, and reliable air-conditioning it ended up being the go-to place for any casualties.

Jenn had been surprised when an unconscious Kathryn had been carried in by one of the bouncers, accompanied by Rebecca.

Rebecca had quickly explained that she seemed to just be overheated and exhausted. Apparently, Echo had been queueing up drinks for her for a while. Rebecca hadn't stayed, wanting to get back to Arabella, and so Jenn had

A.E. RADLEY

watched and waited for Kathryn to come back to the land of the living.

She didn't have to wait long. Brown eyes fluttered open and looked around the room. Soon, they found Jenn, and terror filled them.

Jenn smiled. "Hey."

"Hey," Kathryn replied softly. "What… what happened?"

"Easy! Go easy sitting up," Jenn said as Kathryn gingerly raised herself up from the couch. "You fainted," she explained. She picked up a glass of cold water from the dressing table and handed it to Kathryn without standing up.

Kathryn gratefully took the glass and drank down some of the liquid. She nervously looked around the room as she did. She had barely finished drinking when she asked, "Where's Echo?"

"Your girlfriend? She went to get you a taxi," Jenn said seriously. Kathryn's eyes widened, and Jenn had to laugh. "I'm kidding, she's gone."

"Oh, thank god," Kathryn sighed in relief.

"Remind me," Jenn drawled. "You originally came here to tell me that you're not gay, right? Before you got yourself a girlfriend and watched my burlesque show at one of the most popular lesbian bars in the city. Right?"

Kathryn looked up at Jenn with an exasperated expression. "It's all a misunderstanding."

"You seem pretty good at them," Jenn commented. She stood up and walked behind a dressing screen.

After a few silent moments Kathryn spoke again. "The show was amazing."

"Thank you," Jenn said simply. She didn't wish to be drawn into any further conversation.

"I'd never seen burlesque before."

Jenn removed her kimono and sighed softly. She leant her head on the wall of the dressing area. Why did Kathryn have to faint? Why was she now trapped with the frustrating woman? She was thankful for the tall dressing screen, which meant she didn't have to see her.

"I didn't think you would have," Jenn replied.

"What made you get into it?"

Jenn started to strip out of her stage outfit. Since she was stuck with Kathryn, she might as well make conversation.

"A couple of years after I came to New Orleans, I saw a show. There are a lot of competitions in the city when it comes to burlesque," Jenn explained. "I'd always been interested in dance and performing, and I decided to go to a class, just for me, you know?"

She pulled on a pair of skinny denim shorts. "My teacher said I was good at it, she wanted me to go on at a talent night. It was the seediest place ever, and I hated every second of it. Men were whistling and leering and throwing money at me. I felt like a stripper, and that wasn't what I was there for. Burlesque is an art form."

Jenn put a white tank top on and walked out from the dressing screen, back towards her dressing table. "But I met a woman who worked here at Façade. She asked me to come down and interview. I do one show a week, and I do it because I enjoy it. It's a nice setup here."

Kathryn nodded.

"And I'm sorry I was short with you earlier," Jenn continued. "It's just I knew you had no idea Façade was a gay bar, and Echo, well, she likes to collect fresh babydykes. I wanted to warn you."

Kathryn chuckled. "And then I pissed you off and you threw me to the wolves?"

Jenn laughed. "Yep, pretty much."

Kathryn smiled and took another long gulp of water.

"Are you feeling better? Can I get you more water?" Jenn asked.

"I'm feeling better," Kathryn said. "Just a little overheated and, well… it doesn't matter now."

"Go on," Jenn gently pressed, even though she wasn't sure she wanted to know.

She'd had a lot of time to think about Kathryn's yo-yoing sexuality, and even though she found Kathryn extremely attractive, she'd decided to keep her distance. The last thing she needed was to get her heart broken by someone who hadn't gotten their act together.

While she didn't believe for one moment that Kathryn was straight, she wasn't ready to be the one who got hurt trying to help the woman see that for herself. No, it had to end now.

Kathryn looked at her nervously. She looked like she was mentally weighing up her options before she finally whispered, "I think I'm… confused."

"Confused?" Jenn frowned.

"Yes, confused." Kathryn nodded. "I've seen a lot of things since I came to this city and, well, tonight was an eye-opener."

Jenn suddenly understood what she meant. "Ah, confused. What's so bad about feeling confused?"

"I'm straight," Kathryn explained. "I've always been straight, I have never *ever* looked at a woman in… that way. But now I'm, well, I'm seeing things and feeling things I haven't felt before."

Jenn held her breath for a second as she wondered what to do next. After Kathryn's drunken kiss she had stayed awake all night. *Avoidance is the best strategy*, she reminded herself. *Come on, you can do this.*

She'd previously met women visiting New Orleans who were curious and wanted someone to explore with. And on a couple of occasions Jenn had participated in their experiments.

Each had ended disastrously. For Jenn. Usually when the women went back home to their husbands or boyfriends, having managed to scratch the itch and leave it in New Orleans.

Jenn couldn't stand to have her heart broken again.

"Look, Kathryn," she started. She looked down at the floor, choosing her words carefully. "I—I have feelings for you. You've got to know that. You're smart, funny, and—" She looked up and sighed. "Breathtakingly beautiful. But I can't be your experimental toy. I just can't."

Kathryn blushed bright red and broke eye contact. "I'm not asking you to be."

"I think you are, or at least I think you eventually *will*," Jenn admitted quietly. "I've been here before; straight woman comes to the Big Easy and sees the other side of the coin. Wants to experiment. Then they go home, back to their life. But I'm left here."

"I..." Kathryn started. "You kissed *me*, after the tram—"

"Streetcar," Jenn correctly softly.

"After the *streetcar*, you kissed me. You started all of this!" Kathryn pointed out.

"I know, and I apologised," Jenn said. "I shouldn't have kissed you, but I thought you were flirting with me."

"Maybe I was." Kathryn sighed. She put her head in her hands. "I just don't know any more."

Jenn swallowed hard. "I... you... you're just tired and emotional. Like you said to me earlier."

"I suppose," Kathryn muttered. She looked up again.

Jenn took a deep breath. She had to end this here and now. She was already in pain. Prolonging it would just make things worse. "I think it would be best if we avoided each other."

Kathryn paused for a moment, looking at Jenn in hurt

and confusion. But the confusion slowly faded, replaced with understanding.

"I agree. I'm sorry... I shouldn't have come here."

"It's fine, I appreciate you coming to apologise. And hey, now you know you like burlesque," Jenn pointed out. "Another thing that New Orleans has taught you about yourself."

Kathryn put the empty glass on the dressing table and stood up and looked nervously at the door.

"Do I want to know how Echo got her nickname?"

Jenn laughed. "Probably not."

Kathryn nodded. "Is there another way out of here? I'm not sure I want to see her again... I think we're engaged."

Jenn grinned. She'd miss Kathryn's dry wit. "Sure, I'll walk you through to the fire exit."

She grabbed her bags, and they both left the dressing room. They walked down a small hallway, Jenn saying goodbye to a few members of staff as they left.

She pushed the door open and gestured for Kathryn to step out into the warm night air.

"You know," she couldn't help saying. "If you are curious, then Façade is a good place to hang out. It's more upmarket than some of the other bars, if you don't include Echo."

Kathryn shook her head nervously. "I... I don't think I'll come back."

They walked up the empty alleyway.

"If you are curious, then you should probably explore it," Jenn said sympathetically. "The person we end up with is an important factor in our lives. If you maybe are gay, or bi, then you're opening up your possibilities of finding your true love."

Kathryn chuckled lightly. "True love?"

"Yeah." Jenn smiled. "Don't you believe in true love?"

"No," Kathryn said quickly. "I think that's just a fairy tale our parents tell us to protect us from how lonely the world can be. Something to keep people occupied, millions of people seeking out their true love to prevent them from actually seeing how dire their life is. The concept of true love is just a distraction."

Jenn stopped walking and blinked at Kathryn in shock. "Wow."

"What?" Kathryn frowned.

"That's some heavy shit right there." Jenn chuckled. "But seriously, have you ever been in love?"

"Of course I have." Kathryn shrugged. "I just don't think it's this all-encompassing dream state that we're led to believe it is."

"I take it back," Jenn said.

"Take what back?"

"Don't explore your curiosity. Don't go bringing that doom and gloom attitude into the queer community," Jenn laughed.

Kathryn gently slapped the back of Jenn's arm.

They continued up the alleyway towards the busy road ahead.

Kathryn regarded Jenn curiously. "So, you believe in true love?"

"Yep." She smiled. "I think that there is someone, the perfect someone, out there for everyone. And you know what else?"

"What else?" Kathryn smiled.

"I also believe in fate," Jenn confessed. "So, I also believe that fate will push you towards your true love if you let it. I bet you think that's silly, right?"

"Yes," Kathryn said simply. "But I sometimes wish I could believe in that kind of thing, too."

"Too much of a realist, huh?" Jenn asked.

Kathryn nodded. "Something like that."

They approached the end of the alleyway, coming to a stop before they joined the bustle of the city.

Kathryn sighed. "Thank you. For, well, everything. I'm sorry I've been a constant source of trouble for you."

Jenn chuckled. "It's been fun. I'm glad I met you, Kathryn. And I really hope you enjoy the rest of your time in New Orleans. As I said when we first met, there's something for everyone if you just go out and look for it."

Kathryn looked at her, and Jenn momentarily got lost in the soulful brown eyes. She blinked and looked away. She knew down that road led to heartache. She'd had her own fair share of that over the last few years. This was for the best. For everyone.

"Good night, Jenn," Kathryn said, her bright smile not quite meeting her eyes.

34

A TOUCH OF JEALOUSY

"Well, that was an interesting evening," Arabella said.

"Unexpected," Rebecca agreed.

They walked hand in hand down the street towards the hotel. Rebecca was enjoying feeling Arabella's soft hand in hers. She wondered if this behaviour would continue when they were back home in London.

Nothing had been mentioned about what they would do when they returned home. Rebecca didn't know if Arabella was ready to start introducing her as more than her just a friend, especially to her father.

While she wanted to know, she also didn't want to rock the boat. She'd take what she could get for now. The going-home situation could be a conversation for another day.

"So, you liked the show?" Rebecca asked, trying to take her mind off their eventual departure.

"I did, very much so."

Rebecca furrowed her brow a little. She'd been convinced that Arabella would like the burlesque show. She knew she appreciated other forms of dance, so it wasn't too big a leap.

While some people might attend a burlesque club to see flesh on display, she knew Arabella would understand the complexity of the act and the fitness required.

Although, now she allowed her mind to wander, she did wonder what Arabella thought of Jenn's performance. Did Arabella get turned on by it? She couldn't blame her, Jenn was a very attractive woman. But she was her friend. It would feel weird if Arabella thought of her that way.

"So... you, um, liked the... choreography?" She winced slightly. It sounded ridiculous to her own ears.

"I did. Jenn must have incredible core strength," Arabella said.

Jealously rushed through Rebecca in a way she'd never felt before. Now she wished she'd never gone to Façade. She looked around the bustling street. They'd left soon after the main show had ended, along with many other people from the club.

She suddenly felt extremely possessive of Arabella. They were walking along a street, crammed with women who loved women. Women who would obviously find Arabella attractive. Some who Arabella might also find attractive.

It had never occurred to her before that she might have to compete for Arabella's affections. But it made sense, Arabella was stunningly beautiful. She could easily have her pick of women.

Arabella let go of her hand, and Rebecca looked at her in confusion.

"You were hurting my hand," Arabella explained in reply to her unasked question.

"Oh god, I'm so sorry." She looked at Arabella's hand. It was red from the pressure of her grasp.

"It's okay, you were just holding on a little tight. Are you okay?" Arabella questioned. She placed her hands around Rebecca's upper arm as they continued to walk.

"Do you find other women attractive?" Rebecca blurted out. "I mean, it's fine if you do. I was just wondering."

Arabella laughed that deep throaty laugh of hers. "You ask me that *after* you take me to a lesbian bar?"

"Yeah, I didn't think it through," Rebecca said with a chuckle. "Sorry, you don't have to answer that. It's a silly question."

"Are *you* attracted to other women?" Arabella asked.

Rebecca felt her pulse speed up. She'd really put her foot in it now. She couldn't deny it, she'd dated other women.

"Don't answer that," Arabella replied softly. "I just wanted to make the point. We're both attracted to other women. I may not have dated any, but I can appreciate a good-looking woman when I see one. But, I don't think of it as anything else than that. Appreciation. From afar."

"I'm sorry, I really shouldn't have asked that," Rebecca said. "I just suddenly felt jealous, and I've never felt that way before."

"You've never felt jealous before?" Arabella sounded surprised.

"No. When I've been in relationships, it's always been very secure. We started as friends, became more, and generally lasted a while. I've never been a one-night stand kind of person."

"I see," Arabella said. "Do you think you felt jealous because I'm new to being with a woman?"

Rebecca shrugged. "I don't know. I didn't really get time to think about it like that. The thought was just suddenly there."

Arabella stopped walking. Her grip on Rebecca's arm pulled her to a stop, too. The older woman stood in front of Rebecca.

"I can see another woman and think she is attractive, but I don't want to be in a relationship with her, or kiss her, or sleep with her. I want to be with you. You're like a best friend to me, as well as someone I'm desperately attracted to."

Rebecca's eyes drifted to Arabella's lips. She closed her eyes and shook her head. Now wasn't the time to stare at her beautiful girlfriend's features. Now was the time to talk about something that had been bothering her for a while.

"It's just," Rebecca started. She paused as she tried to think of an appropriate parallel. "You… you wouldn't go into a store and buy the first pair of shoes you tried on."

Arabella's mouth contorted as she tried to smother a grin.

"No," she allowed. "I wouldn't. But, I'm assuming that in this charming analogy, you are comparing yourself to a pair of shoes?"

Rebecca nodded.

"What if I'd passed that shop window every day for weeks? Looking in the window at those shoes, analysing them, thinking about how they would fit? How they would feel? Balancing if they were the right shoes for me. Before, finally, one day going into the store and trying them on. Would that make sense?"

Rebecca felt a bubble of happiness well up in her chest. That did make sense. She'd been so caught up in being Arabella's first that she hadn't considered that Arabella had spent a lot time thinking about this. She wasn't the kind of person to jump into a new situation without thoroughly examining it first. Arabella had thought about being in a relationship, probably far more than Rebecca had.

It wasn't like her to worry about such things. Or things in general, really. She knew exactly why this whole situation with Arabella bothered her. While Arabella had spent the last few weeks and months figuring out if she wanted to date Rebecca, she'd spent the same amount of time falling in love with Arabella. Not that she'd admit that to Arabella just yet.

"That makes sense," she replied.

"Good. I know I'm new to this, but I assure you that I'm not going to run off with some other woman."

Rebecca took her hand again and continued to walk them towards the hotel.

"The jealous streak is cute, though," Arabella pointed out.

"No, it's not." Rebecca chuckled.

"It is," Arabella argued gently. "It's nice to know you want me."

"You have no idea," Rebecca mumbled.

"Hmm? What was that?"

"I have an idea," Rebecca changed the subject. "Let's head down to the river for an evening stroll."

Arabella regarded her suspiciously for a moment, obviously wondering if that was what Rebecca had said. Thankfully, she didn't push the matter. She simply nodded her head in agreement.

3 5

GYM BUDDIES

Kathryn swiped her hotel room key card on the door to
the gym. The light shone green, and she opened the door.
She tossed her towel onto a table by the window and looked
at the view for a couple of moments.

Annoyingly, New Orleans was a pretty place first thing in
the morning. She really did think that she would hate everything about the Louisiana city, but as time went by she had
to admit it had a certain charm.

Unfortunately, she'd learnt that from a person she had
deeply hurt. Someone who had asked her to stay away.
Kathryn didn't think that she'd ever had someone ask her to
avoid them before.

It was a profoundly unsettling feeling.

More so even than her sudden confusion about herself.
She kept trying to push down, but it kept bubbling back to
the surface. She was pretty sure that alcohol wasn't the reason
for her sudden emotional upset, but it was definitely the
reason for her headache.

"Never. Drinking. Again." She selected a treadmill with a

view of the river in the distance and selected a slow walking speed.

She had no idea if it was the fact she was on vacation, the alcohol, the grief swirling through her mind, or even the heat, but something was taking over her thought processes.

She had never looked at other women in a sexual way, but now she couldn't stop thinking about it. Sleep had evaded her most of the night as she wondered about her reaction to the show, and about her general behaviour since arriving in town.

At first, she had thought that it was the burlesque show itself. The whole art of burlesque was of course tantalising and somehow forbidden, so any reasonable person would find it stimulating.

Shaking her head to remove the thoughts, she cranked up the speed a little on the treadmill.

She closed her eyes and focused on her breathing and her steps. She had to get herself together. She felt like she was spinning out of control. Erica had been right, she needed a vacation. Sadly, the vacation was making her realise just how troubled she was.

The air pressure in the cooled room changed. She opened her eyes to see Arabella coming in. She wore a black tank top and shorts.

"Hi," Kathryn greeted her solemnly.

She couldn't remember too much about the previous evening, but she knew Arabella had been there for her embarrassing display.

"Hi," Arabella said. She placed her water bottle and key card in the holders of the treadmill beside Kathryn. "Mind if I join you?"

"Feel free," Kathryn said.

Arabella adjusted the settings, and her treadmill whirred into action.

"How are you feeling?" Arabella asked politely.

"Justifiably terrible," Kathryn replied. "I'm so sorry for how I behaved last night."

"No need to apologise," Arabella said.

"You must think I'm some crazy alcoholic, stirring up trouble all over town."

"The thought had crossed my mind," Arabella confessed. "But I'm not here to judge."

"I don't usually drink a lot," Kathryn admitted. "In fact, I hadn't drunk for over three years, aside from the occasional glass of wine at a work function. I've gone a little crazy here, but I'm not touching another drop of alcohol."

"I see," Arabella said.

She thinks I'm an alcoholic, Kathryn realised. *Of course she would, you told her you didn't drink at all for three years. And now you're proclaiming to not touch another drop.*

"It was a personal choice," Kathryn added. "The not drinking."

"You don't have to explain yourself to me," Arabella said.

"I feel like I do."

Arabella sighed, finally turning her head to face Kathryn. "You don't, you really don't. I'm just… puzzled. Rebecca tells me about you and Jenn, and… I don't know your motives."

Kathryn chuckled bitterly. "Neither do I."

"Why were you in a lesbian bar last night?" Arabella asked.

"I didn't know it was a lesbian bar, and I had no idea that Jenn was performing *that* show there. I found out that was where she'd be, and I went to apologise to her. We had a little fight and she neglected to tell me that I was in a lesbian bar, on the night of her burlesque show, and making friends with a known womaniser."

Arabella laughed softly. "Sounds like she got her own back. What were you apologising for?"

"I... kissed her."

Arabella's brow knitted. "I thought *she* kissed *you?*"

"That was the night before," Kathryn explained.

Arabella slapped the stop button on her treadmill and turned to face her again. "So... you kissed her? The night we had dinner together?"

"Yes, it was a mistake. I was d—"

"Drunk," Arabella guessed.

Kathryn pressed the stop button on her own machine. "Yes. I just... I don't know what I'm doing."

"Well, why did you kiss her? I've had too much to drink on the rare occasion, but I don't randomly kiss people," Arabella said. She picked up her water bottle and took a long sip.

"I don't know," Kathryn said. "At the time, I just wanted to. But I've never been interested in women before. I'm straight."

"You don't sound very straight, if you're kissing women. And I saw the way you looked at Jenn during her routine last night." Arabella looked at her pointedly for a few moments.

Kathryn felt a familiar clenching at her chest. Panic.

"Do you like Jenn?" Arabella asked.

"I don't know," she whispered.

"You do," Arabella pressed. "You do, somewhere deep inside. You know."

She did know. Or, at least, she thought she did.

"I don't understand, though." She leaned heavily on the handrail. "I have never, ever been attracted to women. And then I met Jenn. With her ripped shorts and her messy hair. And now I don't know what I'm feeling. Anyway, it doesn't matter. I'm not going to find out, Jenn doesn't want to see me again."

As much as it hurt, she could understand. It wasn't fair to

ask Jenn to join her in a journey into the unknown. Especially after Jenn had admitted feelings for her.

"She doesn't want to get hurt," Arabella said. "Something which you seem to be—unwittingly—doing to her. Frequently."

"I know, I know. I feel terrible. I want to apologise to her, and somehow make it up to her. But I tried that, and I made things so much worse."

"What did you say to her?"

Kathryn winced. "I told her I'm confused."

Arabella laughed. "Oh, I bet she loved that."

"She told me she had feelings for me and she didn't want to be my *experimental toy*." Kathryn stepped off the treadmill and over to the water fountain. She plucked a paper cone from the stack and filled it with water.

Arabella regarded her silently for a few moments. She stepped off her treadmill, walked over to the chairs by the water cooler, and sat down.

"When I met Rebecca, at the end of last year, I thought I was straight. I was engaged to be married—to a man," she explained. "I'd never looked at a woman in any way other than platonically. Ever."

Kathryn downed the water and poured herself another drink.

"Then, we shared a journey home—which we told you about over dinner. We argued, made assumptions about each other... it wasn't exactly love at first sight. It was more frustration at first, second, and third sight."

"Sounds familiar." Kathryn thought back to her first meeting with Jenn at the bar, then the second at the parade.

"But during the journey we talked. Really talked. I got to see another side to Rebecca, not just the person I assumed she was at the start of the trip, but the real Rebecca, or, at least, part of her. And she opened my eyes. She talked about love and relationships in a way that had me thinking she was a naïve child. I thought she lived in some kind of dream world.

"But her words stuck with me. I started to look at my own life, and I realised I wasn't happy. I didn't want to marry Alastair, and I didn't want to do all the things that had been planned for me since I was a child. I wanted to experience things, see sights, meet people who taught me things."

Arabella laughed as she became lost in the memory. She looked up at Kathryn with a sparkle in her eyes.

"Rebecca told me the purpose of life is to grow as a person." She rolled her eyes. "I thought she was nuts. She said she wanted to be more today than she was yesterday. And it hit me that I hadn't changed for years. And, in fact, what I was was entirely the product of who I *thought* I should be."

Kathryn could recognise that. She herself was the result of stereotypes and family requirements. Only recently had she been forced to take drastic action to keep the status quo. But it wasn't something she was ready to talk about yet. Not with Arabella.

"The last few months have been terrifying," Arabella admitted as she continued. "One moment I felt for sure that I was ready to leap into a new life with Rebecca. The very next I was clinging to my old life as hard as I could. And in between those two extremes, I buried my head in the ground and ignored everything. Hoping that things would somehow resolve themselves."

"What changed?" Despite her bleariness, Kathryn had noticed that Arabella and Rebecca were together at Façade the night before. They'd shared meaningful looks, and, at one point, Arabella had kissed Rebecca. Something had obviously changed since the previous evening. Maybe something had happened when they left early.

"Coming here," Arabella stated, "I made myself stop and think. I couldn't mess Rebecca around anymore. I had to make a decision, even if it wasn't a permanent one. I was stuck in limbo and I didn't want that anymore. I didn't want to do that to Rebecca anymore."

Kathryn smiled. "You two make a great couple. She speaks very highly of you."

Arabella's cheeks reddened. "She's amazing. And I finally realised that I'm lucky to have her in my life and it was time to tell her how I felt. Or else I'd potentially lose her."

"I wish I could be sure," Kathryn said. "I just... I honestly don't know how I feel. I feel so confused." She raked her hands through her hair. "I know that's not a great answer, but it's an honest one. I find all of this so confusing. And I feel so damn old, like there's a new term to explain someone's sexual preference every week and I have no idea what they mean."

Arabella smiled. "It is hard," she agreed.

"Apparently, Jenn is pansexual. Which I didn't even know existed before this week. I keep telling her I'm straight, but how can I be straight? I can't stop thinking about her, and it kills me to know that I've completely blown it with her."

Kathryn's eyes widened as she realised what she said. She gulped down another cup full of water.

"Sounds to me like you have your answer," Arabella said. "You can't stop thinking about her. Is that usually the case with women you've just met?"

"No."

Arabella looked at her watch. She stood up and walked back over to the treadmill. "Maybe you're meant to be with Jenn, maybe you're not," she said as she pushed some buttons on the panel. "But whatever is going on, you need to figure it out for you. You owe it to yourself to know what it is that you're feeling. You can't live your entire life as a lie. Trust me, it doesn't work. Now, I really need to get on with this workout because my *girlfriend* is waiting for me."

Arabella started to jog as the machine sped up. She turned her attention away from Kathryn and focused on her movements.

She's right, Kathryn thought. *I can't bury my head in the sand about this. I need to figure this out.*

36

SEEING THE SIGHTS

"So, we're on this open-top bus and we're freezing," Jenn explained.

Rebecca laughed as she poured some cola from the bottle into her glass. "It was *so* cold," she reiterated to Arabella. "Like, I've never been so cold in my life."

Arabella put a fond hand on Rebecca's and squeezed. Jenn smiled at the action. It was heartwarming to see the new couple interacting.

Her heart clenched. She missed being in a relationship. There had been some offers, but Jenn was getting fed up with playing the scene. She wanted security, a future. She smiled as she watched Arabella's thumb gently rubbing circles on the back of Rebecca's hand. She wanted what they had.

"December in New York," she said. "And your girlfriend had no idea it would be so cold."

"Hey! I checked the forecast before I travelled, and it didn't seem that cold," Rebecca replied.

"It's a different kind of cold in New York," Arabella said as if it were obvious.

"I know that *now*," Rebecca grumped.

"Anyway, the bus is about twenty minutes out from Midtown—where both our hotels are located—and Rebecca looks at me and dead serious says, 'I don't think I'm gonna make it'," Jenn said. "So, we decide to get off at the next stop and find somewhere to warm up. Because being on that open-top bus with the wind blowing? Not fun. Luckily the next stop was by some stores, so we went into this clothing store and bought jackets that you could go *skiing* in and then we went to a coffee shop to defrost."

"And you've been friends ever since?" Arabella asked in admiration.

"Yep, we toured around New York together after that," Rebecca replied. "Had dinner together a few times, and then stayed in touch."

Arabella sipped her orange juice as her eyes darted between them. Jenn knew what was coming, the question she'd ask if their positions were reversed.

"So… did you two… ever?" Arabella asked.

"No," Jenn and Rebecca replied at the same time.

Jenn laughed. "No, we've never been anything more than good friends. We kept talking about travelling together, but I was busy and then Rebecca's mom got sick."

"And she has a billion jobs," Rebecca said. "Like she would ever be able to coordinate all those jobs to get some time off! Which is why I had to fly out here to this… what did she call it?"

Jenn smirked. "A sordid hellhole."

Rebecca burst out laughing.

Arabella frowned, looking between the two of them in confusion. "Have I missed something?"

"When Kathryn first came to town, she was dropped off by her sister in the middle of Bourbon Street. And she loudly stated that she didn't want to be left in this sordid hellhole," Rebecca explained.

Arabella's eyes widened. "That doesn't seem very wise."

"It wasn't," Jenn agreed. "She's lucky it was early in the morning and no one was around. But, I do have to give her some credit and say that she was in an extremely bad mood at the time. Every time I saw her after that, she was much nicer."

Rebecca played with the label on her cola bottle. "I don't know how you can defend her after what she did."

Jenn shrugged. "I liked her."

You like her, her traitorous brain amended.

"I saw her this morning in the gym," Arabella said softly.

Rebecca looked at her in a way that made Jenn think this was the first she was hearing about the meeting, too.

"How was she?" Jenn asked.

"Embarrassed. Confused." Arabella chuckled. "Hungover."

"I told her to stay away from me," Jenn confessed.

"She mentioned," Arabella said. "I think that's wise, she doesn't seem to know what she wants. I..." Her face contorted as she appeared to try to verbalise her thoughts.

"You?" Jenn asked, eager to know.

"I get the impression that there's something else going on with her," Arabella said. "I don't know, she seems like she has a lot on her mind."

"No excuse to act the way she has," Rebecca reminded them both.

Jenn knew that Rebecca was just being protective of her, and she appreciated it. But the truth was, Jenn felt regret at telling Kathryn to stay away. Part of her wondered if maybe Kathryn was close to making a breakthrough in her apparent 'confusion'.

It didn't matter now. She'd made her decision and told Kathryn how she felt. Even if she did see Kathryn again during her stay in New Orleans, it would be nothing more than a passing hello. She needed to focus on other things, like ensuring that Rebecca and Arabella had a fantastic time in the city.

Arabella's phone rang, and she rolled her eyes. "Excuse me, I've been expecting this call."

She got up and walked over to an empty part of the coffee shop. Rebecca watched her, concern in her eyes.

"Problem?" Jenn asked.

"Work keep calling her," Rebecca said. "At first it was emails, then last night they called her twice. I know she's the boss, but it's like they can't cope without her. She's on holiday."

"I don't suppose you can tell her not to answer?" Jenn asked.

Rebecca shook her head. "No, her work ethic is off the scale. I would have thrown my phone in the Mississippi by now."

"I don't think she'll get a signal out in the bayou. Maybe we should suggest heading out there this afternoon, taking a boat trip," Jenn suggested.

Rebecca's eyes shone. "Could we do that?"

"Sure. I know a couple of great companies, as long as you're both okay with gators and snakes?" Jenn had taken a friend from Boston on the tour once, completely forgetting that he was terrified of snakes. He'd screamed so loud she still heard ringing in her left ear, two years later.

"We'll ask her when she gets back," Rebecca said. Her expression became distant, and Jenn knew she was already planning what camera equipment to bring with her to the swamp.

37

GUIDING HAND

A SUGGESTION from the concierge had led Kathryn to a small bistro in Frenchmen Street. The eatery was tiny and only held about a dozen tables. The windows looked out onto the bustling street, the window separating the busy street from the relaxing restaurant.

Just what I needed, she thought. *Some peace and quiet. And good food.*

The waiter approached and handed her a menu.

"Thank you."

She opened the hard-backed menu and looked over what local cuisine they had to offer. She'd only been reading for a few moments when she heard a knocking on the glass window. She lowered her menu and looked up.

Shit.

Echo was smiling at her from outside. She smiled back, hoping it seemed sincere and not terrified. A moment later, Echo entered the restaurant.

Kathryn's heart pounded hard against her rib cage. Echo sat at the table, directly opposite Kathryn.

"I was hoping I'd bump into you again," she said. She looked Kathryn up and down appreciatively.

"Here I am." Kathryn smiled, at a loss for much else to say.

"Are you meeting someone?" Echo asked.

Kathryn knew she couldn't lie. The waiter had already been informed that she was dining alone and had swept away the cutlery and glassware from the other side of the table.

"No, just me," she squeaked.

"Well, I can't have a pretty woman like you eating alone." Echo winked dramatically. She laughed loudly and then waved the waiter over.

Kathryn shifted nervously in her seat. There wasn't much that could be done about the situation, and before long they had both ordered meals and were on some kind of date. Possibly a second date, to Echo's mind.

She'd apologised for getting drunk and vanishing the night before. Echo waved away the concerns as if it were something she was used to. She kept the conversation ticking over, telling Kathryn all about her crazy exploits with various women. She certainly wasn't shy.

But Kathryn felt shy. For the first time in many, many years. She twisted her hands in her lap and wondered if she could escape somehow. She didn't want to be dining with Echo, she didn't want to be dining with *anyone*. She wanted to be left alone to her humiliation. She'd made a mess of the whole trip, and she'd only been there a few days.

She wondered why Erica couldn't have picked a business conference in the Florida Keys to dump her at. At least then she'd have been able to stay out of trouble. Why did it have to be New Orleans? The home of Jenn Cook and of Kathryn's mounting regrets.

It was over the main course that Echo suddenly dropped the bomb on Kathryn.

"So, you're still figuring it all out, aren't ya?"

Kathryn nearly choked on her chicken. She looked up at Echo with confused panic. "Sorry?"

"The gay thing," Echo said. She noisily slurped her beer. "You're not sure, I could see it in your eyes at Façade. You're curious, but you just don't *know* yet."

Kathryn swallowed hard. "Something like that."

Echo nodded knowingly. "You like the dancer, don't ya? Jenn?"

Kathryn could feel the blush rising up her cheeks. She knew lying would be impossible. "I don't know. I think so."

"Ah." Echo chuckled. "You really are having trouble figuring it all out." She interlaced her fingers and rested her chin on them. "So, how far along are we? Any lesbian activity? Touching? Kissing? I mean, I can tell there hasn't been any sex yet."

Kathryn's cheeks felt like they were on fire. She opened and closed her mouth a few times, but nothing came out.

"Oh, wow." Echo smiled sadly and shook her head. "I see, we're in the *very* early stages."

"I'm really not comfortable discussing this," Kathryn tried.

Echo ignored her. "So, let me guess. You're straight, completely straight, never been with a woman, never even looked at a woman. But now, suddenly—" she placed her open palms on her cheeks and looked shocked, "—you wonder if you like girls. Am I right?"

"N—no," Kathryn stuttered. She lowered her cutlery and took a few gulps of water. She couldn't understand how Echo was so spot on. Was she a walking cliché? Did this happen all the time?

"Come on." Echo drank some more of her beer. "I saw the way you looked at Jenn on that stage. That wasn't just someone appreciating the artistic tones of a good burlesque show. That was someone who wanted more."

Kathryn placed her water glass down on the table. She looked around the bistro to see if anyone was watching them. Luckily, it was a quiet day, and no one seemed interested. She looked back to Echo who was staring at her in wonderment.

"You don't *know*, do you?" Echo asked.

"Know what?" Kathryn questioned. She picked up the wine menu and fanned her face.

"If you're sexually interested in women," Echo answered. "You think you are, but you're not quite sure."

"I—I—" Kathryn stuttered.

Echo turned around to face the waiter and shouted for the bill. She turned back to face Kathryn. Picking up her fork, she reached across the table and stabbed at Kathryn's leftover chicken. "You're not going to eat this, are you?"

It was already removed from her plate before she had a chance to reply.

"Why did you ask for the check?" Kathryn was confused.

"Because you and I are going to hit some of New Orleans finest establishments, and we're going to solve your conundrum for you," Echo explained.

Kathryn had many questions. "Why?" was the only one she managed to verbalise.

Echo shrugged as she threw down some bills on a silver dish that the waiter had laid on the table. "I need a new toaster oven. Come on, let's get out of here."

Kathryn didn't know why she was agreeing to this madness, but she did and soon found herself hurrying after Echo as they walked along Frenchmen Street.

"I don't understand," she said.

"I know." Echo nodded. "That's why we're doing this."

"Doing what?" Kathryn pressed.

Echo turned and looked at her, a wide grin on her face.

"Think of it as a scientific experiment. You're not sure if you like women or not. You probably have questions, and the best place to deal with all of this is Heels."

"Heels?" Kathryn looked at Echo with a raised eyebrow.

Echo put her arm around Kathryn's shoulder. "It sounds worse than it is, but you and me are going to work out your sexuality. In order to do that, we need some booze and some dancers. Trust me."

"I'm not drinking anymore," Kathryn protested.

"Fine, then *I* need some booze. Do ya trust me?"

Kathryn didn't know why, but she did trust Echo. There was something about her that Kathryn liked. Probably her no-nonsense attitude. She didn't feel like she needed to pretend with Echo, the woman accepted Kathryn no matter what she said or did.

And the truth was, she needed help and guidance. And if Echo was the only person offering, then she'd accept. She was seeking answers to questions she didn't really understand. Maybe Echo was the answer to finding them.

She gave a vague nod.

Echo turned abruptly and started to enter a seedy-looking club. Kathryn grabbed her hand and pulled her back towards the street.

"Jenn doesn't work here, does she?" Kathryn asked. She tilted her head towards the flashing neon sign.

Echo laughed loudly. "No! Of course not, this is a dive. Your girl is too classy for here."

"She's not *my girl*." Kathryn blushed furiously. She looked around to ensure that no one had overheard Echo's words.

Echo held up her hands. "Okay, okay. Not your girl. Got it."

They entered the club. Kathryn winced at the décor.

Echo hadn't been kidding when she said it was a dive. Her eyes scanned the bar.

"There are men in here," she said accusingly.

Echo nodded. "Yes, unfortunately there are. But as a gay woman you have to learn that you are in a minority."

"I told you—"

"Come on." Echo cut her off by dragging her towards a booth in the corner.

Kathryn looked at the leather bench for a couple of seconds. It looked grimy, and the cracked material showed foam that had seen better days. Ordinarily, she'd never sit on a bench like that. But she was already in a dive bar, so she decided to throw caution to the wind and embrace the entire experience. She sat down opposite Echo.

"So, what's the plan?" Kathryn asked. She examined the table, which wasn't as clean as she'd like.

"Drinks," Echo announced. She waved in the direction of a waitress.

Kathryn looked seriously at Echo. "I don't want to get drunk. Seriously."

Echo nodded. "No, you don't want to get drunk. But a little liquid courage to remove that hetero-filter is going to be essential."

It made sense. And something to dull the smell was probably going to be helpful.

A waitress in a tight and skimpy outfit approached the booth. "Hey, y'all," she said. "What can I get ya?"

"Well, hey yourself." Echo smiled, clearly appreciating the bare midriff on display.

"White wine," Kathryn said quickly. The sooner they ordered, the sooner the poor girl could leave and not have to deal with Echo's leering.

Echo ordered a beer. The waitress promised to be right

back. As she left, Echo leaned out of the booth and watched her walking away.

Kathryn rolled her eyes. "Is that necessary?"

"What?" Echo shrugged. "I'm not getting any tonight, the least I can do is look."

Kathryn felt relieved that Echo didn't have plans to get her drunk and attempt to seduce her. She knew she'd have to be paralytic with drink before agreeing to anything sexual with Echo. She was nice enough, but she certainly wasn't Kathryn's type.

Kathryn frowned. The thought indicated that she did have a type.

"What's with the frown?" Echo asked.

"Nothing," she quickly covered.

Echo chuckled. "Look, if you want to get anything out of tonight, then you're going to have to start opening up."

Kathryn thought for a moment. It was true. Whatever this bizarre experiment was, it would require opening up. She nodded towards the waitress. "You find her attractive?"

Echo grinned mischievously. "Yeah, but I take it you don't?"

Kathryn shook her head. "She seems like a nice girl, but no, I don't see her... that way. Should I?" She looked over at the waitress and squinted. Was this part of the test? What did a lack of attraction mean?

"Aw, the confused mind of a babydyke springing to life. Look, darling, do you find *all* men attractive?"

Kathryn looked at Echo and shook her head. "Of course not."

"So, if a muscular man was walking down Bourbon showing off everything he had to offer, would you automatically be thinking you'd want you a slice of that?"

Kathryn blushed. "No."

"Exactly." Echo's eyes lit up as the drinks arrived. She thanked the waitress.

After a long slurp of beer, she sighed and rested her hands on the table as if she were a news reader about to deliver an important breaking news alert.

"There is much discussion about lesbian types and categorisations," she began. "Some say there are just five main types of lesbian: butch, lipstick, alpha, athletic, and boy babe."

Kathryn blinked and decided to keep silent on the fact she thought there were only two types.

"But," Echo said with a considered pause, "I don't subscribe to that theory. Yeah, you can find all of those types of lesbian, but I think there are more categories out there. You'll hear terms like dyke, power dyke, diesel dyke, butch, stone butch, gold star, lone star, chapstick, femme, pillow queen, blue jeans, stud, stem, futch, boi. It's endless. Thing is, I personally think that those categorisations are off-putting to newly uncloseted members of our group. They wonder what they are, if they need to get some kind of badge, if they can overlap two. Can they be a power dyke during the week and a pillow queen on the weekend?"

Kathryn took a large swig of her wine. Echo had been right, she would need a drink.

"The straights don't categorise themselves like we do. Even the gays have less terms than us. Personally, I think of sexuality as a scale." Echo drew a line along the table with her finger. "Straight, bi or pan, gay. You can be anywhere along that line. Does that make sense?"

Kathryn looked at the imaginary line and nodded her head a little.

"People are obsessed with labels. I know that we fought for the right to use those labels, but I think it's gone far enough," Echo continued. "We're all individuals. Yeah, we may fit into stereotypical groups. I'd be considered butch, but does that define me? Does that mean I can't enjoy a little lip gloss now and then? No."

Kathryn nodded again.

"So, you need to push all of that to one side. Don't worry too much about what you are, don't spend forever looking for the label that fits the best. Think about you and how you feel. What I'm trying to say is, humans don't fit into neat little boxes and neither should your sexuality. You can slap a name on it later if you really want to, but first you need to figure out what it is for yourself."

Kathryn considered the words. They made sense. She'd spent a lot of times wondering if she was gay or straight. But they were words assigned to people. Did they encapsulate her feelings? Not really.

She sipped some more wine and pulled a face. It tasted like acid. Not surprising. She wasn't at an upmarket wine bar in New York enjoying the latest import from New Zealand.

"So." Echo paused, grinning. Kathryn knew it was going to be a personal question. She took a deep breath and held it in preparation.

"When did you first look at a woman as something other than a potential manicure buddy?" Echo asked.

Kathryn knew she was blushing as she considered the question.

Echo patiently waited for her to reply, drinking her beer.

"When Jenn kissed me," Kathryn admitted quietly.

"Damn, girl." Echo leaned back and placed her arms along the back of the booth seat.

"I pushed her away," Kathryn continued. "I... I had no idea she was gay. Or that she thought I was flirting with her."

Echo's eyebrow raised. "I see. And then?"

Kathryn let out a deep breath. "Then I couldn't stop thinking about it."

Echo remained silent, waiting for her to continue.

"I kissed her," she whispered eventually.

Echo's eyes flew wide open. She stared at Kathryn silently.

"I was drunk," Kathryn explained further.

"Of course you were." Echo laughed. "Because you're straight, right?"

Kathryn sipped some more foul wine.

"Like so many straight women: spaghetti."

"Spaghetti?" Kathryn asked.

"Straight until wet," Echo supplied.

Kathryn wished she hadn't asked. She tried to put the conversation back on course. "She said I was drunk and pushed me away."

"And then?"

"And then I couldn't stop thinking about it. About her."

Echo leaned forward. "Thinking about the kiss or thinking about more than the kiss?"

"More."

"More like kissing and cuddling or more like… more?"

Kathryn wondered if it was possible for her cheeks to melt from her face entirely. "More."

"More like—"

"Do we have to do this?" she interrupted.

"I'm afraid we do," Echo said with a mock serious tone which was belied by the spark of humour in her eyes. "What I'm trying to find out is, do you want a roll in the hay, or do you want to be baking cookies for your brood of children?"

Kathryn nearly choked on her wine. Echo laughed at her reaction.

She opened her mouth to reply, but Echo held up her hand. She was looking towards the front of the stage where people were moving to seats.

"Hold that thought, the show is about to start."

"What show?" Kathryn questioned.

"Well, it ain't burlesque."

Before Kathryn had a chance to say anything else, music with a forceful bass line started pumping through speakers and bright lights lit up the stage. The stage which Kathryn belatedly noticed was adorned with silver poles.

Her heart sunk as she realised she was in a strip club. She wondered how she managed to get herself into these situations. This kind of thing never happened to her back home in New York.

Young, lithe women appeared onstage in the skimpiest of outfits. Kathryn turned away to examine the sticky cocktail menu on the table. It wasn't right, she couldn't watch.

After a few minutes, Echo tapped her hand. "You like her?"

Kathryn dragged her eyes from the menu. Her cheeks were so hot she wondered if she was creating the red glow of the stage lights.

"Which one?"

"The one in red."

Kathryn shook her head. She looked away from the stage again. "I'm sure she's a nice girl, but—"

"Yeah, yeah." Echo waved her hand. "What about the natural blonde? Are blondes your thing?"

Kathryn sighed and turned back towards the stage. She wondered how long strip shows lasted, how long she would have to endure the torture.

She sought out the blonde. She didn't know what she was looking for, what she was supposed to look *at*. She could appreciate that the woman was toned and exceptionally fit, but nothing else. In the right light, she looked a little like Jenn. But she wasn't Jenn.

She wasn't interested in any of the women. Nor would

she ever be. It was a waste of time being there, an uncomfortable waste of time.

"Kathryn? Hello?" Echo tried again.

"I don't think I want to be here anymore," she said simply.

Echo regarded her for a moment and then nodded. "Then let's get out of here."

Kathryn threw down some money on the table. She rolled her eyes when it promptly stuck to the surface.

They quickly exited the club and started to walk along the street to get away from the crowds. Once they were in a slightly quieter area, Echo pulled Kathryn to the side.

"Wanna tell me what revelation you just had?"

"I'm not gay," Kathryn said with certainty. "I was just in a strip club, and I felt nothing. Well, I felt extremely uncomfortable. But I didn't feel anything else."

"Okay," Echo drawled. "Not even for the blonde?"

"Nothing. When I saw her, all I could think was that she's not Jenn."

Echo let out a long laugh.

Kathryn frowned. "What's so funny?"

"You know Jenn is a woman, right?" Echo said. "You know that having strong feelings for one woman rather than all woman can still make you gay, right?"

Kathryn clenched her jaw. "I never said—"

"Look, Kathryn," Echo interrupted. "I meet a lot of baby dykes who come to the city to explore their sexuality. A lot of them choose a type they wanna tap and that's it. They don't care about anything other than getting their kicks. They drink, dance, and screw. Simple as that."

Kathryn looked around the street, hoping no one passing by had heard Echo's crass commentary.

"But you, you're different," she continued. "Which makes me think that Jenn is a lucky girl."

"What do you mean?"

Echo sighed, as if explaining something so obvious was paining her. "You're not in town to scratch an itch, you came to town and you fell in love."

A laugh bubbled up and exploded from Kathryn's lips. "I am *not* in love."

Echo folded her arms and stared at Kathryn. "Really? Do me a favour, okay? Pretend that Jenn is a man. Now, replay all of your interactions with her and your internal monologues and whatever as if she was a man. See if that clears things up for you."

Kathryn rolled her eyes. It was the most ridiculous thing she'd ever heard. She was not in love. She'd felt confused, but she'd gone to a strip club and she'd felt nothing. In fact, she felt dirty and like she wanted to leave as quick as possible.

So, what if Jenn were a man? What difference did that really make?

She swallowed hard.

It made all the difference.

"You're gay," Echo announced. "But you're gay for one woman. It happens. Maybe it's a crush, but you don't seem like the kind of woman who has crushes."

"I—I…" Kathryn stuttered.

The world was spinning. She hated to admit it, but Echo's argument made sense. If Jenn were a man, she wouldn't be so confused about her feelings. The confusion was rooted in the fact that she was debating whether or not she was gay. Wondering if she knew her own mind at all, having never previously felt anything like this for women.

But if she ignored gender, it was very clear that she had strong feelings for Jenn. Very strong feelings. Could they be lo—

"Echo, I hope you're keeping outta trouble?"

They both turned. An older, larger lady was smiling at

them. She looked Kathryn up and down. "Well, well, if it isn't Fine Shoes."

"Hey, Miss Mae." Echo smiled. "Just hanging out with my new buddy here."

Kathryn regarded Miss Mae. She seemed familiar. The penny dropped, and she remembered where she had seen her. "You work at the tourist office."

"I surely do," Miss Mae replied. "You didn't like my bus."

"No. I didn't like much that day."

"I thought as much," she said with a knowing smile.

"I'm sorry," Kathryn apologised. She knew she'd been a pain in the ass when she'd first arrived, and she deeply regretted it.

Miss Mae gave Kathryn with a long look. "I'll think about accepting your apology *if* you watch my show tonight."

Kathryn's eyes widened. She wondered what kind of show she was talking about. She'd certainly had her fill of some shows.

"Miss Mae is the best jazz singer in town," Echo explained.

"Oh, well, yes, I guess I could drop by." She was confused as to why she was receiving a personal invitation from the woman.

"Go back to your sinful ladies, Echo," Miss Mae said with soft humour. "I'll look after Miss Fine Shoes here."

Kathryn looked down at her heels and frowned. Her shoes weren't that impressive, but it seemed she'd gotten a reputation and a nickname from them.

Miss Mae took her arm and started to walk down the street with Kathryn in tow. Kathryn turned around and looked over her shoulder. Echo saluted her in farewell.

"Child, you have to be careful who you trust in this city," Miss Mae was saying.

Kathryn noted that the bustling crowds in the street parted for them. Many people greeted her companion as they passed by.

"Can I trust you?" Kathryn said.

"More than you can trust Echo." Miss Mae chuckled. "Girl is trouble. A good heart, but still trouble."

Kathryn wasn't about to argue that fact. She imagined Echo could be a lot of trouble if she put her mind to it.

"Where are we going?" she asked instead.

"The Snug, best jazz venue in town."

"Oh." Kathryn was mesmerised by how friendly people were being to them. It was clear to her that Miss Mae was something of a local celebrity.

"You're going to have a front row seat, I'll see to that," she said.

"Th—thank you." Kathryn couldn't think what she had done to deserve the special treatment she was receiving from the woman.

"I sing for twenty-five minutes, no longer," Miss Mae said. She pulled Kathryn close as though to give her some advice. "Always leave 'em wanting more."

Kathryn chuckled.

"And then you and I are going to talk about my girl, Jenn."

A shiver ran up Kathryn's spine. She felt like a misbehaving schoolgirl who was about to get lectured in the mother of all detentions.

"And don't think about leaving early," Miss Mae said with a shake of her finger. "I know where you staying, Fine Shoes."

Kathryn swallowed and nodded her understanding. She wished, not for the first time that evening, that she had stayed in the hotel.

Miss Mae led her into a small club and guided her to a

seat in the front row. She pointed to her eyes and then to Kathryn. "We'll talk soon," she promised.

Kathryn nodded. Miss Mae walked away, speaking to the bartender before she disappeared behind the scenes.

When will I learn to just stay in the hotel? she chided herself. They have room service. I should just stay there the rest of the trip.

38

EMPLOYMENT

ARABELLA SAT on the sofa and looked around the small apartment. Her professional eye quickly cast over the architectural details of the home, assessing resale potential. Jenn had a good eye for design. The room was sparsely decorated but still homely. She lived on the edge of the French Quarter —convenient for work, Arabella assumed.

Rebecca was in the kitchen with Jenn, helping her make a proper British cup of tea. Rebecca often thought that people needed help in that regard. She'd even taken to watching over Arabella as she made hot drinks, offering nuggets of unwanted advice.

Arabella pulled off her shoes, dropping them beside the sofa. She massaged the heel of one foot. She wasn't used to all the walking they had been doing, but it was worth every second and every potential blister.

New Orleans was beautiful. Vibrant and, at times, chaotic. The thing she enjoyed the most was the constant soundtrack. You never knew when a band would set up in the middle of the road and start playing. And if there was no band, then music was pumped through speakers to keep up the illusion.

She'd added a number of songs to her Spotify list to remind her of the trip when she returned home. Her face fell at that thought. Home. The duration of their stay had seemed perfectly reasonable when they booked flights. Now it seemed painfully short.

How could they possibly see everything, and how would she manage returning to work after realising how much stress it caused her?

Mindlessly, she checked her phone. She'd taken a couple more calls that afternoon, despite being on a boat in a swamp. Three important deals were all tied to each other via a funding scheme, who was refusing to pay out any money until a valuation was complete. Unfortunately, it was hard to value a barren piece of land and a gleam in an architect's eye.

On the smaller end of the scale, two residential sales looked like they were about to fall through. Property deals falling through weren't anything new, they happened all the time in England. But it did mean months of work for nothing and a return to the drawing board, without having been paid.

"I can hear you thinking about work," Rebecca said as she came into the room. She placed a mug of tea on the coffee table in front of her.

"It's hard to turn off," Arabella admitted.

Rebecca looked down at her thoughtfully.

Arabella frowned at the expression. It didn't seem to be a telling-off look. "What?"

Rebecca's shoulders rose slightly. "Nothing, just... doesn't seem like you enjoy your work much sometimes."

Arabella laughed. "Does anyone?"

"I do," Rebecca said.

"I do, too," Jenn said from the kitchen.

"We do." Rebecca offered her a wide smile.

"So I hear."

Rebecca perched on the edge of the table and looked at Arabella seriously. "Do you like your job?"

Arabella sucked in a breath. That was a hard question to answer. Her name was on the incorporation documents. Her family had established the company, and it was a runaway success in its first year. It was now one of the most respected estate agencies in London. She ran a busy office and sat on the board.

It had been her life from the moment she started work. She adored *aspects* of her job, but did she like it as a whole? She didn't know. It was another thing she had never stopped to think about.

The question was ridiculous. As if she would ever walk up to her father and tell him she quit.

She quickly shook her head. "That's not relevant. It's a good, safe job. And my father needs me. I make very good money."

"You're making yourself sick with stress," Rebecca said.

Arabella narrowed her eyes.

Rebecca held up her hands. "Okay, okay, I'll drop it. Just thought I'd mention it."

She returned to the kitchen, presumably to continue helping Jenn. Arabella glanced down at her phone to where she had opened her emails. There were five new messages since the last time she checked, all marked high priority. All about an impending work disaster.

She closed the application and opened her personal email account. As she suspected, no new emails. The last thing she had received was a selfie from Rebecca sent the day before they travelled. Rebecca refused to email Arabella at work, saying she didn't want to rub shoulders with stuffy suit-clad men in Arabella's inbox.

She smiled at the image. Rebecca had angled the phone's camera so her suitcase could be seen on her bed. It was entirely empty except for a bikini. Rebecca issued a thumbs-up and the subject line was 'job done'.

Arabella closed the application down and tossed her phone into her bag.

39

THE SNUG

JAZZ MUSIC PLAYED through The Snug's speakers on a quiet loop. The bartender came over and took Kathryn's drink order. She opted for water and fruit juice in order to remain sober for whatever Miss Mae had to say to her.

In what she was coming to understand was traditional New Orleans style, people started to arrive moments before the show was due to start. They quickly grabbed drinks, and within a few short minutes, the bar was filled to capacity.

Some musicians started to set up on the stage. Kathryn watched with interest how quickly they managed to set up and tune their kit.

A spotlight shone in the middle of the stage, and silence fell over the room. It was the first time in her life that Kathryn had heard a bar completely fall silent. She could hear the ice cubes in her drink chinking together.

A large, worn armchair was brought up onto the stage.

She could feel the anticipation building. The room buzzed with excitement.

Miss Mae stepped onto the stage and the crowd went

wild. Kathryn clapped politely, looking around in surprise at the whoops and hollers coming from all around her.

Miss Mae smiled gratefully at the audience. She raised her microphone to her mouth and turned to wink at the musicians. It was an indication for the music to begin, and a moment later Miss Mae started to sing.

Chills ran up Kathryn's arms. She instantly understood the reverence with which people had looked at the older woman on the street. Miss Mae's voice was incredible. She was easily the best singer that Kathryn had ever heard.

The short set flew by. The majority of the audience knew not to applaud in between songs. Those who tried received a quick glare from Miss Mae and were soon silenced.

When the set was over, Miss Mae whispered a soft "thank you" into her microphone and the audience went wild. Kathryn joined then, standing up and clapping loudly. Miss Mae smiled and waved to the audience before walking off stage.

A few moments later, one of the bar staff approached Kathryn and asked her to come backstage.

She nervously entered the small dressing room where Miss Mae sat in an armchair that looked as worn and well-loved as the one on stage. In front of her was a glass of whisky and a glass of water. She gestured for Kathryn to sit on the small sofa beside the dressing table.

Kathryn sat down. "You're extremely talented. You have an amazing voice."

Miss Mae inclined her head. "Thank you, Fine Shoes."

Kathryn glanced down at her heels.

"My Jenn has been moping around," Miss Mae said.

Kathryn looked up but remained silent. She wasn't sure what to say.

"She won't speak to me." The singer shook her head. "She stubborn."

"Yes, she is," Kathryn agreed.

"And she don't want to get her heart all broken up either."

"I... I know."

"So whatcha gonna do about it?"

"Me?"

"You." Miss Mae picked up her whisky and took a small sip.

Kathryn was baffled. She couldn't fathom what Miss Mae wanted from her. Jenn wanted her to stay away, and that was what she intended to do.

"You want some free advice, Fine Shoes?"

Everyone seemed eager to give her advice, but Kathryn nodded.

"You know they call this here fine city the Big Easy, right?"

Kathryn nodded again.

"That was thought up by some fancy marketing types in the sixties. It's supposed to signify our laidback attitude to life. But New Awlins ain't easy, it's anything but easy. Just like the rest of this country, life is hard. We have to deal with unemployment, natural disasters, and tourists."

Kathryn snorted.

"You may laugh, Fine Shoes," Miss Mae took another sip of her whisky, "but you tourists, man, you cause trouble. Don't get me wrong, we like your money."

Kathryn smiled.

Miss Mae lowered the glass and leaned back in her chair. "You from New York?"

"I am."

"The Big Apple." Miss Mae nodded. "With all your running around, business deals, and coffee to go."

"And our fine shoes." Kathryn indicated her heels.

Miss Mae laughed loudly. "And your fine shoes!" She

looked at Kathryn for a few moments. "I can see why Jenn likes you."

Kathryn wondered if Miss Mae wasn't quite up to date on the latest events in her twisting relationship with Jenn.

"We agreed to avoid each other," she explained.

"I gathered. She said you were confused, still figuring things out."

Kathryn broke eye contact. She wasn't comfortable discussing her sexual preference with someone she'd just met.

"Thing is," Miss Mae continued. "Life is short. We may be laidback down here, but we don't go wasting no time. We live our life to the full. We find our happiness wherever we can and we embrace it. Not like you big city folks. Going to doctors every time you have a feeling."

Kathryn chuckled bitterly. She'd practically paid for her therapist's new car following the recent turmoil in her life. She was sure that therapy worked perfectly well for some people, but it didn't for her. Mainly because she purposefully lied to the therapist so he heard what she thought he wanted to hear.

"The way I see it," Miss Mae said, "you got to talk to her. Tell her that you have feelings for her."

"How can you possibly know that I have feelings for her?"

"I saw it in your eyes the first time I mentioned her name." Miss Mae smiled. "If you were here for some pickup then you would have gone with Echo or stayed at that nasty club I saw you come out of earlier. You not like the other girls. You care for her."

"Echo thinks I'm in love," she confessed.

"What do you think?" Miss Mae asked.

"I don't know," Kathryn said. "The whole thing confuses me."

Miss Mae's eyes narrowed. She stared at Kathryn, seemingly taking stock of her.

"How confused can you be?" the woman asked. "You wanna be with Jenn? It's as simple as that."

Kathryn blinked. "Um. Well—"

"No, no. Don't overthink it. Just ask yourself if you wanna be with her. Do you want to talk to her? Walk with her? See sights with her? You getting too caught up on the idea of the future. Live in the now."

Loose fragments of ideas started to fall together in Kathryn's mind. She'd been looking at the bigger picture. Straight or gay. She'd been so bewildered about her sudden lusting for a woman, that she'd forgotten an important piece of the puzzle. It wasn't about whether Jenn was a man or a woman. It wasn't about whether Kathryn was gay or straight or anything in between.

She liked Jenn. She more than liked Jenn. The rest didn't matter. The idea of hurting Jenn was painful. The idea of not being able to see Jenn was more so.

She couldn't shake the memory of the first kiss from her mind. When she had drunkenly initiated a kiss the second night, it was because she wanted to recreate the feelings again.

It all seemed so obvious.

But she'd ruined everything. She couldn't ask Jenn to give her a chance now. Firstly, she wanted to respect Jenn's request and stay away. Secondly, she couldn't think how she could even begin to convince Jenn of her feelings after all the back and forth that had gone on between them. And, lastly, she couldn't drag Jenn into the mess her life was. How would she ever explain what had happened over the last two years? The decisions she had made?

Addison.

"You overthinking again, Fine Shoes," Miss Mae said. "Love ain't easy. It's one step at a time."

There was that word again.

Love.

"Come to the tourist office tomorrow afternoon," Miss Mae said.

"But I promised—" Kathryn said.

"Jenn doesn't want you to stay away. She wants you to not break her heart. And I don't think you want to break her heart. You may be confused, but I think you're starting to work it out." Miss Mae stood up. "Tomorrow afternoon. Basin Street."

"What time?" Kathryn asked as she stood up.

Miss Mae laughed. "We don't do time around here, Fine Shoes. Afternoon is fine."

40

POSSUM

Rebecca knocked on the interconnecting door. She nervously drummed her fingers on her thigh as she waited for Arabella to open her side.

A few moments passed, she heard soft footsteps, and then the lock being turned. Arabella opened the door and leaned on the frame.

"We literally just said good night. Miss me?"

Rebecca nodded. "Yeah, I did. But I wanted to apologise."

Arabella frowned. "What for?"

"At Jenn's, I asked if you liked your job. I was overstepping." It had played on her mind for the last few hours. Arabella didn't seem concerned about it, but Rebecca wanted to clarify what she had said and why.

Arabella stepped to one side and gestured for her to come in. "Tea?"

"Yes, please." She'd trained Arabella on how to make a good cup of tea. Why people insisted on putting in the milk last, she'd never know.

She walked into the room and sat on the edge of the bed.

It was high, and her feet dangled, which felt appropriate considering her childish behaviour.

"I don't think you overstepped," Arabella said as she set about making two cups of tea.

"I was jealous."

Arabella turned around and frowned. "Oh?"

"You've been taking calls, and I get that you have to. It's your job, and they need you. But I kinda feel like this is my time, and that they are calling and taking you away from me. I asked if you liked your job because I felt jealous that they could so easily take you away, take your attention. But, of course they can, it's your job. And it's not like you have an average job. You co-own the company."

Arabella smiled. "I had no idea you had such a strong streak of jealousy. It even runs to corporations."

Rebecca rolled her eyes and pointedly turned away. She didn't want to be mocked. She was trying to be honest. She'd never really felt jealous before. It was different with Arabella, she kept wondering what would take the impressive woman away from her.

The bed dipped beside her as her girlfriend sat down.

"Sorry, I didn't mean to be flippant," Arabella said softly. "And you don't need to apologise. Asking if I like my job is a reasonable enough question. Arguing with me if I tell you that I do, that would be stepping over the line."

"If?" Rebecca turned to look at her. "*If* you tell me that you like your job?"

Arabella let out a soft sigh. "Yes, if. The truth is; I don't know if I like my job. I love the industry, I find architecture fascinating, as you know. But buying and selling houses, I don't know if that's an interest, never mind a passion."

Rebecca's eyes widened. Arabella didn't like her job. And now Rebecca had opened the floodgates.

"I'm so sorry, I shouldn't have mentioned anything," she

said. "I know you've been struggling with change lately… I didn't mean to make things worse."

The kettle finished boiling. Arabella pressed a quick kiss to Rebecca's cheek and stood up. "I know, you didn't."

Rebecca watched her making the tea. She felt terrible. Watching Arabella taking work-related calls on holiday had eaten at her. She hated that Hanley Estates couldn't cope without their boss, but she shouldn't have mentioned anything. It was Arabella's *job*. Her family business. It had to come first.

"I can hear you thinking," Arabella said. She turned around and grinned. "Possum."

"Possum?" Rebecca raised an eyebrow. "Don't they raid trashcans?"

"It's better than Boo-Boo." Arabella turned her attention back to the drinks. "What are you thinking about?"

"Well, now I'm thinking about the fact you just called me Possum."

Arabella chuckled. "Before that."

Rebecca stood up and walked over to her. "I was thinking that I shouldn't have said anything about your job."

"I thought we'd agreed to speak to each other when things are bothering us? That can't be a one-way street, you know."

"I know." Rebecca peered over Arabella's shoulder and watched the tea being made. *So far, so good.*

"If you don't stop spying on me when I make you a drink, you'll be called worse than Possum," Arabella promised.

"Okay, Boo-Boo." Rebecca turned around. She looked at the bedside table and frowned at the book she saw there. *"Empowering the Unconscious Brain*, huh?"

Arabella was beside her in a second and trying to pull the book out of her hand. Rebecca tightened her grip.

"Give me the book, *Possum*," Arabella ground the name out.

"What are you embarrassed about, Boo-Boo?" Rebecca asked sweetly as she clung to her end of the book.

Arabella let go and Rebecca fell backwards onto the bed.

"I didn't want you to see that book," Arabella admitted. "But you see everything."

Rebecca frowned as she looked at the book, wondering what was so bad about her seeing it.

Arabella noticed her confused expression. "It's a self-help book," she clarified.

"Yeah, I didn't think it was a slice of toast. This is on my to-read list. I'm currently reading one about learning while you sleep, but I'm not sure it will work for me, I toss and turn too much to keep earbuds in at night." Rebecca sat up and placed the book back on the bedside table.

When she looked up, Arabella was looking down at her with something akin to shock.

"What?" Rebecca asked.

"You… read self-help books?"

"Of course I do. You know I love improving myself— wait, are you embarrassed about reading self-help books?"

Arabella's cheeks tinged pink and she turned away. "The tea," she said by way of excuse.

Rebecca watched her retreat. She smiled in wonderment. Arabella really was a complicated, wonderful human being.

"I love self-help books," Rebecca said. "Some aren't that great, but most of them are really useful. They teach you ways to do things, deal with things, understand things. There's no shame in them."

Arabella finished making the drinks and thrust a cup towards Rebecca, keeping her gaze low.

"There's no shame in them," she repeated, refusing to take the tea until Arabella made eye contact with her.

Arabella looked up, her eyes locking with Rebecca's.

Rebecca took the mug.

"My parents would disagree," Arabella said.

"Then you totally need to read *Toxic Parents*," Rebecca told her.

Arabella laughed. "Is that really a book?"

"Yep, the full title is *Toxic Parents: Overcoming Their Hurtful Legacy and Reclaiming Your Life*," Rebecca said.

"I'll put it in my wish list," her girlfriend promised.

Rebecca placed her tea on the bedside table and picked up the book again. She toed off her shoes and sat up, her back against the headboard. She patted the space next to her.

"Come here, I'll read to you."

Arabella looked at her with uncertainty for a moment. Rebecca could practically see the cogs turning in her mind, wondering if it was a good idea. Questioning if she was going to be mocked.

Rebecca patted the bed again.

Arabella nodded, walking around the bed and grabbing her own mug of tea as she went. She curled up beside Rebecca, wrapping her hands around the tea and resting her head on Rebecca's shoulder.

Rebecca opened to the bookmarked page and started to read.

41

MISUNDERSTANDINGS

KATHRYN DECIDED that three o'clock would constitute 'afternoon'. And so, she walked into the tourist office on Basin Street at precisely that time.

She'd lain awake most of the previous night wondering if coming was a good idea. On the one hand, she wanted to respect Jenn's wishes. On the other, she genuinely worried that Miss Mae would track her down if she didn't do as she commanded.

Kathryn had never been a sentimental person, or someone who became swept away with emotions and feelings. She was practical and pragmatic. Sometimes to a fault.

So, her sudden feelings for Jenn had come as a massive shock to her. Once she had stopped fighting herself and accepted that she felt a great deal of affection for Jenn, the floodgates of her emotions crashed down.

At first, she'd found Jenn fascinating. The long journey on the trams had proved that Kathryn and Jenn could talk about almost nothing for hours and have a great time while doing it.

Then the burlesque show proved that Kathryn had a

physical interest. No matter how much she tried to ignore it, she felt sexually attracted to Jenn after that night.

She didn't know if it was love, as Echo had suggested and Miss Mae had implied. She didn't even know if she was capable of love, and she certainly didn't know if Jenn would be able to love her, especially considering her recent history. But that was a bridge she'd cross later, if Jenn would even speak with her.

What Kathryn did know was that she wanted to be honest with Jenn. No matter the outcome.

The outside temperature was becoming more intense, and she was lightly perspiring as she walked into the tourist office. She took a deep breath of cold air.

She knew it wasn't just the weather. It was her growing panic.

"Ah, there you are," Miss Mae called out from behind her desk.

Kathryn looked over to her and nodded nervously. Jenn stood in the large lobby, eyeing her with suspicion.

"So very kind of you," Miss Mae said loudly. She turned to address Jenn, "She giving me a donation for the church."

Kathryn blinked in surprise.

"Hundred dollars, wasn't it?" Miss Mae asked her.

Kathryn narrowed her eyes and approached the desk.

"Excuse me," Jenn said quickly. She walked out of the lobby and into the old station's waiting room.

Kathryn watched Jenn leave. She turned back to look at Miss Mae, who had her hand held out, palm raised to the sky.

Kathryn rolled her eyes. She got her purse from her handbag and started to count some money into the woman's open hand.

"Why am I giving you one hundred dollars exactly?"

"For my church."

"And when did I agree to that?"

"You didn't." Miss Mae folded the money and placed it in her bra. "But now think how kind and generous you look to Jenn. Ain't no one who don't like a philanthropist."

Kathryn sighed. "What now?"

Miss Mae shrugged. "Don't look at me, Fine Shoes. You did the thinking, you came here. You must have something to say."

Kathryn realised she had just been hustled out of hundred dollars by the wily old woman. She shook her head and muttered under her breath as she walked towards the waiting room.

Air left her lungs as she stepped into the beautifully preserved hall. She knew that the building had been a train station in a past life, and she'd seen signs promising an historical experience in the original Basin Street waiting room. But nothing had prepared her for actually seeing the room for the first time.

For a moment, she forgot why she was even there. She looked around in open-mouthed awe.

Old wooden benches, the high and ornate ceiling, and the display cases made it feel like she had stepped back in time. She approached the first of the display cabinets.

"Impressive, isn't it?"

Jenn stood behind Kathryn, and Kathryn tensed. She held her breath, not wanting to react or say something that might cause Jenn to leave again.

"Very," she admitted. "A wonderful restoration."

Jenn took a tentative step and stood beside her. Her gaze was focused on the contents of the display.

Kathryn continued to peer through the glass. Original tickets, timetables, models of trains, and other historical documents were displayed with information cards.

Kathryn smiled, her sight resting on a shopping list.

"Some things never change," Jenn commented.

Kathryn nodded. "We all still need bread, milk, and sugar."

"I often look at that and wonder whose shopping list it was," Jenn said.

"And did they lose it *before* or *after* they bought the items?" Kathryn supplied.

Jenn chuckled. "Exactly. Did they get to the store and pat their pockets down?"

"And then try to remember what they'd written on the list."

"Then forget the most important item," Jenn added.

"Oh, I hate that," Kathryn confessed. "There's always one thing that you forget, and it's the thing you needed most."

"The thing you originally went out for," Jenn said.

Kathryn smiled. They were communicating, and it felt good. She took a breath and exhaled. It felt good, too. Like a weight had been lifted from her chest.

She gestured to the next cabinet, which housed a conductor's uniform from the turn of the century.

"More formal than your tram outfit," she said.

"Streetcar," Jenn corrected softly.

Kathryn could see her smiling reflection in the glass of the case. "Mmm."

"Why did you come here?" Jenn finally asked.

"To donate to Miss Mae's church."

"She's an atheist."

Kathryn pursed her lips and slowly shook her head. She muttered under her breath.

Jenn laughed. "And with a mouth like that I can't see you as the church-donating type."

"I... I came to see you," Kathryn admitted. She turned around to face Jenn.

Jenn's brow knit in confusion. "Why?" she asked in a whisper.

"I had to see you. I tried to stay away. I really did. I was worried about even bumping into you, and then last night I was in a restaurant and I bumped into Echo." Kathryn looked at her feet, wondering how to explain exactly what had happened the night before.

"Oh?" Jenn's voice was tight.

"She invited herself to dinner with me and we talked. She convinced me to go on to some seedy club—"

"Kathryn," Jenn interrupted.

She paused and looked up. Jenn's face was contorted, she looked pained.

"If this is going to be some story about how Echo helped you with your sexual awakening... I don't... I don't want to hear it. I—I've heard it before."

Kathryn blinked as she processed the words. Then she laughed, so loudly it reverberated in the large space.

"God, no!" she exclaimed. "No, absolutely... just, no. We spoke. Nothing more. In fact, we mainly spoke about you."

Jenn's expression morphed away from hurt and back to perplexed.

"Anyway, we were..." Kathryn let out an embarrassed breath. "At a strip club and I didn't feel comfortable, so I asked if we could leave. Outside, we met Miss Mae and, well, I went to hear her perform and then we spoke."

"Look, Kathryn." Jenn shifted from foot to foot nervously.

Kathryn held up her hand. "No, I need to say this. I still don't have all the answers, I wish I did. Being at that club, it made me realise some things. And speaking with Echo. She explained some things to me. She opened my eyes in many ways. Like I said, I don't have all the answers yet. But I have enough to know that I—"

"Hey, babe."

Kathryn turned to see a tall, slim blonde enter the waiting room, half engaged in something on her phone. She approached Jenn and placed a kiss on her cheek, wrapping her arm around Jenn's shoulder. "Shift over?"

Kathryn stared at Jenn in shock. The blonde interloper continued to look at her phone, unaware of what she had just walked in on.

Jenn licked her lips nervously, still staring at Kathryn. Her hand shook as she lifted her wrist to look at her watch.

"Y—yeah, yeah, sorry. I lost track of time."

Kathryn looked at the two of them.

"Stupid fool," she muttered to herself as she spun around and ran towards the exit. She couldn't believe she had actually thought that admitting her feelings to Jenn was a good idea. She barely knew her. And now, it seemed as if she wasn't the only one who had fallen for her charms.

She had to get out of there. The embarrassment was too much to take.

She marched across the road, weaving in and out of traffic without any thought for her safety. As long as she was away from Jenn, she would be all right.

She shuddered as she heard Jenn call out her name. There was no way she would stop now. She didn't want to hear explanations or see Jenn's pitying expression.

She'd made it across two lanes, now she had another two to go and she'd be unhindered by any further traffic on her way back to the hotel. She stood on the grassy central reservation and looked up to cross the next road.

Tires screeched. A horn blared. There was an unmistakable thud.

She couldn't move. Ice cold fear ran down her spine. She

knew what had happened, without even turning to see. She knew.

All she could do was pray that it wasn't the case.

Her body wouldn't move. As if through sheer willpower alone she could stand still and wait for Jenn to catch up to her. To believe that the thump was anything else.

The longer she stood still, the more she became aware of people pointing, cars coming to a stop, and the sound of someone screaming.

She turned around, breaths coming in large uncontrollable pants. She stepped off the kerb. Jenn was in the road, her back to Kathryn.

She heard the bloodcurdling scream again. The blonde from the waiting room was running towards Jenn.

They reached Jenn's prone body at the same time. Kathryn hesitantly brought her fingers to Jenn's neck, seeking out a pulse.

"Ambulance, I need an ambulance on Basin Street, by the tourist office," the blonde cried into her phone. "It's my cousin, she's been hit by a car. She's... she's not moving."

Kathryn felt a stomach-turning blow at the words.

The blonde was Jenn's cousin. Her *cousin*. The kiss on the cheek was an innocent familial peck. How could she have acted so rashly and run away without being sure?

"Lady?!"

Kathryn realised the blonde, Jenn's cousin, was looking at her with a questioning frown. She got herself together, remembering what she was doing, and focused on her search for a pulse.

Her finger shook. She used her other hand to steady her wrist. She closed her eyes and focused.

She sagged in relief. "There's a pulse. It's weak, but it's there."

Jenn's cousin relayed the information down the phone.

Kathryn looked down at Jenn's beautiful face, which was grazed but peaceful. She threaded her fingers through long blonde locks and removed them from her face, tucking them behind her ear.

"What happened?" Jenn's cousin asked as she hung up the call, the ambulance on the way.

Kathryn looked up. She opened her mouth to beg forgiveness, but no words came out.

"Miss Mae called me, and then I saw Jenn running off."

"I—I think she was coming after me," Kathryn said.

"I'm Chloe." She knelt closer to Jenn and picked up a limp hand in her own.

"I'm... just a tourist." Kathryn swallowed. "Kathryn, we... we met a couple of times."

She looked up, wondering where the ambulance was. They were surrounded by onlookers and stopped cars. The driver was getting out of his car and stumbling towards them in shock.

She couldn't believe how surreal it felt. A few moments ago, she was trying to confess her feelings to the woman who now lay unconscious in the middle of the road.

Hot tears streamed down her cheeks.

Where's the damn ambulance?

42

TIME TO LEAVE

ARABELLA STOOD at the hotel reception desk and watched one of the slowest typists ever prepare her final bill.

She could feel herself getting more and more annoyed with each excruciatingly painful keystroke.

Rebecca placed a hand on her forearm. She leaned in and whispered, "If you want to just go, it's fine. I'll deal with your checkout and we can settle up later."

"It's fine," Arabella said. "I have time before the flight. And I don't want to saddle you with the bill."

"It's okay, I know you're good for it," Rebecca replied. She leaned in closer. "I have generous payment plans available."

Arabella felt a shiver run through her. Damn work. Damn the Southbridge account. Damn her office for not being able to deal with things without her constantly holding their hands.

"We can explore that when you get home," she promised.

"Are you sure you don't want me to come as well?" Rebecca asked.

"Absolutely not. You're here to see your friend and

481

explore the area. I won't see your holiday being ruined because my staff are incompetent."

"You're hot when you're all fired up," Rebecca said.

Arabella chuckled. She leant her head on Rebecca's shoulder. "I'll miss you."

"I'll miss you, too," Rebecca promised.

Arabella quickly stood up straight and placed her hand over her pocket. "Damn."

"What's wrong?"

"I think I left my phone in your room. I wanted to fully charge it before the flight, but I left it—"

Rebecca smiled brightly. "I'll go… you carry on…" She gestured towards the slowest checkout in history.

"Thank you. Could you have a quick look in case I left anything else?" Arabella asked. She wondered what had gotten into her, she'd never forgotten her phone before.

"Sure." Rebecca sauntered towards the elevators.

Ah, yes, that's why I forgot, Arabella thought as she watched her girlfriend depart. She turned back towards the desk. "You have two minutes, or I'll assume my room is free. I really don't see what the delay is."

"Sorry, ma'am, it's our computer systems—"

Arabella held up her hand. "Don't talk to me about computer systems."

She could feel the anger coursing through her veins. Her father had called her first thing that morning to give her an update on everything that was falling apart. She'd woken up, fully dressed and snuggled up to Rebecca, to the sound of her mobile vibrating across the bedside table.

At some point the night before, they had fallen asleep while talking. It wasn't something that Arabella had ever done before, and the crick in her neck told her to never do it again. No, the next time she fell asleep on her bed with

Rebecca, she'd take the time to actually lay in the bed, holding Rebecca close to her.

Seeing her father's name flash up on her phone had caused her to jump to her feet like a teenager caught in a compromising position. That thought had quickly left her mind once he started to explain disaster after disaster piling up in her office.

There was only one thing for it; she had to go home.

Rebecca had been understanding, had helped her pack and find the first flight home. She'd even offered several times to go back with her. But Arabella felt terrible enough for having to leave, she didn't want to ruin Rebecca's holiday more than she already had. And what would Rebecca do when they got home? Arabella would be busy with work, and Rebecca would be mourning the loss of the end of her holiday, sad to be missing out on spending time with Jenn. No, it was better that Arabella went alone.

But that didn't mean that she wouldn't miss her terribly.

"Miss Foster, I have a message for you," one of the other receptionists called out.

Arabella was pleased to hear that Kathryn was there. It gave her the opportunity to say goodbye in person. She turned around and let out a gasp.

Kathryn's mascara had smeared, her cheeks were red, and she looked like someone who'd just run an impromptu marathon.

"Kathryn?" She stepped towards her, fearing that the woman would collapse if she didn't take her grasping hands.

"They wouldn't let me go with her," she said, her hands taking Arabella's in a death grip.

"Who?"

"Jenn. She was hit by a car."

"Oh my god!" Arabella helped Kathryn into a nearby chair and sat on the arm.

"She had a pulse and then the ambulance came. They wouldn't tell me anything, and they wouldn't let me go with her. I… I don't know what to do."

The receptionist came over with a folded piece of paper. "I'm so sorry to interrupt, Miss Foster, but they said the message was extremely urgent."

Kathryn's shaky hand took the slip of paper. She opened it up.

Call Erica immediately. RE: Addison

Arabella frowned. She didn't know what any of that meant, but she saw all the colour run from Kathryn's face. The woman grabbed her phone and quickly made a call.

"Erica?" she said the moment the call was connected.

Arabella felt like she was intruding, but Kathryn still held her hand in a vice-like grip so she wasn't going anywhere.

"Michael?" Kathryn asked, her voice tight. "He's… back?"

Arabella looked around, praying for Rebecca's quick return.

"Mother *knows?*" Kathryn cried. "But… you said you wouldn't tell!"

Arabella leaned a little closer. She could hear a woman speaking, presumably Erica, whoever that was.

"Kathryn," the woman was saying, "I didn't tell her anything. Michael came to the office and told her everything he knew. Mother just put the pieces together."

"What is she going to do?" Kathryn asked, her voice barely a breath.

"She's going to Addison. You have to get there first, Kathryn. Before Mother does."

Arabella's head was swimming. *Who's Addison? Or Michael? And what does her mother know?* She could feel Kathryn shivering with fear. She suspected that she was in shock. Whatever was happening couldn't possibly have come at a worse time.

"I... I can't leave, there's been—"

"Kathryn," Erica said sharply. "Mother knows. Do you want Michael to—"

"Of course I don't. You know I don't."

"You have to make a decision, you can't pretend this isn't happening anymore," Erica said.

Kathryn let out a small sob, her hand almost crushing Arabella's.

"I know, I'll leave now. I'll call you when I can." Kathryn hung up the call. She let go of Arabella's hand and rushed over to the reception desk. She picked up a pen and jotted something on a piece of paper.

"Have my belongings forwarded to this address, I'm checking out now. You have my credit card on file, charge what you have to. I have to go... right now."

The receptionist looked confused but took the slip of paper.

Kathryn spun around, and Arabella took her by the upper arms. "What's happening?" she demanded.

"I... I have to go. I'm sorry. I'm so sorry, I can't stay. Tell Jenn I'm so sorry." Kathryn tore herself away from Arabella's grip. She ran towards the doorman. "I need a taxi, right now."

Arabella stood in shock and watched the woman run off. She had no idea what had just happened, but whatever it was, it was important.

"One phone," Rebecca said as she strolled back into reception.

"Jenn's been in a car accident," Arabella told her. "She's been taken to hospital."

"What?" Rebecca's face paled.

"Kathryn just told me… and then something happened, and she's run off."

"Kathryn ran off?" Rebecca asked, pulling her own mobile from her pocket.

"Yes, she just had a strange phone conversation and then… checked out. But, before that she said that Jenn had been in an accident. She was at the scene, but the ambulance wouldn't let her go with them."

"I'll text her, and her cousin," Rebecca said. "Hopefully someone can tell me what's going on."

Arabella noticed that Rebecca was shaking. She reached out and put her arm around her shoulders. "I should stay."

"No, no, you need to get home. You'll go out of your mind if you don't get back to the office and shake them up soon."

Arabella knew Rebecca was right. She already felt her skin itch at being so far away from work. It was a long way home. It would take many hours of travel and many hours to readjust to the time difference.

But she wanted to stay, to make sure that Jenn was okay and to look after Rebecca. Not that the woman would ever admit that she needed looking after. Rebecca was strong and single-minded.

Rebecca sent a couple of text messages and let out a shaky breath. "There, we'll see what they say."

"Miss Henley?" the receptionist called out. "We have your final bill ready."

Arabella gritted her teeth. She tightened her grip around

Rebecca's shoulders. She didn't want to leave, but she knew she had to.

"It's fine," Rebecca reassured. "You have to go. We'll talk or text all the time."

"If you need me to turn around and come back, you call me immediately. You know my flight time, I'll leave it until last second to board."

Rebecca took a small step back and looked her in the eye. "I appreciate that, I really do. But I'll be fine. You need to go and slap some sense into your office. I'll be home before you know it."

43
AWAKE

Jenn opened her eyes and looked around the hospital room. Rebecca was slumped in one of the visiting chairs, asleep. Just as she had been for the last four days. Jenn kept telling her to go back to the hotel where she had a plush bed, but Rebecca remained.

She was a great friend. Of course, other friends had visited in the days since the accident, and Chloe was a semi-permanent feature, but Rebecca hadn't moved. She'd even taken to helping the nurses with Jenn's care. Jenn knew that this was a throwback to when Rebecca had cared for her mum in the hospital back home.

Even though she was surrounded by those who loved her, she was missing one person.

Kathryn.

She couldn't remember much of what happened, but the moment she woke up she'd felt a longing to see her. As if she had been dreaming about her.

Not long after she awoke, disorientated and in pain, Rebecca had explained the conversation that Arabella had overheard. Kathryn was... gone.

The next day, when Jenn felt a little less like her head was going to explode, she'd asked Rebecca to repeat everything she knew. She tried to piece together the mysterious fragments to figure out what would cause Kathryn to leave like that.

The following day, Arabella called Rebecca. Jenn asked to speak to her, listening to the tale from the source. It hadn't helped. She still didn't understand.

Chloe said that Kathryn had been with her following the accident. And then Arabella explained that she had checked out of her hotel and vanished. Jenn couldn't remember much. The nurse said it was common for people who had been in an accident to forget what had happened just before.

She knew that Kathryn had been at Basin Street. They'd spoken about... something. It was hazy, but she felt like it was important. It felt different from the other conversations they'd shared. Maybe it was wishful thinking. Maybe the bump on the head had warped her perception.

Jenn must have run out into the road, but she couldn't remember doing so. She didn't know what would ever make her do something so foolish.

Her heart was heavy. She was struggling to push thoughts of Kathryn Foster from her mind, but she had to. The truth of the matter was that Kathryn had left. She didn't even know if Jenn was alive or dead.

The door to her room opened. She looked up, eagerly. Despite her determination otherwise, she couldn't help it. A part of her still expected Kathryn to walk in, apologising for being delayed. She pictured her fussing with blankets and tweaking the air-conditioning unit. Caring for her, like Jenn knew she did.

"Still just me," Chloe said. She walked over and handed Jenn an apple and a bottle of water. "Sorry, she isn't coming back."

"I know," Jenn said. "I wasn't expecting her to."

Chloe gave her a look of disbelief.

Rebecca stirred in her seat. She sat up and started to stretch.

"Sorry we woke you," Chloe said.

"No problem, time to get up anyway," Rebecca said.

"Can you talk some sense into my cousin? She's still looking out for the woman who nearly got her killed."

Jenn rolled her eyes. "She didn't do anything. I walked into traffic, it's my fault."

"And she defends her," Chloe added.

"Technically," Rebecca said, "you don't know what happened, you can't remember."

"Exactly," Chloe said. "Maybe she pushed you."

Jenn ground her teeth. "I doubt it. Especially if she sat with me until the ambulance came, like you said she did."

"If I'd known she was the one who had messed with you and broken your heart, we would have needed a second ambulance," Chloe promised.

"Anyway," Rebecca interrupted before the two cousins got into another debate over Kathryn. "What did the doctor say?"

Chloe turned to face Jenn, trying to cover up her anger with a smile. "He says you can go home today."

Jenn dropped her head to her pillow. "Thank god."

"But you need to take it easy," Chloe said with a serious tone. "Three broken ribs, and you had a concussion. No dancing, no driving, no drinking while on the pain meds."

"I know, I'll take it easy," Jenn promised. She eyed her arm. She hadn't broken it, but the sprain was so bad that it was in a sling.

"I'll come and stay with you," Rebecca said, practically reading her mind.

"I can't ask you to do that," Jenn said.

"I'm offering." Rebecca stood up and tucked her hands into the back pockets of her jeans. "Chloe has to work, and you'll need help at home. I'm here, so I can help. Besides, I've been offered a couple of quick freelancer jobs while I'm here."

"You're dying to get home to Arabella," Jenn pointed out.

Rebecca smiled, but it didn't reach her eyes. "I can stay here a couple more weeks with you. Besides, absence makes the heart grow fonder, right?"

Jenn regarded her for a few moments. She'd love to tell Rebecca to get on the next plane home and be reunited with Arabella, but she knew that she would need help as she recovered. And she was right, Chloe couldn't take any more time off work. She doubted she could convince Rebecca to leave anyway. She'd been stuck to Jenn like glue since she'd woken up.

"If you're absolutely sure?" she asked.

Rebecca nodded. "I am."

"Great," Chloe said. "Then it's all settled. Maybe you can talk some sense into her about this Kathryn woman."

"I don't need anyone talking sense into me. It's not like I'm ever going to see her again, she left," Jenn said.

"Then why do you keep looking anxiously at the door?" Chloe asked. "You're expecting her to walk in. And, judging by the look on your face, you'd forgive her if she did. Despite the fact that she clearly doesn't care about you. Who leaves town after something like this happens? No one, that's who. No one."

Jenn swallowed. Chloe was right. She couldn't think of one good reason for Kathryn to vanish like she had. And she hadn't attempted to call to see how Jenn was.

Kathryn really couldn't have known if she was dead or alive.

Obviously, she didn't care either way.

Two Weeks Later

44

LONDON CALLING

ARABELLA HUNG up a call and let out a frustrated groan. She lowered her head to her desk, slowly thudding her forehead against the cool wood.

Her assistant, Helen, entered the office and placed a pre-packaged sandwich and a bottle of orange juice in front of her.

"Lunch," she announced.

Arabella looked at the unappealing sandwich and let out a sigh. She sat up straight and stretched out her back. She missed Dhia. The spa technician in New Orleans had been nothing short of a genius. She'd quickly found and eradicated each of Arabella's knots, knots that were so common she had taken to naming them.

"Your father called again. He said he'll be back from Portugal a day later than he originally thought," Helen said. "Something about another meeting."

Arabella rolled her eyes. She doubted it was another meeting at all, more like a round of golf. Not that she could begrudge her father having a holiday. He was in his seventies and deserved a break from work. It was just mildly frustrating that he had refused to postpone his holiday at the same moment she had felt forced to return from her own.

"You have fifteen minutes before Lannaker and Hardcastle get here for their meeting," Helen continued. "We're printing out the amended contracts, and we're trying to get the last of the survey results from the solicitors. Can I get you anything else?"

Arabella half-heartedly reached for the sandwich. *At least it's brown bread*, she noted. She shook her head and started to pull at the packaging.

"It's one-thirty," Helen said.

Arabella looked at the clock on the wall. A smile graced her face before she could cover it. It was finally a reasonable time to be able to call Rebecca. She'd probably wake her, but it would be an *acceptable* time.

Helen returned her smile. "I'll hold your calls and give you some privacy."

She left, closing the door to Arabella's office behind her before she could say anything else. Arabella didn't know how much Helen knew, she didn't exactly spill her heart and soul to her personal assistant, but it was clear that Helen knew enough.

She knew that Arabella's afternoons were infinitely better than her mornings. She knew that Arabella frequently made overseas calls around lunch time. Afternoons meant she could contact Rebecca. She could finally speak to her again and engage in text conversations throughout the rest of the workday.

She pushed her sandwich to one side and picked up her phone. She called Rebecca, waiting for the international dial tone to sound. It was a sound she loved and hated in equal measure. She loved it because the technology allowed her to stay in touch with Rebecca. She hated it because it reminded her that she was thousands of miles away.

"Afternoon," a throaty voice answered.

"Good morning," Arabella said softly, as if she were personally there to witness Rebecca waking up.

"I miss you," Rebecca said. She said it every time they spoke.

"I miss you, too. Very much," Arabella admitted. "How are you? And Jenn?"

"I'm good. Jenn is going back to work today, just a couple of hours in the morning, easing herself back into it."

Arabella's heart soared. Of course, she was happy that Jenn was feeling better and finally able to get back to work. But a part of that happiness was rooted in the knowledge that it meant that Rebecca would be able to return home shortly.

"But one of my freelance jobs I committed to has pushed back the date of the shoot…" Rebecca trailed off.

"But you had a contract in place," Arabella stated firmly. She paused. It wasn't Rebecca's fault, and she could tell from her tone that she felt bad about the delay. "How much have they pushed back?"

"Three weeks."

Arabella took a calming breath. It was the last thing she wanted to hear. She understood Rebecca's taking freelancer roles while she was in town. It was a great opportunity to diversify her portfolio, make some extra money, and keep busy doing something she loved. But she'd been looking forward to when Jenn could get by without Rebecca's help, so Rebecca could come home.

Now that was looking even further away.

"Are you angry?" Rebecca asked quietly.

"No. No, just disappointed. I miss you," Arabella reassured. "But I understand. There's nothing you can do."

"I took another couple of roles. If I'm going to be here, I might as well make the most of it," Rebecca said. "I'm doing some work for the tourism office. I think Jenn convinced her manager to take me on as a way of thanking me for helping her out."

"Sounds nice," Arabella said, trying to insert some enthusiasm into her tone. "It's a wonderful building, and the waiting room is amazing."

"Yeah, I'm looking forward to it. Well, I'm... I'm missing you, and I'm missing home. But I'm keeping busy, you know?"

"I know. I understand." Arabella pushed her sandwich into her desk drawer for later, she'd lost her appetite.

"When's your dad back from sunning himself in Portugal?" Rebecca asked.

"Oh, he's staying another day," Arabella said. "Apparently, he has a meeting."

Rebecca laughed. "Oh, in the golf club restaurant or on the green?"

Arabella chuckled. "It's cheeky, isn't it?"

"Yep," Rebecca said. "He's taking advantage of your good nature."

Arabella leaned back in her chair. Her eyes wandered to the giant prints that adorned her office walls, a gift from Rebecca following their drive home. She'd had many a positive comment about them from clients.

"How come when you help Jenn, you're being a good friend, and yet when I help my father, he's taking advantage of me?" Arabella asked with a wide smile.

"Because Jenn doesn't *expect* me to help her, and she's eternally grateful. And I know she'd do the same for me in a second. Your dad went on holiday not long after you had to cancel yours. And he dumped you with a load of his work. And he isn't grateful, he expects it from you."

Arabella stilled. Her hand reached for her necklace, and she ran the charm along the chain, deep in thought.

"Shit, sorry," Rebecca mumbled. "It's early, I just spoke without thinking."

"No, you're right. He does expect it, he does take advantage," Arabella admitted. "I'd just not thought of it in such black-and-white terms."

There was a knock on the door. Helen poked her head around the corner, an apologetic look on her face. "They're early."

Arabella rolled her eyes and nodded her head. Helen closed the door again.

"My meeting has turned up early, I need to go."

"I had a dream about you last night," Rebecca said. "It was a bit like when we were at the water aerobics, except it was just you and I in the pool. And I think your bathing suit—"

"Rebecca," she growled in warning. She didn't need to sit through a business meeting with *those* thoughts in her mind.

Rebecca chuckled. "I'll tell you another time."

"You better. I'll text you later," Arabella promised.

"Later," Rebecca said.

She hung up the call and tossed the phone onto her desk. It was 4,624 miles from London to New Orleans. She'd checked. Lately, she was feeling every single one of them.

She stood up and brushed down her skirt, checking her appearance in a mirror by the door.

"Back to work," she murmured.

45

ADDISON AND LUKE

JENN SAT on the rickety stool behind the bar at CeeCee's. It was almost three weeks since her crash, and two since she'd gotten out of the hospital. It felt good to be back at work and getting her life back to normal. Even if she could only work at some of her jobs at the moment. She certainly wasn't performing at Façade yet.

She sucked in a deep breath, relishing the fresh air even if it was hot as hell outside.

It was great to be out of the house. Rebecca had been a godsend. Without her care and attention, Jenn wouldn't have been back at work so soon. But Jenn wasn't used to doing nothing. She was used to being busy, running all over the city, and meeting hundreds of people every day.

She'd started morning shifts at CeeCee's a few days earlier. It was nice and casual. Not too many customers, no heavy lifting. She turned her head to face the antiquated fan, trying to enjoy the pathetic breeze from it.

An elderly man entered the bar. Jenn lowered herself gently from the stool.

"Morning, sir," she said with a warm smile. "What can I get you?"

"Just a bottle of water." He looked at the handwritten sign on the bar and put his hand in his pocket to scoop out the correct amount.

Jenn picked up a bottle of water that was floating in the bucket of half-melted ice and placed it on the bar. She picked up the bills as he slowly slid them towards her, one at a time.

"Where is Basin Street Station?" he asked.

"You need to head down Bourbon," Jenn said as she stood on the bottom rung of her stool and leaned over the high bar to gesture the direction. "About another five-minute walk, you'll come to a café with an outside seating area, take the next left. Keep going and you'll see it right in front of you."

"Wonderful." He picked up the water bottle. "And that's where the tourist office is?"

"It is, I highly recommend the open-top bus," a familiar voice sounded from the doorway.

Jenn looked up in shock.

The elderly man turned and regarded Kathryn. "That sounds great, thank you."

"No problem, enjoy your stay in town," she said as he passed by her on his way out.

Jenn continued to stare at Kathryn, belatedly realising that something about her seemed off. Her eyes widened as she realised what it was. She stared at what Kathryn was holding in her arms.

A child.

A boy, she thought. Asleep in Kathryn's arms, balanced on her hip, legs dangling on either side.

"Hello, Jenn," Kathryn said in a whisper.

"You have a son," Jenn said, incredulously.

"Yes." Kathryn nodded. "His name is Luke."

"Luke," Jenn said softly. She continued to stare at the slumbering brown-haired boy.

Kathryn sat at one of the barstools. When Luke started to stir she adjusted her grip on him so they would both be more comfortable. Jenn looked at his soft features and messy hair, stuck to his forehead with perspiration. She swallowed hard at the adorable sight.

"I'm sorry I left without seeing you," Kathryn said.

"You could have called me," Jenn pointed out bitterly.

"I didn't know what to say," she confessed. "I wanted to come and see you, to explain everything... face to face."

Jenn tore her eyes from Luke. She took a protective step back; the bar didn't seem like enough of a barrier between them. She folded her arms.

"Are you married?"

"No," Kathryn said simply.

"Engaged? Boyfriend?"

"No, and no. I'm single."

Jenn frowned, looking at Luke. She wasn't one to judge, but babies came from somewhere.

"I had an affair... with a married man," Kathryn admitted. "It was stupid, and I deeply regret what I did. He convinced me that he would leave his wife, but he never had any intention of that. I thought he loved me. We only slept together twice before I came to my senses, but by then I was pregnant."

Jenn felt her eyebrows raise at Kathryn's bad luck. And poor judgement of character.

"I told him. He'd always told me that he didn't love his wife. I thought the pregnancy would finally make him break the relationship and be with me. But that didn't happen. Instead, he and his wife moved to Europe."

Jenn sat on her stool again. She wanted to be angry, but

she found it impossible. Kathryn was back, and she was pouring her heart out.

"My mother couldn't have stood the scandal of my being pregnant out of wedlock. She's very traditional, and Erica was always the wild child, I was the golden girl. I didn't know what to do, so one day I confided in my father. He was recovering from a minor heart attack. He'd had one years before, so we all thought it was nothing serious."

Kathryn coughed slightly, seemingly trying to keep the tears at bay and remain calm while Luke slept in her arms.

"He came up with a plan. We'd both travel to see my Uncle Addison in Brazil. My father to convalesce and me to join him, to keep him company. Supposedly."

Addison, Jenn thought. She remembered the exchange she'd heard between Kathryn and her sister, Erica. *Tell Mother about Addison.* And then Arabella's retelling of what she had overhead in the hotel lobby.

Luke started to fidget in Kathryn's arms. She adjusted her grip and whispered some soothing words into his ear until he calmed down again.

"I… didn't want to keep him." Kathryn's cheeks burned with embarrassment. "My father convinced me otherwise. He promised me that he would make everything okay. He told me to leave Luke with Uncle Addison for a while, until he had the chance to speak with my mother."

"Is your mother that bad?" Jenn asked. She couldn't imagine a mother who wouldn't be thrilled with a grandson, regardless of the state of the relationship between the parents.

Kathryn looked at her with a smile. "Worse. She would disown me, cut me out of the family business. Freeze my assets. Religion is critical to her. She's not exactly… maternal."

Kathryn wiped her lightly perspiring brow with the back of her hand. Jenn fished a bottle of water from the icy bucket. She unscrewed the cap and placed both on the bar in front of Kathryn.

"Thank you." Kathryn took a sip. "Uncle Addison has been a foster father in Brazil for many years. He adores children. I have fond memories of visiting him when I was growing up. I knew it would be a good life for Luke. And my father seemed convinced that he would be able to tell my mother without her imploding. So, I agreed to his crazy plan. I had the baby and we stayed for a couple of months, then my father and I went home."

Darkness crossed her expression. "A few months later, my father and I were arguing one evening. He wanted to tell my mother, he wanted to bring Luke home, to have a grandson. I was terrified. I felt for sure that he'd have a better life with Addison. Especially if my mother would disown me and leave me penniless. Not that the money made any difference to me personally, but for Luke's sake. I wouldn't be able to provide for him. And I didn't think I could be the mother he deserved anyway. We fought and... my father had a heart attack that evening and died."

Jenn had known that Kathryn's father had passed away, but that didn't prevent the shock she felt at hearing how and when he had died.

"I'm so sorry," she breathed.

"I felt like it was my fault. I guess it *was* my fault," Kathryn continued. "I forced a sick, old man to keep my secret. I fought with him endlessly. It was too much for him."

"You can't blame yourself," Jenn said.

"I did... I do. I couldn't stop thinking that maybe it wouldn't have happened if I'd made different choices. But I messed up my life, and then I ruined Luke's and my father's. My sister suspected that something had happened. Eventually I confided in her because I was losing my mind. She spent the last six months watching me go off the rails, throw myself into work and into an emotionless pit. Which is why she dumped me here. To give me the time she knew I needed to process everything."

"So, you changed your mind and went to get Luke?" Jenn asked.

"No. Well, not exactly," Kathryn admitted. "After your accident, I got a call from my sister. My secret was out in the open. I found out that Michael had told his wife everything. Including that I had been expecting his child. They'd never been able to have children and Michael's wife wanted the baby. They returned to New York to speak to me, but I was here. They spoke to my mother. She put two and two together and realised that I hadn't simply visited Brazil with my father."

Kathryn took another drink of water. Jenn noticed her hand was shaking.

"They were on their way to Brazil to try to take Luke. I realised I couldn't let that happen. Not just because I didn't want *them* to have him, but because he was mine. I did a lot of soul-searching when I was in New Orleans. I realised that I'd spent my whole life doing what other people wanted me to do. Michael wanted a warm body when his wife was out of town. My mother wanted me to be the perfect daughter. My sister wanted me to take the reins of the business, so she could party. And everything I did, every decision I made, was to fit into these roles they had assigned to me.

"I was terrified of losing those roles, as if I would cease to exist without them. I didn't know who I was. If my mother disowned me, who would I be? I didn't know. But the moment I heard that Michael was headed towards Brazil, I knew. I'd be a mother. A single, unemployed mother. And that didn't matter, because it was what I wanted."

Jenn smiled. Kathryn was speaking with such passion, such warmth and love. Something had changed in the last few weeks. It was like the woman was alive again. Jenn had seen hints of it, but this was as if Kathryn was now in full bloom.

"The second I laid my eyes on Luke again, I fell in love with him. I knew I could never let him go," she said.

"He's adorable," Jenn agreed.

"He is." Kathryn looked down at the child wrapped around her. "Addison had shown him photographs and videos of me, so he knew who I was when I got there. I cried for half an hour straight."

"How old is he?"

"Thirteen months," Kathryn replied. "I had him five months into our year in Brazil. For the next few months I… I was in a bad place. I didn't connect with him very well. I didn't want to connect with him because I didn't think I'd see him again."

"And what about Michael and his wife now?" Jenn asked. Her eyes scanned the outside of the bar, fearful that some terrible child snatchers might be lurking there.

"My father was a lawyer," Kathryn explained. "He'd registered Luke's birth in New York, citing me as the sole parent. Michael believed that Addison was fostering Luke, in which case Michael could have had grounds for a custody battle. Of course, it helped that a lot of my communication with Michael took place over email. I had a paper trail proving that he'd abandoned me the moment he heard about the pregnancy." She kissed her son's cheek. "He's mine, and mine alone."

"Motherhood suits you," Jenn said.

Kathryn looked at her over the top of Luke's head. "Not quite the words my mother used."

Jenn winced. "What happened?"

"Well…" Kathryn sighed. "Suffice to say I was right. I got disowned and fired immediately."

"She fired her own daughter?" Jenn asked incredulously. "One who has a baby?"

"Of course." Kathryn chuckled. "My mother is, well, she's a real piece of work. She was appalled to find out that her daughter was an unmarried mother with gay tendencies."

Jenn blinked in surprise. "G—gay tendencies?"

"Yes." Kathryn looked steadily at her. "I told my mother about this amazing woman I met while I was in New Orleans. She was extraordinary, a free spirit with a real zest for life. I explained that she taught me I didn't have to follow some conventional pattern to fit in with the world around me. I should be able to do what I wanted to do, whatever made me happy. I told my mother that the woman had brought me back to life."

"Me?" Jenn breathed.

"You." Kathryn confirmed with a wide grin.

"W—why are you here?"

"I wanted to see you. I know I have been a thorn in your side, but I've had time to reflect on a lot of things and I want to get to know you. Properly. If you would like that?" Kathryn gestured to Luke. "I understand if not, I'm not exactly—"

"I'd love to get to know you. Both of you," Jenn admitted.

46

NEED SOMEONE ELSE TO BITCH
ABOUT

REBECCA ADJUSTED the settings on her camera and lined up for another shot.

"What you up to, shutterbug?" Miss Mae asked.

"Getting some new shots for your website," Rebecca replied.

"Does anyone go on our website?"

"No idea," Rebecca replied. "But your boss wanted some new pictures for it, and for your leaflets, too."

Miss Mae looked around the tourist office lobby. "Ain't much to photograph."

"True," Rebecca agreed. So far, she'd been taking pictures of the signs more than the actual space. The desks were old and beaten up, and the chairs were worse.

"If you need a little glamour then you know where I am," Miss Mae said. She plonked herself down in a chair and grinned at Rebecca.

Rebecca took a couple snaps of her. "I'll get these over to *Vanity Fair* post haste."

Miss Mae chuckled. "I'll take my usual fee."

Rebecca looked down at her camera and started to adjust

the settings again. Her mind kept wandering, back to London to be exact. Jenn was well enough for her to head home once she finished up her contracts in a couple of weeks. But Jenn was still moping about in a depressive funk because of the Kathryn situation. She didn't want to leave her until she thought she was doing better.

But she missed Arabella so much. The video calls, voice calls, and text messages just weren't enough. She wanted to touch her, kiss her, hold her in her arms. She'd never missed anyone so much in her life.

"Good afternoon!"

Rebecca looked up to see Jenn step into the building with a spring in her step and a wide smile on her face. Rebecca frowned. It was the happiest she'd seen Jenn for weeks. She shared a confused look with Miss Mae.

"How is everyone today?" Jenn asked as she unstrapped her backpack and placed it behind the desk.

Miss Mae's eyes narrowed as she looked Jenn up and down. "What up with you, dove?"

Jenn looked at Miss Mae, biting her lip as if debating whether or not to share her news.

"Kathryn's back."

Miss Mae sighed and turned in her swivel chair. She picked up a crossword puzzle and focused on it, so Jenn turned to face Rebecca instead.

Rebecca just looked at her in surprise. She didn't know how she felt about that news. Kathryn had messed Jenn around and ultimately broken her heart. She had probably played a small part in Jenn's accident, even if it was primarily caused by Jenn ignoring basic road safety. But Jenn was obviously deeply smitten with Kathryn... and now she was back.

"She explained everything," Jenn was saying. "She had family stuff happening, she had to drop everything and go and deal with some things."

"She didn't know if you were alive or dead," Miss Mae mumbled, not fully focused on the crossword after all.

"She… has a son," Jenn said carefully.

"A son?" Rebecca's eyebrows rose. She looked over to Miss Mae who hadn't reacted to the news. The older woman counted the boxes in her puzzle with the tip of her pen.

"It's a complicated story," Jenn said. "She had to give him up, but now she's back with him again. His name is Luke, and he is so cute."

"How old is the boy?" Miss Mae asked.

"Thirteen months," Jenn replied.

Miss Mae shook her head ruefully. "She got you wrapped around her little finger. Or if she didn't before, she will now. You love a toddler."

Rebecca nodded her agreement. It was common knowledge that Jenn was obsessed with toddlers. Babies she could take or leave, children she didn't mind, but the certain qualities of a toddler left her weak at the knees.

"Fine Shoes waltzes back like nothing happened and you forgive her?" Miss Mae looked up. "Dove, you nearly died."

Jenn chewed her lip as she looked from Miss Mae to Rebecca. "She had to go, there's this guy, Michael—"

Miss Mae waved her pen in the air to silence Jenn. She turned back to her crossword. "I'm sure she had reasons," she said. "And whatever those reasons were, you have already forgiven her."

Jenn looked at Rebecca hopefully.

Rebecca let out a sigh and shrugged her shoulders. "I want you to be happy, Jenn. If Kathryn does that for you, then great. But don't forget what happened. We don't want to see you hurt again."

Jenn pulled her friend into a hug. "I'll be careful, I promise."

Rebecca chuckled. "You better."

Jenn rushed around to Miss Mae and hugged her, too. Miss Mae didn't move. Instead, she ignored the woman wrapped around her and tried to continue with her crossword. Jenn bent down to look her in the face, grinning at her co-worker's pout.

"Oh, come on, be happy for me. Please?" Jenn smiled.

Miss Mae looked up at her. She let out a sigh and then shook her head as she slammed her pen down on the crossword puzzle.

"Okay, but we need to find someone else to bitch about," she said.

47

YOU DIDN'T CALL

LATER THAT EVENING, Jenn was walking down towards the river to meet Kathryn and Luke for an early dinner. When she woke up that morning, she never thought that this would be the day that Kathryn would walk back into her life. Certainly never with Luke.

She'd not had a chance to properly meet Luke that morning. Kathryn had been eager to get them checked into a hotel, and Luke slept through their entire conversation at CeeCee's.

Dinner would be her first real meeting with him. She hoped her natural ability with children would work on this particular child.

She was still struggling to process everything that happened. Over the hours, her relief at Kathryn's return as well as her understanding of the circumstances had given way a little to anger. Kathryn had never contacted her to find out if she was okay. She had simply vanished, and then turned up again when it suited her. With a child, an explanation, and... what? An assumption that Jenn would accept it?

Jenn took a deep breath and pushed that thought to one

side. She'd deal with it in due course. For now, she wanted to enjoy Kathryn's company before deciding what to do next.

She walked along the boardwalk, spotting Kathryn and Luke at a table covered by a large parasol. Kathryn was speaking animatedly to Luke and laughing happily. Jenn smiled.

She's beautiful.

Miss Mae had lectured Jenn before she left the tourist office that afternoon. She'd spoken about Kathryn's erratic behaviour and asked again how the woman could leave without knowing what had happened to Jenn after the accident. And, most importantly, how she could go from not wanting Luke to suddenly wanting him in her life again.

Jenn could feel her forehead furrow. They were all good points. Points she needed to clarify with Kathryn. As elated as she was to see her again, she needed to ensure that Kathryn wouldn't vanish again.

She couldn't take it if she did.

She approached the table and stood by Luke's highchair. The attached food tray was filled with colourful stacking cups that he was playing with.

"Luke," Kathryn said softly to get his attention.

Luke looked at his mother and noticed that she was looking beside him. He turned and looked up at Jenn.

"Jee-en!" he exclaimed excitedly.

Jenn's heart clenched at the adorable boy mispronouncing her name. And the fact that Kathryn had clearly taught him her name.

"Hey, Luke." She took a seat beside Kathryn, opposite Luke.

"Jee-en," he repeated. He looked at Kathryn as if to assure himself that his mother had seen their guest.

"Yes, Jenn," Kathryn said softly, attempting to correct the boy. "Jenn's having dinner with us."

A waiter approached the table. He handed each of the women a menu and placed a drawing sheet and some crayons beside Kathryn in case she wanted Luke to have them.

"I'm glad you could come," Kathryn started. She cleared the stacking cups and replaced them with the paper and the crayons.

"Me, too," Jenn admitted. She watched Luke pick up a blue crayon and excitedly run it over the paper. "You're good with him."

"Thank you." Kathryn smiled.

"It's quite a change," Jenn said carefully as she flipped through her menu.

"What do you mean?" Kathryn asked as she fondly watched Luke.

"Well, going from not wanting to be a p-a-r-e-n-t to this."

Kathryn's face crumpled. She looked destroyed for a moment before she sat up and picked up her menu. She focused on the page, but Jenn knew she wasn't really reading it.

She felt terrible, wishing she had taken a little more time to think about what she wanted to say. "I'm sorry, that was tactless, I didn't mean it like that." She lowered her menu and regarded Kathryn.

"Yes, you did," Kathryn replied with a small nod of her head. "I understand, I... I sound impulsive and unreliable. You're wondering if I'm suited to this—"

"No! No, not at all," Jenn exclaimed. She reached her hand across the table to take Kathryn's. "I'm sorry, that really came out wrong. I shouldn't have said anything."

"You're right, though. It is a big turnaround. I didn't want to... be a mother. But I think it was more concern about not being a good enough one. Worry that when my mother cut me off, because I knew she would, that I would be alone and wouldn't be able to offer Luke the best. It was fear."

Jenn understood that. It must have been a shock for Kathryn to discover that she was pregnant, especially with a mother who would react so badly to a grandchild out of wedlock.

"But now that I've done it, I wouldn't change it for the world," Kathryn continued. "We'll be a family, no matter what."

"I'm really glad to hear that. I'm sorry about what I implied, though. That was rude."

Kathryn opened her mouth to answer. She looked at Jenn for a moment and then frowned as if realising something. She closed her mouth and turned to see Luke staring at them with a wide grin.

"Nosey!" she said in a playful tone. She removed her hand from Jenn's and gently tweaked Luke's nose. "Nosey Luke Foster, that is your new name."

"Ugg," Luke stumbled over the letters.

"Luke," Kathryn said, exaggerating the first letter.

"Ugg," Luke repeated with a nod of the head. He looked away and continued to massacre his piece of paper with random colours.

"Clearly, I didn't predict this when I named him," Kathryn said as she turned back to Jenn. "But I also didn't predict I'd see him ever again. I was a different person last year. Hell, I was a different person five weeks ago."

"What changed in five weeks?" Jenn asked.

"Honestly?" Kathryn asked before letting out a disbelieving chuckle. "You."

"Me?" Jenn frowned in confusion.

"Yes, you," Kathryn repeated. "You with your own way of tackling this thing called *life*. You with your nonconformity and happiness. You with your twenty-seven jobs—"

"Nine, actually."

"Saving lives, pouring drinks, driving trams—"

"Streetcars."

"You're full of life, Jenn," Kathryn said pointedly. "You are living your life, you're doing the things you want to do, and you're not following the conventional rules. And it's working for you. I didn't know that it could be like that."

"What did you think it had to be like?" Jenn asked with interest.

"Work commitments, family commitments. Find a man, get a house, get married, have children. Work up the corporate ladder."

"Sounds boring."

Kathryn laughed. She caught a crayon that rolled off Luke's food tray and handed it back to him. "It *is* boring, I just never really considered that there were alternatives. You opened my eyes to that, and you made me analyse what I had done, what I was doing, and where I wanted to be. I can never thank you enough for that gift."

Jenn blushed. She didn't think for one second that she had done anything special, certainly not anything life-changing, but Kathryn seemed to think so.

The waiter returned, so they ordered food and non-alcoholic drinks, both wanting to be clear-headed for whatever lay before them. Kathryn ordered a children's meal for Luke, asking about the vegetable options. When the waiter listed the vegetables, Luke looked up and happily started shouting for peas. Peas were ordered.

The waiter left, and as Jenn opened her mouth to speak, Luke sent a piece of paper flying in her direction.

"Jee-en."

Jenn picked up the colourful swirling mess and smiled. "Wow, Luke, this is very good!"

Luke beamed with pride. He held out his hand in a grabbing motion, and Jenn handed him the drawing back. He turned the paper over and started colouring the back of the sheet.

She looked at Kathryn. "The New Orleans creativity vibe has gotten into him already."

Kathryn smiled lovingly at her son. "Yes, obviously I didn't have anything for him when I went to Brazil, so I picked him up some crayons and a blank notebook for the flight to New York. He has been drawing ever since."

Luke quickly ran out of space on the back of his sheet. He turned it over and over again as if expecting a new blank sheet to appear. Kathryn reached into a baby bag—until now tucked under her seat—produced a blank sheet of paper and placed it in front of him.

Jenn watched the interaction and smiled. Her mind was turning with different questions, but the biggest one that kept presenting itself was the next to fall from her lips.

"Why did you come back?"

"To see you."

Jenn swallowed at the serious look in Kathryn's eyes.

"You left, after… after my accident. You left."

Anger flashed in Kathryn's eyes. "You know why I had to leave—"

"But you didn't know if I was dead or alive. You didn't even call!"

"I called every day," Kathryn breathed.

Jenn blinked. "What?"

"I—I called every day. I spoke to the same nurse. I told her I was your aunt from out of town, and she kept me advised of your progress. She told me she shouldn't be telling me anything, but I think she could hear the panic in my voice. She told me when you woke up at six in the evening the day after your accident. She told me about the three broken ribs, numbers 5, 6, and 7. The concussion, and the relief when there was no internal bleeding."

Jenn swallowed and stared at Kathryn in surprise.

"I'm sorry, I know it was a breach of your privacy. But I was too frightened to call you."

Jenn knew she should be angry at her personal medical details being so readily handed out, but she was too overcome with joy. Kathryn had called *every* day. She even remembered details that Jenn herself had forgotten.

"Are you angry?" Kathryn asked, obviously concerned by her continued silence.

It was enough to break Jenn out of her daze. "No, no, sorry I… I thought you…"

"You thought I didn't care."

Jenn winced and slowly nodded.

"Well, I can't be surprised that you would feel that way." Kathryn sighed. "After I left, I thought I should have said something else to Arabella, get her to pass a message on to you. But I didn't know what to say. And, at the time, I was in a state of shock."

Jenn understood. She didn't think she'd be able to, but she did. She often thought of Kathryn coming back, what reasons she might give for her disappearance, but she never really accepted them. Now, sitting beside her and listening to the words, seeing the expression on her face—it made it real.

They both turned to regard Luke and his colouring for a moment.

"I cared… I mean, I care about you. Very much," Kathryn said. For a moment, Jenn thought she meant Luke. She had spoken so softly and was still facing him. "I know that seems ridiculous. We hardly know each other."

"Not at all." Jenn sucked in a quick breath. "I… feel the same."

She cares about me. And she came back, she thought. *But what does that mean?*

It seemed too soon to bombard Kathryn with questions about what would happen next. For now, she was happy to just enjoy her company.

Soon their meals came. Jenn noticed that Kathryn's food was getting cold while she tended to Luke and his meal. She silently stood up and took the seat beside the boy. She took the cutlery out of Kathryn's hands and started to cut Luke's food and feed him herself. They took turns eating their own meals while the other fed Luke before switching again.

The women kept to lighter topics, mainly Luke and Kathryn getting to know each other. Jenn spoke of her recent return to work. It was casual, light, and airy, but there was an undercurrent of all the things left unsaid.

When the meal was finished Kathryn insisted on paying despite Jenn's protests. They stood, and Jenn helped to put Luke into his stroller. It hurt her ribs, but she already knew she'd carry him for miles if it would make him or Kathryn happy.

"Sorry," Kathryn apologised. "Dinner with a child isn't exactly a long affair, and I need to get him ready for bed."

"It's okay, I understand," Jenn replied. She remained crouched in front of Luke and gently tickled his stomach.

"Maybe we could see each other again soon?" Kathryn asked hopefully.

"Sure, I'd really like that," Jenn said. "Maybe you and Luke would like a trip on the steamboat tomorrow? I'm working, but I can spare some time for my favourite visitors."

They began to walk along the boardwalk.

"That sounds wonderful, as long as you're not going to throw yourself in the Mississippi after some worthless drunk again," Kathryn said.

"I can't make any promises," Jenn joked.

They walked silently. A question that Jenn was dying to ask kept tossing over and over in her brain. She eyed the calm waters of the Mississippi, so she didn't meet Kathryn's gaze.

"So…"

"So?" Kathryn questioned.

"Was there… anything else I opened your eyes to? You mentioned something about gay tendencies?"

Kathryn chuckled softly. "I think you know."

"I'd like to hear it."

Kathryn paused. She pointed Luke's stroller towards the railings, so the boy could see the ships passing. She turned to face Jenn. "I like you. A lot."

"Is that what you meant by gay tendencies?" Jenn asked.

"Yes," she admitted. "I'm still struggling with the labels."

Jenn felt herself deflate. Was she still just going to be an experiment? "I see, so… you're still confused?"

"Well, I don't know if I'm straight, bi, pan, gay… but I do know one thing with absolute certainty."

Jenn frowned. "What's that?"

"I'm Jenn-sexual," Kathryn replied with a flirtatious grin.

"J—Jenn-sexual?" she stammered.

"Yes," Kathryn replied mock-seriously. "I realised I was getting too caught up in the more conventional questions again. Things like, am I interested in men or am I interested in women? But the answer was staring me in the face all along. I'm interested in the person who caused me to initially question myself. So, I decided. I'm Jenn-sexual."

Jenn felt her mouth turn dry. She stared longingly at Kathryn's lips as her brain attempted to catch up with events and process data. The last kiss she had initiated was devastating in its aftermath, and the last thing she wanted to do was make another error.

"Car!" Luke cried as he pointed at a large cargo ship.

Both women looked at him and chuckled.

"Your kid's broken," Jenn joked.

Kathryn slapped her arm playfully. She knelt beside his stroller and pointed at the ship.

"That's not a car, Luke, that's a ship. Can you say 'ship'?"

Luke stared at it for a long while. Kathryn tried again, and eventually, Luke mumbled something that could have been anything at all. The boy let out a long yawn and looked expectantly at Kathryn in an attempt to convey his boredom.

"We should go," Kathryn said sadly as she stood up. "He's had a lot of travel and excitement, and I want to get him into a normal routine as quickly as possible."

"I understand." Jenn nodded as she looked down at the adorable boy who was staring up at her.

Kathryn stepped closer and placed a light and yet lingering kiss on her cheek. She handed Jenn a business card. "Here's my new number, let me know when and where to meet you tomorrow."

Jenn nodded. Kathryn turned Luke's stroller and continued along the boardwalk. Luke leaned out of the stroller and waved goodbye to her.

She waved back.

48

CERTAINTY

REBECCA WAITED for Jenn to get home. The moment she'd left the tourist office, she'd called Arabella and told her all about Kathryn's return and the appearance of a child. Arabella had known there'd been something going on with Kathryn, she'd called it quite early on.

Rebecca had caught her up on all the gossip she had, which wasn't enough for Arabella's liking. She promised that she'd find out everything and would report back as soon as she could. Now she was waiting for Jenn to return from dinner with Kathryn, hoping that her friend wouldn't be dismayed again by something Kathryn had said or done.

She mindlessly flipped through television channels while plucking kernels of popcorn out of a bowl. She heard a key in the door and turned the television off. She turned expectantly in her seat, watching as Jenn entered the apartment.

"Hey." Jenn put her keys on the hook by the door.

"Hey, how did it go?" Rebecca asked.

Jenn regarded her suspiciously. "You really want to know? Or are you about to try to convince me to stay away from her?"

Rebecca shrugged. "I've not decided yet. Depends on what you tell me. But I do really want to know how it went."

Jenn pointed to the kitchen. "Want a drink?"

Rebecca pointed to her bottle of cola on the coffee table. "I'm good, thanks."

Jenn vanished for a few minutes, probably longer than she needed.

She's stalling, Rebecca thought. *She thinks I'm against this.*

She couldn't blame Jenn for thinking that. She'd not exactly been complimentary about Kathryn since she'd left. But then, she did think that Kathryn left her friend for dead in the street. That was not a great quality in a person.

When Jenn did finally return she sat in the armchair and opened her bottle of water. She took a few long sips.

"She's interested in me. She apologised for her behaviour. She called a nurse every day to check on me in the hospital. She wishes she didn't have to leave, but she had to go and get her kid. She loves that kid with all her heart, I can see it in her eyes. She kissed me, on the cheek. She says she's Jenn-sexual," Jenn listed.

Rebecca stared at her. "Wow… right, I need a recap on some of that."

Jenn started to laugh. "Bex, it was great. She… she likes me… like, really likes me. We're seeing each other again tomorrow. I don't have all the answers yet, but I really think this is going to work out."

"What is Jenn-sexual?" Rebecca asked, latching on to the point that had stuck in her mind.

"She said she'd been hung up on figuring out labels. Wondering if she's straight, bi, et cetera. But she's decided she's Jenn-sexual. She has feelings for me. She even told her uptight, religious, bitch of a mother that she had 'gay tendencies.' She then proceeded to fire her and disown her."

"For being gay?"

"That and having a child out of wedlock."

Rebecca couldn't fathom it. "What kind of mother doesn't want a relationship with her daughter and grandson?"

"One who is making a big mistake. Kathryn said she wants nothing more to do with her. She's fully focused on her and Luke now. He calls himself Ugg. It's so damn cute, Bex."

"Ugg?" Rebecca laughed.

"Yeah, can't pronounce L's or K's yet. Ugg."

Rebecca smiled. "I'll have to meet this kid."

Jenn nodded quickly. "You should, he's adorable. And... I think this is serious. I mean, she came all this way to talk to me. We didn't discuss the future yet, it's been a full-on day. But I think that's where it's heading."

"Are you ready for that?" Rebecca asked. "Remember how badly she hurt you."

"I do." Jenn took another sip of water. "But she hurt me because I really liked her, and I was sure she liked me despite her protests. And now, I know she likes me, and she's ready to admit it."

"She has just appeared in town again, suddenly assured of her sexual preference, with a child and no job," Rebecca pointed out.

Jenn nodded. She pointed around the small apartment. "If she was looking for a sugar momma to take her and Luke in, do you really think she would seek me out? I'm hardly a target for that kind of thing. Some young nothing from NOLA with a load of part-time jobs and no savings."

"You're not a nothing," Rebecca argued.

"You know what I mean. No one is going to use me for the money I don't have."

It was true. Jenn lived a comfortable life, but she didn't have much money. She worked low-paid part-time jobs because she enjoyed them, but they didn't leave much for a nest egg.

"Okay…" Rebecca ran her hand through her hair. "But, do you really know her? You've hardly spent any time with her."

"We have talked *so* much in that time," Jenn said. "When she was here before, and today. I feel like I know her inside out. She was born in Brazil, though she's never been able to get used to the heat of the country because she left when she was a small child. She idolised her father. Her mother is a hard-ass, but she feels duty bound to appease her."

Jenn took another sip of water, smiling as she remembered the details of past conversations.

"She works with her mother and sister at a PR company in New York. She doesn't like it much, but she's good at it, so she stuck with it, mainly for her mom. She's travelled to a lot of places in Europe. She takes a lot of photographs, but she never has time to look at them, so she reckons she has over ten thousand pictures to organize someday. She loves animals and donates her time to an animal sanctuary in Jersey every other weekend."

Rebecca held up her hand. "Okay, I get it…"

"She's hot-headed and quick to judge, but when she gives something a chance she's fair. She's very honest—in a refreshing way. She'll tell you if she doesn't like something and she'll explain why. She likes to read biographies because she thinks it's interesting to understand why people make the choices they do."

"Jenn," Rebecca said.

"She has a lot of money, but she doesn't treat herself much. She's too practical for that. She buys nice clothes because she needs them for work. When she travels to Europe, she always ties it in with seeing a client. She never thought she'd be any good at being a parent, and, although she looks like the best mother in the world, I know that she's analysing every single decision she makes one hundred times over."

She stopped and looked up at Rebecca. "I know everyone thinks that this was just some vacation fling. I know people think that she's hot and I lusted over her and that was it. But you know what? I'm a big girl. I'm an adult and I spoke to her, I got to know her, and I fell in love with her. I hated her when I first saw her, it wasn't love at first sight. I got to *know* her."

"It's not you I'm worried about," Rebecca said quietly.

"I know," Jenn said. "But... I have a good feeling about this. Really. She's the one for me. I'm so happy right now. So incredibly happy."

Rebecca let out a sigh and reluctantly smiled. There would be no stopping Jenn now. She was completely enamoured with Kathryn. Rebecca just hoped that Kathryn felt the same way. It wasn't her place to tell her friend what to do. She needed to be the best friend she could be and support her either way.

"So... Luke's adorable, right?" she asked.

Jenn grinned widely and nodded her head. "Oh, man, he's amazing. So fucking cute."

Rebecca laughed. "Better stop swearing if you're gonna be a mommy."

The grin vanished from Jenn's face. "Mommy?"

Rebecca stared at Jenn. "Has it escaped your notice that your new girlfriend has a kid?"

Jenn blinked a couple of times. Rebecca could tell that Jenn hadn't had time to put two and two together yet. It was only now falling into place that she was potentially about to enter into a relationship with someone who had a child. Which meant she'd have a child, too.

"If things work out," Rebecca said, "you'll be Mommy Two. Maybe even Mama."

"Mama," Jenn whispered as her eyes glazed over.

Rebecca grinned. "You have been saying that you were looking for something serious."

"Yes," Jenn whispered in agreement.

"When is she going back to New York?" Rebecca asked.

Jenn's eyes snapped up to meet hers. "I— I don't know. She didn't say anything."

Rebecca felt terrible for bringing it up. It was obvious that Jenn was only just catching up to the fact that Kathryn was in town. She hadn't properly considered the point that she'd presumably soon be leaving again.

"Long-distance relationships aren't that hard," Rebecca said. "With Skype and stuff. Or maybe you could move to New York?"

"I doubt there are many open positions for streetcar drivers or steamboat hosts in New York," Jenn said with a sigh.

"You need to talk to her," Rebecca said. "Before you get in too deep."

"I know, I know." Jenn flopped back into the sofa. She winced.

"Mind your ribs," Rebecca said.

"Screw my ribs," Jenn mumbled.

"Hey." Rebecca came to sit on the arm of the sofa. She wrapped her in a one-armed hug. "You'll work things out, I know you will."

49

BACK ON BOARD

As she had so many times before, Jenn entertained the passengers waiting on the dockside with jokes and stories, but her heart wasn't really in it. Not because of the pain in her ribs, nor the lack of sleep she'd had the night before. It was because of the heavy black cloud that she felt hanging over her.

Rebecca had been right, of course. Kathryn would have to go home at some point, and Jenn couldn't live in New York, even if she wanted to. She loved New Orleans too much, and she'd never be able to find employment in New York, nor the funds to rent an apartment.

That was if Kathryn would even want her there. The possibility that this was a fling, an experiment, weighed heavily on her mind.

Out of the corner of her eye she saw Kathryn arrive with an excited Luke bouncing in his stroller. "Excuse me a moment," she said to the couple she'd been talking to.

She weaved her way through the rope maze that contained the queue. She approached the little party and smiled as warmly as she could. It was a tough sell considering she had been up all night with Rebecca drinking and agonising over what to do.

Jenn was sure that there was something important between her and Kathryn, something that deserved to be explored. But she was also adamant that she didn't want her heart crushed when Kathryn finished her vacation and went home.

"Jee-en!" Luke said excitedly.

"Hey, little man," Jenn said as she smiled down at the cute boy.

"Are you okay?" Kathryn asked. She frowned slightly as she looked at Jenn. Clearly her concerns were written all over her face.

"Yeah," Jenn said, quickly brushing off the concern. "Just tired. Didn't get much sleep last night."

"Ah." Kathryn nodded. "That makes three of us."

"Oh?" Jenn looked at Luke to see if something was obviously wrong that would have prevented him from sleeping.

"I think it was the room," Kathryn explained quietly. "He's not used to there being any noise at all when he sleeps. We're close to Bourbon Street, and when all that died down even the hum of the minibar kept him awake."

Jenn smiled in understanding. "I'm the same. There's no electronics in my bedroom. I hate the noise they make."

"Maybe we'll have to stay at your place," Kathryn said. She blushed as she looked up at Jenn. "Oh! I didn't mean…"

Jenn laughed and waved off the rest of Kathryn's apology. "It's fine, I know what you mean."

A crackling from the walkie-talkie caught her attention. She turned to face the boat and nodded her head at the captain on the deck. "We're ready to start boarding," she said. "Ready, Luke?"

Kathryn looked at the crowd of people by the dock. "Shouldn't you let them on first?"

"Lady," Jenn said with a serious tone, "I'm in charge of boarding the ship. Brunettes with cute kids are first. Sorry but it's a safety thing."

Kathryn bit her lip and grinned. "Sorry, I don't understand these things. Lead the way."

Jenn unhooked a rope and gestured for Kathryn to follow her up the ramp and onto the steamboat.

Kathryn held onto Luke's hand as they walked around the ship for a second lap. On their way, they had made a number of friends as Luke stopped and waved to everyone they passed. Kathryn would usually have hated the attention but seeing how enamoured everyone was with her son was heartening.

As they circled the ship, Kathryn watched Jenn interacting with the other passengers. She frowned, noticing Jenn's eyes glaze over a little with sadness whenever she spotted them.

Kathryn knew something was up. Jenn's whole demeanour had changed from the previous night. It was clear they needed to have a conversation sooner rather than later.

"Luke, let's go in here," she suggested when she saw Jenn in the dining area where the jazz band was playing.

Luke happily turned. A passenger held the heavy door open for them as they entered. Kathryn thanked him, but the man was too busy smiling from ear to ear at Luke to notice.

Her son's eyes lit up at the first strains of the jazz band. He stopped in the middle of the room and began to stomp his little feet in an attempt to dance along to the tune.

A few passengers noticed, and their interest got Jenn's attention. She walked over to them at the same moment that Luke pulled his hand away from Kathryn's and walked towards the band. He stood right in front of the drummer, staring up at the man in awe. His chubby legs thudded up and down in time with the beat.

"A career in dancing?" Jenn asked with a smile as she stood beside Kathryn.

"Doubtful." Kathryn grimaced at the terrible, wobbling thrusts Luke was attempting. She turned to Jenn. "May I ask what's wrong?"

"Nothing," Jenn said unconvincingly.

"Oh, please, you look at me and Luke like you might cry," Kathryn said softly. "What is it?"

Jenn swallowed and looked around the room. When she seemed satisfied that everyone was focused on the band, or on Luke, she spoke again. "I… I guess it occurred to me yesterday that I'll miss you."

"Miss us?" Kathryn frowned.

"Yeah, when you go back to New York," Jenn explained.

"Oh." Kathryn nodded. Her eyes drifted to Luke. "What if I didn't go back to New York?"

Jenn's jaw dropped. "What?"

"There's nothing for me there. I… I hadn't intended to go back."

Jenn continued to stare at Kathryn open-mouthed.

"This is why I didn't say anything last night," she acknowledged. "I know it looks odd, suddenly uprooting my life and moving to a city I hardly know. I hadn't made any firm plans. My father's inheritance money means I'm able to take some time off of work and spend it bonding with Luke. I figured it doesn't matter where that happens, and New Orleans is as good as place as any."

"You're… staying?" Jenn confirmed.

"I'd like to, if that's okay with you," Kathryn continued. "Besides, Luke's taken to jazz. I can't tear him away from his passion."

Jenn turned to a colleague. "Watch that kid as if your life depends on it," she instructed.

She grabbed Kathryn's hand and pulled her towards a staff door. Kathryn allowed herself to be dragged along, watching as Jenn's colleague approached Luke and started to dance along with him.

Once they were alone, in a dimly lit corridor, Jenn let go of her hand and turned to face her. "I need to know, for sure," Jenn said breathlessly. "Because I'm ready for this. I need to know if you are. If I've misread this, tell me now."

"I'm trying to give you space and time to be sure of things," Kathryn said. "I don't want to bombard you with this, me being here, *Luke* being here. I don't want you to feel pushed into anything."

"Are you staying?" Jenn asked, a forceful undertone to her voice.

"Yes."

"You and Luke, staying in New Orleans... for, like, more than a week."

"We'll be here for no less than six months. Hopefully more, if you'll have us."

Jenn's eyes sparkled. "And... you... want to be together?"

"I want to take you out, on a real date. Where we will kiss, and no one will claim it was a mistake," Kathryn confessed. "If you can find a babysitter, that is."

Jenn lunged forward, lips connecting with hers. Kathryn threw her arms around Jenn's shoulders, careful to avoid pressing against her ribs. She returned the kiss with everything she had, wanting to express her true feelings as best she could through the act.

She pulled back. "If I upset you again, I'll leave," she promised. "This is your city. If you don't want to see me again, just tell me."

Jenn cupped her face, her expression dark and serious. "Never. Leave. Again."

"I won't. Fate keeps bringing me to you, and who am I to argue with fate?" Kathryn whispered.

"You don't believe in fate, or true love," Jenn reminded her.

"Things change," Kathryn said.

She threaded her hand through Jenn's locks and pulled her in for another kiss.

50

SURPRISE

REBECCA LOWERED HER CAMERA. She walked over to the curtains of the luxury hotel suite and adjusted them slightly. She returned to her spot in front of the open door and brought her camera back to her face.

Much better, she thought. It was the little details that made the difference between a good shot and a great shot. Picking up on all the small things that combined to make an image. Especially places that were supposed to denote luxury such as the five-star hotel she was currently freelancing for.

Rebecca took a couple of pictures of the new layout. She stepped further into the room and tried for a different angle. She placed her camera down on the desk and walked over to the bed. She fluffed the pillows up a little and ran her hand over the sheet to iron out the few tiny creases.

"How the mighty have fallen."

She spun around.

Arabella stood in the doorway, watching her with a smirk. "A professional photographer, now a hotel maid," she continued.

Rebecca looked around in shock. "What—what are you doing here?"

"Seeing you."

"You're supposed to be in London!" Rebecca rushed across the room and pulled Arabella into a hug.

"I missed you," Arabella whispered in her ear.

"You couldn't tell me that you were coming?" Rebecca asked. She stepped back and looked Arabella up and down. She took another step back and folded her arms, trying to look disagreeable. "I can't believe you didn't say anything."

"Surprise?" Arabella was grinning from ear to ear.

"No, you don't get away with it that easy," Rebecca said. "I'm very annoyed with you."

"Oh? Then why are you smiling so much?" Arabella asked.

Rebecca narrowed her eyes. "I've been missing you so much. How long have you been planning this? I could have been happily *expecting* your arrival, not miserably *missing* you. I could have... have picked you up from the airport!"

"They have taxis," Arabella told her. "And I honestly thought you'd enjoy the surprise. That, and I only made the decision last night. Which meant I had to fly to New York yesterday and get a connecting flight today."

Rebecca shook her head. "Wait, what? You only decided last night? What about work?"

"This isn't the greeting I expected at all," Arabella said, but she was still smiling. Presumably she was happy that she had Rebecca so off kilter. It was so like her to enjoy something like that.

Rebecca smiled. "You're unbelievable, you know that?"

Arabella stepped forward, raising her arms. "Does this mean you forgive me?"

Rebecca nodded and stepped into the hug. She squeezed her momentarily before kissing her, cupping Arabella's face in both hands and showing her just how much she'd missed her. She pulled away only when she'd used up all the air in her lungs.

"How long are you here for?"

"As long as you need," Arabella said.

Rebecca's brow furrowed. "I don't understand."

The last time they spoke, Arabella was just as busy with work as she'd always been. Deals were failing all around her, her father was useless, a key member of staff had left, and they still couldn't find a receptionist who didn't cut off calls when transferring them.

"I hired a very expensive expert," Arabella explained. "I poached him from a rival company in an act of brilliant corporate sabotage. I told my father that I was taking a sabbatical, and that my replacement is called Kevin. And then I told Kevin that I'd be in New Orleans if he needed me, and if he needed me there would be a high likelihood that he'd be fired for not being the expert he claimed to be."

"You got a Kevin," Rebecca said happily.

"I got a Kevin," Arabella confirmed. "They're marvellous, I highly recommend them. Running costs are high, but that can't be avoided." Her tone turned serious. "I needed to see you."

"I'm so glad you're here. Sorry I reacted like that... I've just been missing you so much that I've been feeling depressed lately."

"Noted. In the future, I'll give you some notice. This just seemed romantic, somehow."

"Romantic?" Rebecca bit her lip. It wasn't like Arabella to try to be romantic, but this was a side to her that Rebecca looked forward to exploring.

"Silly, I know." Arabella flushed.

"Not silly." Rebecca kissed her again. More chastely this

time, now that she remembered the door to the corridor was still open. "I am so glad you're here. Where are you staying?"

"Here."

"Here, here?" Rebecca asked.

"Yes. I told the manager I needed a room immediately after seeing some fabulous photographs on Instagram from a top London photographer I follow. He seemed very pleased."

Rebecca chuckled. "You don't have an Instagram account."

"No, but you told me you uploaded some snaps to Instagram the other day before you started your project here… I listen." Arabella smothered a yawn behind her hand. "Sorry, I'm still not a very good traveller. I'm told I get grumpy when I travel."

Rebecca noted the dullness in her eyes and the blush on her cheeks and neck. Now she was looking, she realised that Arabella looked exhausted. Then she heard Arabella's stomach rumble lightly.

"Go and get some rest, I can catch up with you later," Rebecca instructed.

"I'm not going to argue. There's a protein bar in my bag with my name on it," Arabella said. "I'm in room 521. Come and see me when you're done."

"Sure you don't want to sleep?" Rebecca asked. She didn't want to interrupt her.

"I'd rather see you," Arabella said. She looked around the room. "There's a cobweb in that corner."

Rebecca turned around and followed Arabella's pointing finger. Sure enough, there was a cobweb in the corner of the room. Trust Arabella's eye for detail to pick up on it.

"Damn," she said, wondering how she hadn't noticed it herself.

"If you want to photograph my room…" Arabella winked.

"I'll take you up on that later," Rebecca promised.

Arabella let out a tired yawn. "Right, I'm going. Room 521."

"Room 521," Rebecca confirmed. "Thank you for coming, I can't tell you what it means to me."

"You can tell me over dinner, I have expensive tastes," Arabella told her. She gave her a peck on the cheek and turned and left the room.

Rebecca smiled so hard her cheeks started to ache. She couldn't believe that Arabella had chosen her over work. And surprised her with the romantic gesture of just showing up like that.

She reached for the phone and called down to the hotel reception.

"Hi, it's the photographer. I'm in room 802 and there's a cobweb in here, and the bedding needs sorting out. Can you ask someone from housekeeping to come up? That's great. Oh, and is the kitchen still open? Brilliant. There's a really important property developer from London staying in the hotel. And I know she loves an egg white omelette with spinach. One word from her would put this place on the map! Fantastic, I'll come down and get the omelette and deliver it to her myself. Also, I'm going to order some flowers to be delivered to the front desk... can you let me know when they arrive?"

When she was finished, she lowered the phone.

If she wants romance, I'll show her romance, she thought.

51

BLUBBERBYES

ARABELLA LET OUT a breath and looked up at the blue sky. It was another beautiful New Orleans day. She'd not heard a word from work, only a quick email from Helen informing her that Kevin was coping wonderfully and reminding her to have a lovely holiday.

She'd taken the advice to heart, spending the next few days bolted to Rebecca's side and spending every waking moment with her. Some days they saw sights, some days she accompanied Rebecca on her freelancing jobs, some days they sat outside coffee shops and read books in companionable silence.

"Bella. Play."

She tilted her head to regard Luke who was staring at her, a grubby tennis ball in his hand. She lifted herself from the picnic blanket, placing her drink away from him.

"Play? I don't know how to play," she joked.

He giggled. "You do."

She turned around and looked at Rebecca. "This young man wants me to play, I must now leave you," she said formally.

"Farewell," Rebecca replied in between mouthfuls of a portion of beignets she was sharing with Jenn.

Kathryn gestured for Luke to come closer to her. She pulled a wet wipe out of her baby bag and gave his mouth a clean. "Mucky," she teased him. "How did you get to be so mucky?"

Luke shrugged. He strained to turn around to check Arabella was still there and still intending to play with him. She gave him a smile, reassuring him that she wasn't going anywhere.

She looked around the park while she waited. It was a quiet weekday. There were a few other picnic blankets around, and some children playing in the distance. It was sheer bliss.

"Before you go," Kathryn said to Arabella, "help me figure out the ninth job."

Arabella laughed. She looked at Jenn with a curious expression. "I don't know what it could be, I think we've guessed just about everything there is."

Rebecca snorted a laugh. "I don't think astronaut, belly dancer, and oil tycoon could really count as reasonable guesses."

Kathryn looked at Luke. "Luke, ask Jenn what her ninth job is. She can't deny you anything."

Luke frowned. He turned to Jenn and opened his mouth. His eyes dropped to the beignets between Rebecca and Jenn. Jenn tore off a piece of a beignet and handed it to him. He put the sweet treat in his mouth and sat down in front of her.

"Traitor," Kathryn whispered.

"Remember, you only have one guess per day," Jenn reminded her.

Arabella laughed as Kathryn rolled her eyes. She'd been limited to one guess per day after endless guesses threatened to derail a cinema trip a couple of days before. Arabella had loved watching Luke that night, as well as cuddling up on the sofa with Rebecca while they waited for Jenn and Kathryn to return home from their date.

"And remember she told you that it's not anything like any of her other jobs," Arabella added.

"True." Kathryn nodded. She held up her hand and listed the jobs she knew. "So, we know you are a steamboat host, bartender, tram driver—"

"Streetcar," Jenn and Rebecca corrected.

Kathryn smirked and then continued. "Voodoo museum attendant, casino worker, burlesque dancer, water aerobics instructor, and a tour guide. So... it's not like any of those."

"Right." Jenn dipped her finger in powdered sugar and then put her finger on the end of Luke's nose. He giggled and brushed it away with his hands.

Arabella smiled. Jenn was so good with him, and Luke adored her. Rebecca had told her that Jenn was planning to cut back on some jobs in order to spend more time watching Luke while Kathryn set up her new PR company in the city.

"Oh, I don't know." Kathryn threw her hands in the air. "Zoo keeper."

"Nope! You're close, though." Jenn darted a hand towards Luke's tummy and tickled him. He fell to the ground and giggled.

"Stop, stop!" he cried through laughs.

Arabella swept in and picked him up. "I'll save you from that evil tickle monster," she told him. He put his chubby arms around her neck and smiled down at Jenn.

Arabella noticed Rebecca watching her wistfully. She knew that look. It was the 'you'd make a great mother' look. She'd seen Rebecca use it a few times recently. Not that she minded. She felt the same way when she saw Rebecca playing with Luke.

"Close?" Kathryn asked. She scooted closer to Jenn. "How about another clue?" She fluttered her eyelashes.

Jenn melted.

Arabella rolled her eyes. "You're not actually going to fall for that are you, Jenn?"

"She is," Rebecca said.

"Bella. Play," Luke reminded her.

Arabella looked at the adorable boy in her arms. "Of course. What would you like to play?"

"Blubberbyes."

Arabella blinked. "I'm sorry, sweetie. What was that?"

Jenn was on her feet and taking Luke from Arabella's arms. "No, no, that's our secret, remember?" she told him as she stepped away from the picnic blanket. Her cheeks were red.

Arabella and Kathryn shared a look.

"Luke, honey," Kathryn asked. "What did you say? Blubberbyes?"

"Yes, like Jenn!"

Jenn shushed him and took a few steps away. Rebecca was howling with laughter at the whole display.

Arabella's eyes widened. "This is something to do with the ninth job," she realised.

Kathryn got to her feet. "Blubberbyes… what could he mean?"

Arabella shook her head. "I don't know, but she's stolen your son." She watched as Jenn playfully ran away with the boy in her arms. She turned to Kathryn. "What letters does he struggle with most?"

Kathryn chuckled. "Most of them. There's a speech therapist in his future. But L's, T's, G's, F's."

A grin crossed Arabella's face. She walked over to where Rebecca lay giggling on the blanket. She bent down and pushed Rebecca onto her back, straddling her stomach.

"Tell me what you know, Edwards," she demanded. "What is Blubberbyes?"

Rebecca looked up at her. "I'll never tell."

Arabella raised an eyebrow. She picked up the last beignet on the plate.

"Fine, eat it," Rebecca said. "It would be an honour to see you eat sugar."

"Oh, I'm not going to eat it." She picked up a half-drunk takeaway coffee mug. "Tell me, or this beignet... the last of the beignets... goes for a swim."

Rebecca looked at her in horror. "You can't do that! It's the last beignet. You know I save the best beignet to the end."

"It's not my fault you're a slave to tradition," Arabella told her.

"Butterflies!" Rebecca cried. "Blubberbyes are butterflies."

Arabella looked at Kathryn in confusion.

"She's... a butterfly?" Kathryn asked.

"You clearly don't think I'm serious," Arabella said. "Say au revoir to Monsieur Beignet." She dangled the pastry over the cup.

"No, wait! She *is* a butterfly. She dresses up as a butterfly at the Audubon Butterfly Garden. You know, for kids' parties and stuff. She wears a leotard and some big papier-mâché wings and paints her face."

Kathryn laughed loudly. "That is priceless, no wonder she didn't want to tell me." She looked up to where Jenn was hiding behind a tree. "I'm coming to mock you!" she shouted before running towards her.

Arabella lowered the beignet and the coffee cup.

Rebecca looked up at her, a sparkle in her eye. "I won't lie, this is kinda hot," she admitted.

Arabella reached down and picked up the beignet, taking a big bite of it. She moaned as the sugar and doughnut mixed on her tongue. She chewed slowly and then swallowed. It was pure heaven.

She put the rest of the beignet down on the plate. "You're right, they are good."

Rebecca reached up for her arms and pulled her down into a kiss. After a moment, Rebecca pulled back, held Arabella's face still, and, painfully slowly, traced her tongue around Arabella's lips.

"Sugar," she explained when she was done.

"I'm hungry," Arabella whispered.

Rebecca's eyes widened.

"You told me to tell you in the future when I was hungry," Arabella reminded her. "Rebecca, I'm hungry." She stared at the woman beneath her, impressing upon her that she didn't mean food.

"Let's go back to your hotel," Rebecca suggested.

"Excellent suggestion," Arabella agreed.

PATREON

I ADORE PUBLISHING. There's a wonderful thrill that comes from crafting something and then releasing it to the world. Especially when you are writing woman loving woman characters. I receive messages from readers who are thrilled to discover characters and scenarios that resemble their lives. Books are entertaining escapism, but they are also reinforcement that we are not alone in our struggles.

I'm passionate about writing books that people can identify with. Books that are accessible to all and show that love —and acceptance—can be found no matter who you are.

I'm at the beginning of my writing career and have already published over ten books. I have plans to write many, many more. However, writing, editing, and marketing books take up a lot of time... and writing full time is a treadmill-like existence, especially in a small niche market.

Don't get me wrong. I feel very grateful and lucky to be able to live the life I do. But being a full-time author in a small market means never being able to stop and work on developing my writing style, it means rarely having the time or budget to properly market my books.

This is why I have set up a Patreon account. With Patreon, you can donate a small amount each month to enable me to hop off of my treadmill for a while in order to reach my goals.

My Patreon page is a place for exclusive first looks at new works, insight into upcoming projects, monthly Q&A sessions, as well as special gifts and dedications. There are tiers to suit all budgets. My readers are some of the kindest and most supportive people I have met, and I appreciate every book borrow or purchase. With the added support of Patreon, I hope to be able to develop my writing career in order to become a better author as well as increase my marketing strategy to help my books to reach a wider audience.

https://www.patreon.com/aeradley

JOIN THE FUN!

I love connecting with my readers and one of the best ways to do this is via my Facebook Group.

I post frequent content, including sneak peaks of what I am working on, competitions for free books, and exclusive easter eggs about my work.

I'd love to see you there, so if you have a Facebook account please join us.

https://www.facebook.com/groups/aeradley

ABOUT THE AUTHOR

A.E. Radley had no desire to be a writer but accidentally turned into an award-winning, best-selling author.

She has recently given up her marketing career and position as Managing Director in order to make stuff up for a living instead. She claims the similarities are startling.

She describes herself as a Wife. Traveller. Tea Drinker. Biscuit Eater. Animal Lover. Master Pragmatist. Annoying Procrastinator. Theme Park Fan. Movie Buff.

Connect with A.E. Radley
www.aeradley.com

Published by Heartsome Publishing
Staffordshire
United Kingdom
www.heartsomebooks.com

ISBN: 9781912684144

First Heartsome edition: November 2018

Made in the USA
Monee, IL
09 April 2021

65278695R00319